Dragonwatch

As the kingdoms of the north negotiate a secret alliance, the Wytch Council attempts to discredit and replace the rebellious Wytch Kings. Can Tristin of Ysdrach and Prince Mikhyal of Rhiva get to the bottom of the plot? Or will the Northern Alliance be torn apart before the ink on the treaty is dry?

Also by Jaye McKenna

Guardians of the Pattern
Prequel: Facing the Mirror
Book 1: Psi Hunter
Book 2: Gremlin's Last Run
Book 3: Ghost in the Mythe
Book 4: Wildfire Psi
Book 5: Eye of the Storm
Book 6: Closing the Circle

Wytch Kings
Book 1: Burn the Sky
Book 2: Blackfrost
Book 3: Shadowspire
Book 4: Dragonwatch

Middle Kingdoms
Leythe Blade

Complete list of titles at
www.jayemckenna.com

Dragonwatch

Wytch Kings, Book 4

Jaye McKenna

Mythe Weaver Press

Chapter One

Tristin was wholly dragon.

The treetops rushed by as he soared down the mountain on wings of brilliant ruby red, reveling in the perfection of his dragon form. When he was dragon, he was strong and whole. When he was dragon, he didn't have to put up with horrible feelings shivering through his human form every time he touched something that had been handled by someone else.

The anzaria his uncle had dosed him with for years might have dulled his mind and plagued him with hallucinations, but it had also blocked his cursed Wytch power. Addiction, at least, had brought him peace.

Now, with his human body purged of the last remnants of the drug, Tristin sought refuge in his dragon form more and more often, much to the consternation of those overseeing his recovery.

The late afternoon sun was warm on his back, and a thrill of joy suffused him as the ground sped by below. There was Dragonwatch, where he'd been taken to recover from his addiction and learn to control the Wytch power that had kept him in isolation for over half his life. And there, at the foot of the mountain, lay Castle Altan, home to the cousins he'd only recently learned he had: Garrik, the Wytch King of Altan and Prince Jaire, Garrik's younger brother.

Tristin had yet to set foot in the castle itself, but he hoped he'd be well enough to do so one day soon. His cousins seemed genuinely concerned about his welfare, and once he'd fully recovered, he planned to spend some time getting acquainted with them. He'd had no one to call family since the death of his mother, half a lifetime ago.

His uncle, Wytch King Altivair of Ysdrach, could no longer be counted as family; not after the things he'd allowed to be done to Tristin.

A flash of emerald green on the roof of the watchtower caught his eye as he went past, and Tristin banked and came around at a lower altitude to get a closer look.

The green was a cloak, whipped by the wind, worn by a figure with hair gleaming like copper in the sunlight: Ilya, Wytch Master of Altan. Across the watchtower from the Wytch Master was Prince Jaire, in his opalescent white dragon form. As Tristin watched, Jaire reared up on his hind legs and breathed a snapping, glowing ball of lightning down into the river valley below. Tristin felt the tingle of it in the air even from this distance.

Lightning.

Prince Jaire was unusual among dragon shifters in that he could breathe fire and ice. The lightning was new. If war was coming to Altan, the prince's versatility would certainly be a valuable asset on the battlefield, although Tristin cringed at the thought of his gentle cousin going to war.

Prince Jaire blew out another ball of lightning, and moments later, took to the sky. He winged his way up to Tristin and leveled out so he was flying on Tristin's left.

<Did you see, Tristin?> Jaire spoke directly into his mind, a convenient ability the dragon form allowed. *<I did lightning! We've been working on lightning for days. It's much more difficult than fire or ice, but I've finally got the pattern right!>*

<I did see. I felt the charge in the air from here. Most impressive.>

<Vayne's the one who finally figured it out. He's really good at designing new patterns.> Jaire gave him a toothy dragon grin. *<Master Ilya wants a word with you. He says to land on the roof.>*

<Thank you, Cousin,> Tristin replied, not bothering to hide his dismay at the Wytch Master's request.

<It'll be all right, Tristin. You're doing better every day.>

Tristin didn't respond. The only thing he was getting better at was hiding his despair. Jaire peeled away and glided down the mountain toward the castle. Tristin watched him for a few moments, then blinked hard to bring down his inner eyelids. He quickly located a downdraft, a swath of cool turquoise, and rode it in a lazy, spiraling descent toward the roof of the watchtower. His landing was perfect, but it gave him no satisfaction, and he didn't make the shift back to human form.

Wytch Master Ilya stood before him, a cloak draped over his arm. "Would you shift for me, Tristin? I would have words with you, and we cannot speak properly when you are in dragon form and I am not."

Tristin snorted, but didn't shift. If Ilya wanted to speak to him so badly, the Wytch Master could shift. He knew exactly what Ilya wished to talk about, and the thought of it made his dragon belly writhe and twist in dread.

His gaze drifted away from the Wytch Master to the slope of the mountain beyond the watchtower. He could have been safe in his cave by now, if he hadn't been curious and come to investigate.

"Tristin... it's been three days since I've seen you in your human form. If you insist on spending all your time as a dragon, you risk losing yourself to the beast entirely. You will forget your humanity and truly become dragon."

Tristin stared down at his wicked, ruby-red claws. Forgetting his human life would not necessarily be a bad thing.

"If you lose yourself to the dragon," Ilya continued, "you will be a danger to the folk of Altan. Garrik would have no choice but to order your death, though it would grieve him to do so."

Ilya was right, of course, and Tristin knew it. He'd already experienced signs of the dragon within him overshadowing his human self: losing track of the days, reveling in the hunt, the smell of blood transporting him into ecstasies the likes of which he'd never known as a man.

"Won't you try?" Ilya coaxed. "Your cousins are both very concerned about you, as am I."

His cousins, yes. He owed them his life, his freedom... and, he thought, with a mixture of resentment and guilt, his current condition. Which, truth be told, they *were* trying hard to help him with.

"I know the watchtower is particularly difficult for you," Ilya said. "If you'd be more comfortable, you may glide down to the courtyard, and I will meet you there."

With a heavy sigh, Tristin dipped his head in acquiescence and nodded toward the courtyard.

Ilya smiled. "Very good. I shall see you in a minute, then. Would you like to take the cloak with you?" He offered it to Tristin, laid across his outstretched arms so it would be easy for the dragon to take it. Tristin carefully wrapped his claws around it and hopped to the edge of the watchtower roof on three legs. He spread his wings and glided down to the courtyard.

Shifting back into human form was easy, but the mental onslaught that came with it was always a shock, no matter how well prepared he thought he was. Visions of armed men running to do battle flooded his mind. Shouted commands and screams of pain filled his ears, and he felt the bite of steel on flesh and the searing pain of fire. The smell of smoke and the taste of blood were almost enough to choke him. It didn't matter how many times he reminded himself it wasn't real, the sensations were too intense for him to remember that when he was caught up in them.

The empathic resonances bled from every surface he touched, and those first moments after shifting back into human form were always overwhelming, especially after the peace he experienced as a dragon.

Dragonwatch stood on the site of an old fort which had been home to the men who guarded the kingdom of Altan from the winter raids of the mountain barbarians. The barbarian tribes were gone now, thinned out or driven off nearly a century ago, during the Ten Winters of the Dark Ice, but the empathic resonances of the men who'd fought here remained. The violence, fear, and pain experienced by those ancient warriors had permeated the stones of the watchtower and the surrounding landscape as their blood had soaked the dirt.

Most people were blissfully unaware of the savage history resonating through the land beneath their feet.

Tristin wasn't most people.

The fears and hopes of those long-dead souls who once defended the kingdom sliced through his head like millions of tiny daggers. Each alone was barely noticeable, a drop of rain in a raging storm. But the combined onslaught was so overwhelming that for a moment, Tristin froze, feet glued to the sun-warmed stone, cloak in a blue puddle of fabric on the ground in front of him.

"Tristin?" Master Ilya's voice broke him out of a haze of pain so intense, he forgot to hide his arms. "You will be well again, I promise you. But I cannot teach you the shielding patterns if you insist on spending all your time in dragon form."

The Wytch Master's pale blue eyes fixed on Tristin, his expression remaining calm and composed. He didn't look the least bit disgusted at the sight of Tristin's gaunt frame, or the terrible scars on his arms.

Ilya bent to retrieve the cloak, and though Tristin wanted to tear it from Ilya's hands and whip it around himself to cover his body, he forced himself to wait while the Wytch Master gently draped it over his shoulders. When the cloak was in place, Tristin pulled it tight, holding it closed with shaking hands in an attempt to cover as much of himself as possible.

"Come. You'll feel better once you're inside." The Wytch Master's voice was cool, a soothing contrast to the painful chaos of empathic resonances swirling in Tristin's head.

By the time they reached the school's entry hall — the *new* hall, built from freshly hewn planks, thank the Dragon Mother — Tristin's skin was slick with cold sweat. The moment his bare feet touched the smooth, polished floorboards, the sensations absorbed by the stones in the courtyard faded to a dim noise in the background, leaving him weak-kneed and trembling.

Master Ilya escorted him to his suite and waited in the sitting room while Tristin staggered into his bedroom to find some clothing.

Now that the worst of the resonances were blocked by the relatively new floor, Tristin's mind was as quiet as it ever got. He dressed quickly, in breeches and a shirt with sleeves long enough to hide his scars.

Outside, the sky was a clear, lavender blue, and Tristin stared longingly at it. He could be out the window and gliding — without pain — high above Dragonwatch in a moment, if he dared.

The Wytch Master's words threaded through his mind: *Garrik would have no choice but to order your death...*

For one brief moment, he thought perhaps that was the answer. But no — Tristin wasn't quite ready to give up yet. Not quite. Though he feared if things didn't improve, it wouldn't be long before he reached that point.

Casting one last look of regret at the sky, he left his bedroom.

A tray of bread, fruit, and cheese was waiting on the little table in the sitting room, along with a pitcher full of water. Ilya bade him sit and began loading a plate with food.

Tristin arched an eyebrow when the Wytch Master handed it to him. "You're serving me?"

"I'm seeing to the needs of a wounded man who has come under my care," Ilya corrected. He sat down opposite Tristin. "Eat. I should like to see you gain a bit of flesh. You will not have the focus or the energy to learn the shielding patterns if you are not at full strength."

"You're starting to sound a lot like one of my hallucinations." Tristin eyed Ilya suspiciously. "You haven't been talking to them, have you?"

"I wouldn't presume," Ilya said drily. "I'd much rather talk to you. Although at the moment, I'd prefer you had your mouth too full to speak."

Tristin shifted his gaze to the food and wrinkled his nose. The thought of putting anything into his mouth made his stomach turn. Even the bread, still warm from the oven, did nothing to tempt him.

"Tristin." Ilya's voice was gentle, but there was a determined edge to his tone. "I want to help you, but there is little I can do if you will not meet me halfway."

"I can't imagine why you care enough to do so," Tristin said, glancing up in time to see Ilya's pale eyes narrow.

"Can you not? First and foremost, I am a healer, and I cannot bear to think of any creature in pain. In addition to that, you are the only living relative Garrik and Jaire have. And Jaire has taken quite a shine to you. He asks about you every day, you know."

A faint smile curved Tristin's lips. He'd liked Prince Jaire from the moment he'd met the young man.

"Try to eat something, Tristin. If not for yourself, then for Jaire. He would be devastated if anything were to happen to you."

Tristin started to reach for the bread, then let his hand fall into his lap. "I see little point."

"You are giving up already? You have barely begun."

The Wytch Master was right, of course, but Tristin saw no point in getting his hopes up only to have them dashed once more. Mordax had tried for years to teach him the simplest of shielding patterns, and Tristin had never been able to master even the first one. "I have so far to go," Tristin said wearily. "The mere thought of it is exhausting."

"That is because you are focusing on the end point," Ilya said gently. "You need a more easily achievable goal. Something you can accomplish quickly, if only you put your mind to it."

Tristin shrugged. The only goal he was interested in was whichever one would leave him free of the resonances that soaked every surface, to have his mind quiet for once. Even here in his bedroom, the resonances were there. Muffled, yes, but still there, an ever-present noise in the back of his mind. By the end of the day, he'd have a skull-splitting headache.

"What about going a whole day without shifting?" Ilya suggested. "Do you think you can do that?"

Tristin blinked. Could he? "I... I don't know," he whispered. "When it gets too much, shifting is the only escape I have."

"Hmm, well, perhaps we need to give you some incentive. If you could do anything — anything at all — what would it be?"

"I... I don't..." Tristin frowned. No one had ever asked him that before, and he hadn't the faintest idea how to respond.

"Let me put it another way. Looking back over your life, when were you the happiest?"

Had he ever been happy? Not at Shadowspire, certainly. And not in the years since his Wytch power had awakened and filled his mind with feelings and sensations he didn't want, but couldn't shut out.

He had to think back further than that, to a lonely childhood. Raised in isolation at Falkrag, one of his uncle's estates, Tristin had very few happy memories. The only person who'd paid any attention to him had been old Thom, the gardener.

A faint smile curved his lips. "Rooting about in the dirt in Falkrag's gardens," he murmured. "The sun on my back, the rich smell of the living earth all around me. Watching the green, growing things poking their heads up out of the dirt. Seeing the leaves unfurl and reach for the sun..." Falkrag's gardens were more for growing herbs and vegetables than for show, and old Thom had allowed Tristin to have his very own patch of earth. Tristin had chosen to grow flowers in as many colors as he could. "I was happy then." His smile turned wistful. "Or... as close to happy as I've ever been, I suppose."

Ilya looked pleased. "Very good. Ambris grows herbs in the garden behind the school, and cares for the flowers in the courtyard. If you can go all of tomorrow without shifting, I will speak to him about finding a bit of earth for you to work. Would that be sufficient encouragement?"

Tristin's eyes widened and his heart beat a little faster. It would never have occurred to him to ask for such a thing. "I'd like that. I-I'll try, Master Ilya." With a tiny smile, Tristin lifted a chunk of buttered bread to his lips.

Mikhyal, prince of Rhiva, lay flat on his back in the corner of the practice yard and stared up at the sky. A smattering of applause came from around the yard, where a growing number of Rhiva's guardsmen had paused in their own sparring matches to watch their captain give their commander a thorough trouncing. He pretended he didn't hear the clink of coins changing hands.

Captain Rhu's pale blue eyes crinkled as she grinned down at him. "All right, Commander?"

"Ai. Surprised is all. And a bit winded." Mikhyal took the offered hand and gave the watching guardsmen a rueful grin. "Go on," he called across the yard. "Back to work with the lot of you."

Chuckling and calling out insults, the men returned to their practice bouts. The captain hauled Mikhyal to his feet with strength that always surprised him, given how small she was.

Once he was standing, Rhu let go of his hand and gave his admittedly soft belly a hard jab. "Too many rich meals at your father's table." The critical edge to her tone said she wasn't entirely joking.

"Ai, and not enough time away from the desk to balance it." He rubbed his bruised backside and returned her grin with a sardonic one of his own. "Thank you, Rhu. You'll have to show me that maneuver." He'd seen something coming, but hadn't been quick enough. The moment he'd moved to block her attempt to disarm him, she'd kicked his feet out from under him. He'd landed hard on his arse, losing both his blade and his dignity.

"Not until you've got your edge back, Commander. You've let yourself get too soft and slow to manage it without hurting yourself."

"I'm not sure I'll have the time to—"

"Then don't expect to survive your next armed encounter," she said bluntly. "A year ago, I'd never have got that move past you."

"A year ago, I believed all Shaine needed was a bit of guidance." Mikhyal stared down at the packed dirt and lowered his voice. "Now, however, I fear my hopes were misplaced. I dread to think what happens when he becomes king."

Rhu said nothing. It was more than her position was worth to speak badly of the heir, but Mikhyal knew her fears echoed his own. She'd told him so over too much wine on several occasions in the last year.

"You're right," Mikhyal conceded. "I'm badly out of shape. Perhaps it's time I stopped spending so much energy opposing Shaine. None of it's going to matter once he's crowned. He'll do just as he pleases, then. Or rather, as Wytch Master Anxin pleases. I'll see what I can do about making one of the practice sessions a daily habit."

"This is a good time, if you can manage it," Rhu said. "I'll be able to work with you myself in the mornings. The afternoon session is mostly new recruits, and they need all of my attention."

"I'll have to rearrange my schedule. The only reason I managed to find the time today was because Shaine canceled our morning meeting at the last minute. No promises, but I'll try to be here first thing tomorrow morning."

She grinned. "Very good, Commander. I'll look forward to crossing blades with you tomorrow."

Mikhyal gave her a sharp nod and collected his practice blade. On his way back to his suite, he considered how he might present the schedule change to his brother. Shaine had little patience with Mikhyal's friendship with Rhu, or with his efforts to keep himself fit. Mikhyal already knew exactly what his brother would say: *That's what we have guardsmen for. Your job is to assist me. Their job is to protect us.*

Which sounded too much like something Wytch Master Anxin would say.

He'd just turned down the hallway leading to the royal apartments when he caught sight of his brother's red hair, a bright stream of flame against the soft, muted blues and greys of the family wing of Rhiva's summer palace.

"There you are," Shaine said, eyes narrowing as they moved from Mikhyal's sweat-damp, disheveled hair to his torn breeches, and finally, to the practice blade he still held in his hand. "What in Aio's name have you been doing?"

"When you canceled our meeting, I thought I'd get in some practice with the guards." Mikhyal slowed, but didn't stop, forcing Shaine to turn and fall into step beside him if he wished to converse.

"Whatever for?" Shaine sounded mystified.

"Well, I *am* the commander of Rhiva's army," Mikhyal replied. "I ought to at least keep up appearances, don't you think? In fact, I've been meaning to resume my daily weapons practice, so I won't be available during the hour before breakfast. We'll have to change our meeting time to later in the day. Before lunch, perhaps?"

Panic flashed in his brother's eyes, there and gone again so fast, Mikhyal decided he must have imagined it. "I'll check my schedule.

I'm sure I can juggle it to accommodate you, if I must, though I don't see why you're bothering." Shaine's voice was cool and full of disdain. "A waste of your valuable time, if you ask me."

"I didn't."

Shaine didn't respond. Nor did he turn away. Instead, he continued on down the corridor with Mikhyal. At the door to his own suite, Mikhyal paused and faced his brother. "Was there anything else?"

A soft shadow flickered behind Shaine's hard green eyes, an echo, perhaps, of the boy he'd been, the brother Mikhyal had loved, before the accident last summer had turned him into a stranger. "Mik, please, I—" Shaine stopped, a strangled sob escaping his throat.

Mikhyal started at the sound of the nickname Shaine hadn't used in over a year. "Are you all right, Shaine?"

Shaine squeezed his eyes shut as if he were in pain. A moment later they opened, and whatever fleeting emotion Mikhyal thought he'd seen was gone, leaving his brother's face as cold and composed as ever. "I'm fine," he said flatly. "I only came to inform you that Father requests your presence at breakfast. Apparently he has an announcement to make."

"I see." Mikhyal resisted the urge to sigh at the thought of all the time formal breakfast would take from his morning.

Shaine said nothing more. He turned and headed back down the hall, his movements stiff and jerky. Mikhyal slipped into his suite and closed the door, leaning heavily against it.

Eight years it was, since the Wytch Council had confirmed Shaine as Wytch King Drannik's heir. Eight years since Mikhyal's younger brother had taken the place he'd always assumed would be his. It had been long enough for Mikhyal to have come to terms with the cold reality that he would never be king, that the best he could hope for would be a position as one of Shaine's advisors.

Only fifteen at the time, poor Shaine had been terrified at the prospect of ruling the kingdom. Mikhyal had thrown himself into the task of helping his brother prepare for the role. Shaine might not have been groomed to be king like Mikhyal had, but with Mikhyal's guidance, he'd been slowly growing into it. After much hard work,

Mikhyal had come to believe that although it wasn't what Shaine truly wanted, his brother would be a good king.

Last summer, all that had changed.

Up until the accident, Mikhyal had counted Shaine as his closest friend as well as his brother. But ever since Shaine had woken up a week after being thrown from his horse, a stranger wore his brother's body and spoke with his voice. The healers could do nothing but patiently explain that it was not unheard of for a man's personality to change completely following such a serious head injury. Mikhyal was told it was only by the Dragon Mother's grace that Shaine had survived without more serious effects, but Mikhyal thought his brother's personality change to be quite serious enough. The accident had changed the heir of Rhiva, and not for the better. Shaine was Wytch Master Anxin's creature now, and Mikhyal feared the day his brother took the throne.

Swallowing down his bitterness, Mikhyal headed for his bedroom. His valet, Senn, was waiting for him. Senn took one look at Mikhyal and said, "Ah. You'll be wanting your bath then, Your Highness."

"Sorry, Senn. Rhu caught me snatching a bit of last night's cake for breakfast in the kitchens, and the next thing I knew, she had me working it off in the practice yard."

Senn's sniff communicated his disapproval perfectly as he inspected his prince. "Those breeches weren't meant for sword practice, Highness. The stains will never come out."

"Ai, well, when I dressed, I wasn't expecting to spend half the morning on my arse in the dirt. I shall endeavor to treat my wardrobe with more care in future, shall I?"

"Please." Senn gave another pained sniff, then continued, "His Majesty requests that you attend him at breakfast as soon as you're presentable."

"Ai, Shaine came and told me. You wouldn't have any idea what it's about, would you?"

"I really couldn't say, Your Highness, though rumor has it His Majesty received a visitor last night. *Late* last night."

"Oh?"

"One of the dragon-men from Altan, apparently."

"Wytch King Garrik?"

"No, Highness, I believe it was his Wytch Master, Ilya."

Mikhyal frowned. "I wonder what he wanted. Well, I suppose I shall find out at breakfast." He glanced longingly toward his bathing chamber. "And I suppose that long soak in the bath I was looking forward to will have to wait."

"As you say, Your Highness."

With Senn's capable assistance, Mikhyal set about making himself presentable.

"Garrik of Altan has just announced the betrothal of his brother, Prince Jaire," Drannik said. He took a sip of his tea and regarded his breakfast thoughtfully.

"It's about time," the queen murmured. She was, as always, the picture of cool beauty, with her pale blonde hair and her ice-blue eyes. "I do feel for Lady Bria. Poor woman, she was supposed to marry Garrik years ago. What a disappointment *that* must have been. Imagine, growing up thinking you'll be queen, and then having to settle for the younger prince." She turned to Shaine and beamed. "Not like your Kirali, ai, Shaine? Promised to Mikhyal all those years, she must have thought her life was over when the Council confirmed you as the heir. I can only imagine her joy and relief when she learned the Council had withdrawn their approval of her marriage to Mikhyal and given her to you instead."

Mikhyal suppressed the urge to roll his eyes. He imagined Kirali's relief would have had more to do with being betrothed to a man closer to her age than his status. At nineteen, she was only four years younger than Shaine, but nearly a decade separated her and Mikhyal. She'd been a babe in arms when she'd been promised to him.

Drannik made no comment. He and the queen had never been close, and while they played their roles to perfection in public, the king and queen had lived in separate apartments for as long as Mikhyal could remember.

"At Wytch King Garrik's request, I shall be attending the festivities," Drannik announced, "accompanied by Mikhyal."

Silence settled around the table while the family digested that. Wytch Master Anxin was the first to break it. "There's been no official word of a betrothal."

"I understand it will be a very small ceremony, with only a few guests," Drannik said. "Prince Jaire is quite shy and fragile, if you'll remember, and Garrik fears that making a huge production of it will be too great a strain on him."

"Very good," Anxin said, inclining his head. "When does Your Majesty wish to depart? I can be ready at your convenience."

"The ceremony is still a month away, but I'll be stopping at Brightwood on the way. I've not yet had a chance to have a look at the new breeding stock the horse master acquired at the spring Faire in Askarra. I'll be leaving in a week, but I should like you to remain here, Anxin, and watch over Shaine. This seems like an excellent opportunity for him to try taking the reins for a short period, and you are the only one I trust to guide him."

The Wytch King's sincere delivery would have fooled anyone who wasn't in his confidence. In truth, Drannik despised Anxin, but the only member of the royal family who was aware of that was Mikhyal. He shifted his gaze to his brother in time to see an expression of alarm flash across Shaine's face. A moment later, Shaine's body tensed, and he bowed his head and fixed his eyes on his breakfast.

"Of *course*, Your Majesty," Anxin said. "It would be my honor." In his early forties, with not a streak of grey to mar his sable hair, Anxin was young to have been granted the honor that came with the station of Royal Wytch Master, and wasn't above a little preening. "I am humbled that you would entrust the guidance of your heir and the oversight of your kingdom to me."

Drannik's smile might have fooled Anxin, but it looked more like a grimace to Mikhyal. Into the silence that followed, the queen said brightly, "I do believe I shall accompany you, my dear."

"Will you, indeed." Drannik's voice and his expression were perfectly neutral.

"This summer has been *entirely* too dull. The Midsummer ball at Mir was *dreadfully* disappointing. A royal betrothal ceremony will be a lovely diversion. And it's been ages since I've seen Brightwood."

"I was not planning to bring an entourage," the Wytch King said patiently. "As I said, it will be a small ceremony. I had intended to cut through the forest with a small contingent of guardsmen in order to minimize my time on the road."

"Don't let me stop you," Icera said pleasantly. "I am quite content to go alone. I'm sure Mikhyal would be happy to escort his mother."

"If it would please Father, I would indeed," Mikhyal said, heart sinking at the prospect of escorting his mother's carriage. On horseback, a small group of skilled riders could make the journey to Altan in a week, but with the carriage and the frequent stops the ladies would require, it would take over two weeks, and that was assuming the weather, the horses, and the ladies cooperated.

"Very well," Drannik said in a clipped tone. "If we are to arrive on time, we will depart in two days, and we'll delay the visit to Brightwood until after the ceremony. I shall need at least two weeks to see to matters at the estate, and there simply won't be time for it if we are to be shackled to the pace of the carriage. If you cannot arrange for your baggage to be packed in that time, I regret that you will have to remain behind, my dear."

Icera arched a perfectly shaped golden eyebrow. "As you say, dear. Two days. I look forward to it."

A cool silence descended over the breakfast table. Mikhyal noted that Shaine didn't eat, only pushed the food around on his plate. Anxin watched the young man with narrowed eyes, and Mikhyal would have given a lot to know what the Wytch Master was thinking.

Tristin was trembling when he presented himself to Ilya in the Wytch Master's study the next afternoon. His head ached from the relentless barrage of muffled emotions seeping up from the stone and earth underneath Dragonwatch's floorboards. Though the intensity was nowhere near the level it was in the ancient watchtower, it never let up. Having agreed not to shift into his dragon form, in which he mercifully could not sense the resonances, he could find no respite.

"Are you all right, Tristin?" Master Ilya's brow wrinkled as he studied Tristin's face. "Come, sit down."

Tristin took the seat across the desk from Ilya, and sat hunched over, hands clasped tightly in his lap. "I think," he began, licking his lips, "I think if I am to keep my promise not to shift, I need something to occupy my mind. Something to stop me from focusing on my discomfort. Can you... do you think you could show me the patterns I need to shield myself?"

"Is the pain so bad?" Ilya asked softly.

"It is... not unbearable, but there is no longer any drug fog to retreat into, nothing to lull me into the depths of sleep. There is a constant noise in my head. It never lets up, not for a moment. Even my hallucinations went away every so often." He gave Ilya a thin, bitter smile. "It nibbles and bites at the edges of my awareness, and frays my determination so thin, I fear I shall break. The sooner I can learn to block it out, the better."

"I'm not convinced you've the strength yet to focus." Ilya's pale blue eyes were soft with concern. "I'd hate to start before you're ready. Failure now is only going to shake your confidence."

"Confidence?" Tristin's bark of laughter was brittle. "I can promise you cooperation, Wytch Master, but confidence? That, I fear, I lost long ago."

Ilya regarded him in thoughtful silence for a time. "Mordax gave you no encouragement?"

Tristin couldn't quite suppress a cold shudder when he thought about the Wytch Master who had been in charge of his training and later, his captivity. "I was not a good student," he said flatly. "And Mordax was... a harsh teacher, and not very patient."

The Wytch Master's eyes narrowed as he frowned. "Tristin... did Mordax hurt you?"

Heart pounding, Tristin stared down at his hands. "Only when I couldn't perform to his satisfaction. Which was most of the time, actually. He... he told me it was for my own good."

Ilya cursed softly, almost under his breath. Tristin risked a glance up, and found the Wytch Master's eyes still on him. His cheeks heated, and he quickly averted his eyes.

"We shall start at the very beginning," Ilya said. "With the most basic lesson of all — finding your center."

"My… my center? Is that… is it anything like the place where the patterns for shifting go?"

"Exactly so." Ilya arched a coppery eyebrow. "He never showed you your center? No wonder you couldn't master it." He rose and beckoned to Tristin. "Having the shifting patterns as a template will help. Come, then. If you are serious about getting started, let us retire to a more comfortable spot. Your sitting room, I think, since I'd like you to feel as safe and relaxed as possible."

The tiniest glimmer of hope kindled in the dark recesses of Tristin's mind. If shielding was anything like shifting, perhaps he *could* master it, after all. Curious, Tristin got to his feet and followed the Wytch Master.

Despite the lingering aches and pains from his practice bout with Rhu, Mikhyal chose to make the journey to Altan on horseback. The alternative was to spend day after day shut up in the carriage with his mother and her ladies, forced to endure endless rounds of interrogation regarding his own marriage prospects.

The relative quiet of the forest and the cool breeze on Mikhyal's face were a relief after the two-day panic that had ensued when Queen Icera had made known her intention to accompany her husband and son to the betrothal ceremony.

Preparations for the journey to Altan had become rather fraught at that point, with the queen insisting she would need far more than two days to prepare, and the king telling her he would depart on time, with or without her.

They were several hours out from the summer palace when Wytch King Drannik pulled his black gelding up near Shirra, Mikhyal's bay mare, and said, "Drop back with me. We need to talk."

At forty-eight, Drannik cut an impressive figure, especially armed and on horseback. Like many men of the north, he was tall and powerfully built. Though twenty years younger, Mikhyal could have been Drannik's brother, with his broad shoulders and black hair. The only real difference was their eyes. While Drannik's were an impenetrable black, Mikhyal's eyes were the same as his mother's: a pale, icy blue.

"Your mother is convinced poor Prince Jaire has landed himself in the middle of a scandal," Drannik said as they waited by the side of the road for the rest of the party to pass by.

"Well, it *was* rather short notice," Mikhyal observed. "Every betrothal ceremony I've attended has been announced at least a season in advance. They've given us, what, four weeks?"

"Ai, something like," Drannik said. "She's working herself into a froth of disapproval over his imagined expectant wife-to-be. I'm rather looking forward to seeing her face when she learns that Prince Jaire's intended is a young man."

Mikhyal smothered a laugh. "She'll never forgive you if she finds out you knew."

"Won't be the first time," Drannik muttered. "Perhaps the gossip will keep her too occupied to wonder."

The last of the guardsmen but for the rear scouts had passed, and Drannik urged his horse back onto the road. Mikhyal guided Shirra after him. As he drew up beside his father, Drannik said, "The reason for such haste is that the betrothal ceremony is merely an excuse to bring the Wytch Kings of the north together for negotiations."

"If you're intending to involve Rhiva in something that requires negotiations," Mikhyal said with a faint frown, "wouldn't you have been better off having Shaine accompany you? He won't thank you for excluding him."

"I don't want Shaine involved in this," Drannik said grimly. "And nor will you, once I've explained. The messenger who brought the invitation was none other than Altan's Royal Wytch Master Ilya."

"Oh?" Mikhyal pursed his lips; Senn's information had been correct. "What warranted a visit from the Wytch Master?"

"The necessity for secrecy. Ilya said the Council attempted to force Garrik to step down in favor of an unknown cousin, using his own brother as leverage. Prince Jaire was kidnapped and held hostage, apparently at the Council's order."

"I see." Mikhyal barely managed to keep his alarm off of his face. Council interference in the governing of the kingdoms of Skanda was a major bone of contention between Mikhyal's father and brother. Since the accident and his dramatic change in personality, Shaine would support the Council's actions unquestioningly, whereas Drannik... should Drannik's views ever become common knowledge, Mikhyal could see the Wytch Council moving to hurry along Shaine's ascension to the throne. "Has the situation been resolved?"

"For the moment. With one Wytch Master dead, and another collared and chained in Altan's dungeon. Garrik expects Council retaliation, and from what Ilya said, it sounds as if he welcomes it. He requests our aid in the defense of his kingdom. He and Wytch King Ord of Irilan have invited us to a meeting of the northern kingdoms to discuss an alliance that could see the entire north break with the Council. Edrun of Miraen has been invited, too."

Mikhyal's gut clenched. "Who else knows of this?"

"No one but you and I," Drannik said softly, sharp black eyes holding Mikhyal's gaze. "And I plan to keep it that way. If an agreement can be reached and we do break with the Council, my choice of heir will no longer be subject to Council approval, and you, not Shaine, will be Wytch King of Rhiva after me. Shaine will not take such news well."

"To say the least," Mikhyal murmured. "Do you really think it will be that easy? The Council will not stand for it. An alliance of this nature can only lead us into a war we cannot win. Even combining their strength, the northern kingdoms do not have the resources to support a protracted military venture."

"So I told Master Ilya. He said Altan possesses knowledge that could change that, and Garrik asks only that we hear him out."

"He must be confident, indeed, to even suggest such a meeting. What sort of knowledge have they unearthed?"

"That, I cannot say."

"I suppose we will find out soon enough."

"That is exactly what Ilya said." Drannik gave his son another grim smile as he urged his mount forward.

Tristin felt sick. This was only his third lesson with Wytch Master Ilya, but the first two had gone badly enough that he'd been dreading it all morning.

"What is the most important thing for you to remember?" Ilya's voice was cool and steady, nothing like Mordax's sharp tones, which had become more clipped with Tristin's every failure.

Tristin swallowed. "That we start fresh every day. That I must not think about yesterday or the day before, but only of this moment. I must see this as my very first lesson." *Beginner's mind.* That was what Master Ilya wanted, and that was what Tristin must strive for.

"You must also make the attempt to actually change your mindset, rather than simply parroting back the words you think I want to hear," Ilya said drily.

"Sorry, Master Ilya. I'll try."

"Close your eyes, then."

Tristin closed his eyes and reminded himself yet again that Mordax, Royal Wytch Master of Ysdrach, was dead. Enraged and wholly dragon at the time, Tristin had dragged him from the top of the watchtower and thrown him to his death after he'd threatened Prince Jaire.

Ilya's soft voice broke into the memory, reminding Tristin that he needed to focus. "There, in the darkness of your mind, in the same place you focus on when you shift, is your center."

Tristin focused inward and willed himself to relax and sink back into the darkness. There it was, the blazing core of fire and fury deep inside him, where the heart of his dragon self lived. Ilya said it was a conduit leading straight to the raw mythe, the place from which he drew the power he needed to build the patterns that allowed him to shift.

In theory, he ought to be able to use that energy to build any pattern he was capable of using, but Tristin had yet to break his instinctive ability to shift into steps he could apply to learning other patterns.

He wished Prince Vayne was able to burn the patterns for shielding into his mythe-shadow as easily as he had done the patterns for shifting.

"Finding my center isn't the problem," Tristin said with a grimace. "It's the same place I go when I shift. The problem is knowing what to do once I get there. I keep wanting to shift, and there doesn't seem to be room for anything else."

"I'll show you the pattern," Ilya said. "Relax and watch. You should see it hovering in front of you, like a snowflake made of light and shadow."

Tristin attempted to relax, but the tension across his shoulders wouldn't ease. The dull headache arising from his constant awareness of the low-level empathic resonances increased in intensity, making it difficult to concentrate.

He managed to still his mind enough to see the pattern hanging in the air before him. Ilya's description was accurate — it looked like an intricate snowflake made of light and dark. He might have thought it beautiful once, before Mordax had turned the patterns he couldn't seem to learn into symbols of failure and pain.

Focus, boy!

Mordax's voice lashed at him from across the years, and Tristin hunched over, tensed for the blow he could never perform well enough to avoid.

Ilya's calm instructions were drowned out by the vivid memories: the barrage of insults, the riding crop coming down sharply across his upper back, and Mordax's demands that he stop being lazy and try harder.

Do you want to spend the rest of your life in torment? How will you manage if you cannot bear to walk across any ground where others have trod? You cannot. Focus! Focus! Focus!

Each one of those last three words was punctuated with a sharp blow across the shoulders. Tristin whimpered with each one, clamping his lips together to minimize the sounds of his distress. Crying out would only enrage Mordax and make his punishment that much worse—

"Tristin? Tristin, it's me, Ilya. It's all right. Come on. Come back from wherever you've gone. You're safe."

Ilya's words penetrated the haze of fear and pain, and Tristin blinked, surprised to find his eyes full of tears.

"Deep breaths," Ilya said gently. "That's it, slow and easy."

Tristin struggled to do as he was told. His chest felt tight, every breath a hard-won victory. When he was able to speak, he raised his eyes to meet Ilya's. "S-sorry, M-Master Ilya," he stammered. "I... c-can't help it. Every t-time..."

"Mordax again, was it?"

"Ai, Master." Tristin shivered, aware suddenly of the cold sweat trickling down his back.

"I think, perhaps, it is too soon for us to be attempting this," Ilya said slowly. "You need more time to recover. I know you're eating well, and you've even put on a bit of weight since you left your bed, but the memories are still very close to the surface and very raw."

Tristin said nothing. The Wytch Master was right; his memories of Mordax were still far too vivid to make this anything more than a futile, painful exercise.

"There is no reason for us to rush this," Ilya said.

"No reason but my own comfort." The bitterness in Tristin's voice made the Wytch Master wince. "I don't suppose... Master, I've kept my promise for three days now. I haven't shifted once, though I've been sorely tempted. Might I shift? Just until sunset... just to have a bit of peace?"

Ilya frowned. "Your work in the garden hasn't helped?"

"It helps in the sense that I now have something to occupy my time," Tristin told him. "But I'm not strong enough yet to work for very long. I know you hoped that doing something I enjoy might distract me, but... the noise seeps into my mind wherever I stand, and I am aware of it no matter what I'm doing. When I am dragon, I cannot feel the resonances of all those lives and deaths. I can fly into the mountains and find places where no one has stood. There, I can shift into human form, and I can be at peace for a time. Please, Master Ilya. I promise you, I am not giving up, and I will not lose myself to the beast." He stared down at his arms, and turned them to display his scars. "If I wanted to be finished, there are far easier ways to do it than risk the lives of those who have cared for me by becoming a rogue dragon."

Ilya looked down at the scars on Tristin's arms, then raised his eyes to study Tristin's face for a long time before finally giving him a single, sharp nod. "Very well, Tristin. Go and be dragon. Be at peace for a time. But if you do not return by sunset, I will come and fetch you myself."

Tristin smiled, the first real smile he'd given anyone in three days. "Thank you," he whispered. "I will return. I promise." This time, at least. If things didn't improve soon, though, he might just choose to fly far, far away, and seek out a place devoid of history and memory, a place where simply existing wouldn't hurt so much.

Chapter Two

"At this rate, Prince Jaire will be betrothed, married, and a father several times over before we ever reach Altan," Rhu grumbled to Mikhyal as they followed the carriage at a sedate pace that wouldn't upset the ladies' digestion.

"Ai, I'd forgotten how much I hate traveling with Mother's entourage." Though the ladies rode in a closed carriage to protect them from the damp forest air, Mikhyal still kept his voice low enough not to carry. "We could have traveled this distance in a day or so if we didn't have to keep to the pace of the carriage."

They were five days out from the palace, and even though he'd at first appreciated the slow pace, he was now more than ready to be finished with the journey. The ladies tired easily, forcing the party to stop in the late afternoon, and though they rose at a reasonable time in the morning, it was usually several hours of primping and powdering before they were ready to resume the journey.

A shout from up ahead had Mikhyal and Rhu exchanging an anxious glance. A moment later, the distinctive sound of steel ringing against steel reached them, followed by the king's voice barking orders.

"Stay here, Your Highness," Rhu ordered, and urged her mount toward the front of the line, where the king rode.

Mikhyal stared after her for only a few moments before touching his heels to Shirra's flanks. The mare surged forward. When he reached the carriage, which had stopped at the first sign of trouble, he dismounted and tethered her to the door.

The dark curtains at the carriage window parted, and his mother's face appeared, shockingly pale against her brightly painted lips. Her blue eyes were wide as she stared at her son.

"Stay here!" Mikhyal shouted through the glass.

The queen nodded once and let the curtain fall closed.

Mikhyal hurried forward on foot. He was already winded when the trees thinned abruptly. The melee appeared to be contained in a large clearing up ahead. Keeping to the cover of the forest, Mikhyal circled the open space until he caught sight of his father engaged in combat with a scruffy-looking man in worn, dirty leather armor.

Drannik appeared to be holding his own, but the king wore only a breastplate for protection. Mikhyal drew his sword and rushed to Drannik's defense. Before he could reach his father's side, a huge man stepped out from the cover of the forest, sword raised to strike. With only a moment to react, Mikhyal brought his blade up to parry a powerful stroke that might well have split him in two. The force of the blow sent a numbing shock from shoulder to fingertips. Mikhyal's fingers spasmed, and before he could regain his grip, his opponent twisted his own blade to wrench the hilt from Mikhyal's hand. Out of the corner of his eye, he saw his sword go sailing into the underbrush.

His focus narrowed, and his senses sharpened as he reached for his dagger. Not fast enough. The sword was arcing around to slash his belly open.

Time froze. Mikhyal braced himself for agony, certain a killing blow was coming. In the next moment, a streak of green and grey flashed past. One of Rhiva's soldiers barreled into the man from the side, knocking him off of his feet. Mikhyal caught a glimpse of Rhu's black braids flying past before his attacker fell heavily to the forest floor, blood streaming from his cut throat. Rhu paused long enough to give Mikhyal a nod before springing back into the fray.

Mikhyal stared down at the dagger in his hand. He needed a better weapon, something with more reach. He turned toward the underbrush where his sword had disappeared. A glint of bright steel on the ground at his feet stopped him. His sword? No... this was the blade that had nearly killed him: a longsword that looked oddly familiar. Mikhyal bent to pick it up.

The moment his fingers closed on the grip, a tingling shock went up his arm, and a great ringing sound resonated through his whole body, rattling his very bones and shaking him to the core. The world went white, and a loud buzzing filled both his ears and his mind.

When his vision cleared, the fighting was still raging around him in the clearing. Before he could dive into the chaos, all was covered in a whirling storm of mist and light, full of claws and teeth. Mikhyal caught brief flashes of teeth rending and blood spattering. Screams rang in his ears, and a terrible feeling of pressure began to build in his head.

The realization that someone must be weaving the mythe froze him. The only mythe-weavers in the royal party were his parents, and neither one of them was capable of anything like this.

Before he could make himself move, the storm was over, though the horror remained. The light-suffused mist lifted, and Mikhyal's gorge rose as he took in the blood-soaked grass and the gleaming piles of white bone that had once been men.

On top of the still form of a dead horse reclined a shimmering, silver creature about the size of a small house cat. It looked vaguely dragon-like, with four clawed feet and a long, tufted tail. A white mane started at the top of its head, and flowed down its back. Thick white whiskers drooped around its mouth, and tufts of shaggy white eyebrow fur twitched above its eyes.

The creature surveyed the carnage with a satisfied nod, then raised its head and grinned, displaying a fearsome array of sharp, glittering teeth. Eyes like shiny black beads fixed on Mikhyal, and one shaggy eyebrow lifted.

Mikhyal swept his gaze around the clearing, seeking his father. All around him, the men of the King's Guard were staring at the carnage, eyes wide with shock. He didn't see his father among them, but before he could call out to anyone, a wave of darkness crashed over him, and he knew no more.

Tristin sat on a stone bench in the courtyard, soaking up the sun. The bench was a new fixture, carved by the royal stonemason out of freshly quarried stone. It had been placed beside the raised flower bed he was in the process of building, so he'd have somewhere to sit when he tired. Somewhere not pulsing with the lingering resonances of his ancestors and those who'd served them.

The building of the flower bed was a slow process. The thick, flat pieces of stone he was using for the walls that would contain the dirt were located behind the herb garden, and Tristin was not strong enough to carry more than one at a time. Kian and Ambris, his healers, had agreed that the exercise would help speed his recovery, so he'd resigned himself to having to carry the materials he needed all the way from the herb garden to the courtyard.

He'd been at it for nearly a week, and every muscle in his body burned and ached. Ilya said it was a good ache, and that as time went on, the pain would fade and his strength would increase. Already, his stamina was improving; each day he was able to work a little longer than the day before. Seeing the labor of his own hands slowly take shape was enough to spur him on. In another day or two, he might finish the walls and begin hauling the dirt he would need to fill it.

A cool mountain breeze brushed his skin, and Tristin closed his eyes, inhaling deeply. The sharp scent of the fir trees covering the lower slopes filled the air, softened by the lighter, sweeter notes of the pink and white flowers planted in the already established flower beds around the courtyard.

When he'd been imprisoned in Shadowspire, he'd never been allowed outside. Not that there had been much of an outside to enjoy; located deep in the Iceshards, the tower of glittering black mythe-stone was surrounded by snow, ice, and bare rock, even in high summer. Once Tristin had arrived there, he'd never left. Fifteen years, he'd been confined to the same suite of rooms, and during that time, he'd seen no one, unless one counted the myriad hallucinations that kept him company, punctuated by rare, perfunctory visits from Wytch Master Mordax.

Here, at Dragonwatch, there were real people to talk to, though it was not so crowded that he found it overwhelming. At the moment, there were only himself, Master Ilya, Kian and his husband Ambris, Alys the housekeeper, and a few guardsmen. Tristin had come to know all of them during the long weeks of his recovery.

A piercing, draconic cry of pure joy sounded in the distance, and Tristin opened his eyes to see a dragon winging its way up the slope. Pale, opalescent scales gleamed in the sunlight. The magnificent creature soared high in the air and executed a flawless loop before swooping low over the courtyard. It circled and touched down lightly just beyond the arched stone entrance, then shifted smoothly into a pale, slender young man with white-blond hair hanging to his waist.

Blushing a charming shade of pink, Prince Jaire of Altan passed through the archway into the courtyard in all his naked glory. He flashed a shy smile at Tristin as he passed. "Good afternoon, Cousin."

Tristin returned the smile as Jaire headed straight for the wooden chest by the main door. "And to you, Your Highness."

Jaire wrinkled his nose. "Don't *Your Highness* me, Tristin. We're cousins and friends, and I shall have none of this standing on ceremony." He gave Tristin a rueful smile as he bent to rummage through the chest. "I was so busy thinking about coming to see you and wondering how far you'd gotten on your flower bed that I forgot to bring some clothes with me. They're still lying in a heap on top of the north tower."

"Ilya's probably got something in his suite that would fit you," Tristin suggested. "I think you'll find him in his study."

"This will do." Jaire pulled a green cloak from the chest and wrapped it around himself. "I've had quite enough of clothes for today. Mistress Nadhya accosted me outside the dining room after breakfast, and I spent the entire morning standing in her fitting room in that ridiculous piece of frippery they want me to wear for the betrothal ceremony. That woman must have worked in the dungeons at some point, though Garrik swears up and down she's never set foot in them. I'm certain he's lying; she enjoys poking me with her pins far too much."

Tristin laughed at that. After having no one to talk to for so long, he found Prince Jaire's company quite enjoyable. Jaire was always happy and bright, and he did most of the talking, which took the burden of thinking of something to say off of Tristin.

"This is really coming along," Jaire said as he came to inspect Tristin's work on the flower bed. "Did they really make you carry all those stones by yourself?"

"Every single one of them. They said it would be good for me."

Jaire wrinkled his nose. "The same way eating horrible vegetables is good for you, I suppose."

"They've even got the guardsmen in on the plot," Tristin said mournfully. "They're allowed to watch and talk to me if they like, but they mustn't lift a finger to help unless I hurt myself."

"You'll have to fake an injury, then," Jaire said, eyes twinkling with mischief. "Though I suppose with three healers here, there's not much chance of getting away with that. I'd stay and help you if I could, but Master Ristan's got the afternoon reserved to go over all the etiquette for the betrothal ceremony with me and Vayne. We have to learn all the official titles of the guests, and who outranks whom. At least I already know most of them. Poor Vayne doesn't know anyone except the family. Honestly, I shall be glad when it's over. Do you think you'll be able to come?"

Tristin swallowed. Jaire and Vayne had saved both his life and his sanity, and he owed it to them to make every effort to attend their betrothal celebration. But Castle Altan was old enough that every stone must be soaked with the emotional resonances left by countless generations of Wytch Kings and their families and servants. Without anzaria — which Master Ilya would not allow him to have under any circumstances — he wouldn't be able to bear it. Not when a single touch of his foot to the floor was enough to overwhelm him with all the toils and travails of those who had walked the halls before him.

"It's only three weeks away, isn't it?" Tristin asked.

"Ai, and it can't come soon enough for me. *Will* you come? Please?"

"I'd very much like to, Jaire," he said gently, "but the last thing you want on your special day is your bastard cousin with the traitorous father tripping all over the dance floor and causing all manner of scandalous talk."

Jaire's face fell. "You always think everything will turn into a disaster if you're there. It won't, you know."

Tristin immediately regretted his offhand remark. "I'm sorry if I've offended, Cousin. I didn't mean to. I'm afraid being locked up alone for so long has made my sense of humor a bit too dark for polite company. I... I've learned to make light of difficult things because if I did not laugh at them, I should surely weep."

At Jaire's look of alarm, Tristin continued quickly, "At any rate, I really would like to be there at your betrothal, but until I've learned the patterns to protect myself, I don't think I could bear it. Ilya tried to start teaching me last week, but it's not going very well. He thinks I just need some time to settle in, but... I rather doubt I'll be ready by the ceremony. I *am* sorry."

Already a diplomat at the tender age of twenty, Jaire covered his disappointment quickly with a smile that looked only a shade too bright to be real. "That's all right. I understand. Surely you'll have managed it by the wedding, though. That's not until after the harvest, and it will be ever so grand! Ilya and Garrik are getting married the same week. There will be parties every night, with entertainments and dancing. And Mistress Nadhya's making me a different suit of clothes for every one of them."

"And you'll have to endure numerous fittings for each one, no doubt," Tristin said. "I'm sure Mistress Nadhya can barely contain her excitement at the prospect."

Jaire scowled and opened his mouth to say something, but no sound came out. The color drained from his cheeks, and he clutched his head. "Aio's teeth," he said from between clenched teeth. "Whoever's caught in the middle of that is in trouble..."

"The middle of what?" Tristin asked.

But Jaire didn't answer. Still clutching his head, he dropped to his knees and let out a low moan. Tristin leapt to his feet. Visions of flame and violence locked in the stones beneath him pushed into his mind, and he gritted his teeth. He'd only taken two steps toward Jaire when the prince slumped over and fell limp on the flagstones. Sweat broke out on Tristin's body as he fought to stay calm in the midst of the chaos of the ancient battle his mind insisted on showing him. With a whimper, he struggled to lift Jaire. The prince was quite a bit smaller than Tristin, but even after several days of lugging rocks, Tristin still couldn't manage Jaire's slight weight.

He was debating whether or not he should leave the prince alone and go for help when Ilya burst into the courtyard. "What's happened?" he asked, moving to help Tristin.

"I don't know," Tristin said as he helped Ilya lift Jaire onto the bench. The Wytch Master knelt beside the prince, eyes unfocusing as he examined Jaire's mythe-shadow with his healer's sight.

Tristin stepped back out of the way and shifted from foot to foot as he sought a comfortable spot to stand on. He recalled a spot he'd noted just yesterday, next to that fine crack in the darker flagstone — a place where the empathic impressions weren't quite so strong — and moved over to it, sighing with relief as the noise faded into the background once more.

"We were talking," he explained to Ilya, "and all of a sudden, Jaire stopped and clutched his head as if he was in pain. He said whoever was caught in the middle of it was in trouble. I'm not sure what he meant, though."

"Something stirring in the mythe. I felt it too, though obviously not as keenly as Jaire did. Whatever it is, it's a long way off." Ilya placed a hand on Jaire's shoulder and gave him a gentle shake.

At Ilya's touch, Jaire stirred, eyes fluttering open. He stared about, looking quite lost. A few moments later, his eyes widened, and he clutched at Ilya's robe. "Ilya, they're hurt! We must go and help!"

"Who is hurt? And where?" Ilya asked. "I sensed a disturbance, but nothing specific."

"I... I don't know. There was a clearing... and men with swords. Some of them wore Rhiva's colors. I felt... fear and pain and... and..." He stared at Ilya, pale grey eyes huge. "A storm in the mythe. A storm of blood and death. It was horrible..."

"A battle?" Ilya looked grim.

"It felt like something more than a battle," Jaire said. "Like the mythe itself had been stirred into a terrible storm. There are people hurt... I can still feel the echoes of it. Can't you feel it, Ilya? Like the ripples on a pond when a stone is dropped into still water..."

"I cannot feel anything of the sort, Jaire," Ilya said gravely, "but if men of Rhiva are in need, it is our duty to go to their aid."

"I can guide you to them," Jaire said. "It's that way." He pointed east, across the river valley that formed the border between the kingdom of Altan and its ally, Irilan.

Ilya turned toward the valley, eyes unfocused. After a short time, he frowned and shook his head. "I still sense nothing, but you are much more sensitive to such things than I. I'll fetch Kian. Wait here."

"You're going?" Tristin asked. "Is Jaire all right to fly?"

"He is shaken, but otherwise sound," Ilya said, stripping out of his clothes right there in the courtyard. "And as I cannot sense the echoes of the disturbance, Jaire is the only one who can lead us to those who are in need of our aid. Alys is in the kitchen, Jaire. Go and ask her to pack some food for us to take with us. Depending on what we find, it may be a number of hours before we can return." Ilya strode through the stone arch. He didn't break stride, not even as he shifted, and quickly took wing.

Jaire stared after the lithe silver-blue dragon gliding down to the castle.

"*Are* you all right?" Tristin asked.

"I'm fine," Jaire said, sounding much stronger now. "As Ilya said, a bit shaken. That surge at the beginning was the strongest thing I've ever felt in the mythe. I'm surprise Ilya only got a whisper of it. I suppose I'd better go and see Alys about some food."

"At least let me help you up." Tristin offered Jaire his arm. "You still look a bit unsteady."

"I'll be all right." He accepted Tristin's help, though, and rewarded him with a rueful smile. "When I said I wanted to escape Master Ristan's etiquette lessons, this wasn't exactly what I had in mind."

Tristin stood in the courtyard next to the dark flagstone with the hairline crack, eyes fixed on the eastern sky. The purple shadows of twilight crept across the flagstones, and the first stars of evening were just visible. Of the three dragons who had taken off from the top of the watchtower earlier in the day, there was no sign.

Shifting his gaze to the tower, Tristin contemplated climbing to the top. The view from the flat rooftop would be much better, but he'd promised Ilya he wouldn't shift while he was gone, and he didn't think he was ready to face the violence of the empathic resonances absorbed by the worn stone steps. The watchtower was far worse than the courtyard, and even if he could reach the top, he'd still have to come down again.

"Alys says dinner's ready."

Tristin started and turned to see Ambris, the gentlest of the healers who'd been caring for him, approaching. He wasn't feeling particularly hungry, and started to say so, but the words died in his throat as he recalled his promise to Jaire that he would do his best to be well enough to come to the prince's wedding in the fall. "Yes, of course. Thank you, Ambris."

Ambris pursed his lips, as if he'd guessed the direction of Tristin's thoughts. "I'd be happy to keep you company if you'd like," he offered.

Only a few weeks ago, Tristin would have refused, unused to spending time with anyone who wasn't a figment of his drug-addled imagination, and unwilling to put himself on display. But Ambris had been there while he'd been deep in the throes of withdrawal. Ambris had already seen him at his worst, but still treated him as if they might be friends.

"I'd be glad of your company, if you think you can stand mine," Tristin ventured. "It's been rather strange, not having any hallucinations to talk to."

"I'm sure I can manage to be a bit more interesting than a hallucination," Ambris said with a gentle smile.

Tristin turned his head to glance up at the sky one more time, and when he looked back at Ambris, the healer's pale gold eyes had also turned skyward. "It's early yet, to expect them back," Ambris said mildly. "If there was a battle of some sort, there will surely be injuries to see to."

"Of course," Tristin said, and turned to follow Ambris inside to his small suite. "Jaire did say he thought there were people injured."

Dragonwatch had never been intended to house a large number of students, and only contained half a dozen suites. Ilya kept permanent rooms here, and Ambris and Kian had been using the suite next door to Tristin's, as they'd spent a fair amount of time here in the weeks since Tristin's arrival.

They settled at the small table in Tristin's sitting room, and Alys soon brought in their dinner. She'd done a roast with tender baby carrots and new potatoes sprinkled with herbs and butter.

"Thank you, Alys," Tristin said. "This looks wonderful."

Alys set her hands on her hips. "Master Ilya left instructions that you were to clean your plate, m'lord, so I shall be reporting to him upon his return."

"If Master Ilya is so intent upon my plate being cleaned," Tristin said, "perhaps we should await his return so he can witness it for himself."

"You'll not be getting out of eating your dinner that easily," Alys told him, twinkling brown eyes belying her otherwise stern expression. She turned to Ambris and added, "And you're not to be eating it for him, brother, or you'll be for it, as well."

Ambris laughed. "As if I would dare! Worry not. I'll see that he eats. I shall have Ilya to answer to if I don't!"

"And me," Alys said, giving Tristin another stern look. "I'm on to your tricks, m'lord, so don't think you'll be slipping it out the window, either."

"Why, Alys," Tristin teased, "I'm shocked and hurt that you think me capable of such duplicitous behavior."

"After last week's attempts to get out of eating, I'd not put anything past you," she said drily. "Master Ilya said you were clever, but I'll warn you right now — I'm cleverer."

Ambris laughed again, and when Alys had gone, Tristin said, "I didn't realize she was your sister. You look nothing alike." Ambris was pale and blond, with intriguing golden eyes, but Alys, with her dark brown hair and eyes and her dusky, dark gold skin, looked almost like a female version of Kian.

"Sister by marriage," Ambris clarified, taking a bite of roast. "She's the eldest of Kian's younger sisters."

"How many sisters does he have?" Tristin asked. Hidden away at Falkrag with his mother, who had scandalized Ysdrach's Court by having a clandestine affair with the late Prince Vakha of Altan, Tristin had never had siblings. He couldn't imagine what it might have been like growing up with other children.

"Three," Ambris said. "Two younger, one older. And an older brother. I've often envied him his family. They truly enjoy one another's company, and seem to genuinely care for one another. My own family is... well. I have two elder brothers, but I've not seen either of them in years. And my father..." Ambris trailed off, shaking his head. "He's coming for the betrothal ceremony, which means I shall be staying here in hiding for the duration. I hate to miss it, as I'm very fond of Prince Jaire, but the last thing I want to do is make things awkward for Garrik. It's best for all concerned if my father continues to believe I'm dead."

Ambris looked so grim, Tristin didn't quite dare ask any of the questions dancing on the tip of his tongue. Instead, he said, "Jaire very much wants me to be there, too. He asked me again this morning. I felt dreadful telling him I couldn't, but after my last lesson with Ilya, I just don't think I can."

"You aren't ready," Ambris said, expression softening. "You're still not completely recovered from the withdrawal. It doesn't surprise me at all that you haven't picked up shielding yet. You're under a great deal of stress, you know. Not just the physical stress of the withdrawal, but the mental stress of having your whole world turned upside down. It's no wonder you can't focus. Do you want me to have a word with Jaire?"

"I don't think that's necessary," Tristin said. "He's disappointed, of course, but he understood. If the courtyard here still gives me headaches, I dread to think what it would be like setting foot in the castle. I doubt I could bear it."

"I shouldn't think so. Not until you can protect yourself, at any rate." Ambris flashed him a quick smile. "Very well, then, you and I shall have our own celebration here while everyone else is down at the castle. I'll have a word with Alys. I'm sure she'll make sure we've something nice to eat, at least."

"Are you sure?" Tristin could hardly believe Ambris would want to celebrate with him. "I mean… I just… I'm sure I'm not very good company, and if you've something better to do—"

"Tristin," Ambris said, gently cutting him off. "It's all right. I really would like to spend the evening with you. I enjoy your company."

"Oh. Oh. Well." Pleased beyond words, Tristin flushed and ducked his head. "Um. Thank you, Ambris. That's… that's very kind."

"Now, tell me about your plans for the flower bed you've been working so hard to create."

They finished the meal with a discussion of what flowers might look nice in the new bed. Ambris promised to see if Master Ludin, the royal gardener, had any suggestions, and invited Tristin to come and help him with the herb garden if he felt like taking a break from lugging rocks and dirt.

It was quite late when Ambris finally took his leave, and Tristin felt more encouraged than he had since he'd arrived. Perhaps one day, he would be able to have something approaching a normal life… whatever that was.

For the first time in many years, Tristin fell asleep thinking of what he might do tomorrow, and actually looking forward to waking.

Dawn was just breaking when terse voices and hurried footsteps in the hallway woke Tristin from a sound sleep. He dressed quickly and eased his door open a crack, peering out in time to see Kian striding down the hall with the limp body of a dark-haired man slung over his shoulder. Behind him came Prince Jaire. Both men were barefoot and dressed in cloaks, and Jaire was dragging a saddlebag in one hand, and had a sheathed sword in the other.

When Jaire caught sight of Tristin hovering in his doorway, he stopped. "Wait until I tell you!" Jaire's grey eyes were alight with excitement.

"Tell me what?" Tristin asked.

"I was right — something *enormous* was happening in the mythe. I'm just going to help get Prince Mikhyal settled, and then I'll be back to tell you all about it."

Prince Mikhyal?

Tristin didn't know enough about Skanda's royal families to have the vaguest notion who Prince Mikhyal might be. He retreated to his room and sat at the table to await Jaire's return. Alys would doubtless be in with breakfast soon enough; he couldn't imagine anyone sleeping through this racket, and if they'd brought a prince back with them, the staff would be falling all over themselves, making certain everything was just so.

Hopefully, the prince wouldn't be staying very long. After years of isolation, Tristin had found it hard enough adjusting to the presence of even the small staff here at Dragonwatch. A royal entourage would be unbearable.

It wasn't long before Jaire arrived, cheeks flushed pink with excitement. He'd taken a few moments to pull on breeches and a shirt, both rumpled enough that Tristin guessed they'd been crammed into the bottom of one of his saddlebags.

"Alys said breakfast will be ready soon." Jaire sat down at the table across from Tristin. "She said she'd bring it here, if that's all right. Ambris is seeing to Prince Mikhyal, and Kian and Ilya have gone off to bed. They're both exhausted. Kian flew all the way back from Rhiva with Prince Mikhyal strapped to his back, and Ilya spent most of his time healing the wounded. It was—"

"The *wounded?*" Tristin echoed, heart beating a little faster. "What in the Dragon Mother's name did you walk into? A battle?"

Jaire grimaced. "The aftermath of one, anyway. Wytch King Drannik's entourage was attacked on their way here. He's the king of Rhiva, remember? He and Queen Icera and Prince Mikhyal were coming here for the betrothal. Anyway, it wasn't so much a battle as a massacre, to hear Wytch King Drannik tell it."

"Oh, dear." Tristin couldn't help but wince. "How... how many people...?"

"Fifteen bandits killed — or at least, that's what they thought. It was a bit difficult to tell. None of Drannik's party were killed, although a few of his guardsmen were wounded. Prince Mikhyal saved them all. His Wytch power awakened, and he killed every last one of them. All that was left was their bones!" Jaire's eyes were wide, and a visible shiver rippled through the young prince. "By the time we got there, they'd cleaned up the battle site, and the guard captain and half the guardsmen had escorted the queen's entourage and some of the wounded to the nearest village. There wasn't much left for us to do except, have Ilya and Kian heal the worst of the wounded."

"Prince Mikhyal killed fifteen bandits? What sort of Wytch power can do that?"

"I'm not exactly sure," Jaire said. "But whatever he did, it was powerful enough that Ilya and I both felt it all the way from Rhiva. Drannik said the bandits ambushed them in a clearing. They were fighting for their lives, when all of a sudden, a fog came down and covered everything. There were screams and flashes of light, and when the fog lifted, all that was left of the bandits were little piles of polished bone, carefully arranged in strange patterns. They found Mikhyal unconscious and suffering from mythe-shock. Drannik thought Mikhyal's Wytch power must have awakened, and Ilya said that was a possibility, but he'd have to examine him more thoroughly to be sure."

"So this Mikhyal is what, fifteen or so? He looked a bit big for fifteen, if he's the one I saw Kian carrying in."

"No, I think he's about Garrik's age," Jaire said. "Twenty-seven or twenty-eight? It's been years since I've seen him. He's the eldest of Drannik's sons, but the Wytch Council wouldn't consider him for the throne because his Wytch power never awakened. Like your father. And like Garrik, until Master Tevari woke his power. So Mikhyal's younger brother, Shaine, is the heir now. I suppose that'll change, once Mikhyal gets control of his power. If he ever does. Well, Ilya will teach him. He's good at that, though he had to argue with Wytch King Drannik for hours about bringing him here at all."

"The king didn't want his son to come here?" Tristin asked. "Why ever not?"

"Well, I think he was a bit worried about having Mikhyal go on dragonback, what with him being in mythe-shock and all. I can understand him being a bit nervous. Kian *is* quite big, and rather fierce looking, if you don't know how soft he is underneath. Ilya told Drannik with a Wytch power that deadly, the Wytch Council would send Mikhyal to Dragonwatch anyway, and it would save everyone a lot of time and bother to just bring him here straight away. I thought Ilya was going to have to play Wytch Master and invoke Council Law — he *hates* doing that — but Drannik did finally see the sense of it. He even agreed to let Kian and Ilya come back for him in a week, so he can escort the queen back to the palace and still get here in time for the ceremony. I don't think he was looking forward to it, though. He looked a bit green when they were strapping Mikhyal in for the journey. Oh, and there was a sword, too! It glowed in the mythe, and there's a glowing thread connecting it to Mikhyal. Ilya says it's a mythe-blade, and Mikhyal is freshly bonded to it, and Drannik didn't look at all happy about that. He wanted to take it back to the palace with him, but Ilya told him separating Mikhyal from it would kill him, so we brought it with us."

Tristin listened as Jaire rambled on about his adventure. All that was required of Tristin was the occasional question or murmur of agreement, and he was quite happy to supply that.

Jaire didn't stop talking until Alys brought breakfast. Tristin watched in amazement as the young man devoured two huge stacks of flat cakes smothered with cream and strawberry jam. Tristin barely managed a single cake with a light scraping of butter and a drizzle of honey.

When he'd finished his breakfast, Prince Jaire rose and said, "Sorry I can't stay longer, Tristin, but I need to get some sleep, and I promised Ilya I'd go and report to Garrik as soon as I'd had something to eat." He hurried off, promising he'd be back just as soon as he could manage it.

After he'd gone, Tristin stacked the plates on the tray and carried them to the kitchen. Alys would probably appreciate the help, what with having an unexpected royal guest to run around after.

With everyone else either asleep or seeing to the new arrival, Tristin found himself at a loose end. Recalling his dinner conversation with Ambris, he thought perhaps he'd go and have a look at the herb garden. While building the new flower bed was satisfying, he found himself longing to get his fingers into the dirt. Working in Falkrag's gardens had always soothed him, and he'd certainly learned enough from Falkrag's gardener during his childhood that he'd be able to see what was needed in the herb garden easily enough.

Determined to start immediately, he went straight to his bedroom to change. He stopped in the doorway, brought up short by the sight of a small creature curled up on his pillow. For a moment, he thought it was a little silver cat, but upon closer inspection, he realized it had more in common with one of the dragons than a cat. Its features were certainly draconic, and instead of fur, it was covered in delicate silver scales that glinted in the sunlight.

Unlike the dragon forms of the shifters he knew, this creature had fluffy eyebrow tufts, long, luxurious whiskers, and a flowing, silky mane running halfway down its back.

It couldn't possibly be real. As Tristin squinted at it, one of its back legs began twitching in a way that reminded him of his uncle's hunting dogs, running down rabbits in their dreams.

What did a dragon that size dream about chasing?

"You can't possibly be one of my hallucinations." Tristin's voice cracked and wavered. "I've not had any of Mordax's damned drug in weeks."

"Hallucination?" The creature cracked open gleaming black eyes, twitched its long whiskers, and gave him a flat stare. "Guess again, Human."

A moment later, it vanished into thin air.

Tristin sank down slowly on his bed, bitter disappointment crushing his chest and tightening his throat. Just last night, Ambris had commented on how well he looked, and how much good working outside was doing him. But the fact that he was hallucinating again suggested that he wasn't doing nearly as well as Ambris thought.

Was he finally going mad? Or was this just a lingering remnant of his addiction?

Tristin squeezed his eyes shut. For a moment, all he wanted to do was shift into dragon form and flee. It wouldn't help, though;

while it might make him feel better in the short term, he would never learn to stand on his own two feet if he fled at every setback.

So instead of tearing his clothing off and running outside, Tristin rode out the urge to shift, imagining instead Ilya's cool, soothing voice talking him down: *Deep breaths, Tristin. It's not real. You're just under too much stress. Ambris even said so last night, and he's a healer. He would certainly know.*

When he opened his eyes again, the bed was still empty, and Tristin breathed a little easier. Perhaps he'd had a bit too much sun yesterday. Or... or perhaps something he'd eaten hadn't agreed with him.

He'd wear a hat today to protect himself from the sun. And he'd watch what he ate.

There was a simple, logical explanation for this, and it had nothing to do with hallucinations.

Chapter Three

Tristin knelt on a low wooden platform and dragged a hand rake over the dirt in his new flower bed. He'd put the platform together himself after he'd discovered that wood insulated him from the worst of the empathic resonances. It was roughly built and not quite square, but Tristin was rather proud of his first attempt at carpentry. Better yet, it seemed to be helping; his headache today was barely noticeable.

The sun was warm on his back, and he paused in his work to wipe the sweat from his brow. The last few days had been more peaceful than he might have guessed. In the cold light of day, he'd managed to convince himself that the little dragon he'd thought he'd seen was simply the product of an overwrought imagination. Too much stress, he'd decided; Ambris had suggested as much the other night.

So Tristin had thrown all his energy into working in the garden, and it seemed to be helping. The rich smell of the earth calmed him, bringing to mind some of the few happy memories of his childhood. Getting his fingers into the dirt was satisfying in a way that nothing else was. Today, he felt more in tune with his body than he had since his arrival. He'd slept deeply and well last night, and best of all, he'd had no more hallucinations of any sort.

He'd spent the last few days lugging buckets of dirt from the back gardens to fill his flower bed. By the time he stopped at the end of each day, his legs were shaking and his muscles were burning, but he couldn't complain. The stiffness of his limbs in the mornings reminded him he was still alive. Indeed, it often felt as if he was only just waking up from a nightmare that had consumed years of his life.

It gave him no end of satisfaction that he'd accomplished this task all on his own. Now, he stared down at the dark, rich earth and considered what he might plant there. It was too late in Altan's short growing season to start anything from seed, but Alys had said he might split some of the larger plants from the beds in the back near the kitchen. And there was that pretty purple creeper that spread so quickly. Alys had wrinkled her nose and called it a weed, but its flowers were a lovely shade of violet. It would at least fill the bed for the rest of the summer. Then, next spring he could—

Tristin blinked.

Next spring…

Would he even be here next spring?

He sat back on his heels and stared down the mountain at the castle. He'd been so ill when he'd first come here that he'd given no thought to what might come after his recovery. Now, with his addiction behind him and his body becoming stronger with every passing day, he ought to think about what he was going to do with the rest of his life.

Assuming, of course, that he could learn to protect himself from the empathic resonances that still haunted his every step. Ilya seemed to think he could, even though his attempts thus far had all been failures.

Going back to Ysdrach was out of the question. There was no place for him in his Wytch King uncle's kingdom, and even if there was, he'd never trust Altivair again. Not after his uncle had been complicit in a plot that would have put Tristin on Altan's throne as a puppet-king and seen Garrik and Jaire dead or in chains.

Where *would* he go?

He could hardly stay here. Bastard son of a man who'd tried to murder his way into a regency… No. Prince Jaire might have taken a shine to him, but Wytch King Garrik had no reason to trust him.

"That's going to look lovely, overflowing with flowers." Ambris's voice came from behind him. "Have you decided which ones you want?" The healer looked weary, the dark circles under his eyes a striking contrast to his pale skin. Prince Mikhyal was very ill, requiring constant care. Ambris, Kian, or Ilya had been with him every minute since he'd arrived.

Tristin rose and dusted off his breeches, keeping his feet firmly on the wooden platform. "I'm not sure. Something bright and cheerful, I think. Reds and yellows, perhaps, though it's too late to do anything much with it this season, other than transplant some things from the kitchen gardens. I don't suppose my favorites from Ysdrach would do very well up here in the mountains."

"I haven't had a chance to talk to Master Ludin yet." Even in his exhaustion, Ambris managed to sound as if he truly regretted not having done so.

"Of course you haven't," Tristin replied. "You've been busy with Prince Mikhyal, and he's much more important than my flowers."

"Perhaps you'll be able to go down to the castle and speak with him yourself before long."

"I... I'd like that, but..." Tristin trailed off. Given his current lack of progress, it would be a long time before he could even think about braving the castle. He'd tested himself on the watchtower steps just that morning, and the mental onslaught had been every bit as bad as it had when he'd first come.

Things might improve once he started working with Ilya again, but with Prince Mikhyal to care for, and the betrothal ceremony just over two weeks away, Tristin had hardly seen the Royal Wytch Master.

Ambris reached out and gave Tristin's shoulder an encouraging squeeze. "It will come, Tristin. Ilya might have some time to work with you in the next few days. Prince Mikhyal has improved a great deal since yesterday."

"Has he? That must be a relief."

"I must admit, I am rather looking forward to a full night of unbroken sleep," Ambris said. "Next to my husband, if I'm lucky. In fact, that's what I came to see you about. Mikhyal is out of danger and sleeping normally now. Kian and I have hardly seen each other since he flew out to Rhiva, and I wondered if you wouldn't mind watching over Mikhyal this afternoon in case he wakes up. He'll be in need of some reassurance."

"I wouldn't mind," Tristin said, "only I don't suppose I'd be much good at reassuring him. I've not had much experience with that sort of thing."

"That's all right — if he stirs, you can send for me and Kian. We'll do all the explaining. I'd just rather not have him waking up alone in a strange place. The Dragon Mother only knows what he might think, or what sort of horrible dreams he's been having. There's no danger. We've been giving him anzaria, so he won't be capable of unleashing his Wytch power even if he does wake up frightened and disoriented."

"All right," Tristin said, pleased that there was something useful he could do to help the healers who had taken such good care of him.

"You might want to stop by your room for a book," Ambris added as they went inside.

Tristin followed Ambris in and stopped in his own rooms for the book Prince Jaire had brought for him only yesterday morning. The prince's thoughtfulness had touched Tristin's heart; Jaire had found a book on plants and flowers he thought Tristin might enjoy in Altan's library. He'd taken the trouble to have the castle scribes copy the text and the drawings so Tristin wouldn't have to worry about the book having absorbed any disturbing emotional resonances from its previous owners.

In Prince Mikhyal's room, Tristin settled himself in the armchair drawn up beside the bed and opened the book.

"We meet again." The voice was male, familiar, and pleasant. Tristin started, eyes going straight to Prince Mikhyal, but the prince's eyes were closed, his dark lashes a shocking contrast to his pale skin.

Tristin set his book down and glanced about the room. A glimmer of light at the foot of the bed caught his attention, and he rubbed his eyes, certain he was seeing things again.

There, curled up next to Prince Mikhyal's feet, was the little silver dragon he'd imagined a few days ago. It got to its feet and stretched, arching its back like a cat. Its jaws opened wide in a yawn, pink forked tongue curling. It turned around several times, like a dog, before settling itself, this time facing Tristin.

"You're not a hallucination," Tristin blurted out before he could stop himself.

"What a coincidence," the dragon said tartly. "Neither are you." It lifted one sharp, black claw, licked it, and dragged it through long, flowing whiskers.

"I suppose I shall have to tell Ilya I'm seeing things that aren't there again," he murmured. "It seems to be the only thing I'm good at, just lately."

The dragon finished grooming itself and crossed its little front feet neatly. It looked exactly like Tristin's memory of it: a slender, sinuous thing with a long snout, impressive whiskers, and far too many teeth. Now that he looked more closely, in addition to its fluffy eyebrows and flowing mane, Tristin noted a pair of delicate wings folded against its back, a small, white tuft at the end of its tail, and just a hint of white fuzz at the tips of its little pointed ears.

Glittering black eyes, bright with intelligence, caught Tristin's gaze and held it. "Or perhaps you're rather good at seeing things that *are* here. I don't suppose I could persuade you to tell me where here is." The dragon sounded a bit mournful, and when Tristin didn't answer, it let out a heavy sigh and rested its chin between its front feet, much like his uncle's hounds did when they were begging for a bit of meat. "It would save us both a lot of time and aggravation."

"Don't... don't you know?"

"*Humans*," it muttered, making the word sound like an insult. "If I knew, there would be no point in asking, would there?"

"I... suppose not." Tristin glanced at Prince Mikhyal to make certain he was still asleep. It wouldn't do to have the prince wake up and catch him talking to himself. He'd been looking forward to meeting someone who didn't have any preconceived ideas about his sanity, but the prince wasn't even awake yet, and he was already off to an unfortunate start.

"You're at Dragonwatch," Tristin said in a low voice, "in the kingdom of Altan. If you're looking for the castle, it's just down the mountain. It's not far. Well. I mean, it's probably not far for you, assuming those wings of yours are actually functional and not just decorative." No point in being polite to a hallucination. Besides, if he offended it, perhaps it would go away. It was a tactic that had rarely worked in the past, but one could always hope.

The dragon laid its ears back and regarded him with a level stare before saying very softly, "Decorative?"

Tristin shrugged, but didn't offer an apology. "You're rather prickly for a hallucination. Or... perhaps not. I'm usually too drug-mazed to recall the details of these sorts of encounters."

"Prickly," it mused. "Let me show you *prickly*." It flashed him a wide grin, displaying a glittering array of needle-sharp, crystal-clear teeth.

"Charming," Tristin commented, certain he'd never held a conversation this long — or this coherent — with any of his hallucinations. "I suppose next you'll be threatening me."

"Not much point. You don't look bright enough to take heed."

Tristin frowned, perplexed. His hallucinatory visitors didn't usually insult him.

The dragon got to its feet, stretched again, then hopped lightly up on the window sill and gazed out over the mountains. "The Iceshards or the Dragon's Spine? If memory serves, Altan borders both, though these look a bit high and sharp to be the Dragon's Spine."

"The Iceshards," Tristin said.

"But Altan, not Rhiva. Interesting." The little dragon turned to face him and sat neatly on its haunches, tufted tail curling around its dainty, clawed feet. "Well, then. What shall I call you? *Human* seems a bit too general, if the parade in and out of here is any indication of how many of you there are wandering about. Have you a name that distinguishes you from the rest of them?"

"Tristin," he said promptly. "Prince Tristin of... well. Of the new flower bed, I suppose. There was some talk of me being king at one point, but that appears to be off the table for good." Tristin paused for a moment, then added hastily, "Not that I'm complaining, what with all the bloodshed that would have ensued... and the fact that I'm completely unsuited to be..." He trailed off as he remembered his manners. "And you are...?"

"You may call me Dirit."

"Dirit. That's a rather odd name." Tristin cocked his head as he studied the creature in the light. "Doesn't fit you at all. More the sort of thing you'd call one of those brightly colored songbirds. Or perhaps a type of shrew. Or one of those little hopping insects with the lacy—"

"*Insects?*" Dirit's tail lashed back and forth, and its eyebrow tufts drew together in a scowl.

"Father?" The voice came from the bed, and Tristin looked down to see Prince Mikhyal's eyes fluttering open. Before he could come up with something helpful and reassuring to say, Dirit hopped down off the window sill and onto the bed. The little dragon marched up the prince's body, stood upon his chest, and stared down at him.

The prince's pale blue eyes widened as they fixed on Dirit. "No... you can't be real..." Prince Mikhyal's voice broke, his words ending on a low, choking sob.

Tristin leapt to his feet, but before he could call for anyone, the prince's eyes rolled back in his head and his body went limp.

"Well." Dirit turned to Tristin, whiskers twitching with something that looked perilously close to amusement. "That went better than expected."

Mikhyal was on his knees surrounded by a bloody fog. The screams of the dying sliced through him like razor-edged steel, and a cold far deeper than the bite of a winter wind out of the Iceshards froze him from the marrow out.

The murderous dragon-creature followed him into his dreams. Its black eyes fixed on him in a mocking stare, and its needle-sharp teeth dripped blood. Seeking to escape the nightmare, Mikhyal struggled to wake, only to find the thing had followed him.

With a sob, he fled back into the icy darkness.

"Mikhyal? Prince Mikhyal, can you open your eyes?"

The voice wasn't at all familiar, and with vague memories of a battle flashing through his mind, Mikhyal's first instinct was to feign sleep.

"It's all right," the voice soothed. "You're safe. You've been brought to Altan for healing. I'm Ambris, and you've been in my care ever since you arrived."

Mikhyal forced his eyes open to find himself staring into a pair of kind, pale gold eyes set into a thin face framed by short, golden-blond hair.

Blood-drenched images of the ambush filled his mind: armed men charging across the clearing, more emerging from the trees; his father, sword in hand, mouth set in a grim line as he fought to protect his queen and his men.

"My... my father..." Mikhyal struggled to sit, but a firm hand on his shoulder pushed him back down.

"Your father is quite safe," Ambris said matter-of-factly. "As is your mother. You saved their lives. Saved all of them."

"Where..." He glanced around, taking in the unfamiliar furnishings. "Where am I?"

"You're at Dragonwatch, a little way up the mountain from Castle Altan. You've been suffering from mythe-shock, but I think you're going to be all right now."

"Mythe-shock? But..." Mikhyal blinked at Ambris, trying to understand what could have happened to bring him here. He remembered the ambush and being certain he was about to die... then Rhu had been there, and after that, the fog. When it lifted, a dragon-like creature with gleaming black eyes and teeth like little glass needles had been staring at him...

But no... that part couldn't have been real. In his illness, his mind had woven nightmares from threads of memory drenched in the lurid shades of fever dreams.

"Try to relax," Ambris said. "Wytch Master Ilya will be here later, and he will explain everything. For now, it's enough for you to know that you and your family are safe. Your father will be arriving in a few days."

But Mikhyal couldn't relax. Not until he knew how much of the nightmare was real. "You said I saved them... but... how? We were attacked on the road... there were far too many..."

"Ah. Well. It appears that your Wytch power may have awakened. That is why you were brought here to Dragonwatch instead of taken home to Rhiva."

"Wytch power? But... I don't... I don't have any Wytch power..."

"Master Ilya can explain it far better than I can. He will come and see you later."

"But I need to know what happened," Mikhyal insisted. "The guardsmen who escorted us... how many dead? How many injured?"

"There were no deaths," Ambris said. "Not among your folk, at least. The worst of the injuries were seen to by Ilya and one of his assistants."

Ambris took a wooden cup from the bedside table and held it out to Mikhyal. "Drink this." He used the same tone of voice Rhiva's healers did, full of confidence that in the sickroom, at least, he was in charge, regardless of his patient's social standing.

The bone-deep cold still lingered, and Mikhyal shivered as he hauled himself up to sitting and accepted the cup. The liquid inside was thick and had a floral scent. "What is this?"

"Anzaria," Ambris said as he settled a dark blue knitted blanket over Mikhyal's shoulders.

"Anzaria?" He couldn't imagine why Ambris thought he needed that. Anzaria was used to shut down a Wytch's access to the mythe. But Mikhyal couldn't touch the mythe; if he could, he'd be the heir, not Shaine.

"Ilya thought it safer to keep you drugged until he's had a chance to examine you properly and decide what to do with you. There are some... ah... *uncertainties* as to what, exactly, your condition is."

Ambris was clearly not going to explain. Mikhyal raised the cup to his lips and drank down the contents. It was warm and sweet, and tasted much like it smelled, like wildflowers and honey. He handed the empty cup back to Ambris and settled back against the pillows. Something knocked against his leg as he shifted position, and he looked down to see a sheathed longsword lying next to him. It looked vaguely familiar.

"Why is this here?" he asked.

"*That* is one of the uncertainties," Ambris said. "Master Ilya will explain—"

"Later, I know." Mikhyal sighed and resigned himself to waiting. "Well, if you cannot tell me what's happened to me, perhaps you can tell me what happened to my men. How is it that healers from Altan saw to their injuries when the ambush occurred within the borders of Rhiva?"

"You have Prince Jaire to thank for that," Ambris said, sinking down in the armchair next to the bed.

"Prince Jaire? How?"

"He sensed something stirring in the mythe, all the way across Irilan and Miraen to Rhiva. He's the one who led Master Ilya and Kian to your side. Like Prince Jaire and Master Ilya, Kian is a dragon shifter. The three of them flew out to find the source of the disturbance. What they found was the aftermath of a battle. A few of your men were injured, and you were deep in mythe-shock. They did what they could to aid your party, and then strapped you to Kian's back and brought you here, so Master Ilya could oversee your recovery."

"Strapped me to... I came here on *dragonback*?" Mikhyal searched his mind, but he had no memory of such a thing. Was he truly conscious, or was this, too, part of the nightmare?

As if reading his thoughts, Ambris said quietly, "You were in no state to remember. You were so deeply unconscious, we feared for your life at first."

"But... but... *dragons*? I thought Wytch Master Ilya and Wytch King Garrik were the only ones."

"Ah. Well." Ambris cleared his throat, and his expression became guarded. "That, too, is something to be discussed at another time. After your recovery."

"But—"

"Your Highness, I've probably already said more than I ought, and I'd really rather not have to deal with the Wytch King when he's in a temper. I fear your questions will have to wait. You are still recovering, and rest is more important than anything else at the moment."

The determined set to Ambris's jaw told Mikhyal further argument would be futile. "And you are the healer."

"Exactly so. Mythe-shock is no laughing matter. It very nearly killed you."

"I shall do my best to follow your orders then, Master Ambris. It wouldn't do for you to have to give my father an unfavorable report, now, would it?"

"No, it would not." Ambris's lips twitched. "I appreciate you saving me the trouble of issuing the threat myself."

"What do your orders say about how long I must lie abed?"

Ambris considered that for a moment. "You may get up tomorrow, I think. But only for a short time, and only if you can manage to eat something today."

"That sounds more than fair. Since I appear to be at your mercy, I shall endeavor to do my best to please you."

"If only all my patients were so accommodating." Ambris smiled as he got to his feet. "I'll go and speak with Mistress Alys about putting together a tray for you. Soup to start with, but if you're feeling up to it, you can try a bit of bread for your dinner tonight."

Mikhyal's stomach growled at the thought of food, and Ambris's smile widened. "Perhaps I'll send along some bread, after all."

When Ambris had gone, Mikhyal pulled the blanket tighter about his shoulders and surveyed his surroundings. The room was simply furnished, but comfortable, with stone walls and a polished wooden floor. The weapon rack hanging on the wall opposite his bed held his own sword, which reminded him of the one lying on the bed next to him. Mikhyal lifted it and studied the hilt, trying to think where he'd seen the thing before.

"About time you woke up," said a male voice that sounded as if it came from both everywhere and nowhere.

Mikhyal's gaze went first to the closed door, then traveled around the room, seeking the speaker.

"Four days, it's been," the voice continued, "with no one to talk to except that half-mad fellow down the hall, and *he's* written me off as one of his hallucinations." The long pause that followed was punctuated by a pained sniff. "Hallucination, indeed."

A flash of silver near the end of his bed caught his eye. He blinked, and there, curled up in a patch of sunlight near his feet, lay the dragon-like creature of his nightmares. About the size of a small house cat, it wasn't nearly as big as it had been in his dreams, but Mikhyal's heart still stuttered, and a wave of cold dread crashed through him. He threw the covers back and scrambled out of bed, still gripping the sword.

"*Do* calm down, Your Highness." Unblinking black eyes regarded him with an expression that looked very much like disapproval. "And get yourself back into bed before you fall over. Do I look big enough to eat you?"

"Y-you ate at least a d-dozen armed men the other day. I'm n-not sure size has much to d-do with it."

"Ah. *That.*" The little dragon sounded almost regretful. "I'd rather hoped you hadn't seen that. Pity."

"What..." Mikhyal's throat went dry. "What do you want?" he whispered.

"I want you to get back into bed. And then I shall answer all the questions the healer would not."

Mikhyal considered that. If the creature meant him harm, it could easily have killed him while he'd lain here, helpless. Not taking his eyes off of it, he moved cautiously to the bed and slowly got in, still gripping the hilt of the sword tightly.

Once he was settled as far away from the creature as he could get without falling off the bed, the dragon sat up on its haunches and cocked its head, regarding him from gleaming black eyes. "It's time we were properly introduced. I am called Dirit, and I am bound to protect you and your line, Prince Mikhyal of Rhiva."

"Me and my line?" Mikhyal's voice cracked. "You want the heir, then, not me. I'm nobody." He stared down at his hands. "Nobody important, anyway."

"You are *most* important to me," Dirit said matter-of-factly. "You are my bond-mate." The dragon's eyes fixed pointedly on the sword Mikhyal still clutched.

Mikhyal stared down at the blade. "This?" He dropped it down on the bed. "What has the sword to do with anything?"

"It's very simple, really. I am bonded to the sword, as are you. That makes you my bond-mate."

"*Bonded?*" A ripple of unease went through Mikhyal. As a child, he'd heard fantastic tales of swords that could form bonds with men, but he'd never seen anything to make him think those stories could have any basis in fact. "Are you telling me this is one of those mythe-blades?"

The little dragon's tiny forked tongue flicked out for just a moment. "Is that some sort of trick question?"

"But I... I thought... but those are just *stories*, aren't they? I mean, I just... I picked this up on the battlefield after I lost my own. It belonged to one of the bandits. Wouldn't you have been bonded to him?"

"Even if he hadn't been quite dead when you picked up the blade, he was of *common* blood." Dirit flattened his ears and let out a disdainful little sniff. "*Not* of the royal bloodline of Rhiva. Not even remotely. I couldn't have bonded to him if I'd wanted to." The dragon grinned, showing its teeth. "And I didn't want to."

Mikhyal opened his mouth to say more, but at that moment there was a knock on the door. It opened to reveal a tall, slender man with the black hair and dark eyes so common to the royal lines of Skanda.

"Oh, time for another formal introduction!" Dirit grinned broadly, displaying even more glittering fangs. "Prince Mikhyal of Rhiva, allow me to introduce Prince Tristin of... of the New Flower Bed, was it not?"

Prince Tristin took one look at Dirit, blanched, and promptly dropped the tray he was carrying. It hit the floor with a clatter, and the poor man looked so distraught, Mikhyal's heart went out to him.

"It's all right," Mikhyal said quickly. "Accidents happen."

Dirit lifted one of his front feet and waved it dismissively. "Oh, don't worry about him. He's overly sensitive. He's still trying to decide whether or not I'm a hallucination."

Tristin's wide-eyed gaze shifted from Mikhyal to Dirit and back again, then dropped to the floor to fix on the broken crockery at his feet. His cheeks colored, and he stammered, "I'm t-terribly s-sorry, Your Highness. I'll j-just go and g-get someone to c-clean this." With that, he bolted into the hallway, slamming the door shut behind him.

Mikhyal stared after him for a few moments, then turned to Dirit. The dragon appeared to be smirking. The moment Mikhyal met his eyes, Dirit's ears drooped, and he looked away.

Face flaming, Tristin slammed Prince Mikhyal's door shut and fled back to the kitchen. The dragon. The little cat-sized dragon he'd been hallucinating had been right there in the prince's bedroom, lounging on the bed, bold as brass.

And the prince had been *talking* to it, as if he could actually *see* it.

Which meant it *wasn't* a hallucination.

It should have made him feel better, but instead, Tristin felt sick.

"That was fast." Mistress Alys turned from the stove, a wooden spoon in her hand. "Was His Highness satisfied with the tray, then?"

"Um. I... I had... there was... a bit of an accident..." Tristin started to stammer out an apology, which quickly turned into a rambling, incoherent explanation.

Mistress Alys merely raised a dark eyebrow and waited. When he'd finally wound down, rather than asking him to repeat himself, she said, "You'll be wanting some rags and a bucket, then, won't you?"

Before Tristin could respond, she'd plucked a pile of rags and a bucket from a shelf, and handed them to him. Tristin was too surprised to do anything but take them. He'd been intending to finish his flight to his own suite, and take to his bed for the foreseeable future. Midwinter, perhaps, he might think about venturing out again, about the time when—

"Pick up as much of the crockery as you can," Mistress Alys ordered, "and wipe up the mess. Then come back for the broom and sweep the floor. It won't do for His Highness to cut his feet." Her tone was firm, but she didn't appear angry. "I'll prepare another tray while you're tidying up."

"Y-yes, Mistress Alys," Tristin stammered, and backed out of the kitchen.

In the hallway, he stared down at the rags, let out a heavy sigh, and trudged back to the prince's bedroom. He dithered outside the door for several minutes before finally plucking up the courage to ease it open just a crack.

From the safety of the hallway, he peered in. The little dragon was no longer lounging on the bed. Taking that as a positive sign, Tristin opened the door a bit more.

"It's all right," Prince Mikhyal said from the bed. "You can come in."

"I've, ah, come to apologize for throwing your lunch on the floor. And to tidy up the mess I made." Tristin edged into the room and peered about.

"He's gone. The dragon, I mean. Dirit, he calls himself."

"Ai, we've met," Tristin mumbled. He dropped to his knees and began picking up bits of broken crockery. "I was certain I was imagining him."

"So he said."

Tristin's hand froze on the way to the bucket. "He..." He gulped air and had to fight to keep his voice steady. "He told you about me?"

"He mentioned you when he was complaining about having no one to talk to. He seemed rather affronted that you thought he was a hallucination." The prince didn't sound at all concerned about the fact that a small dragon had been sitting on his bed. Tristin risked a glance up. Prince Mikhyal gave him an encouraging smile. "I'm Mikhyal," he said. "And if Dirit is to be believed, you are Tristin."

"Prince Tristin of the New Flower Bed, apparently," Tristin murmured. "At your service. Only, I'm not really. A prince, I mean. My father was a prince, but I'm just a bastard with no—" He snapped his mouth shut, realizing that he'd probably just said far too much. Talking to real people, he'd discovered, was far more fraught than talking to hallucinations, which were there and gone again in the blink of an eye, and didn't remember all the stupid things that came out of one's mouth.

Prince Mikhyal laughed, a deep, rich sound, and Tristin looked up to find his gaze caught by a pair of pale blue eyes in a very handsome face, framed by tousled black hair. Several days' worth of dark beard covered a strong jaw, giving him a rugged look that Tristin found rather intriguing, much to his dismay.

"It... it doesn't bother you?" Tristin finally managed to say as he dropped the last of the crockery into the bucket.

"What? The questionable circumstances of your birth?"

"No... well, yes, *that*, but I meant the... Dirit. The... the... d-dragon."

Prince Mikhyal blinked. "To be honest, I'm still not convinced I'm actually awake. The things I saw... and... and if I *am* awake..." His eyes darted down to the bed covers, and Tristin followed his gaze to see the sheathed sword lying alongside him. "I suppose I might be mad," the prince mused.

Their eyes met, and Tristin gulped. "Then we can be mad together," he said gaily, and tore his gaze away from Prince Mikhyal's. He bent forward to hide his flaming cheeks and began wiping up the spilled broth.

"If I *am* going mad," the prince said slowly, "I suppose I would rather do it in company than alone."

Tristin didn't dare reply. He finished mopping up the mess, got to his feet, and left the room as quickly as he could. The hall was empty, thank the Dragon Mother, because his face was still burning, and surely if anyone saw him, they'd ask about it. He stopped by the kitchen long enough to deposit the bucket full of broken crockery and soaked rags just inside the door.

Mistress Alys was nowhere to be seen, so, feeling vaguely guilty, Tristin crept back to his own room. Hopefully, she wouldn't remember that she'd asked him to deliver another tray.

It was with vast relief that he closed his bedroom door and leaned heavily against it. He squeezed his eyes shut, but he couldn't get Prince Mikhyal's face out of his mind. His rich laughter, his rugged good looks, and those kind blue eyes...

With a shiver, Tristin pressed his hands to his face and hoped Prince Mikhyal wouldn't be here for very long.

Dirit didn't return, not even after Tristin's hasty escape, and Mikhyal began to wonder if he'd imagined the strange encounter. Perhaps the dragon and the bastard prince were both figments of his imagination. It did all seem like some very odd fairy tale.

Mikhyal had little knowledge of healing, but if he was suffering from mythe-shock, surely it wouldn't be unheard of for him to be having odd, waking dreams.

Not long after Tristin's departure, Mistress Alys brought him some lunch. Mikhyal ate the bread with great enjoyment, and the moment he'd finished the broth, a great wave of sleepiness overcame him. He closed his eyes for just a moment, but when he opened them, twilight was darkening the room. Mikhyal stretched luxuriously. His head felt much clearer now, and his body tingled with restless energy.

"Oh, finally," said a familiar voice. "You've been asleep again."

Mikhyal turned slowly to see Dirit sitting on the wide window ledge, long tail curled neatly around his tiny, clawed feet.

"You haven't been a very interesting bond-mate thus far." The dragon sounded petulant. "But I suppose I shouldn't complain, since you *are* at least talking to me. Not like my last bond-mate, who refused to even acknowledge my existence. Very rude of him, I thought."

"I must still be dreaming," Mikhyal murmured to himself.

There was a knock on the door. Dirit didn't move, but his grin widened.

"Come in!" Mikhyal called out.

The door opened and in came Wytch Master Ilya. Mikhyal knew Altan's Wytch Master a little, having met him several times over the past few years at various royal gatherings. Ilya was slender, and with his delicate features, he could almost be called pretty. He had long, coppery hair, currently hanging loose to his hips, and rumor had it he was far older than the twenty years he appeared to have lived.

Master Ilya made a brief gesture with his fingers, and a ball of yellow light floated up from his hand to hover near the center of the ceiling, bathing the room in a soft, golden glow. "That's not too bright for you, is it?" he asked.

"No, it's fine. Thank you for asking." Mikhyal pulled himself up in the bed and shoved the pillows higher behind him.

"Ambris said you'd improved, but I must say, I hadn't expected to find you sitting up and talking sense quite so soon." The Wytch Master pulled the room's single chair close to the side of the bed and settled himself there. "How are you feeling?"

"Better, at least in the physical sense," Mikhyal said. "Although there are some rather odd things going on. Ambris said you would explain."

"*Odd things,*" Dirit muttered. "Oh, *very* nice."

Mikhyal glanced at the dragon, and then at Ilya. "You didn't hear that, did you? And you can't see it, either."

Ilya looked toward the window, frowning. "Should I see something?"

"A dragon. Small, about the size of a house cat. He's... he's in here now. On the window ledge. He calls himself Dirit, but... you can't see him, can you?"

The Wytch Master followed Mikhyal's gaze and peered at the window. His pale eyes unfocused, and Mikhyal held his breath, waiting for Ilya to pass judgment. If he was mad, he'd rather know it now than struggle to hide it. His father would need better counsel than a madman could give him, especially if he intended to ally with Altan and the other northern kingdoms. Mikhyal only hoped this wouldn't ruin the alliance they'd come to negotiate.

"I see nothing, Your Highness," the Wytch Master said softly. "Nothing with my eyes, and nothing in the mythe."

"I see." Mikhyal swallowed. He didn't *feel* mad.

"But then, I wouldn't expect to see anything. *You* are the one bonded to the sword. In all the accounts I've read of mythe-bonds, only the blade's bond-mate hears its voice. I must admit, however, in all my reading, I've not come across any accounts involving visual manifestations."

"*Manifestations?*" Dirit sounded appalled. "Well, I never! I'm not sure I like this Wytch Master."

Mikhyal ignored the dragon. "So I didn't dream it. The... the dragon — Dirit — he called me his bond-mate. I suppose that means I'm bonded to the sword." He glanced down at the blade, which still lay on top of the bed, alongside his leg.

"You are," Ilya said gravely. "I can see the bond clearly in the mythe. I was not certain at first whether we were dealing with a mythe-bond, an awakening Wytch power, or both, but once we got you away from the site of the manifestation and the resulting disturbance in the mythe, it became clear to me that you were, in fact, bonded to the sword. That's why it's lying on the bed near you. Close proximity to the blade during the first few days helps ease the bonding process."

"I'm not sure if I should be relieved or terrified," Mikhyal said. "And I don't understand how a sword that claims its purpose is to defend the royal line of Rhiva ended up in the hands of a bandit."

"Did it?" The Wytch Master's thin, coppery eyebrows drew together in a faint frown. "It was in your hand when they found you. Your father recognized it, and assumed you'd taken it from one of the vaults beneath the palace. He said it had been there since his father's grandfather's time. He seemed quite surprised to see it."

"But... I didn't," Mikhyal said slowly. "Take it from the vaults, I mean. The first I saw of it, the bandit captain was about to take my head off with it. He... he disarmed me, and I thought he was about to kill me, but Captain Rhu intervened. My own blade was nowhere in sight, lost somewhere in the underbrush, I suppose, though it looks as if someone found it." Mikhyal's eyes strayed briefly to the weapon rack hanging on the wall opposite the bed.

"I grabbed the captain's sword," he continued, "and the moment I touched it, I felt this... this tingling feeling that ran up my arm and... covered my whole body. It felt as if I were standing inside a great bell, and someone had struck it. It rang all through me, right down to my bones, and then everything went white. When I came back to myself, the fighting was still raging around me. I'd just started across the clearing to aid my father when a cloud of fog and light descended, covering the entire clearing. When it lifted, all that was left of the bandits were little piles of bone."

A cold shudder went through Mikhyal as he turned his head to look at Dirit, who was now lounging on the window ledge. The dragon grinned and winked.

"Ai, it frightened your father's men terribly," Ilya said. "Once we got you here, and I had a chance to examine the blade, I came to the conclusion that they were never in any danger. It was quite selective in its choice of victims."

Mikhyal turned back to Ilya. "Are you certain?" he whispered. "How can we be sure it won't do the same thing here?"

"You said its purpose was to defend your line," Ilya said calmly. "And that sense of purpose is written clearly and deeply in the blade's mythe-shadow. Since it was found in the vaults under the palace and once belonged to one of your ancestors, I do not believe you have anything of that nature to fear from it."

"You most certainly do *not*." Dirit's whiskers drooped. "You wound me with your doubt, Your Royal Suspiciousness. It is my sacred *duty* to protect you. I was *chosen* for this task by one of the greater dragons, bonded to the blade of my own free will when I learned that I, Dirit, might play a most important role in the restoration of the Balance."

Mikhyal bit his lip. "It says... it says it was chosen. Bonded to the sword to... to help restore the balance?" He shifted his gaze from the dragon to the Wytch Master. "I don't understand what that means."

"Nor do I," Ilya said gravely. "But if you require further reassurance, perhaps a visit from Prince Vayne and Prince Jaire is in order. Prince Vayne is far more skilled than I at reading and interpreting mythe-shadows. He could, perhaps, examine the blade and set your mind at ease. And Prince Jaire is a voracious student of history. It wouldn't surprise me if he holds the entire contents of the royal library in his head. It's quite possible he's read something about this blade, in particular."

"Ai, that... that might help," Mikhyal said.

"I shall ask them to accompany me here tomorrow. Until then, I'd like you to continue resting and recovering your strength. You're not long out of mythe-shock, and if you attempt too much too soon, you will have a relapse."

"Don't worry, I'll do as I'm told." Mikhyal forced a smile. "Ambris has already made it quite clear that he's in charge."

When the Wytch Master had closed the door behind him, Mikhyal turned to Dirit. "Tell me more about this bond that joins us. Can it be broken?"

"Quite easily, in fact." The dragon hopped off the window ledge to land lightly on the bed, where he curled up facing Mikhyal.

"How?" Mikhyal asked eagerly.

"You must leave the sword somewhere and then travel a long distance away. It will strain the bond, and eventually break it. It won't do you much good, though, because at that point, you'll be dead of mythe-shock, and I'll be rather uncomfortable, so I'd be much obliged if you didn't."

"So I'm stuck with you, then."

One tufted eyebrow twitched. "Or *I'm* stuck with *you*. Rather depends upon which side of the bond you're on, doesn't it?"

Mikhyal considered that. "What else can you do?"

Dirit tapped one claw against a crystalline fang, as if deep in thought. "Well… if you ever need to sneak about, I can scout ahead and let you know what I see and hear. And of course, I can assist you in combat."

"The way you assisted me the other day, murdering all those men?"

Dirit's glare was decidedly sulky. "They would have killed your entire party. Your royal father. Your royal mother. Your royal—"

"You stripped their bones clean."

"I was hungry." The dragon cocked his head. "It *was* a rather impressive display, wasn't it?"

"Impressive isn't exactly the word I'd have chosen," Mikhyal said flatly. "They'll all be terrified of me, after this."

"*Humans*," Dirit huffed. "So concerned about appearances. You command Rhiva's army, do you not? Surely a bit of terror isn't out of keeping. Does wonders for one's reputation. Imagine it… the very sound of your name striking fear into the hearts of the bravest warriors. Think of the songs they'll—"

"You must promise you won't do anything like that again."

Gleaming black eyes narrowed, and Dirit laid his ears back against his head. "Why?"

"Because I order it," Mikhyal snapped.

"Order?" Dirit sounded most affronted. "*You*, a mere human, think you can order *me*, a creature of the mythe — one *chosen* for a most important mission, no less — to do *anything*? I am most pleased to inform you that anything I do or do not do will be done in the service of my mission. Unfortunately, protecting Your Most Ungrateful Royal Self is part of that mission."

"That may be so," Mikhyal said firmly, "but I cannot have you destroying my reputation. I've worked hard for the good of my people, and I cannot bear to see them run from me in fear."

"Hmm." Dirit's eyebrow tufts drew together in a frown. "Given the speed at which rumors spread, it might be a bit late for that."

"Which is another reason why you mustn't do such a thing again. Especially not in public."

The dragon huffed out a huge sigh. "They never appreciate the *artistry* of the thing. All they see is a pile of bones. They never ask how it was done. Or marvel at the way the bones fall in such clever patterns. Or notice how beautifully polished they are."

"Dirit. Please."

"Oh, very well. If I should have occasion to devour anyone on your behalf again, I shall take pains to do it... *surreptitiously*. Will that suit Your Royal Squeamishness?"

"I'm not—"

"You're a soldier, aren't you? You ought to be used to such things."

"It's not a question of—"

"Oh, stop being so dramatic," Dirit said, waving a front claw at him. "I shall endeavor to behave myself. Unless your life is threatened. *Then* I will use every weapon I have at my disposal: claws and teeth, tail and mythe. My sacred duty is to see to it that you survive, and I am sworn to uphold that duty. Keep yourself out of danger, and your shining reputation shall remain, ah, untarnished. You might consider locking yourself in a tower. That's rumored to be quite safe." And with that, he flashed Mikhyal a toothy grin and faded from sight, leaving Mikhyal uncertain as to whether he should be relieved or concerned.

Tristin cringed, waiting for a blow that never came. The pattern he was starting to build shattered into scintillating shards of fire and shadow, glittering in the darkness before winking out.

"I'm sorry, Master Ilya." He glanced across the table at the Wytch Master. "I *am* trying." If he'd been in a better frame of mind, he was certain he could have completed the pattern this time. He'd done quite well during his last two lessons. Twice now, he'd managed to find his center and meditate quietly upon it without once thinking about Mordax and his punishments. Tonight, he'd tried to take it a step further, and begin building the very simplest of shielding patterns.

After the day he'd had, he should probably have guessed it wouldn't go well. Seeing Dirit again had been bad enough, but learning that the all-too-intriguing Prince Mikhyal could also see the little dragon was enough to put Tristin into a panic. And finding out the prince had yet to decide whether Dirit was a product of his own madness hadn't made Tristin feel any better at all. If they could both see Dirit, then Dirit *couldn't* be a hallucination, and if that was the case—

"You seem distracted," Ilya observed. "If you don't feel up to working tonight, we can stop early. You've done well with the last few lessons, and I'd hate to push you further before you're ready. That would be far more of a blow to your confidence than stopping now and picking up again tomorrow."

"I... it has been a rather difficult day," Tristin admitted, staring down at the table.

"*Difficult*, was it?" said a voice behind him. "You don't know the meaning of the word."

Tristin twisted around in his seat to see Dirit balancing precariously on the edge of a tall bookcase. The dragon took several mincing steps along the very edge, then leapt from the shelf to land lightly on the back of the empty chair at the foot of the table. He settled himself there, adjusting his delicate little wings.

Ilya followed Tristin's gaze and frowned at the back of the chair. "What do you see, Tristin?" Ilya's voice was soft and full of curiosity.

Tristin wrenched his head away from Dirit to stare at the Wytch Master.

"Yes, Prince Tristin of the New Flower Bed, what *do* you see?" Dirit asked.

"It's all right to tell me," Ilya said. "Prince Mikhyal spoke to me earlier about observing a... a disturbance in the mythe."

"Disturbance, indeed," Dirit muttered, shaking his head. "Thank you, Dirit, for saving the entire royal family of Rhiva from certain death. As a token of our undying gratitude, please accept this nice silk cushion to lay your head upon, and all the blackberry tarts you can eat. But no, it's not good enough, is it? Silk cushions and lovely pastries have not been forthcoming. Instead, I'm a *disturbance*."

If Tristin had any doubts regarding the Wytch Master's awareness of Dirit, they were certainly laid to rest now. Ilya gave no sign of having heard the little dragon's lament.

"If there *is* a disturbance in the mythe," Tristin said carefully, "surely you can sense it, Master Ilya."

"I cannot, and I'm curious to know if anyone else can. If you think you're hearing things, or seeing things... it doesn't necessarily mean you're hallucinating. Just as some people have exceptional vision or hearing, you may have exceptional mythe-senses."

"Well... I suppose I *did* see Prince Vayne when he was trapped in the mythe," Tristin said slowly. "I thought at first he was another of my hallucinations, but... but he didn't act anything like a hallucination. At least, not like any I remembered having up until then."

"Ai, and Prince Jaire saw him, too," Ilya said encouragingly. "And he's always been able to sense things I cannot."

"Go on, go on," Dirit said. "The nice Wytch Master has practically *invited* you to tell him all about your Dirit-shaped hallucination."

Tristin shot a scowl at the dragon, and reminded himself that Prince Mikhyal could see Dirit, too, and he'd known the dragon's name without Tristin having to tell him.

"Did it speak to you?" Ilya asked. "Just now, I mean?"

"Ai, it did, and its manners are beyond appalling." Tristin clapped a hand over his mouth and stared at Ilya with wide eyes, cringing as he waited for the Wytch Master to call for the guards to drug him senseless and lock him away.

But Ilya only leaned forward, pale eyes fixed on Tristin. "Tell me."

Tristin swallowed and glanced at Dirit. The dragon was grinning broadly and picking his teeth with a single, sharp claw. He pulled something stringy from between them, examined it closely, and flicked it in Tristin's direction. Tristin leaned aside to avoid it, but there was nothing there. "It's… it's a little dragon, about the size of a house cat. It looks a lot like Prince Jaire does in his dragon form, only… only it's silver, and it has fluffy bits. Whiskers, eyebrows, and a mane. Oh, and a rather sweet little tuft at the end of its tail."

Dirit rolled his eyes. "Sweet, indeed," he muttered. "I'll give you *sweet*."

"And does it have a name?"

"It calls itself Dirit."

Ilya looked pleased. "That is *exactly* what Mikhyal said. That should set your mind at ease regarding your sanity."

Tristin gave him a dubious look. "I'm not sure how sharing a hallucination with the prince of Rhiva is supposed to make me feel better."

"It is most certainly *not* a hallucination," Ilya said firmly. "It is a manifestation of the mythe-blade Mikhyal is bonded to."

"So, you don't…" Tristin had to force himself to finish the question. "You don't think I'm mad?"

"Aio's teeth, no." Ilya gave him a reassuring smile. "The mythe is a most fickle mistress. She shows different sides of herself to all who can see her, and no mere mortal can possibly know all of her secrets."

Some of the tension in Tristin's body eased. "And... and I can see Dirit for the same reason I could see Vayne?"

"Exactly. I shall be most interested to find out if Prince Jaire can see it, too. He made no mention of it while we were assisting Mikhyal's entourage."

"Why don't you just invite the entire castle up to have a look?" Dirit said with a sniff. "Only my bond-mate is *supposed* to be able to see me. Honestly, having all these extra-sensitive mythe-weavers about is a bit like relaxing in your own home in your underthings, and then discovering everyone's been peering at you through a window you'd never noticed before. I feel so very... *exposed*."

Tristin merely shook his head slightly and turned his attention to Master Ilya.

"... see why your day might have been difficult, if you believed you were hallucinating again," Ilya was saying. "I'm not surprised you're having trouble concentrating. I think, perhaps, with all the excitement, we should take a few days to allow you to rest and recover before we try again. If you're in no hurry?"

"No, no hurry at all." Hurrying was pointless; Tristin had nothing to go back to and nowhere he belonged. He was just beginning to feel safe here at Dragonwatch, and once he learned to protect his mind from the empathic resonances contained in the objects he touched, there would be no reason for him to stay. Then he would have no choice but to confront his future.

Master Ilya bade Tristin a good night and took his leave, promising he'd stop by tomorrow, when he brought Jaire and Vayne to see Prince Mikhyal.

When Master Ilya had gone, Tristin looked about for Dirit, but the dragon had disappeared. Probably off frightening the local wildlife or causing mischief elsewhere.

Heaving a huge sigh of relief, Tristin headed for his bedroom. Though he'd done less physical labor today, he found himself exhausted. Tomorrow would be better; Prince Jaire was coming tomorrow, and Tristin did enjoy spending time with his cousin. The prince was interested in so many different things, they could always find something to talk about. Tristin thought perhaps he'd ask Jaire to have a word with Master Ludin and find out what sorts of flowers might grow best in his new flower bed.

A knock sounded on the door of his suite, and Tristin paused with his hand on the bedroom door. Who besides Master Ilya had reason to come to his rooms at this hour? Perhaps Alys needed help with something.

But it wasn't Ilya *or* Alys. Standing out in the hallway looking rather pale and drawn was Prince Mikhyal.

"Your Highness." Tristin glanced up and down the hallway, and was both relieved and alarmed to discover the prince was alone. "Should you be out of bed? You... you look as if you're about to fall over." He offered his arm, and Prince Mikhyal took hold of it gratefully, leaning heavily on Tristin.

"I fear I've overestimated my strength," the prince said as Tristin helped him to the armchair next to the hearth.

"Ai, I've done rather a lot of that, myself, just lately. One of the more frustrating phases of a long recovery: thinking you can do things and discovering the hard way that you're not quite ready. Can I fetch you something from the kitchen? I've nothing here to offer you at the moment but a drink of water."

"No, thank you. And please don't stand on ceremony. Just Mikhyal will do quite nicely."

"Well, then, you must call me Tristin, and you can kindly leave off the *Lord of the Flowers* bit, or whatever it is that bloody dragon's decided to call—" Tristin snapped his mouth shut, face going so hot, he was certain he must be a brilliant crimson.

Mikhyal's lips twitched. "He does have an infuriating way about him, doesn't he? Actually, that's why I braved that deceptively long hallway in the first place. I wanted to apologize."

"Apologize? What... whatever for?"

"For what I said earlier, about going mad in company. I didn't mean to imply that I thought *you* were mad. I... I'd just woken up, and I'd had such odd dreams while I was ill. Ambris tells me that's not unusual with mythe-shock. When you came to my room, I still wasn't certain whether or not I was dreaming, and you must admit, given the choice, Dirit is the sort of thing one would prefer to relegate to the dream world."

"Nightmare, more like," Tristin muttered under his breath.

Mikhyal broke into a grin. "Ai. Nightmare fits much better. Only it's not one I'll be waking up from, I fear. Dirit is tied to a sword forged by my ancestors. Only the royal bloodline of Rhiva can wield the blade, and Dirit claims that I'm now bonded to it."

"Ai, that's what Wytch Master Ilya said when I told him about Dirit." Tristin sank down in the chair opposite Mikhyal. The fire in the hearth was blazing merrily, but it did nothing to warm him. "Have you any idea what this bonding entails?"

"According to Dirit, it means I'm stuck with him."

"I see," Tristin murmured. "Do you gain any benefit from this… uh… relationship?"

"Why, His Most Fortunate Royal Gloriousness is blessed with the pleasure of my company, of course," Dirit said from the mantelpiece, where he lay stretched out full length, tufted tail dangling down in front of the fire. "What more could a prince of the blood ask?"

Both men turned to look at the dragon.

"Do you see it?" Mikhyal whispered.

"Ai," Tristin whispered back. "Draped over the mantel, as if it hasn't a care in the world."

The dragon's ears went back and glittering black eyes flicked from one to the other of them. "It's the height of rudeness to talk about someone as if they're not present. Especially someone whose most heroic efforts saved you from certain death. Don't those fancy royal tutors of yours teach manners anymore?"

Mikhyal looked contrite. He inclined his head and addressed Dirit. "I do believe you're right, Dirit. I haven't thanked you properly, have I?"

"No, you have not." The little dragon sat up on the mantle and cocked his head, regarding Mikhyal expectantly.

"I apologize for being so slow to express my gratitude." Mikhyal's tone was grave. "I fear my only excuse is that I've been recovering from the effects of our bonding. Thank you, Dirit, for saving my life and the lives of my family and my men."

"Truly, it was nothing," Dirit said, preening. "A mere fraction of what I'm capable of when my full power is unleashed. I was specially chosen for the task, you know, because *I* was the most powerful and the most trustworthy. Also, the most beautiful. You're very lucky I chose to bond to you."

Mikhyal glanced at Tristin long enough to roll his eyes. "My understanding is that you didn't have much choice in the matter, tied to the royal bloodline as you are."

"Oh, well, *that*," Dirit blustered. "Well, of course, there is *that*. But I could have refused to bond with you. I don't *have* to, you know."

"He's all fire and wind, isn't he?" Tristin said in a low voice.

Mikhyal smiled, and in the warm glow of the firelight, he was even more handsome than Tristin had first thought. "Ai, that he is."

"Fire and wind, indeed." Dirit managed to convey his wounded feelings in a single sniff. "I shall give you fire and wind, I shall, *just* when you least expect it."

Mikhyal's smile widened. Pale blue eyes sparkling with mirth caught Tristin's gaze and held it fast. Time froze, or perhaps it stretched. The air between them sizzled, and Tristin felt his ears growing hot.

When he finally managed to look away from Mikhyal, he found Dirit watching him with apparent interest. The dragon grinned, displaying needle-sharp teeth. "He is rather handsome, isn't he?"

"Quite," Tristin said before he could stop himself, but at almost the same moment, Mikhyal murmured, "Oh, yes."

Tristin turned his head slowly to face Mikhyal, mortified. "Sorry. I'm sorry, Your Highness. It just... um. Popped out. That is, my, ah, my mouth often keeps going even when my senses of propriety and self-preservation are screaming at it to stop." Face flaming, he got to his feet, prepared to flee, until he remembered that he was already in his own rooms, and there was nowhere to flee to.

"Then I think, perhaps, this would be an appropriate moment for me to make a dramatic exit." Mikhyal's mouth curved in a rueful grin. "I'd very much like to leave you with some witty, yet frustratingly ambiguous remark to ponder over. Unfortunately, I'm too exhausted to think of anything witty *or* ambiguous. I don't suppose you'd care to help me back to my rooms?"

"Dramatically?" Tristin couldn't help but ask.

At Mikhyal's warm chuckle, Tristin ducked his head so the prince might not notice his flaming cheeks.

As he walked Mikhyal back down the hall with one arm around his waist to steady him, it occurred to Tristin that not long ago he'd been the one needing help. He really had come a long way since he'd been brought to Dragonwatch. He hadn't realized how much his addiction had dulled his senses. Coming off the drug had been a painful ordeal, but it had opened up a world of sensory experience Tristin had almost forgotten.

Now, he was finding it very difficult not to be aware of the solid warmth of Mikhyal's hip pressed against his own, and how very broad and strong Mikhyal's back felt against his arm. They were roughly the same height, though Mikhyal felt as if he was mostly muscle, with perhaps just a hint of extra padding around his middle, whereas Tristin was all bones with a bit of scarred skin and stringy sinew holding everything together.

"Thank you, Tristin," Mikhyal said as they reached the door of his suite. "Pleasant dreams to you."

"And to you, Your... I mean, Mikhyal."

The door closed quietly behind Mikhyal, and Tristin turned and made his way slowly back to his own room, body still tingling pleasantly from the close contact.

Mikhyal slept late the next day. It was the middle of the afternoon when he finally woke to see Dirit pacing about on top of the wardrobe looking quite put out.

"About time you woke up," the dragon grumped. "That healer's poked his nose in here three times already. You're going to catch it for overdoing it yesterday, see if you don't."

Indeed, Mikhyal had only just finished dressing when there was a knock at his door and Ambris looked in. "Oh, good, you're awake.

And ready for the day, or what's left of it, at least. How are you feeling? The effects of the anzaria should be mostly gone by now."

"My head is much clearer today, for which I'm grateful," Mikhyal said, "but I fear I may have overdone it a bit last night. I paid a visit to Tristin, and the hallway ended up being quite a bit longer than it looked."

"I see." Ambris's lips pursed. "I thought I told you to stay in bed, and we'd see about you getting up today. You've been very ill, Your Highness, and mythe-shock is nothing to be trifled with."

"Ai, and I wouldn't have trifled with it, only there was... a bit of an incident when Tristin brought me my lunch. I feared I might have upset him, and I wanted to offer him an apology."

Ambris's brows drew together. "Oh?"

Mikhyal gave the healer a rueful smile. "I might have implied, indirectly, of course, that he and I were both mad."

"Ah. I can't imagine that going down at all well."

"He did seem a bit sensitive about it," Mikhyal admitted. "But it's all right now. He accepted my apology quite graciously."

"So it was worth exhausting yourself and risking a relapse?"

"Oh, ai, I think so." Mikhyal smiled to himself, remembering the moment when their eyes had locked and something had passed between them. Something that made him want to see more of Tristin. Much more.

Ambris sighed. "I can see you're going to be every bit as difficult a patient as Garrik is." His pale gold eyes unfocused as he examined Mikhyal with his healer's sight. "Well, your adventure doesn't appear to have caused you any harm. Which is just as well. Ilya would be sorely vexed if I had to send you back to your bed. Prince Vayne and Prince Jaire are waiting in his study, if you'd like to join them. He asked me to come and fetch you, and requested that you bring the sword with you."

Mikhyal stood and lifted the sword from the bed. "Let us not keep the Wytch Master waiting." He glanced up at the top of the wardrobe. "You had better come along too, Dirit. Master Ilya was quite interested to know if Prince Jaire would be able to see you."

Ambris must have already been briefed regarding Dirit, for he said nothing, only followed Mikhyal's gaze, the slight frown puckering his brow suggesting that, like Ilya, he saw no sign of the little dragon.

Dirit's eyebrow tufts twitched. "On display again," he muttered, hopping down off the wardrobe to land lightly on Mikhyal's shoulder. He was weightless, and indeed, when Mikhyal reached up to try to touch him, his hand passed right through the creature, with only a brief sensation of intense cold to suggest there was anything there at all.

"Stop it." Dirit hissed and laid his ears back. "How would you like to have someone poking about inside you?"

Mikhyal grinned broadly. "That would depend entirely on who was doing the poking, Master Dragon."

Ambris gave him an odd look and started out the door.

"*Master Dragon.*" Dirit preened, offended dignity apparently forgotten. "I could get used to that."

"Don't," Mikhyal said under his breath as he followed the healer out the door.

"It would be most fitting, don't you think? I must say, *I* rather like it... *Master* Dragon, yes, *very* nice."

In the hall, Ambris offered his arm, but Mikhyal waved him off. "I'm feeling much stronger today. I'd like to see if I can manage on my own."

Master Ilya's suite was just a bit farther down the hall than Tristin's, and Mikhyal walked the entire distance unassisted. Though he felt much stronger than he had the day before, he was just as glad not to have to turn around and walk back immediately.

Ambris ushered him into Master Ilya's sitting room and settled him in a padded armchair in front of a low table holding a tea pot and a tray piled high with an assortment of pastries. Mikhyal leaned back gratefully and rested the sheathed sword across his knees.

On the couch opposite him sat Prince Jaire, who'd grown from boy to man in the years since Mikhyal had last seen him. The prince was still immediately recognizable, with that bright, white-blond hair of his. Sitting next to Prince Jaire was a man with thick black hair and dark eyes. This must be Prince Vayne.

"Good afternoon, Your Highness," Master Ilya said after Ambris had gone. "You're looking quite a bit better than you did yesterday."

"Thank you, Master Ilya. I'm sure that's to do with the most excellent care I've received here."

"And the fact that your bond-mate can help you heal," Dirit whispered in his ear. The dragon hopped down onto the table to inspect the pastries. "You'll want to watch how many of *those* you eat, Your Royal Voraciousness."

"Ilya, you didn't tell me it was so beautiful!" Prince Jaire leaned forward, examining Dirit closely.

"No, well, I can't see it like the rest of you can," Ilya murmured, watching Prince Jaire with a bemused expression.

"Can you see it, Vayne?" Jaire asked.

"No, I can't." Prince Vayne looked as bemused as the Wytch Master.

"It's got the prettiest silver scales," Prince Jaire said, "and a beautiful white mane. It has tufts of fur over its eyebrows and at the tip of its tail. And such dainty little feet! I don't think I've ever seen anything quite so lovely."

"Oh, now, *you* I like." Dirit displayed glittering, needle-sharp teeth in what Mikhyal hoped was a grin. "I can see we're going to be the greatest of friends. At least *someone* appreciates my numerous charms." He threw Mikhyal a baleful glare before continuing, "I am Dirit, and you must be Prince Jaire. I am most charmed to make your acquaintance."

Much to Prince Jaire's delight, Dirit marched across the table, traipsed over the pastries, and climbed up onto the prince's lap, where he settled himself, curling his tail around his body like a cat.

Prince Jaire smothered his laughter behind his hand and shifted his attention to Mikhyal. "Sorry, Your Highness. I didn't mean to ignore you, it's just..." He smiled down at Dirit. "I had no idea. Welcome to Altan and to Dragonwatch, Dirit. And welcome to you, too, Prince Mikhyal. It's good to see you awake and on your feet, Your Highness. I'm Prince Jaire, and this is Prince Vayne of Irilan, my intended husband."

"Ai, I remember you from a harvest festival some years ago," Mikhyal said, starting to rise, but Prince Jaire waved him back, and Mikhyal nodded gratefully and sank back down in his chair. "You were just a boy, hanging about the dessert table and doing your best to avoid your nurse."

"I'm afraid not much has changed," Jaire said with a rueful grin. "The dessert table hasn't lost its appeal, but up until very recently, it's been noblemen with eligible daughters I've had to avoid. They're quite a bit trickier than Mistress Polina ever was."

Mikhyal shifted his gaze to Prince Vayne. "Prince Vayne, I am very pleased to make your acquaintance, though I must confess, I didn't realize Ord had another son."

"I'm not his son, Your Highness," Vayne said. "More like a very distant cousin."

"Vayne was trapped in the mythe for years and years," Jaire explained. "His father was Wytch King Urich, the same Urich who was put to death by the Wytch Council for leading the Irilan Rebellion. Urich hid Vayne in the mythe, but was killed before he could tell anyone what he'd done, so poor Vayne was trapped there all that time — over two hundred years — until I set him free."

Vayne gave his intended an indulgent smile as Jaire wrinkled his nose and continued, "It sounds rather like one of those soppy romantic ballads that go on and on, but it was really very exciting. Vayne rescued me, Kian, and Tristin after the Wytch Council kidnapped me and tried to make Garrik step down in Tristin's favor."

Mikhyal eyed Vayne with interest. "You learned about mythe-blades while you were trapped in the mythe?"

"No, my father taught me," Vayne said. "My own skills lie in the manipulation of living mythe-shadows, but my father was capable of burning patterns into raw mythe-stones. As a student of both my father and his Wytch Master, I had a great deal of practice at reading the mythe-shadows of the objects created from those stones." He looked questioningly at the sword still lying across Mikhyal's knees, than back up at Mikhyal. "If I might?"

At Mikhyal's nod, Vayne rose and took the sword from him. He pulled it from the scabbard and examined it closely, eyes unfocusing slightly as he studied its mythe-shadow. "The bond is strong," he murmured. "And tied to the bloodline of Rhiva. Some of the patterns in the blade's mythe-shadow echo the inherited patterns in yours. Passed down from your father, was it?"

"No, strangely enough, it wasn't," Mikhyal said. "According to Dirit, it hasn't had a bearer since my father's grandfather died."

"Hated me, he did," Dirit muttered. "Fought the bond, damaged it to the point where I could not manifest physically to prove my existence. Always arguing, he was. And of course, since he had damaged the bond, no one but him could see me, so they all thought he was quite mad by the time he died. On his deathbed, he ordered the sword sent to the vaults. And there it stayed until... well. Until *someone* removed it. Recently."

Prince Jaire's eyes widened and he bit his lip as he stared down at the little dragon. "That must have been horrible," he murmured, hand hovering over Dirit as if he would stroke the creature. "Poor Dirit."

The little dragon looked mournfully up at Prince Jaire. "Most horrible," he agreed. "Poor Dirit, indeed. Charged with a sacred task, and then not allowed to perform it."

At Ilya's questioning look, Mikhyal repeated what Dirit had said, then went on to ask, "You don't know who took the sword from the vaults?"

Dirit's ears flattened. "I've no idea. The sword is my gateway to this world, but unless I have a bearer, the gate is shut tight. All I know for certain is that it cannot have been anyone of the line of Rhiva, or the bonding would have been initiated the moment they touched the blade."

Mikhyal repeated Dirit's reply for the benefit of Vayne and the Wytch Master.

When he'd finished, Dirit cocked his head. "Perhaps this would make it easier."

A moment later, Prince Jaire let out a squeak of surprise. "It has weight now!" Jaire stared down at the little dragon in wonder and reached out a tentative finger to stroke Dirit's mane.

Dirit flinched at the contact and shot him an irritated glare. "I *can* manifest in the physical world, but I find it *most* uncomfortable."

He rose gingerly to his feet and lifted each of his claws in turn, as if finding himself ankle deep in something disgusting. "Breezes and *smells* and all manner of *things* ruffling my fur and poking at my feet. The mythe is *so* much cleaner and more civilized." His tail twitched, and he hopped onto the table. Tiny claws tapped delicately on the polished surface as he minced across it to the pastry tray, where he helped himself. "I am rather partial to blackberry tarts, though."

Jaire was watching in rapt fascination. "Can you see it now, Vayne?"

"Ai." Vayne nodded, his eyes fixed on the little dragon. "It looks very much like some of the creatures I encountered when I was trapped in the mythe."

Dirit devoured the pastry with a few quick snaps of his jaws, apparently oblivious of his audience. When he was finished, he took one step, then lifted one of his front feet and inspected it, snout wrinkling. "*Sticky.* I cannot abide *sticky.*" And with that, the little dragon set about licking every scrap of blackberry jam from his claws with a long, forked tongue. He went on to groom his whiskers. When he was finished, he settled on the table with his front feet crossed primly before him. "Ask your questions, then, humans. Quickly, for I am not prepared to tolerate all these odd textures and disturbing *smells* for very long."

"Are you trapped in the mythe like Vayne was?" Jaire asked.

"No," Dirit said. "I can roam freely in the mythe, though I am tethered to the sword. I can only manifest physically a short distance from it, and then only if my bond-mate is also nearby."

"Did someone capture you in order to bond you to the blade?" Vayne asked. "The method of forging mythe-blades I'm familiar with involves trapping the personality bonded to the blade within a mythe-stone."

"That is the way it is done when a human personality is used to create the blade. It works differently for creatures of the mythe." The little dragon's chest puffed out a bit, and he sat up straight. "I was *chosen* for the honor of defending the royal line of Rhiva because I was trusted to carry out my duties most faithfully. *Mortified,* I was, to discover I had been barred from carrying out my sacred duty because of the whims of a mad Wytch King who refused to accept me as his protector."

"Who chose you?" Ilya asked quietly.

"Why, one of the Greater Dragons, of course, second only in power to the Dragon Mother, herself. His name is Ashna, and he is one of the more influential creatures in the mythe." Dirit drew himself up even more. "He said there was important work to be done, and *I* was uniquely qualified to do it. Those were his exact words: *uniquely qualified*."

"Ashna," Vayne said thoughtfully. "Of course. I encountered him a number of times during my exile. He spoke in riddles much of the time, and I got the impression he toiled at some great task far beyond human understanding. What sort of work did he intend for you to do?"

"I was *personally* chosen to help restore the Balance." Dirit turned to look at each of them in turn, perhaps to gauge how impressed they were. "Seeing to it that the line of Rhiva remains unbroken is a *very* important part of it. Perhaps the *most* important."

Mikhyal frowned. "The balance of *what*, exactly?"

Dirit blinked. "Well, I *never*. These questions are becoming *entirely* too personal, Your Royal Inquisitiveness." And with that, the little dragon simply faded from sight.

"Can you still see it, Mikhyal?" Ilya asked.

"No, he's gone," Mikhyal said. "I seem to have offended him. Again."

"Offended or not, I see no reason for concern, Ilya." Vayne said. "There is nothing to be read in the mythe-shadows of either the sword or of Prince Mikhyal that suggests to me that the blade is anything other than what Dirit claims. I did, however, see patterns in Mikhyal's mythe-shadow very much like some of those possessed by both Jaire and Tristin."

"Does that mean—" Jaire started, but Vayne elbowed him and he pressed his lips together.

"I see," the Wytch Master murmured, and turned a speculative gaze upon Mikhyal. "Well, then. We shall have much to discuss when the Wytch Kings arrive."

"Meaning what, exactly, Master Ilya?" Mikhyal asked.

"All in good time, Your Highness," Ilya said smoothly. "You have enough to think about at the moment, what with recovering from mythe-shock and adjusting to the bond. You understand, of course, that we needed to be certain the blade posed no danger to anyone before we moved you to the castle."

"Of course," Mikhyal said. "Most sensible of you, to isolate me until you knew for certain what sort of bond it was."

"Now that Vayne has confirmed my observations, I see no reason for you to remain here," Ilya said. "You are out of danger now. All that remains is for you to continue resting and recovering. Kian is standing by, ready to ferry you down to the castle, where a suite has been prepared for you and your father."

"I..." Mikhyal trailed off, thoughts spinning as it occurred to him that once his father arrived tomorrow and the negotiations began, he might not see Tristin again before he had to return to Rhiva. He hoped they wouldn't rush him off to the castle too quickly; he'd like to at least have the chance to say goodbye.

Tristin knelt on the stones at the edge of the bed of coldroot and plucked out the weeds that were valiantly trying to gain a foothold in the rich soil. The task was simple. His hands remembered weeding the herb beds when he'd been a child helping in the gardens at Falkrag, leaving his mind free to wander.

Jaire and Vayne had arrived a little while ago. Tristin had seen them playing up in the sky above the watchtower before they'd landed in the courtyard and gone inside to meet Mikhyal and Dirit. He wondered what Jaire would think of Dirit. Imagining his cousin's delight brought a smile to his lips, and he hoped Jaire would be able to see the little dragon.

"You missed a bit."

Tristin turned to see Dirit eyeing him from the middle of a patch of coldroot. He was about to admonish the dragon when he realized that Dirit wasn't actually crushing the flowers, but only looked as if he were. He glanced across the garden to see if anyone else was about, but the herb garden was deserted.

"I thought you were supposed to be in there with Mikhyal." Tristin sat back on his heels and regarded the little dragon soberly. "Prince Jaire said something about Ilya wanting to make sure you're not dangerous."

"Of course I'm *dangerous*." Dirit's nostrils flared in an offended sniff. "I wouldn't be much use as a protector of the royal line of Rhiva if I wasn't *dangerous*, would I? Anyway, they've had all the answers they're going to get from me. The questions were getting *entirely* too personal, so I took my leave."

"You can't blame them for asking. I should think anyone would be cautious around a force that can strip the flesh off of a man in a few moments and leave behind naught but a pile of bones."

"They told you about that, did they?" Dirit preened.

"Prince Jaire did. And you needn't look so pleased with yourself. I find the idea rather horrifying."

Dirit flattened his ears. "You would." His lip curled in disgust, revealing long, needle-like teeth glittering in the sunlight like tiny crystalline knives. "In case no one told you, mythe-weapons *do* tend to be a bit horrifying by human standards, although I'm sure you must agree, they don't normally come in such an *appealing* little package."

Before Tristin could think of a suitable retort, someone called, "Tristin!"

Tristin looked round to see Prince Mikhyal making his way toward him. Frowning slightly, he stood, dusted off his hands, and took a few steps closer. "Are you all right to be up and about, Your Highness? Last night you were about to collapse after a short walk down the hall."

"Whether I am ready or not, my father will be arriving tomorrow," Mikhyal said. "He will have need of me. I had a very long sleep, and I'm feeling much stronger than I was last night." His gaze shifted to Tristin's shoulder. "Dirit, I'd like to apologize if I offended you with my questions."

Tristin looked over to see the little dragon perched on his own shoulder.

Dirit blinked. "Apologize?"

"Ai. I must admit, I'm as curious as anyone about your origins, but I will refrain from asking. If you choose to share your past, it should be because you wish to, not because you feel you are bound to."

Dirit cocked his head. "Why, thank you. I do believe that's the first time anyone's acknowledged the fact that *I* might have feelings in the matter." The little dragon blinked again, then hopped down off of Tristin's shoulder and disappeared halfway to the ground.

"He's a funny little fellow, isn't he?" Mikhyal said when he'd gone.

"He is," Tristin said, smiling hesitantly. "He, ah, seems to think rather a lot of himself."

"That, he does." Mikhyal smiled. "I think he's had a difficult time of it, though. His last bearer was my great grandfather, and they didn't get along at all. But that's not why I'm here. Master Ilya says I'm ready to move down to the castle. I've come to say goodbye, and to inquire as to whether or not I'll see you again."

"Oh... I-I... um..." Tristin stammered. His ears burned as he struggled to think of something to say.

"You seem to be on very good terms with Prince Jaire," Mikhyal continued, "and I wondered if you might be planning to attend the betrothal ceremony."

"Ah. I... well... you see, I... um. Yes?" The final word was out before Tristin could clap a hand over his mouth, and he'd just started to try and explain that he hadn't really meant *yes* at all, when Mikhyal's face broke out in a smile so beautiful it nearly stopped Tristin's heart.

"Oh, very good! I suppose it would be rather too forward of me to ask if you might save a dance for me?"

"Um. I... well. That is, I haven't ever danced before, but I'd very much like to dance with you if it wouldn't be too much trouble, and I'd really like to see you again if that's all right, only I've not been properly introduced to anyone, and I'm afraid I might cause a bit of a scandal if anyone finds out where I'm really from and who my father was, and it might not do your reputation any good to be seen with someone who still talks to hallucinations, and if Dirit shows up I can't promise I won't make a scene, and it really might be better for everyone if we just... um..." The words ran together until Tristin ran out of breath, and when he finally stopped to take in a great gulp of air, Mikhyal's lips were twitching, as if he was trying to hold back his laughter.

"I shall assume that's a *yes*, since it sounds as if you'd like to. I shall be very much looking forward to it. Until we meet again, Prince Tristin of Dragonwatch." And with that, Mikhyal executed a formal bow and made his exit.

Prince Tristin of Dragonwatch? Tristin stared after him, mind racing through all the things he ought to shout after the prince. Like that he wasn't even sure if he'd be capable of going down to the castle.

Before he could settle on a suitable response, the kitchen door banged shut and Prince Mikhyal was gone. Tristin sank down to his knees on the sun-warmed flagstones, staring after him. What had he done? Only promised to go down to the castle for the betrothal. And dance with a prince of Rhiva.

A shadow fell across him. "Are you all right, Tristin?"

Tristin looked up to see Ambris staring down at him, brow furrowed in concern. "Yes, yes, I'm fine," he hastened to reassure the healer. "Or, well, no, I'm not fine. No. Not really. Actually, not fine at all. Rather miserable, in fact, now that you mention it."

"Oh?"

Tristin got to his feet and spread his hands helplessly. "I've just promised Mikhyal... um, I mean *Prince* Mikhyal, a dance. At Prince Jaire's betrothal ceremony. I'm not sure how it happened. One minute he came to say goodbye to me, and the next thing I knew, he asked if he'd see me again, and I opened my mouth and words came out and now he's expecting to see me at the ceremony." Tristin shook his head sadly. "Only I won't be going anywhere near the ceremony. How can I set foot in the castle when I can't even manage the watchtower stairs?"

A great draconic cry cut through the air, and Tristin and Ambris both looked up to see a great black dragon — Kian in his dragon form — circling the watchtower with a rider on his back. Mikhyal's long, black hair streamed behind him like a banner, and his face was alight with an expression of boyish exuberance. Kian swooped low over the garden, and Mikhyal lifted a hand to wave as they passed by.

Tristin raised his own hand and gave Mikhyal a shy smile.

"Well, you've certainly made an impression," Ambris said, watching his husband glide down the mountain.

"For all the good it'll do me," Tristin grumbled. "I suppose I shall have to ask Master Ilya to take a message to him telling him I won't be able to manage the betrothal ceremony."

"Nonsense," Ambris said firmly. "If you hold thoughts like that in your head, you've failed before you've even begun. Now listen: you've just over two weeks until the celebration, and Master Ilya has several hours scheduled to work with you after dinner tomorrow. I'm sure if you tell him how much it means to you to be able to attend the ceremony, he'll find more time to work with you. Two weeks is plenty of time to master the basics."

"Mordax spent two *years* trying to teach me the basics." A heavy gloom settled over Tristin. "He eventually gave up, said I was hopeless and I'd never learn."

"Master Ilya is the best teacher the Wytch Council has." Ambris's voice brimmed with all the confidence Tristin lacked, and Tristin's spirits rose a little in spite of the enormity of the task lying before him. "Why do you think they gave him his own school? He trains the students no one else can, as well as the ones who are so dangerous no one else dares. I despaired of ever learning to shift properly, but Master Ilya taught me in a single afternoon what I'd struggled with for years. I believe he can help you, too, Tristin."

"I'd like to believe that, but our last lesson didn't go at all well."

Ambris snorted. "When you had your last lesson, Prince Mikhyal of Rhiva hadn't caught your eye. Nor had you promised him a dance. I think the prospect of dancing with a man as handsome as Prince Mikhyal might inspire even the most reluctant student, don't you?"

Tristin allowed himself a small smile as he stared down the mountain at the castle, but he found it impossible to believe it might be that easy.

"You can do it, Tristin."

"I hope so, Master Ambris. I truly hope so." Tristin's face grew hot again. "I should very much like to claim that dance."

Chapter Four

"Someone's coming." The voice was a low hiss, right in his ear.

Mikhyal woke with a start and sat up on the couch, frowning as he stared at the unfamiliar surroundings. It took a moment for him to realize he'd fallen asleep in the main room of his guest suite at Castle Altan. He'd polished off a marvelous lunch sent up from the kitchens, and had only intended to close his eyes for a few minutes.

"Up here," the voice said. Now it came from behind him.

Twisting around, Mikhyal saw Dirit materialize. He was lying stretched out along the top of the couch, tail swishing lazily through the air. "Ah. Dirit. There you are. Sorry, I didn't see you at first."

"You weren't supposed to," Dirit said loftily. "I was in hiding."

"Hiding? From what?"

"Anything that might want to eat me, of course. Very difficult to eat someone if you can't find them."

Mikhyal frowned. "No one here wants to eat you."

"Not *here*. In the mythe." The little dragon's wings vibrated with his delicate shudder. "There are things. Bigger things than me. Things with sharp teeth and sharper appetites."

"I suspect you'd give anything that tried to eat you a rather bad case of indigestion," Mikhyal said mildly.

"At the very least," Dirit agreed. "But by that time it would be a bit too late for me."

Mikhyal was about to get to his feet when he heard voices in the hall outside. The door of the suite flew open, and in stepped Han, the castle steward, followed by his father.

Wytch King Drannik's eyes went straight to his son. "Mikhyal! Kian said you were much improved, but it does my heart good to see it with my own eyes."

Mikhyal stood and went to embrace his father. Two servants carrying heavy saddlebags edged past them. "What of you, Father? You weren't hurt? And mother? Is she all right?"

"I was not injured, nor was your mother, though she was quite frightened. Once we arrived safely back at the summer palace, she was too nervous to settle. I sent her back to Castle Rhivana with some of the staff and a large detachment of guardsmen."

"I'm sure she'll feel safer there," Mikhyal said. "The castle is much more secure than the summer palace. What of Shaine? Did he remain at the palace?"

"Ai, he did. I suggested he might accompany your mother, but he didn't seem overly concerned about his own safety. Anxin, of course, remained with him."

"Of course."

Han waited in the doorway in respectful silence while the bags were taken to the largest of the suite's three bed chambers. After the servants had gone, Han waited until Drannik and Mikhyal had drawn apart before saying, "If Your Majesty should require anything, just pull on the red cord by the door, and someone will be with you. An informal supper will be served in the Wytch King's private dining room at six. Shall I send someone to guide Your Majesty?"

"No, thank you, Han," Drannik said. "I remember the way."

Han bowed and retreated, closing the door firmly behind him. When they were alone, Drannik looked Mikhyal up and down. "How are you really?"

"I'm well, thank you. I'm told I was suffering from mythe-shock, but Master Ilya and his healers took very good care of me. I'm still a bit tired, but other than that, I think I'm fully recovered."

"That is very good news," Drannik said warmly. "There was talk of your Wytch power finally awakening. Is that true?"

"Alas, no, Father, it's not. Master Ilya first thought it was the most logical explanation for what happened in the clearing, but we've since learned that was not the case."

"No Wytch power, then?" Drannik looked disappointed.

"No, what happened was the work of the sword. The one I picked up after I lost my own in the attack. Master Ilya said you recognized it."

"Ai, I'd nearly forgotten about it until we found you holding it after the ambush. It belonged to my grandfather, but it was forged long before his time. They called it the Wytch Sword of Rhiva, and its power was legendary. The story I was told was that if the Wytch Sword found the right bearer, its powers would awaken, and it would answer the call of its master."

There was a very distinct *humph* from Dirit. "Master, *indeed*," the dragon muttered. "No human is *my* master. I serve the Dragon Mother and protect the line of Rhiva at *her* behest." Mikhyal looked around to see the dragon clinging to the chandelier above the suite's dining table.

"Ah. Yes. About that... it appears that I am its... ah... master." Mikhyal glanced at Dirit, whose eyebrow tufts drew together in a fierce scowl.

"Oh, *very* presumptuous," Dirit protested. "*I* never called you master."

"And what, exactly, does that mean?" Drannik inquired.

"It... it speaks to me." Mikhyal's shoulders tensed in anticipation of his father's reaction.

But Drannik only raised an eyebrow. "Indeed. My grandfather said the same. Most of the family thought he was quite mad, though the Royal Wytch Master always said there was something odd about the sword."

"Odd, indeed," Mikhyal murmured, glancing at Dirit. The dragon flattened his ears, rolled his eyes, and flopped over onto his back, draping himself over the chandelier with his head hanging down so he could stare at Mikhyal. "It... according to Master Ilya, the sword is a mythe-blade. It acts as a conduit for a creature of the mythe, which is bound to protect the line of Rhiva."

"Who *chose* to protect the line of Rhiva," Dirit corrected. "I'm not *bound* to do anything."

"Is it speaking to you now?" Drannik asked, squinting as he followed Mikhyal's gaze upward.

"Ai," Mikhyal said with a small sigh.

"What's it saying?"

"He's correcting me. He says he is not bound to protect the line, but rather *chooses* to. The distinction seems quite important to him."

"*He?*"

"His name is Dirit, and he appears to be a small dragon, about the size of one Mother's cats. He's... an interesting companion, to say the least. At the moment, he's draped over the chandelier over there." Mikhyal pointed, and Drannik squinted in that direction.

"I see nothing of the sort." The Wytch King of Rhiva gave his son a dubious look.

"That doesn't surprise me. Master Ilya can't see him, and neither can the healers, Ambris and Kian. Prince Jaire was able to see him, though. And Tristin."

"Master Ilya did say there was some connection between you and the Wytch Sword when he and the others came to our aid. But who is this Tristin?"

"He calls himself the bastard prince," Mikhyal said, "but to be honest, I'm not entirely sure who his father was. He never said. Perhaps he doesn't know. At any rate, he's up at Master Ilya's school, Dragonwatch. It's where they brought me when they thought I might have some sort of out-of-control Wytch power."

"So Ilya said." Drannik rubbed the back of his neck. "If you don't actually have Wytch power, and the Wytch Sword was responsible for the slaughter, what caused you to fall into mythe-shock so deep that Master Ilya feared for your life?"

"Apparently the process of bonding to the sword can be rather a shock to the system."

"For *some* people," Dirit put in. "Your great grandfather didn't even bat an eye. You must have an extremely delicate constitution, Your Royal Frailness. The bloodline has clearly thinned in recent years. Too much inbreeding, I imagine." He glanced at Drannik appraisingly. "You're certain he's your father?"

Mikhyal sputtered at the insult, and Drannik gave him a sideways look.

"I've just been insulted," Mikhyal explained, once he'd caught his breath. "Or, rather, *you* have."

"By a creature only *you* can see, apparently." Drannik shook his head. "They all thought my grandfather was mad, you know. He hated the Wytch Sword, but he kept it with him all the time."

"You can speak to Wytch Master Ilya if you require confirmation of my sanity," Mikhyal said, a little stiffly. "Dirit most graciously performed a physical manifestation for the Wytch Master. Apparently, he finds the physical world to be quite uncomfortable, so I am disinclined to ask him to do it again."

Dirit froze, black eyes going wide as they fixed on Mikhyal, and for once, the little dragon had nothing to say.

"My apologies, Mikhyal." Drannik gave him a smile that looked more resigned than anything. "I didn't mean to give you the impression that I don't believe you. I've already spoken to Wytch Master Ilya, and he has given me all the reassurance I need as to the soundness of your mind. Now that I know you are well, my main concern is what effect any rumors about this might have on the negotiations. As for the rest of it, if what happened to those bandits was any indication of the Wytch Sword's power, then I am well pleased. Given what may be coming, you might find yourself grateful to have the extra measure of protection. It seems fortuitous that you chose to bring this particular blade along."

"I didn't," Mikhyal said flatly. "Choose it, I mean."

"Then who did? As far as I knew, it was down in the vaults, in storage. When we found you after... after it had... I assumed you must have removed it, though I'd have thought you would have asked first."

"I most certainly would have. The first I saw of it, it was lying on the ground at my feet, dropped from the hand of the bandit captain. I recall thinking it looked familiar, but I didn't have time to ponder it. He'd disarmed me and was about to take my head off when Rhu intervened. I had no blade, and his was there on the ground in front of me, so I picked it up and... and there was a ringing sensation, like a great bell had been struck, and the next clear memory I have is of waking up at Dragonwatch."

"I suppose Shaine might have taken it," Drannik mused, "but I can't imagine what he'd want it for — he's always hated weapons practice with a passion."

"Ai, I wouldn't have thought Shaine would have any interest. I can ask Dirit. He might know."

The dragon stared down at him from the chandelier. "Dirit might, if he'd had a bearer at that point, but he didn't. He has no more idea who removed the sword from your vaults than you do."

"Ah. No. Dirit says he is unaware of anything that might have happened before I picked up the sword."

"Pity," Drannik said, glancing in the direction Mikhyal had been looking and shaking his head.

"Actually, it can't have been Shaine," Mikhyal said. "If it had been, his touch would have woken Dirit, and Dirit would have bonded to him." He frowned. "But that leaves us with a greater mystery — who else has access to the vaults? The only keys are in the hands of you, Shaine, and myself. Who else could have gone down there?"

"Perhaps no one," Dirit said.

Mikhyal stared up him. "What's that supposed to mean?"

Dirit's ears flattened. "Well, only that you're operating on the assumption that your brother Shaine is of the line of Rhiva."

Mikhyal blinked. According to whispered rumors, Shaine was the very image of a certain guard captain who had been dismissed shortly after the prince's birth. The queen had done much to quiet the rumors by announcing that Shaine looked very much like her own dear grandfather on her mother's side, and when Shaine's Wytch power had awakened and Drannik had been forced to declare him his heir, the rumors had died completely.

But what if those rumors were true?

It would certainly explain Drannik's coolness toward his youngest son, and his reluctance to have Shaine take the throne after him.

"What did it say?" Drannik demanded.

"Only that it has no idea who else might have access to the vaults," Mikhyal said, casting a sharp glance at Dirit. Drannik had never said anything to him to make him question his brother's legitimacy, and Mikhyal wasn't about to bring it up now.

"Ah," Dirit said gaily, "the plot thickens. I shall be watching with interest most avid and breath most bated to see how *this* all unfolds."

"Well, then," Drannik said. "If there is a thief in our midst, I shall post a guard on the vaults the moment we return home. For now, I suppose we had best prepare for supper with the Wytch King of Altan. Hopefully, we shall learn more of this alliance he's proposing. Has Edrun arrived yet? Will Garrik present his plans for the alliance over dinner, do you think?"

"I'm not certain. I haven't seen any sign of the delegation from Miraen, but I came down from Dragonwatch late yesterday, and other than Master Ilya coming to check on me this morning, I've seen no one else."

"Then we must be prepared for anything," Drannik said.

"I'm *always* prepared for anything," Dirit chirped.

Tristin concentrated on the pattern he was trying to build. Circular, with lines here, and a spiky bit there... His heart raced as the pattern slowly took shape in his mind.

Could he really do this?

"Yes..." Master Ilya murmured from across the table. "Exactly so. And the little hooked part... yes. Now hold on to it in your mind and study how it *feels* as well as how it looks. Both the look *and* the feel of the pattern will serve as your guide the next time you build it. You'll know when you're getting close, and when you've got it wrong. Now dissolve it, and we'll start from scratch again, but this time, you'll do it without my guidance."

"It's much easier than I expected," Tristin said, opening his eyes to focus on the Wytch Master.

"Especially when you don't have a troublesome little mythe-dragon distracting you, hmm?"

Tristin offered him a shy smile. Ilya had believed him even before he'd seen Dirit with his own eyes. "Yes, that does make a difference. But more importantly, you explain everything so clearly.

Mordax had a way of making it all seem so difficult and complicated."

"Given what the Wytch Council had planned for you," Ilya said drily, "it may not have been in Mordax's best interests to have you learn to protect yourself. If you'd been able to master the patterns, he'd have had no reason to keep you locked up in Shadowspire."

"And if he hadn't made me dependent on that damned drug of his, he'd have had no hold over me." Tristin stared down at the table. "I feel so stupid for just blindly accepting it all. I never questioned him, never even tried to escape."

"You were a child, Tristin." Ilya's voice was gentle. "And you were isolated. You had no reason to think they were using you, and not enough experience to question the situation. And once you were taking the anzaria regularly, your mind was too clouded to come to any such conclusion, no matter how much evidence was presented."

"Do you really believe that?" Tristin found himself unable to meet the Wytch Master's eyes. "Or are you just being kind?"

"I truly believe it, Tristin. I cannot see what the future holds for you, but I believe it will be bright. And you will not be alone with no one to turn to, not ever again. You have family and friends here in Altan. Prince Jaire thinks the world of you, Ambris speaks highly of you, and you seem to have struck up a friendship with Prince Mikhyal easily enough."

Tristin's ears began to burn, and he finally risked a glance up. He saw no disapproval or censure sharpening the Wytch Master's delicate features. "Ah. Yes. Well. Prince Mikhyal is… he's very kind. I wasn't expecting him to even speak to me. I'm not really very…" He trailed off, cringing as Ilya's lips twitched, certain he was about to be reprimanded for behaving inappropriately. Mikhyal was a prince of the blood, after all, and Tristin, the bastard son of a murdering traitor.

"I'm glad to hear you're getting on well with him," Ilya said, and Tristin stared at him in surprise. "I worried that after so many years in isolation, you would have trouble forming friendships. I am happy to learn I was wrong."

"Ah. Well. Um." Tristin pressed his lips together to keep any other awkward confessions from slipping out, and tried not to think too hard of the promise he'd made to Mikhyal yesterday.

"Shall we try again?" Ilya asked.

"Yes. That would probably be for the best." Relieved, Tristin closed his eyes, banished the image of Mikhyal's face alight with joy as he rode down to the castle on dragonback, and started building the pattern Ilya had taught him.

At the stroke of six, Mikhyal followed his father into Wytch King Garrik's private dining room to find the table set for three. Garrik was already there, and rose to greet them when they entered. At twenty-seven, he was only a year younger than Mikhyal, though he'd taken the throne at the tender age of twenty, after the murder of his father, Wytch King Dane.

"Drannik, Mikhyal, welcome to Altan," Garrik said, coming forward to clasp arms first with Drannik and then Mikhyal. "I hope you don't mind a quiet, private dinner. Edrun will be arriving tomorrow, and there'll be a formal reception tomorrow night. Tonight, I wanted to speak with you alone, without any servants about. I trust you've found your suite satisfactory?"

"Quite, quite," Drannik said, "and your staff most accommodating. You must thank Kian again for coming to fetch me. Though the journey here on dragonback was a bit nerve-wracking, it was certainly faster than horseback, and much more comfortable than that damnable carriage my wife prefers."

"I will indeed pass the message along. I'm told Kian is far more considerate of his passengers than I am." Garrik gave him a rueful grin before turning to Mikhyal. "And how fare you, Mikhyal? I apologize for not stopping by to see you when you arrived yesterday, but preparations for my brother's betrothal ceremony are taking up every spare moment of my time."

Mikhyal bowed his head slightly. "I understand, Garrik. To be quite honest, I wouldn't have been very good company last night. I was still quite exhausted, and Wytch Master Ilya only allowed me to leave Dragonwatch on the understanding that I wouldn't overdo it."

"He'll hold you to that, too," Garrik said with a grin, and gestured toward the sideboard, where a generous buffet was set out. "Ilya would have joined us tonight, but he's working with a student up at Dragonwatch, and with all that's going on here, he hasn't had as much time for him as he ought."

"Is this Tristin you speak of?" Mikhyal asked.

"Ai. You met him, did you?"

"I did. Is he a relative? He reminded me very much of both you and your father."

"Ai, he's cousin to Jaire and me," Garrik said. "Vakha's bastard, apparently. Cenyth and her cronies on the Wytch Council thought they'd put him on the throne in my place, but we managed to disabuse them of that notion quite handily."

"So Ilya said when he came to me in Rhiva," Drannik said, taking a plate and looking over the offerings. "He also said you had hopes for an alliance. The one you hinted at rather obliquely last year, I assume?"

"Indeed," Garrik said. "And that is what I wished to speak to you of tonight, before we meet formally with Edrun and Ord."

When they had all filled their plates and were sitting, Garrik began. "My father was an outspoken opponent of the Wytch Council, and one of his goals was to find a way to unite the northern kingdoms and break with the Council and the south. I know he spoke of it at length to you, Drannik, and I also understand the main reason nothing ever came of it was that you both feared the Council would raise the entire south against us. Even with the combined military force of all four of the northern kingdoms, we could never hope to defeat the armies of the southern kingdoms and the Council's Drachan troops."

"You'll find us all in agreement with that assessment, I think," Drannik said.

"Ai, and that situation has not changed appreciably," Garrik said. "But what if I were to tell you that I have come into possession of knowledge that will give us an advantage the Council cannot hope to match, even with the combined might of the south behind them?"

"I *do* hope he's not talking about *me*."

Mikhyal looked down to see Dirit curled around his plate, head appearing to rest upon a leg of roast duck. He gave the dragon a very slight shake of his head and turned his attention back to the conversation.

Drannik's dark eyes revealed nothing as he slowly chewed his mouthful. "A weapon, then?" he said finally. "Whenever the Wytch Kings of the north grow restless, there's talk of caches of weapons buried in the deepest vaults of the oldest holdings of the royal families, hidden before the Wytch Council banned the possession of such things."

"Not a weapon." Garrik's eyes glittered in the candlelight. "An army."

"We have an army," Drannik said flatly. "Between the kingdoms of the north, we have *four*. It still wouldn't be enough. Even if we were able to choose our ground for every battle, we simply cannot raise the numbers we'd need. The northern kingdoms have never been able to support the kind of population the southern kingdoms can."

"What about an army that can cross a kingdom in hours rather than days? An army that isn't hampered by rough terrain or foul weather, and will not require long supply lines. An army that can strike a devastating blow out of a clear sky." Garrik leaned forward, his voice barely a whisper. "An army the mere sight of which will strike terror into the hearts of those who oppose us."

"Oh, my ears and whiskers!" Dirit exclaimed. "How exciting! He's talking about *treason*." The dragon minced across the table and lay himself down, settling his head between his little front feet like a dog, and stared up at Garrik. "He looks much too kingly to be a rebel, don't you think? I wonder if history will paint him as a hero or a traitor. I suppose it depends upon which side emerges victorious once the dust has settled."

Mikhyal kept his mouth shut and hoped Garrik couldn't hear Dirit any more than Drannik could.

Drannik was silent for a time, regarding Garrik from hooded eyes. "What sort of army?" he finally asked.

The grin that lit Garrik's face was almost feral. He rose from his seat and threw open the double doors of the dining room. "Come with me. This will only take a few moments."

Mikhyal and his father exchanged a frown and a shrug and rose to follow the Wytch King. Not content to be left alone, Dirit made a show of scurrying up Mikhyal's sleeve and perching on his shoulder.

Garrik only took them as far as the Grand Hall, where Prince Vayne, Prince Jaire, and the healer, Kian, awaited them. All three men wore cloaks and were barefoot.

"My, my, what have we here?" Dirit murmured in Mikhyal's ear.

Jaire executed a formal bow. "Good evening, Your Majesties and Your Highness." His gaze drifted to Mikhyal's shoulder, and he grinned, presumably at Dirit.

"Good evening, Your Highness," Dirit chirped. "Are you going to give us a demonstration?"

Prince Jaire glanced over at his brother and Drannik, then gave Dirit the slightest nod.

"Whenever you're ready," Garrik said.

As if they'd rehearsed the maneuver, Vayne and Kian both turned and walked a few paces away from Jaire, then all three men faced forward and whipped off their cloaks. None of them wore a stitch of clothing underneath, but there was hardly time to register that before all three of them began to change.

Their shifts were so smooth and so fast, Mikhyal barely caught any details. His attention was on Prince Jaire, and he had a momentary impression of the prince's slender body lengthening, his face elongating and changing, and the next thing he knew, in place of Prince Jaire stood a dragon with gleaming opalescent scales and violet markings. Next to him, where Vayne had stood, was a slightly larger emerald-green dragon, and at Jaire's other side stood a much bigger black dragon.

"Oh, they're *very* good," Dirit said admiringly. "And what pretty colors. Though Jaire and Vayne don't look nearly big enough to carry you, Your Royal Immenseness. Even though you were quite restrained with those blackberry tarts yesterday."

Mikhyal opened his mouth to throw back an acid retort, but snapped it shut before a single word could slip out.

Drannik's eyes narrowed in a calculating expression as he watched the three men shift back to human form. Blushing furiously, Jaire snatched up his discarded cloak and whipped it over his shoulders. Kian and Vayne followed suit at a more leisurely pace, clearly less bothered about exposing themselves.

Jaire focused on his brother. "If that's all, Garrik, Master Ristan's expecting me in the library to go over titles and such."

"Evening lessons?" Garrik inquired.

"Making up for spending yesterday afternoon at Dragonwatch," Jaire grumbled. "I thought I was getting out of it, but apparently I was just delaying it."

"Go on, then. Off to your lessons," Garrik said. "Better you than me."

Jaire shot his brother a scowl, flashed a quick, shy smile at Mikhyal — or perhaps it was Dirit he was acknowledging — and hurried off across the hall.

"Nice boy," Dirit commented. "I like him."

"Vayne, Kian, thank you," Garrik said. "That's all I need for the moment."

Vayne and Kian nodded to the Wytch King and followed Prince Jaire out at a leisurely pace.

Drannik turned his speculative gaze upon the Wytch King. "I saw Jaire's dragon form when Ilya brought him to our aid in Rhiva. I knew you had inherited the gift of the Dragon Mother, but until that moment, I did not realize your brother had, too. There's been no talk of it among the Wytch Masters."

"No, there wouldn't have been," Garrik said. "Jaire did not inherit the gift. None of them did. Prince Vayne transformed both Jaire and Kian by burning the patterns into their mythe-shadows. He can confer the ability to shift upon anyone who can touch the mythe, as well as some who cannot, if certain patterns are present in their mythe-shadows."

"Can he, now?" Drannik glanced at Mikhyal, then focused on Garrik, eyes alight with interest. "Let's hear about this alliance you're proposing. And this army."

"Let us return to our meal, then," Garrik said, "and I'll tell you what Wytch King Ord and I have in mind."

Tristin drew in a deep breath, squared his shoulders, and stepped out into the hall. Ambris had been encouraging him to join him, Kian, and Alys for meals ever since he'd been well enough to eat solid food. Thus far, Tristin had always politely declined, but yesterday, he'd announced to Ambris that he was going to try to be more sociable. He would have to be, if he intended to venture down to the castle. Lunch with Ambris and the others seemed like a sensible first step.

He'd almost reached the dining hall when he heard voices drifting out. It sounded as if an argument was going on, and he hesitated in the doorway.

Should he intrude? Perhaps he should just turn around and go quietly back to his suite…

"I'm just saying you can't possibly know for certain until you've talked to him." Kian sounded irritated.

"Taretha was his *sister*," Ambris snapped. "Of *course* he knew."

"You don't know that," Kian said stubbornly. "And you won't, unless you ask him."

"Gently, Kian," Alys said. "Not everyone is lucky enough to have a family like ours."

Ambris looked as if he was about to launch into a tirade, but stopped when he caught sight of Tristin, still dithering in the doorway. "Come in, Tristin! I was hoping you'd come. Alys has set a place for you."

Tristin edged in, suddenly very aware of the three pairs of eyes fixed on him. "Um. Sorry. I… ah… didn't mean to interrupt anything. You did say I should join you sometime, but if you're having a private discussion…"

"Hardly," said Ambris. "And it's *not* a discussion." He shot a glare at Kian. "I happened to mention to Kian that you were keen to go down to the castle for the betrothal, and now he's got it into his head that *I* ought to go, as well."

"I only suggested that since Tristin was going, you might go together," Kian said.

"And risk being recognized?" Ambris scowled. "There's too much at stake to risk alienating Miraen. Garrik needs all the northern kingdoms working together, and if my father should find out Garrik's been sheltering me here..."

"And it makes such a fine, noble excuse, doesn't it?" Kian muttered.

"*Kian.*" Alys kicked her brother under the table, and Tristin suppressed a smile. Having never had a sibling, he found Kian and Alys's interactions both fascinating and amusing.

Ambris grimaced. "I've had plenty of time to consider it, Kian, and my mind is made up. I shall remain here at Dragonwatch until the ceremony is over and the guests have gone home."

While Ambris spoke, Tristin took a seat at the table, opposite Ambris and next to Alys, who offered him a kind smile as she lifted a slice of meat pie onto a plate for him. "You're looking much better this morning, Master Tristin."

"Thank you, Alys. I'm feeling better, too. I had a very encouraging lesson with Master Ilya last night."

"*And* an invitation to dance with Prince Mikhyal at the ball following the ceremony," Ambris said.

Heat crept up Tristin's cheeks. He ducked his head and took a forkful of the pie Alys had set before him. The flavor was rich, the pastry flaky and buttery, and the meat practically melted in his mouth. "Alys, this is lovely," he said.

"Why, thank you, Master Tristin." Alys smiled happily. "You're very kind to say so."

"Are you changing the subject, Tristin?" Ambris teased.

"No, but you are," Kian said. "Honestly, Ambris, you need to confront him, if only for your own peace."

"I *have* peace," Ambris muttered. "Or I would, if you would leave it be."

"Peace," Kian said flatly. "Ai, that's just what it looks like when you're whimpering in my arms after a bad dream."

"They're just dreams."

"They haunt you."

Ambris stared down at his plate and applied himself to his lunch, and the rest of the meal passed in long silences punctuated by brief attempts at awkward conversation. When he'd finished eating, Ambris excused himself, saying he had work to do in the garden. Tristin had already promised he'd help with the weeding this afternoon, so he trailed after Ambris, wondering what to say.

Ambris saved him from having to think of anything by speaking first. "I'm sorry you had to listen to that, and on the first day you felt brave enough to join us. It's not usually like that."

"It... it sounds as if Kian cares a great deal for you," Tristin ventured.

"Oh, he does," Ambris said quickly. "That's what makes it so difficult. I know he's trying to help. He truly wants to see me happy. But Kian is lucky enough to have been loved and wanted his whole life. He hasn't quite grasped the concept of abandonment and betrayal by one's own flesh and blood." Ambris shook his head and forced a smile. "But enough of me. What of you? You said you had a good lesson, and Ilya sounded very pleased when he left last night. He said you've made great progress."

"I'm not sure I'd call it *great*," Tristin said, "but progress, certainly. I managed to build the basic shielding pattern he's been trying to teach me. It turned out to be far less difficult than I expected, although all the credit for my success must go to Ilya. He's a marvelous teacher. Once I got over my fear of failing, it wasn't nearly as difficult as I'd been led to believe."

"Ilya *is* a marvelous teacher, indeed." Ambris's smile looked a lot less forced now. "He taught me, too, and like you, I'd been told I was too hopelessly broken to ever learn so many times, I never questioned it."

"Ilya suggested that it wouldn't have been in Mordax's best interests to have me learn to protect myself," Tristin said with a shudder. "I can't help thinking that if Ilya had been the one to teach me from the beginning, perhaps I'd never have ended up spending half my life shut up in Shadowspire with only my hallucinations for company."

"We have much in common, it seems," Ambris said. "I was kept prisoner at my father's estate at Blackfrost for five years while my aunt stole power from me under the guise of trying to teach me. Only... once Kian helped me escape, Ilya took over my training, and I learned that Taretha hadn't been teaching me the correct patterns to help me control the shift." Ambris's golden eyes took on a distant look. "I still don't know if my father was complicit." He glanced at Tristin. "That's what the fuss over lunch was about. My father is Wytch King Edrun of Miraen, and he's coming for the betrothal ceremony. Kian thinks I should talk to him."

"Ah. And you would rather not. Do you think you will?"

Ambris swallowed hard and looked away. "I don't think so. I... don't think I could bear to find out that he knew what she was doing. How much she was hurting me. I think I'd rather not know. That way, I can go on believing the best of him."

Slowly, hesitantly, Tristin reached out to put a hand on Ambris's shoulder. As he squeezed gently, Ambris turned his head and gave him a thin, watery smile. "Besides," he said in a quavering voice, "I don't want to cause an incident of any sort. I'd feel dreadful if my presence here harmed Altan's relations with Miraen. Garrik's been very kind to me, and I refuse to do anything to complicate things for him. It's better if my father continues to believe I perished in the fire."

They'd reached the garden now, and Tristin was grateful to have something else to focus on. It was all terribly awkward; he had no idea what to say to the healer. He knelt at the edge of the flagstones and began searching through the clumps of rabbit-bane planted around the edges of the garden.

Ambris knelt beside him. "We've a gap here," he said, his voice sounding much steadier. "That won't do."

Tristin looked down at the spot where Ambris was pointing. "We can transplant some from the edge of the coldroot bed," he suggested. "It's gotten rather thick there."

"Then we can solve two problems at once," Ambris said. "I shall go and thin out the plants on that side and bring some of them over here for you to plant." He got to his feet and headed off toward the garden shed, spine stiff, shoulders tense.

Tristin stared after him, wondering if he'd done something wrong. Real friendships were turning out to be far more complicated than his hallucinatory ones ever were.

Movement in the dressing table mirror had Mikhyal glancing up to see his father entering his bed chamber.

"How are you feeling?" Drannik asked.

Mikhyal kept his gaze fixed on the mirror, gritted his teeth, and with effort, refrained from tossing off the first biting reply that came to the tip of his tongue. The constant inquiries after the state of his health were becoming tiresome. Ilya had been in not half an hour earlier to deliver an invitation to a meeting in the library, and he had asked the same question.

"Much better, Father," he said patiently. "In fact, I feel quite well. Ilya says I've made a remarkable recovery."

From his perch on the dressing table, where he was busily inspecting and adjusting his admittedly magnificent whiskers, Dirit said, "No thanks necessary. No, *really*, I'm channeling the healing energy of the mythe to my bearer out of the supreme goodness of my heart. Not that I really *expected* anyone to notice. Oh, no, it'll all be credited to Prince Mikhyal's Remarkable Constitution or the Manly Blood of Kings flowing through his veins. It's all right, don't bother apologizing or thanking me. I'm quite used to being taken for granted." The little dragon turned to face Mikhyal. "How do I look?"

"Petulant," Mikhyal said mildly.

"Really?" A tuft of eyebrow fur twitched and Dirit turned to survey himself in the mirror once more, though Mikhyal saw no evidence of a reflection, not even a shadow.

"It rather suits you."

"I *do* believe I've been insulted." Dirit let out an offended sniff and turned away, lashing his tail at Mikhyal. "See if I help you the next time you get yourself into a mess, Your Royal Ungratefulness."

"Given that you've admitted to being bound to defend my line, I'm afraid I can't quite find it in me to see that as much of a threat."

"*Chosen,*" Dirit hissed.

"Chosen to be bound," Mikhyal countered.

"Well, *really!*" Dirit huffed.

"You're going to have to watch that, Mikhyal," Drannik said. "You keep speaking to thin air, and people are going to talk."

Mikhyal looked up and met his father's eyes in the mirror. "I'll be careful, Father. And I'll keep my mouth shut at the meeting this morning unless I have something important to contribute."

"Oh, if *only* you could be persuaded to make that a permanent state of affairs," Dirit muttered. "I wonder what it would take?"

"Leaving the Wytch Sword here doesn't make a difference, does it?" Drannik asked hopefully.

"No, it does not," Mikhyal replied. "The sword's been here in the suite since I arrived, but Dirit seems quite able to follow me about wherever I go. Prince Jaire took me... er, I mean *us*, on a tour of the castle grounds yesterday, and Dirit was perched on my shoulder the entire time."

"Well, I wouldn't be much of a defender of the bloodline if I was stuck in a sword, would I?" Dirit asked. "There is a limit to how far I can go from the sword, but it's a bit farther than the edge of the castle grounds." He flitted up to the top of the mirror, coiled himself up, and leapt toward Mikhyal to land on his shoulder.

Mikhyal felt nothing when the dragon landed, but it appeared to be kneading his tunic with its claws like a little cat. Once it had itself settled, it wrapped its tail around his neck and said, "*I'm* ready. Shall we be off, then?"

When Mikhyal turned around, Drannik was giving him a speculative look. "I don't suppose it might be encouraged to spy for you? Listen in on conversations, tell us where trouble might be brewing?"

Before Mikhyal could answer, Dirit whispered in his ear, "It *might* be persuaded. Possibly. For a price."

"Of course there would be a price." Mikhyal rolled his eyes. "What would it want?"

"A nice fish." Dirit smacked his lips. "Or perhaps the occasional compliment."

"Or a blackberry tart?" Mikhyal suggested.

"Ooh, yes, that would do *very* well. *Much* nicer than those bandits. They were altogether too *stringy* for my liking. Could have done with some tenderizing. And a nice bit of sauce or gravy... something with lots of garlic would have been *just* the thing."

Mikhyal's stomach roiled as he thought of what Dirit had left of the bandits in the clearing. "Compliments and blackberry tarts, then," he murmured. He turned to his father and said, a little louder, "Apparently, it might be persuaded. If I'm nice to it, and feed it pastries."

Drannik's dark eyebrows drew together. "Well, then, you had best endeavor to be civil, had you not?"

Dirit chuckled. "Yes, *do* try to be civil, Your Royal Beastliness. I shall be most intrigued to observe your attempts."

Mikhyal didn't answer the dragon, but said to his father, "I'll do my best."

A guardsman waited in the hallway outside the suite to escort them to the library.

"I don't know how Garrik manages without a queen to oversee the household," Drannik commented as they crossed the Grand Hall, where servants were busy cleaning and polishing in preparation for the betrothal ceremony. "Your mother works herself to the bone for weeks before any event held at Castle Rhivana."

"Extremely competent staff, I'd imagine," Mikhyal said, trying to ignore Dirit, who was chattering in his ear about all the changes he'd noticed since he'd last visited Castle Altan, which must have been at least a century ago.

They were the last to arrive in the library. The gathering was not large. Each of the Wytch Kings had brought only a single advisor with him, and Mikhyal immediately noted there were no Wytch Masters present, not even Ilya. Garrik had Prince Jaire at his side of the table. Ord had Vayne with him, and Edrun had brought Prince Bradin, the second eldest of his sons. Drannik, too, had made note of the conspicuous lack of Wytch Masters. He scanned the faces at the table, then glanced at Mikhyal, one eyebrow raised.

"This looks like a council of war!" Dirit exclaimed. "How intriguing!" He hopped down from Mikhyal's shoulder and settled himself near Prince Jaire to listen to the proceedings. An expression of delight crossed the prince's face, but he quickly concealed it, giving the little dragon a surreptitious nod, then directing a shy smile at Mikhyal, who grinned in return.

"Where is Ilya?" Drannik asked. "I expected to see him here."

"Depending upon what we decide," Garrik replied, "he and Wytch Master Ythlin of Irilan, both of whom are sympathetic to our cause, may be joining us later. I thought this first meeting should not involve any Council representatives, no matter which faction they favor." He folded his hands in front of him and cast his gaze around the table, meeting each man's eyes in turn. "I've spoken to each of you in the past of uniting the northern kingdoms and breaking free of the Council's grip, and I am aware that my father also approached you during his reign, so the alliance I will propose to you is nothing you haven't considered or discussed before.

"My understanding from speaking to each of you individually is that the biggest objection to forming an independent alliance is the fact that our declaration of independence would be met with force. The Council and the southern kingdoms will not wish to lose their access to the metals, gems, and mythe-stones than come out of the mines in the Iceshards.

"Up until now, there has been no reason to think we could be victorious in such a conflict. With our harsher climate, difficult terrain, and shorter growing season, the mountain kingdoms have never been able to support the number of people — or raise the kind of armies — that the southern kingdoms can.

"But we now have a course of action open to us that will swing the balance in our favor. Prince Vayne of Irilan has revived an ancient technique of mythe-shadow manipulation that could help us build an army the likes of which the Council cannot hope to match. You've all witnessed Prince Jaire's transformation into a dragon shifter. The gift of the Dragon Mother, it has been called, and yet it was not given to Jaire by the gods, or by chance, but by Prince Vayne. Furthermore, this transformation can be performed on anyone who can touch the mythe, or anyone who has certain patterns already present in their mythe-shadow. Indeed, Vayne has already successfully performed it on a number of volunteers. I have therefore bestowed upon him the title of Royal Dragon Master."

All eyes turned to Vayne, who bowed his head in acknowledgment.

Wytch King Edrun cleared his throat. "Not all who possess the gift of the Dragon Mother are able to use it effectively. Garrik's own experience in learning to control the shift was not so pleasant. How can you be sure those you transform can control the power you give them?"

"I burn the patterns to control the shift into their mythe-shadows when I give them the ability to shift," Vayne said. "Thus far, none have had any difficulty controlling their abilities."

"What are the risks of the procedure?" Drannik asked.

"As with any process involving the manipulation of mythe-shadows," Vayne said, meeting Drannik's eyes, "the primary risk is mythe-shock. The risk can be minimized if I work closely with a healer. I have, in fact, found a healer here in Altan who works extremely well with me. Together, we have performed the transformation on nine volunteers, including Prince Jaire. None of them suffered any ill effects, and all of them now have the ability to shift, which means they have the ability to fly."

"Think about it," Garrik said softly into the silence that followed. "It means we can observe troop movements from the air, and get word back to our commanders long before the armies meet. Knowing what the enemy is planning will allow us to meet them on the ground of our choosing, and our ability to react to enemy tactics will be far greater than their ability to react to ours. Not to mention the fact that most of our dragon shifters turn out to be fire breathers. Imagine the terror of the enemy soldiers, knowing that fiery death could rain down from above with little warning."

Mikhyal listened with increasing interest. This was exactly the advantage the northern kingdoms needed, and the murmurs of approval coming from around the table suggested the others were in agreement.

"Wytch King Ord and I have spent the past several weeks combing the archives and drafting a preliminary document laying out the framework of the Northern Alliance," Garrik continued. "If I've piqued your interest, we can present our draft to you as a starting point. I am hopeful that we might be able to come to an agreement before the betrothal ceremony."

Beside him, Drannik nodded thoughtfully. "It is time. The Council overstepped their authority when they kidnapped Prince Jaire. Which of us will be next, hmm? The heir they have saddled me with is not the heir I'd have chosen. Wytch power should not be the sole qualification for rule. I, for one, am with Garrik. I say we break free before the Council attempts to tear our kingdoms apart and fill our thrones with puppet kings."

Ord nodded, but Edrun said, "What of our Wytch Masters? Ilya and Ythlin may be willing to throw their lot in with the north, but Miraen's Wytch Master Rotham was hand-picked by Council Speaker Taretha. She may be gone, but Rotham is still loyal to the Council. He would betray us."

"As would Rhiva's Anxin," Drannik murmured. "Indeed, I fear my own heir, Shaine, has become a puppet of the Council, and would also betray us, were he to learn of our plans."

"I, too, have a Wytch Master to be rid of," Garrik said. "Wytch Master Faah was involved in the plot to usurp Altan's throne. He is currently in a cell beneath the castle. I suggest we send him, Rotham, and Anxin to Askarra in a prison coach, with the declaration of our independence chained around their necks."

"A bold move, indeed," said Edrun. "But perhaps it is time. Let us see this document you and Ord have drafted. I would be well pleased to help devise a plan to rid ourselves of those who would betray us." He glanced at his son, Prince Bradin, before addressing Drannik. "Your own heir would betray you?"

Drannik grimaced. "He was not my choice of heir. Mikhyal, here, would be my choice. He is my firstborn and was trained to rule after me, but his Wytch power never manifested, and without that, the Council would not confirm him."

"That could be changed," Vayne murmured. "Even though he possesses no active Wytch power, Prince Mikhyal carries latent shifter patterns in his mythe-shadow. It would be a simple matter to bring them to the surface, thus giving him the power to shift. With such power, he would be considered an acceptable heir by the Council."

Mikhyal's heart leapt at the thought. How much easier the job of a commander would be if he were to have a bird's-eye view of the combat. He turned to look at his father, expecting eagerness to match his own, only to be met with a frown of consternation.

"Ooh…" Dirit chirped, picking his way across the table to sit in front of Mikhyal. "Heir to the throne. So my sacred task of preserving the line of Rhiva becomes much more important. It seems I chose my bond-mate wisely after all."

"I see the same latent patterns in Wytch King Edrun and in Prince Bradin," Vayne said quietly. "If any of you are interested, I could perform the transformation on you."

"Imagine *four* dragon kings," Jaire murmured. "The Council would be paralyzed."

"Imagine four dragon kings leading an army of dragons," Garrik said. "The Council and their Drachan soldiers would flee, tails between their legs, like the dogs they are."

Around the table, the Wytch Kings nodded their agreement, their eyes alight with interest. Drannik clearly spoke for all of them when he said, "Bring forth these documents, Garrik. Let's have a look at what you and Ord have worked out, and see if we can come to an agreement."

"Yes, please get on with it," Dirit said, crossing his front feet primly before him. "I *do* love a good rebellion."

No one seemed the least bit surprised when Prince Jaire suddenly burst out laughing.

Drannik was quiet as he and Mikhyal made their way back to their suite to get ready for dinner. Once the door was shut behind them, he said, "Garrik has thought out this alliance extremely well."

Indeed, every one of the concerns expressed by the gathered Wytch Kings had been answered to their satisfaction, almost as if every objection that could possibly be raised had been anticipated and prepared for. Each of the kings had been handed a copy of

Garrik's proposal to be looked over before they reconvened the following morning.

Mikhyal let out a barely audible sigh as his father spread the documents out over the suite's dining table. The two of them would, no doubt, be combing over the papers into the wee hours of the morning. Bed, though it beckoned already, would have to wait.

"Master Ilya said you must rest," Dirit whispered in his ear from his perch on Mikhyal's shoulder.

"Not likely, tonight," Mikhyal muttered under his breath. Though he was feeling better every day, he still tired easily. The mere thought of having to focus on the details of the alliance for half the night was enough to make him want to skip the formal dinner.

"Let me see if I can help," Dirit said, and a moment later, a surge of energy tingled through Mikhyal. His mind sharpened, and he suddenly felt as rested as if he'd just woken from a full night's sleep.

"What did you... was that you?" he asked the dragon.

Dirit looked very pleased with himself. "One of my many talents. No thanks necessary. Of course, you cannot survive on mythe-energy alone — you do actually *need* real sleep — but a bit of help now and then will not harm you, and this should be enough to get you through the evening."

Drannik looked up from the papers he was perusing. "Did you say something, Mikhyal?"

"No, Father, I was just talking to Dirit."

"A dragon army," Drannik said. "Imagine. That was not at all what I expected to hear when Garrik sent Ilya to invite us to negotiations."

"Nor I. It sounds like exactly the advantage we need." Mikhyal went to the window and stared out. "Imagine that sky full of dragon warriors."

"Ai." Drannik set the papers down and came to join him. "A truly fearsome prospect." His gaze became distant as it swept the sky.

"What did you think of Vayne's offer to transform me?"

Drannik turned to face him. "I think it is worth our consideration," he said slowly, as if he was carefully choosing each word. "But we must exercise caution. I would have to be reassured regarding the safety of the procedure. If we can make this alliance a reality, my choice of heir will no longer be bound by Council dictates. With the succession no longer an issue, there is no reason for us to rush into anything."

"I disagree," Mikhyal said. "I think there is every reason to move forward with it, and quickly. Think of the advantage it would give us in battle. I could survey my troops and the progress of the conflict from the air. We'd be able to see our enemy's every move. They'd never be able to flank us. Not to mention how useful it would be in terms of sending messages and coordinating with our allies. Do not tell me it won't come to that, Father. If Rhiva joins this alliance, there will be war."

"I am aware." Drannik's smile was grim. "Believe me, I've studied enough military strategy to see the advantages. I'm certain we won't be short of volunteers for the transformation. I'm just not convinced that *you* should be one of them." He returned to the table where he began shuffling through the papers again, apparently considering the matter closed.

Mikhyal scanned the sky once more and imagined himself gliding through the air, an entire unit of dragon warriors at his back.

"You're not giving up that easily, are you?" Dirit whispered in his ear.

"You would have me ask my men to submit to a procedure that I, their commander, will not risk?" Mikhyal said softly. "That is not the way to maintain the loyalty and trust I have striven to build over the years."

Drannik looked up from his papers. "It is the risk to you that concerns me. Vayne sounds confident that the procedure is safe, but he admits he's only performed it on a handful of people, and he cannot see all eventual outcomes. If you do not survive the process, what then? I will be left with Shaine as my heir, and we both know where that will lead."

"I've never understood why you've always been so opposed to Shaine taking the throne. Up until the accident, it was my belief that with the right guidance, Shaine could make a fine king. And yet you have been dead set against the idea ever since the Council confirmed him as your heir. What, exactly, are your objections?"

"You know my objections. They are the same as yours: he has become the Council's creature."

"That's a recent development," Mikhyal pointed out. "What were your objections *before* the accident?"

Drannik's dark brows drew together. "You were always my first choice. You know that."

"There is more to it than that, is there not?" Mikhyal pressed. "The rumors—"

"Are true," Drannik said flatly. "As I'm sure you've already gathered. Shaine is not mine. Had he been mine, I would have been far less resistant to the idea of accepting him as my heir. As it is, whenever I look at him, all I see is the end of my line." The bitterness in his father's voice was enough to take Mikhyal's breath away.

"Does Shaine know?" Mikhyal asked quietly.

Drannik spread his hands and shook his head. "Not from me, but I've no idea what your mother has told him." He stared down at the documents, but Mikhyal guessed he wasn't seeing the carefully formed letters inked on the parchment.

The silence stretched between them until finally, Mikhyal said, "We had best prepare ourselves for dinner. Think upon what I've said. We have time to come to a decision, but do not close the door on Vayne's offer. It could be crucial to our success." Dirit, still perched upon Mikhyal's shoulder, was, for once, mercifully silent.

Chapter Five

The mountain air rushed by, crisp and cold. Mikhyal pulled the fur-lined cloak more tightly about his shoulders, thankful he'd taken Prince Jaire up on his offer to loan it to him for his ride to Dragonwatch. Garrik's muscles shifted and bunched beneath him as the dragon's powerful wings lifted them higher, and the air grew colder as they glided up the mountain.

Unbeknownst to the Wytch King, Dirit rode upon his head, standing on his hind legs, front feet wrapped around the dragon's horns, whiskers trailing behind him in the strong wind.

Mikhyal's heart was still pounding with a mixture of wild joy and sheer terror after Garrik's leap from the top of Castle Altan's north tower. For one heart-stopping moment, they'd plummeted into the valley below. Mikhyal had let out a most unmanly squawk, and from the shaking of the dragon's ribs as he caught an updraft under his great wings, Mikhyal guessed Garrik found his reaction amusing.

Early that morning, the Wytch King had sent word to Mikhyal that he was heading to Dragonwatch for breakfast, and Mikhyal was welcome to join him if he would like. The tone of the note had been most formal and correct, but Mikhyal had to wonder why he'd been invited.

It had been well over a week since he'd seen Tristin... was it possible Tristin had asked his cousin about seeing Mikhyal? His heart leapt at the thought, and he had to remind himself that there had been nothing in Garrik's message to indicate anything of the sort.

The flight was over far too quickly, and Mikhyal found himself almost disappointed when Garrik landed in Dragonwatch's courtyard.

Ambris was waiting near the door, and came forward immediately. "Good morning, Your Highness." The healer reached up to unbuckle the safety straps holding Mikhyal securely in place. "I trust you had a good flight?"

Mikhyal couldn't stop grinning as he slid down to the ground. "Absolutely amazing! Though I must say, that initial headlong dive off the north tower was enough to make me thankful for the harness. It was a good thing I hadn't eaten breakfast yet."

The Wytch King snorted, a sound that was suspiciously close to laughter.

"*I* certainly found it entertaining," Dirit chirped, picking his way down Garrik's neck. "Your squeal of terror as we took to the air was particularly endearing, Your Royal Anxiousness."

Mikhyal gritted his teeth and refrained from comment.

"Yes, I'm afraid our Wytch King does seem to enjoy frightening the life out of his passengers." Ambris removed his own cloak and laying it across one of the stone benches. "Until someone's sick all over him. Then it's not nearly so amusing, you understand."

Dirit chuckled as he hopped down to the ground and scampered toward the front door, fading from sight halfway there.

"There's a cloak for you on the bench, Your Majesty," Ambris said. "I don't see any saddlebags, so I'll assume you couldn't be bothered to bring any clothing for yourself. If you'd like to stop by our suite, you can borrow something of Kian's, just so you don't frighten poor Alys. Give me a moment to get this saddle off you and... oh... well. If you're in that much of a hurry, I shan't bother."

Mikhyal turned to see the Wytch King in his human form, untangling himself from the straps, apparently unconcerned about his lack of clothing.

"You can accompany me to your suite Ambris," Garrik said to the healer, who reached for the cloak and settled it over the king's shoulders. "Mikhyal and I have a meeting to attend later this morning, so we'll be leaving shortly after breakfast, but I wanted to have a word with you alone."

"Very well," Ambris said. "Mikhyal, if you'd like to go on to the dining room, I believe you'll find Tristin there. We'll join you once Garrik is presentable." He eyed the Wytch King critically, and added, "Or, if not presentable, at least *clothed*."

Garrik's black eyes glittered, and he barked out a laugh. "I'll have you know Ilya finds me quite presentable, *especially* unclothed."

"Yes, I imagine he does," Ambris said drily, "though I must admit, I've always found Ilya to be somewhat lacking in taste."

Chuckling at their easy banter, Mikhyal followed them inside and headed toward Dragonwatch's dining hall, which was hardly a hall. The school only boasted six suites, and accordingly, the dining hall contained two tables each surrounded by enough sturdy chairs to seat six.

Tristin was sitting at the table nearest the window, chatting with Dirit, who was perched on the back of the chair next to him. Alys was nowhere to be seen, though the clatter of dishes from behind the kitchen door suggested she'd be along presently.

The shy smile Tristin gave him as he approached made Mikhyal's heart beat faster. Tristin looked almost well; he was still slender, but his face had lost that gaunt, haunted look, his dark eyes were bright, and his cheeks were no longer quite so pale.

"You're looking much better, Mikhyal." Tristin bit his lip, eyes darting down to the table and then briefly, back up to Mikhyal's face.

"I was just thinking the same of you." Mikhyal returned the smile and took the seat opposite him. "You look much brighter. Working in the garden seems to agree with you. I wish I had time to join you. And I'm sorry I haven't had a chance to come and see you before this. It must be at least a week since I was here last."

"Ten days, actually," Tristin muttered, then flushed, and Mikhyal hid a smile. He was counting the days? "But you're doing important, kingly sorts of things," Tristin added quickly. "Things that make a difference. You're busy discussing treaties, determining the fates of entire kingdoms… and I'm just… sort of flailing about in the dirt."

"Oh, don't tell him he's *kingly*," Dirit said. "He'll become bloated with self-importance."

"I don't think I'm in nearly so much danger of that as some others, who shall remain nameless," Mikhyal said.

"What, *Tristin*?" Dirit inquired. "Never!"

Mikhyal didn't bother to hide his smile this time. "I've not been so busy that I've forgotten about the dance you promised me. I've thought about it every day since I left Dragonwatch."

"Ah. Well." Tristin flushed even pinker. "I, um… about that… um… I mean, I was…" A faint frown puckered his brow. "Did you really? Think about dancing with me, I mean?"

From his perch on the back of the chair, Dirit heaved a dramatic sigh. "Oh, you two are just *too* much. Any more sweetness, and I shall be ill. I'm off to see if Alys has anything nice for me."

"Alys can't even see you," Tristin said, "so how are you going to ask her?"

Dirit gave him a toothy grin. "She most certainly *can* see me, if I choose to show myself to her. But I never said I was going to *ask*." And with that, the little dragon trotted off.

"Finally, a bit of peace," Mikhyal murmured.

"Been a bit of a trial, has he?" Tristin asked.

"You have no idea," Mikhyal said. "The little monster rides about on my shoulder, commenting on everything. It's all I can do not to answer, especially when I'm in meetings with the Wytch Kings and their advisors. My father and Garrik know about him, though neither of them can see him. I catch them watching me every so often. And Prince Jaire sometimes bursts out laughing at something Dirit's said or done at the most inopportune moments. He says they're all used to him talking to himself, so nobody thinks much of it. But me… well. I have to watch myself, or rumors will start flying." He grimaced and added, "If they haven't already."

From the kitchen came a shriek and the sound of pottery shattering on the floor.

"Oh, dear," Tristin said. "It sounds as if Alys has made Dirit's acquaintance. I wonder if she needs any help."

Mikhyal got to his feet, ready to lend assistance. Before he could take a step toward the kitchen, the door flew open, and Dirit skittered out, pastry clenched firmly in his little jaws. He was followed by a broom-wielding Alys. Nimbly dodging a blow from the broom, Dirit dove under the table and disappeared with his pastry.

Alys shot a baleful glare after him and lowered her broom before dropping a low curtsy. "Apologies, Your Highness, m'lord. The little devil frightened me."

"I'm terribly sorry, Mistress Alys," Mikhyal said, trying his best to look contrite. "I... suppose Ilya mentioned him to you, did he?"

"Ai, he did. Said I might see him slinking about, and warned me of his penchant for blackberry tarts. Of course, that's where I found him, lounging on the window sill, pretty as you please, devouring my fresh pastries before they were even cool."

"She threw a teacup at me." Dirit's plaintive voice came from under the table.

"Can you blame me?" Alys demanded. "I thought you were a rat. I'd have offered you a pastry, had you but asked."

Loud eating noises followed. "Rat, indeed," Dirit said, smacking his lips. "If it pleases you, madam, I *did* burn my tongue."

"Serves you right," Alys said. Her dark eyes settled on Mikhyal. "Rat or not, I'll thank you to keep it out of my kitchen, Your Highness."

Mikhyal dared not look at Tristin as he struggled to keep his lips from twitching into a smile. "I'll speak to him, Mistress Alys," he said gravely. "He won't bother you again."

"Thank you, Your Highness. I'll be back shortly with your breakfast."

As soon as her back was turned, Tristin shot him a dubious look. Dirit slunk out from under the table and clambered up on top of it. "A rat, am I?" he muttered, and proceeded to settle himself by Tristin's elbow, where he made a show of licking his claws clean.

"Dirit, a little more caution, if you please," Mikhyal said. "I'd rather not make your presence known to all and sundry. And for the sake of all of us, please leave Mistress Alys alone."

"Blackberry tarts," Dirit said, by way of explanation. "Fresh and hot, all flaky and steaming and delicious."

Mikhyal rolled his eyes. "I can just see the history books now. A Scholarly Treatise on the Role of Blackberry Tarts in the Fall of the Prince of Rhiva."

Dirit scowled, eyebrow tufts twitching. "Oh, very well, Your Royal Circumspectness. I suppose it will only cause trouble if I keep frightening the help. I shall limit my appearances to you and Tristin. And Prince Jaire, of course. *He* appreciates me, at least."

With a heavy sigh, Mikhyal turned to Tristin. "Enough of Dirit. Tell me, what have you been up to while I've been stuck in endless alliance negotiations?"

"Oh, well... I've been practicing," Tristin said.

"Practicing what?" Mikhyal gave him a sly smile. "Dancing, by chance?"

"Oh..." Tristin's cheeks turned pink. "Um. I... well, you see, Mordax didn't teach me properly... I mean, he tried to, or at least, he pretended to try, but he might not have actually wanted me to master it, and I always thought I was hopeless because I couldn't even walk across the floor of the keep at Falkrag without going into fits. And then Mordax gave up on me, and Uncle sent me to Shadowspire, and I spent fifteen years there with no one to talk to except my hallucinations."

Mikhyal frowned, struggling to follow what Tristin was trying to tell him. "You're not talking about dancing at all. You... you're talking about mastering your Wytch power, aren't you?"

Tristin blinked. "Yes. That's what I just said."

"That would explain why you're here at Dragonwatch, then."

"Well, yes. Sort of. Mordax and Faah actually brought me here with Prince Jaire after they kidnapped him... they were planning to exchange Jaire's life for Garrik's agreement to step down in my favor. The way they spoke of it, the plan was approved by the Wytch Council."

"Garrik told us of their plot to put you on the throne, though he didn't go into any details regarding your history, other than to say you would have been the Council's puppet."

"That... that's correct." Tristin swallowed hard and stared down at the table. "I was... I was addicted to the drug Mordax was giving me to stop me from feeling the empathic resonances in everything I touched. It... it was supposed to be a temporary measure, just until he could teach me, but I proved to be a hopeless student, and by the time he gave up on me, I was addicted. That's the other reason I'm here. The school is new."

At Mikhyal's blank look, he added, "There haven't been enough people living here for long enough for the floors and the furnishings to have absorbed much in the way of empathic impressions. The watchtower, on the other hand..." Tristin trailed off, shuddering. "That place is awful. The very stones are steeped in pain and violence, bloodlust and fear. I get swept away in the memories of those who fought and died in that place. I lose my grip on the moment, and... well, it's... it's not good. And the courtyard isn't much better. Though I have found if I kneel or stand upon a thick chunk of wood, it blocks out enough of the resonances that I can work in the herb garden. Or... or on my new flower bed."

Mikhyal stared at him as he tried to fit all the pieces together. "You were kept in isolation all that time? Fifteen years, you said?"

"Ai," Tristin nodded.

"And you've not yet mastered your power?"

"Um. I'm... that is, I... well, I've had some small successes. Recently. I've at least managed to weave the most basic shielding pattern Master Ilya knows. I... I'm not sure it will be enough, though."

"Enough?" Mikhyal's eyes widened as Tristin's meaning slowly dawned on him. "Oh... you mean enough to allow you to... Oh, Tristin, why didn't you say? I'd never have asked you to come to the betrothal ceremony if I'd realized. I'm sorry. You don't have to come — of course you don't."

Tristin's face fell. "But... I thought... I thought you wanted to... to dance with me. Oh, but... right. I'm a bastard, you're a prince... no point in even thinking about it, is there? I mean, you're not free to marry where you will, and I'm too much of a mess for anyone to want to bother with, aren't I? I mean, look at me! I can't even—"

"Tristin." Mikhyal reached across the table and laid a finger against Tristin's lips to stop the flow of words. "I *do* want to dance with you." He took Tristin's hand in his own, ignoring Dirit, whose beady black eyes were fixed upon him with avid interest. "I'd like to dance with you very much. My only concern is that setting foot in the castle might be distressing for you, and I would hate to think I was to blame for causing you pain of any sort."

Tristin glanced down at their joined hands and then back up at Mikhyal. "I... I'd like to try," he said, his voice barely a whisper. "I've been practicing, and I think, by the day of the ceremony, I might be able to manage it."

Mikhyal was about to protest, but upon seeing the hope and determination in Tristin's eyes, decided against it. Instead, he squeezed Tristin's hand and said, "Then I will look forward to seeing you there. And if you are unable to come for any reason, I will come to you here, as soon as I am able. We *will* have that dance, even if the only music is the whisper of the wind through the fir trees." Keeping his eyes on Tristin's, he lifted Tristin's hand to his lips and pressed a gentle kiss to it.

Tristin's eyes went wide, and his fingers trembled in Mikhyal's hand, but he didn't let go.

Tristin couldn't believe Mikhyal still wanted to dance with him, even after he'd heard the truth about his past, his captivity and his addiction, and the fact that even now, he struggled to control the Wytch power that had taken so much from him.

When Mikhyal kissed his hand, it was all Tristin could do not to pull it away. He clenched his teeth and pressed his lips together to hold back the tide of nonsense that would pour forth if he dared allow himself to speak.

He was saved from having to make a response by the dining hall door opening. Mikhyal turned to see who had come in, and Tristin took the opportunity to snatch his hand back, cheeks coloring as he glanced up to see a man who could only be the Wytch King, watching him from the doorway, a slight smile curving his lips.

Wytch King Garrik looked nothing like his brother. Where Jaire was slender and delicate, Garrik was tall and powerfully built. Where Jaire was pale, Garrik was dark, having the black hair and black eyes that so often appeared in the royal lines of the northern kingdoms.

"Well, he doesn't look at all kingly, does he?" Dirit chirped, slithering across the table and climbing up Mikhyal's shoulder to observe.

Tristin had been far too awed to pay attention, but now that Dirit mentioned it, the Wytch King did look a bit shabby. His feet were bare, his long black hair unbound, and Tristin was certain he'd seen Kian wearing the same shirt only a few days ago.

"Good morning, Cousin." Garrik's smile broadened as he approached the table. "You're looking much better. I apologize for not finding the time to come and see you before now. With all the guests here for Jaire's betrothal ceremony, I've had very little time for anything else."

Tristin rose and bowed low to his cousin. "Your Majesty. I... I appreciate your concern, though I can't imagine why you'd want me anywhere near you or your family, given who my father was and what he—"

"Enough." Garrik didn't raise his voice, but his tone was implacable, and that one word was all it took to make Tristin snap his mouth shut. "Your father's sins do not reflect upon you, Tristin. From what I've been told, you never even met the man."

"That... that's true. Your Majesty is most—"

"And you can dispense with the honorifics. You are my cousin, and you will call me Garrik. Unless I'm being particularly beastly, in which case *that pain in the arse warming the throne* will do nicely."

"I... ah..."

Dirit chuckled. "I think I approve of this cousin of yours, Tristin. He's a breath of fresh air compared to most of the royal windbags of my acquaintance."

Tristin cringed for a moment, before recalling that Mikhyal had mentioned that Garrik couldn't see or hear Dirit. He glanced at Mikhyal, whose mouth twitched as he struggled not to laugh.

The kitchen door opened, and Alys appeared, carrying a tray. She set it down on the sideboard and bobbed a quick curtsy to Garrik before setting two platters piled high with flat cakes on the table. Pots of jam, cream, butter, and honey followed, and then Alys retreated to the kitchen.

"Ah, flat cakes," Garrik said, taking a large helping. "Jaire's favorite. He'll be sorry he missed this, but he had an early appointment with the head seamstress. You should have heard the whining. You'd think she was dragging him down to the dungeons for an interrogation."

Tristin smiled. "Would this be the infamous Mistress Nadhya?"

"Ai, it would. He's been whining at you, too, has he?"

"Not whining so much as suggesting she might have been in charge of the dungeons in a former life."

Garrik laughed. "He's said as much to me on several occasions. Poor Mistress Nadhya is getting a completely undeserved reputation."

Tristin smothered butter and honey over his flat cakes and took a forkful. Alys's flat cakes were crisp and light, and Tristin closed his eyes as he savored the texture. Food was so much more interesting now that his senses were no longer dulled by the drug.

"Ilya seems very pleased with your progress," Garrik said.

Tristin opened his eyes to focus on his cousin. "I... well, I still have a long way to go," he said slowly, "though I did have a minor success in my lessons the last time Ilya was here."

"Excellent. We'll have you down at the castle in no time. I've had a suite prepared especially for you."

"I... you have?" Tristin wasn't sure what to make of that.

"Ai, it was Jaire's idea. The work was just finished yesterday. I inspected it myself, and I believe all is in order. You are welcome to move in whenever you feel ready."

Tristin couldn't help his smile. He was used to being a nuisance; no one had ever put themselves out to make him feel welcome, and he found himself liking his cousin very much. "Thank you, Your... I mean, Garrik. I can't tell you how much I appreciate that. I... I'm not certain how long it will be." He cast a furtive glance at Mikhyal. "I've reason to hope it won't be long at all. Prince Jaire invited me to his betrothal ceremony, and I'd very much like to go, if I'm able."

Garrik looked pleased. "We'd be happy to see you there, if you can manage it. I look forward to you joining the rest of the family at the castle. Not until you are ready, though. Please don't push yourself. We all understand that these things take time. The Dragon

Mother knows, it took me long enough to master my own power. I wish we'd had someone like Vayne around then… although, I suppose if I hadn't needed training, I'd never have met Ilya, so I can hardly wish that, can I?"

After breakfast, Garrik excused himself, saying he'd wait for Mikhyal in the courtyard. When he'd gone, Mikhyal rose. "I shouldn't keep him waiting. We do have a busy day ahead. Probably a lot of busy days. I… don't know when I'll be able to come and see you again."

"Don't worry about it." Tristin got slowly to his feet. "You attend to your duties, and I shall do my best to come to you. I intend to dance with you at the betrothal ceremony."

As they walked down the hall, Mikhyal caught Tristin's hand in his own. Mikhyal's hand was warm, and it felt nice the way it encircled his own and squeezed just a little. No one had ever held his hand before, unless it was to drag him somewhere he didn't want to go.

Outside, Garrik was waiting, already shifted into a great orange-gold dragon. Garrik let out an impatient snort and stamped one foot as Kian set the saddle on his back and began fastening the straps.

Mikhyal turned to face Tristin. "Take care of yourself, Tristin. And don't forget — you owe me a dance. If you cannot come to the castle to claim it, then I shall come to you." And with that, Prince Mikhyal leaned forward very slowly, giving Tristin every opportunity to pull away.

Tristin's heart nearly stopped, but he didn't move. He couldn't. Mikhyal's lips brushed against his own, warm and soft. It was Tristin's first kiss, and it was over much too quickly. All too soon, Mikhyal was giving his hand one last squeeze. He let go, fingers slipping away from Tristin's, and turned toward the waiting Wytch King.

When Mikhyal was safely secured, Garrik took to the air. As he watched them disappear down the side of the mountain, Tristin pressed his fingers to his lips, imagining he could still feel the lingering warmth of Mikhyal's kiss.

"Very good," Ilya said when Tristin had woven yet another new shielding pattern flawlessly on the first try. "You're much more focused tonight than you have been."

Tristin, who had thought of little other than Mikhyal's kiss all day, found it difficult to believe Ilya thought he was focused. He blushed and said quietly, "It helps to have a goal, something I want very much, to work toward."

"It does, indeed," Ilya said with a tiny smile. "What do you want badly enough to make such a difference, if I might ask?"

Tristin flushed and turned his face to the window, letting the gentle evening breeze cool his flaming cheeks.

"You don't have to say, if you'd rather not."

"Ah. Well. I... um." Tristin risked a glance at the Wytch Master, but Ilya didn't look at all annoyed with him. Could he tell Ilya about Mikhyal asking him for a dance? No... perhaps not. The last thing he wanted was to follow in his father's footsteps by putting himself at the heart of a scandal.

He settled for telling only part of the truth. "Cousin Garrik was here this morning. He said I might move down to the castle when I'm ready. He's had a suite prepared for me, and... well... I thought... that is, considering that my father murdered Garrik's father, and... and my uncle kidnapped his brother... it's not at all the reception I was expecting. I'd not have thought he'd want me anywhere near himself or his family, and yet... he welcomed me this morning, and told me he was looking forward to seeing me at the castle. I... I'm not used to that. People wanting me near, I mean. All my life, I've been a nuisance and an embarrassment, something to be shut away and not spoken of, except in whispers. I'm finding it rather refreshing to be given a chance. Although..." Tristin stared down at the table. "I expect it won't be long before I ruin it all by saying the wrong thing to the wrong person at the wrong time."

"I don't think you need to worry about that," Ilya said gently. "Garrik's never been one for formality or ceremony. And family is very important to him. You won't drive him off that easily. Wait until you see the suite he's prepared for you."

"How long do you think it will be before I'm ready?"

Ilya regarded him soberly. "That, I cannot say. It will depend on how much of the emotional resonance the shielding patterns block out. That will depend both on your sensitivity and on the strength of the resonances in each separate item you might be exposed to. It is something you will not know for certain until you try."

Tristin's heart skipped a beat, and he sat up a little straighter. "Could we try? Now, I mean? I could go to the watchtower."

"You could, though I would caution you against doing so this soon."

"Why?"

"If the shielding patterns I've taught you thus far don't prove sufficient to protect you, it may shake your confidence badly. You've made tremendous progress today, and I would hate to see you set back simply because you lacked patience."

"On the other hand," Tristin countered, "a successful trial today could give me a great deal *more* confidence. And I honestly don't think a failure would set me back too far. In fact, I think, now that I'm starting to understand how the patterns work, it would only make me even more determined."

Ilya looked as if he were debating with himself, but he finally nodded slowly and said, "Against my better judgment, then. Come. We might as well try it now."

"Really? Now?"

"I've come to know you well enough to realize that if I don't capitulate, you'll simply wait until I've gone and try it by yourself. And given what a difficult time you had last time... Well. Since you insist on doing this experiment, I would prefer you at least do it in my presence."

Tristin waited, bristling with impatience, while Ilya lit a lantern. Once outside, Tristin had to force himself to keep to Ilya's shorter strides.

At the base of the tower, Ilya opened the door for him. "Whenever you are ready, Tristin. Take your time."

Tristin already had the most complex of the shielding patterns he'd learned in place. He stared at the barely-illuminated stone stairs, then steeled himself and stepped into the tower.

He was ready for the same things that had assaulted his senses the last time — visions of terrified men in torn bloody clothing fleeing down the stairs, great gouts of fire chasing them — but this time, he sensed only a whisper of fear. Tristin examined his shielding pattern and noted a spot where the shape of it wasn't quite right. He drew on the light at his center and adjusted the pattern the way Ilya had shown him.

The fear trickled away, leaving him alone in his head and in complete control of his emotions. His heart beat faster as he took his first tentative steps toward the stairs.

"How do you feel?" Ilya asked, his voice coming from right behind Tristin.

"The shielding pattern seems to be holding," Tristin said, not even trying to disguise his joy. "I didn't have it quite right to begin with, but I didn't panic. I made an adjustment, like you taught me, and now I feel none of the violence or the terror that swept me away before."

"That's very encouraging," Ilya said. "Shall we try the stairs? I will be right behind you."

Tristin turned to eye the smaller man. "That's not much comfort, Ilya. We'd both end up at the bottom of the stairs, if I should take a tumble."

"You underestimate the speed at which I can shift," Ilya said mildly.

"Ah. Well then, let us proceed." Tristin stepped onto the first stair and waited, taking careful stock of his senses to make certain he felt nothing of the violence of battles past.

When there were no flames, no screams, no sword thrusts coming from all sides, he dared another step, and then another. Soon, he had reached the top of the stairs. Giving Ilya a triumphant grin, he strode to the center of the tower's roof and spread his arms wide. "I've done it!" he exclaimed. "No one ever thought I could, but I have!"

The shadows cast by the swinging lantern danced across Ilya's face, but Tristin could see his teacher's smile, almost as broad as his own. "Very well done, Tristin. *Very* well done! This is certainly cause for celebration."

"Might we celebrate at the castle?"

Ilya's smile faded a little. "We might, only you may still find that some things — and some places — will leak through the shielding pattern. There are still more patterns for you to learn, so even if you do move down to the castle, our lessons will continue."

"Tomorrow?" Tristin asked eagerly. "Might I go tomorrow? And… might I… might I shift? And go myself?"

Ilya's smile widened again. "You may, indeed. You have kept your word most admirably, and I think you have recovered sufficiently that I need not worry about you hiding in dragon form, ai?"

"No, you needn't worry," Tristin said softly. "I've reason to be much more interested in my human form at the moment."

Ilya gave him an appraising look, then clapped a hand on his shoulder and said, "Let us go down and fetch Kian and Ambris for a celebratory drink. I've a bottle of excellent wine in my suite that I've been saving for a special occasion. I cannot think of a better use for it."

Tristin smiled and followed the Wytch Master down the tower steps.

Tristin was up with the sun the next morning. He had very little to pack. A few changes of clothing and the book Jaire had given him were the only possessions he'd managed to accumulate during the weeks he'd spent at Dragonwatch. He stuffed his things into a leather pack Ilya had found for him, and went to join Alys, Kian, and Ambris for breakfast.

"I hear it's a big day today." Ambris piled eggs and sausages onto his plate while Tristin dug into the fried onions and potatoes.

"Ai," Tristin said, giving him a bright smile. "Ilya says I might move down to the castle today."

"Good for you, m'lord," Alys said, bobbing her head. "You've worked hard for it."

"Thank you, Alys." Tristin's cheeks heated only a little as he smiled at her.

"He spoke to me about it last night," Kian said, "and asked me to escort you down after breakfast. You'll need someone to show you around. It's a bit of a maze until you get used to it."

"What of you, Ambris?" Tristin asked, recalling the breakfast conversation of a few days ago. "Will you be coming with us?"

But Ambris set his fork down and shook his head. "I dare not," he said softly, eyes darting briefly to his husband's face. "Though Kian thinks I ought."

"You needn't worry, Ambris." Kian reached across the table for Ambris's hand and stroked the back of it with his thumb. "I meant it when I said I wouldn't bring it up again. What you do about your father is entirely up to you."

"Thank you." Ambris squeezed Kian's hand and smiled up at him, then turned back to Tristin and continued, "I'll be staying here until after the ceremony. Kian's promised Jaire he'll be there."

"Then I shall make a point of coming to see you when I've time," Tristin said.

"I'd like that," Ambris said. "And you're very welcome to come and visit us in Aeyr's Grove whenever you like, once we've gone back there."

"That's very kind of you." The words nearly clogged behind the lump in Tristin's throat. No one had ever invited him anywhere before, and he was deeply touched that Ambris and Kian would even think to ask him to come and see them in their home. "I'll come for a visit as soon as I'm able."

"Which might not be as soon as you think," Kian said. "If I know Garrik, he's already got something in mind for you to do."

"Really?" Tristin frowned. He hadn't given much thought to how he might spend his days at the castle. "What sort of something?"

"I've no idea," Kian said, "but you can be sure he won't allow you to sit idle."

"I hope he doesn't mean for me to attend Court," Tristin murmured. "I shouldn't like that at all."

"You'll have to wait and see, won't you?" Ambris said, giving him a secretive smile.

After breakfast, Tristin stood beside Kian in the sun-drenched courtyard and shifted into dragon form. Kian had offered to carry his pack for him, so Tristin launched himself into the air completely unfettered, a cry of joy cutting through the cool mountain air as he climbed higher and higher.

A hard blink lowered his inner eyelids, allowing him to see the air currents in all the shades of the rainbow. He caught an orange updraft and climbed higher, then spiraled halfway down the mountain on a river of indigo. By the time he was finished playing, Kian had reached the castle and was circling the north tower, apparently in no hurry.

Not wanting to keep him waiting, Tristin shot the rest of the way down the mountain. A dark-haired figure tall enough that it could only be Garrik, awaited them on top of the tower. Tristin landed gracefully beside Kian, who shifted immediately and grinned at the waiting Wytch King. Kian quickly went to a small chest near the wall and extracted two cloaks. He swept one over his own broad shoulders, brought the other to Tristin, then tactfully positioned himself between Tristin and Garrik.

Tristin shifted and quickly covered himself. "Thank you," he murmured.

"Are you all right?" Kian asked in a voice low enough that only Tristin could hear. "Is your shielding holding up?"

"Yes, it's fine. Only… it's a bit intimidating, being surrounded by all these terribly fit men, and here's me, looking like an underfed chicken."

"You're looking much healthier than when you first came here," Kian told him gently. "And you are still recovering. I expect you'll put on weight right quick if you're eating at Garrik's table. Melli is a wonderful cook. She's the one who taught Alys, you know."

"I shall look forward to my next meal, then."

"Good morning, Tristin," Garrik said, striding toward them. "I'm not interrupting, am I?"

Kian stepped aside. "No, I was just giving Tristin some final instructions from his healers. He's to eat well and put some more weight on."

"I'll be sure to let Melli know," Garrik said, eyes twinkling. "She'll enjoy fattening you up, Cousin, and will consider it a personal challenge. You're in for a treat."

"S-so I've heard, Your — I mean, G-Garrik." Tristin flushed, feeling at a distinct disadvantage standing before his very important cousin wearing only a cloak.

"If that's all, Your Majesty, I'll be heading back up to Dragonwatch," Kian said. "Ilya's said he'll be taking charge of Tristin's recovery while he's here, but tell him to send for me if he needs me. You've enough shifters at the castle now that you ought to be able to spare someone for the few minutes it takes to get up the mountain and back."

"Ai, our dragon army is slowly growing, though I fear between the transformations and the preparations for the betrothal, we're running poor Vayne quite ragged."

"I suspect he's enjoying himself immensely," Kian said. "It must be a nice change to be busy after sitting idle for over two centuries." He shuddered as he removed his cloak and handed it to Garrik. "I can't even imagine it." Kian strode to the center of the tower, shifted, and was airborne within seconds.

Tristin watched Kian wing his way up the mountain before turning to his cousin. "Dragon army?"

"Indeed." Garrik's smile was grim. "I'm in the process of uniting the northern kingdoms. We plan to challenge the Wytch Council and put an end to the sorts of practices that saw my family torn apart, you locked up in Shadowspire, and poor Ambris tortured at Blackfrost."

Tristin swallowed, stunned both at the enormity of such a task and at the lack of concern with which his cousin spoke of defying the Council. "Do you... do you really think you can win a war against the Council?"

"Not a protracted struggle, we can't. Not unless we can bring some of the kingdoms of the south around to our way of thinking, which is doubtful. But I believe if we do enough damage in a short enough period of time, the Council could be persuaded to see the wisdom of allowing the kingdoms of the north to break with the rest of Skanda."

"I would join in the fight," Tristin said softly. "Let me swear fealty to you."

Garrik's dark eyes met his, and the king searched his face for a good, long time before nodding once. "You may do so at the betrothal ceremony, when I announce the formation of the Northern Alliance. It will give me a chance to introduce you to the nobility and to our allies. Although" —the smile he gave Tristin turned wicked— "you seem to be on quite good terms with Rhiva already. Or at least, with its prince."

Tristin flushed and bent to pick up his pack, mind flailing for a suitable response. Before he could come up with anything, Garrik changed the subject. "Would you be more comfortable changing here? I can wait for you just inside the door, if you'd rather not go parading through the castle in nothing but a cloak."

"Ah… yes, that's very kind, thank you," Tristin said, blushing even more furiously. "I think I would be more… comfortable."

Garrik dropped Kian's cloak into the chest and slipped inside without another word, leaving Tristin to pull on the breeches, shirt, and boots he'd packed for himself. When he was dressed, he went through the door. Garrik stood on the landing just inside, waiting to lead him down the tower stairs.

In spite of feeling nothing from the tower, Tristin was braced for an onslaught of emotional resonance. To his surprise, nothing penetrated the protective shield he'd woven around his mind. He was doing well indeed, given that the worn steps leading down from the top of the tower had to be significantly older than those of Dragonwatch.

As they descended, Garrik explained that the north tower was located near the royal apartments, and let out into the private family wing of the castle.

"Let me show you to your suite first," Garrik said as he led Tristin down the hall. "And then I'll be putting you to work."

"Work?" Tristin echoed, a little uneasily.

"Don't look so frightened. I've already discussed it with your healers. I won't be making you do anything too strenuous."

"Oh... um. That's... well." Tristin wasn't sure what to say to that. He only hoped Garrik didn't intend for him to be put on display for the entire Court.

His fears were forgotten the moment Garrik opened the door to the suite he'd had prepared. "Here you are, Cousin. Your home for as long as you'd like to stay here with us. And whenever you wish to visit, should you eventually choose to make your home elsewhere."

Tristin walked in and stopped dead, eyes wide as he took in the sumptuous surroundings. Everything looked new, from the polished wooden floor to the blue velvet curtains to the furniture. Tristin had never had such luxury before — he'd never been able to bear the touch of anything that might have been owned by someone else.

"It's all been newly done, just for you," Garrik said. "When Ilya told me how much trouble you've had with emotional resonances and such, I had the suite gutted. The floors are several inches thick, made of new wood. Same with the wall panels. And the furniture is all new as well, as are the linens and curtains. I wasn't sure what you'd want for decorations, but if you think of anything you'd like, there are plenty of craftsmen down in the town who would be very happy to make whatever you desire, on my order."

"Garrik, this is..." Tristin took a few tentative steps in and turned around slowly, admiring the view of the mountains — he could see the watchtower perched high above them from here — and the heavy draperies hanging at the windows. Everything looked fresh and clean. "You did all this... for *me*?" His voice was barely a whisper.

"I wanted you to have somewhere comfortable to stay," Garrik said earnestly. "I hoped it might encourage you to make your home with us. Jaire and I have so little family. Of course it's up to you. No one will ever force you to stay where you don't want, not ever again. I just thought, perhaps..."

"Thank you," Tristin breathed. "I... no one's ever done anything like this for me before. I... I don't even know what to say."

"Say you'll stay. At least until you decide what you want to do. I'd like a chance to get to know you. And I know Jaire would be happy to spend more time with you. He truly enjoys your company, and there aren't many people I can say that about."

"I... I'm honestly not sure where else I'd go. Thank you, Cousin. So very much."

Tristin spent the next half hour or so exploring his rooms. Garrik followed along, pointing things out and explaining how things worked in the castle.

When the clock struck nine, Garrik said, "I've a meeting in half an hour. Let me give you a quick tour of the castle, so you know how to find the dining room and the library, and then I'll take you to see Master Ludin."

"Oh, yes!" Tristin exclaimed. "I've been hoping to talk to him."

"Ambris mentioned how much you enjoyed working in the garden at Dragonwatch. I think you and Master Ludin will get along very well, indeed. I've told him about you, and he said if you're interested, he'd be glad of your help redesigning some of the gardens here at the castle."

Tristin smiled happily as he used the key to lock the door of his very own suite. A home of his own, a family that wanted him, and a chance to work in the royal gardens... he could only think of one thing that would make things better: a dance with Prince Mikhyal of Rhiva.

"That's the last of it, then," Garrik said, leaning back and meeting the eyes of each man around the table in turn. "Gentlemen, I think we have an agreement we can all live with."

The Wytch Kings of the north all looked very pleased with themselves as they got to their feet for a round of congratulatory forearm clasps.

Dirit, curled up on the table next to Mikhyal's elbow, raised his head and blinked blearily. "Did I miss something?" He peered about, whiskers drooping at the sight of the jovial group. "Oh... they've managed to come to a peaceful agreement, have they? How disappointing. I was hoping for a bit of bloodshed over the bargaining table. Your descendants would surely appreciate the extra effort; makes for much more interesting history lessons."

"Bloodshed will come soon enough, I fear," Mikhyal murmured, getting to his feet as Wytch King Edrun of Miraen turned to clasp his arm and clap him on the back. Dirit ran up his other arm and perched upon his shoulder.

While Dirit might be surprised at the efficiency and civility of the negotiations, Mikhyal was not. The Wytch Kings of the north had long chafed under the dictates of the Wytch Council. The main objection to uniting and declaring their independence had always been that the south had far more military power than the north could ever hope to muster. Until now, any rebellion they might contemplate would eventually be crushed by the sheer numbers against them, and would ultimately only hurt the very people it sought to protect.

With Vayne's ability to confer the gift of the Dragon Mother upon anyone who could touch the mythe, the balance of power had shifted enough that the kings of the north were, if not eager for war, at least willing to entertain the notion. Indeed, Prince Bradin of Miraen had already announced his intention to undergo the transformation.

At the far end of the table, Master Ristan, who served as Altan's historian, scribe, and librarian, gathered up his notes and said to Garrik, "I shall have the documents ready for signing by midday tomorrow, Your Majesty."

"Very good, Master Ristan," Garrik said. "Thank you."

Master Ristan executed a precise formal bow and left the library.

When he was gone, Garrik addressed the group. "It is late, and I have kept you all from your beds for long enough. I appreciate your willingness to work around the preparations for the betrothal celebrations, and I am most pleased that we've managed to come to an agreement that suits us all."

As the group drifted apart, Mikhyal said to Drannik, "You see, Father? Prince Bradin has already volunteered."

"Prince Bradin is not Edrun's heir," Drannik responded.

"Technically, I'm not yours, yet," Mikhyal countered.

"Ai, but you will be, and I'll not have you risking yourself on an unproven procedure that could well kill you. Just because nothing *has* gone wrong yet doesn't mean nothing *can*."

Across the library, Mikhyal caught Vayne's eye and waved him over. "Perhaps a few words with Prince Vayne will set your mind at ease," he said, smiling broadly at Vayne as he approached. "Vayne, I am most interested in hearing more about this transformation procedure you've developed, but I fear my father might take some convincing."

Vayne turned to Drannik. "What is it about the transformation that concerns you, Your Majesty?"

Drannik shot a withering glare at Mikhyal before answering. "The risk, mainly. I have no other heir. None I'm willing to see on the throne after me, anyway."

"I understand your concern," Vayne said smoothly. "I can assure you that working closely with a healer eliminates the risk of mythe-shock. Perhaps a word with Ambris, the healer I've been working with, would set your mind at ease?"

"Perhaps," Drannik said gruffly, though he didn't sound convinced.

"I'll make arrangements for you to meet with him before the ceremony," Vayne said.

"Thank you, Vayne." Drannik nodded politely. "Now, if you'll excuse me, I'm off to have a word with Ord."

When he'd gone, Mikhyal said, "I apologize for that. It seems if I wish to take advantage of what you offer, I must either fight him or defy him."

"Perhaps once Prince Bradin has undergone the transformation, your father will be more open to the idea," Vayne suggested.

"Ai, perhaps. I dared not say so to him, but I must admit to no small amount of trepidation regarding the procedure."

"If it would help to ease your mind, I am certain Jaire would be happy to tell you all about it — in great detail. Of course, he will also tell you all about the thrill of flying, which he still finds enthralling."

Mikhyal smiled at that. He could just imagine Prince Jaire waxing poetic about the joy of flight.

"Or you might speak to Tristin about it," Vayne continued. "Or Wyndra, Altan's assistant weapons master, who was one of my first volunteers. I'd suggest Kian, but his transformation did not go smoothly. I was... still learning at that point."

"Tristin?" Mikhyal frowned. "Tristin is a dragon shifter?"

"Ai," Vayne said with a nod. "I transformed him at the same time I worked on Jaire and Kian. I had to, or he could never have escaped Shadowspire."

"Of course." Mikhyal had heard some of the tale, though he hadn't realized Tristin, too, was a dragon shifter. Tristin had spoken only a little of his years-long ordeal at Shadowspire, and Garrik had been rather vague about the details of both his confinement and his escape.

"I shall say no more about it, for it is Tristin's tale to tell," Vayne said quietly. "If you cannot learn what you wish from Tristin or Jaire, let me know, and I'll arrange for you to talk with one of the others."

"That's very kind of you," Mikhyal said. "I shall consider it."

"And I'll make sure Edrun and Ord drop some words of encouragement in your father's ear, too, shall I?"

Mikhyal smiled. "Ai, I think their support might prove more helpful than any argument I can muster."

He was making his way across the Grand Hall toward the guest wing when Dirit sat up straight on his shoulder and chirped, "Well, well, what have we here? It looks like a rather excited Prince Tristin of the New Flower Bed."

"Mikhyal!"

Mikhyal looked up to see Tristin coming across the hall. The man's face was alight with excitement, and Mikhyal's heart stuttered at the sight of him.

"Look at me! I'm walking! On the floor! In the castle! Look at me, Dirit! I've been all over the place, exploring, and now that Garrik's secret alliance meeting is over for the day, I'm off to the library to see if I can manage to touch a book without going into fits. Imagine, being able to choose any book I like, and read it without having to feel whatever horrible things the previous owner felt."

Mikhyal couldn't help smiling. "You've learned the shielding patterns?"

"I have. Ilya was most pleased with my progress. Well. It helped tremendously to have something to look forward to. Something I could think of as a reward. You... you *would* still like a dance, wouldn't you? I shall be able to attend the betrothal ceremony."

He looked so hopeful and so happy that Mikhyal reached for his hand and squeezed it. "I've been looking forward to it ever since we spoke of it."

Tristin's answering smile brought even more light to his face, if that was possible.

"How long have you been here at the castle?" Mikhyal asked. "Are you returning to Dragonwatch tonight?"

"I arrived this morning, and I'm here to stay. Garrik's had the most lovely suite prepared for me. I'm a bit overwhelmed at all he's done, to be honest. But you must come and see!"

"Yes, please, *do*," Dirit said with a pained little sniff. "Let us take this most touching reunion to a more private venue. All these public displays are *most* unsettling."

Tristin glanced about, clearly afraid he'd offended someone, but Mikhyal said, "Enough, Dirit. I don't suppose you could be persuaded to... to go for a walk, or something?"

"A *walk*?" The little dragon's ears flattened. "You don't have to be so polite, you know. I'm not stupid and boorish, not like *some* people. I *do* know when I'm not wanted." And with that, Dirit vanished from his perch.

"Oh, dear," Tristin said. "I think you might have hurt his feelings."

"Never mind," Mikhyal said. "The properly contrite apology I shall be expected to deliver will be worth it if I can have a few hours free of his most charming commentary. He's probably gone off to bother Prince Jaire, who doesn't seem to find him at all annoying."

Tristin led Mikhyal to his suite and opened the door with a flourish.

Mikhyal stepped inside, turning around slowly as he took in the polished floor, the crisp curtains, and the paneled walls. "Is this all new?"

"It is. Cousin Garrik had it done specially for me, so I'd have a place where I'd be comfortable. Every surface I might touch is new. He even had the floors torn up and replaced so I could walk on them without fear. I can hardly believe he would go to such trouble for me. I mean... he hardly knows me, and... after all the horrible things my father did, I thought... but Garrik said those things were nothing to do with me."

Those wide, dark eyes, filled with such uncertainty, tugged at Mikhyal's heart. "Your cousin is very kind."

"He is. He's not at all what I expected."

"Neither are you," Mikhyal said. "What I expected, I mean. Vayne said... well, he offered to transform me. Into a dragon shifter. He said I should talk to you to find out what it's like. I had no idea. I knew he'd transformed Jaire and Kian, but no one said a word about you."

Tristin flushed. "Garrik's been keeping my presence here quiet, and I-I didn't say anything at first because... because well, to be honest, I'm... a bit ashamed of allowing them to use me the way they did. I should have realized, but... but I didn't. Ilya says I mustn't think that way, that I was only a child, but... but I can't help think none of it would have happened if I'd only been a bit cleverer... or perhaps a bit stronger." Tristin wrung his hands. "I'm sorry," he whispered. "I didn't mean to lie to you, by omission or otherwise. It was just... you're one of the first people I've met who didn't know anything about me from before. And... and I rather liked it like that, being able to make a fresh start without rumors and pretense."

"It's all right, Tristin," Mikhyal hastened to reassure him the moment he paused for breath. "Really. Whatever happened in your past, it's your business. You'll tell me when you're ready, or you won't. It's not up to me to decide that."

"Oh... oh, th-thank you, Your Highness." Tristin gave him a shy, hesitant smile. "I... I *can* tell you about being dragon, though. If you'd like."

"I would," Mikhyal said. "Very much. But only if you're comfortable telling me."

Tristin's eyes took on a distant look, and his smile grew soft and dreamy. "You cannot imagine how glorious it is! All the world spread out below you... all the sky, your playground... I flew down the mountain this morning, and it was so beautiful." The happiness of that memory completely transformed Tristin's face. "Well... you probably can. Imagine it, I mean. You rode up to Dragonwatch on Garrik's back. But... to be the one in control, to feel the wind beneath your wings and see the colors of the air currents, and know instinctively which way they will take you..." He focused on Mikhyal again. "It is truly wondrous."

Mikhyal's breath caught in his throat at the joy in his voice and the brilliance of his smile. "Show me?" he whispered.

"Show... show you?"

"Shift for me? If you would. I'd like to see you in all your dragon glory."

Tristin flushed again and lowered his eyes. "Ah. Well... I... I suppose there's no reason why not. We could... we could go to the north tower. No one's likely to happen by up there."

Tristin led the way, alternately hurrying and dragging his feet. The top of the tower was bathed in moonlight, and Tristin seemed reluctant to leave the shadows near the door.

"Are you sure this is all right?" Mikhyal asked.

"It's... I can do this." It sounded almost as if he was trying to convince himself. Before Mikhyal could tell him it really wasn't necessary that he shift, Tristin swallowed, then took a deep breath and moved to the center of the space. "Would you mind terribly if I asked you to, um, turn your back?"

The sweet, shy request made a fierce protectiveness swell in Mikhyal's chest. "Of course I wouldn't mind," he said quickly, and turned to face the closed door they'd just come through. He froze for a few moments, listening for any sound, but all he heard was the soft rustle of cloth as Tristin removed his garments. Much as he would have liked to catch a glimpse of Tristin unclothed, he remained facing the door until a low rumble followed by a snort had him turning slowly around.

In the spot where Tristin had stood was a dragon. It wasn't nearly as large as Kian's dragon form, certainly not large enough to carry a man Mikhyal's size. Where Kian and Garrik were big and bulky, this dragon was sleek and slender, like Ilya and Jaire, built for speed and grace rather than raw power. Dark scales glinted in the silver-violet moonlight. Mikhyal couldn't tell what color they might be in daylight, but they looked much darker than Ilya's pale silver-blue, or Jaire's opalescent white.

"You're magnificent!" Mikhyal said, completely taken with the creature's beauty. He edged closer and reached out a hand, then froze and asked, "Might I… may I touch you?"

Tristin dipped his head, and Mikhyal drew closer and lay his hand on the dragon's neck. The scales were smooth, like a snake's, but warm to the touch, despite the coolness of the night air. He slid his hand down Tristin's neck in a long stroke, and then moved it to his head.

"Do you like to be scratched?" Mikhyal rubbed the delicate scales around the dragon's snout and eyes, and Tristin's eyes slid shut as he leaned in. A low rumble came from his throat, and Mikhyal laughed. "Are you *purring*?"

Tristin's eyes opened and fixed on him. He bobbed his head up and down and leaned in closer, nudging Mikhyal's hand with his head, clearly wanting more.

Laughing, Mikhyal indulged him, paying close attention to which strokes and scratches seemed to elicit the most favorable response.

It wasn't long before Tristin indulged in a great yawn, showing long, sharp teeth. Mikhyal waited until he'd finished to pat his head and give his eye ridges a final rub. "You're tired," Mikhyal said. "It sounds as if you've had a busy day, and you are still recovering. Perhaps it's time for me to see you off to bed, hmm?"

With a sleepy nod, Tristin shifted back, then squawked in surprise as he stared down at himself. He gave Mikhyal a brief, wide-eyed look of horror, gathered his clothing, and fled. The tower door slammed shut behind him, and Mikhyal stared after him, wondering what he'd said.

"Well," Dirit said, appearing on Mikhyal's shoulder, "*that* didn't go very well, did it?"

Chapter Six

Mikhyal's first instinct had been to run after Tristin and blurt out an apology for whatever gross insult had sent the poor man fleeing from the top of the tower. The only thing that stopped him was the look of abject despair in Tristin's eyes. This was more than simple embarrassment, and the last thing Mikhyal wanted was to make things worse.

Back in the guest suite, he found himself alone. Drannik was either visiting one of the other Wytch Kings or had already gone off to bed. Mikhyal retired to his own room and undressed for bed, but found himself unable to settle.

"What *are* you doing?"

Mikhyal spun around to see Dirit balanced precariously atop the oil lamp on the dressing table. The little dragon's tail lashed back and forth as he peered at Mikhyal. "Getting ready for bed. What does it look like I'm doing?"

"Pacing about in indecision," Dirit said bluntly. "How disappointing. Weren't you raised to be decisive and diplomatic? Go and talk to him."

"I don't think that would be a good idea," Mikhyal said.

Dirit wrinkled his snout in apparent disgust. "If you can't even manage to communicate with a man you'd like to bed, how do you expect to deal with the southern kingdoms and the Wytch Council?"

"It's not the same thing at all," Mikhyal protested.

One eyebrow tuft twitched, and Dirit hopped down from the lamp and settled himself on the dressing table. "Oh, *do* explain, Your

Royal Obtuseness. I'm eager to hear how it's different." The little
dragon's eyes fixed expectantly on Mikhyal.

Mikhyal glared at him. "If you want to be helpful, go and check
on Tristin for me. Otherwise, go and bother someone else."

"Oh, *very* nice. I do my best to assist you and it's, *go away, Dirit,
go and find something useful to do.*" Dirit let out an offended sniff. "We
shall see how *useful* I can be, indeed, we shall. I'll give your regards
to Prince Tristin of the New Flower Bed, shall I? Along with a very
personal message…" And with that, the little dragon flounced off,
disappearing into the mirror.

"Oh for…" Mikhyal muttered several curses under his breath
before extinguishing the lamp and throwing himself down on his
bed. He closed his eyes, but sleep refused to come. In the darkness,
all he could see was the look on Tristin's face before he'd fled.

Tristin hadn't even paused to dress before fleeing down the tower
stairs with his clothing clutched against his middle. Fortunately, it
was late enough that no one was about in the hall leading to the
royal apartments, and Tristin reached his suite without frightening
the servants or causing any unfortunate incidents. He closed the
door firmly behind him and let his clothing fall to the floor.

What *had* he been thinking?

Well, he *hadn't* been thinking, had he? He'd been half asleep,
enjoying the feel of Mikhyal's hand rubbing his head and neck. It
had felt so nice to be touched, even in dragon form, that he'd let
himself forget everything else.

Mikhyal must have been absolutely horrified when he'd shifted
back. Tristin knew very well he was no prize. He'd avoided mirrors
for the most part, but he'd caught enough glimpses to know that his
body was still gaunt and wasted, and the scars…

In the brilliant wash of moonlight, his scars would have been so
painfully visible that Mikhyal couldn't possibly have missed them.
The prince wouldn't even want to dance with him now, and he'd
been so looking forward to that.

Maybe he should have stayed at Dragonwatch, after all.

Tristin trudged into his bed chamber where he curled up on the bed and squeezed his eyes shut. The things that had pleased him so much when he'd first stepped into the suite now seemed only that: things. They wouldn't keep him company when he was lonely. Nor would they gently rub his head and neck, or tell him how beautiful he looked in the moonlight.

A hot tear trickled down his face.

"Oh, this is rich. Honestly, you two."

Tristin started and sat up. Dirit was perched on the foot of the bed glaring at him. The little dragon was bathed in silvery moonlight, making him look like some sort of glowing spirit.

"W-what... what d-do you w-want?" Tristin stammered.

Dirit tapped a long claw on the bedpost, and a glowing ball of yellow light appeared over his head, illuminating the room. "I want you to go and speak to His Royal Restlessness. He's been in a dreadful state ever since he returned from the tower, pacing and muttering, muttering and pacing." When Tristin didn't respond, the dragon added, "He is simply *wallowing* in misery. It's most uncomfortable. I shall *never* be able to fall asleep."

"Ah. Well. If he's wallowing, I'm sure it's because I disgust him."

"*Humans.*" The dragon rolled his eyes and twitched his whiskers in apparent disgust. "*So* dramatic. You think you disgust him, and he's certain he's frightened you off. Matchmaking really isn't part of my mandate, you know, but it appears that neither one of you is bright enough to realize that you've had a misunderstanding."

Tristin stared at him, open-mouthed, as he tried to work out whom Dirit was insulting. Both of them, it sounded like.

The little dragon peered at him, eyebrow tufts drawing together in a frown. "You *do* know what a misunderstanding is, don't you?"

"Of c-course I do. I'm j-just not sure what I can do about it."

"You could start by putting some clothing on," Dirit prodded.

Heat rushed to his face, and Tristin scrambled off of the bed and went to fetch his clothing from the main room of the suite.

"Not *those*." Dirit materialized in front of him for just long enough to grab a mouthful of Tristin's breeches and yank them from his hand. He spit them out on the floor as if they tasted bad, then wrinkled his snout. "They're all rumpled and dusty. You simply *cannot* go courting in dirty things."

"Who says I'm going—"

"Have you *no* sense of decorum?"

"Decorum isn't exactly a priority when you've been locked in a tower for most of your life," Tristin explained. He snatched the rumpled breeches from the floor and clutched them against himself in a vain attempt at preserving both modesty and dignity. "Anyway, I haven't got anything else."

Dirit swarmed across the floor and disappeared into the bed chamber, taking the ball of light with him and leaving Tristin in darkness. A moment later, the dragon — and the light — returned. "You've an entire dressing room full of clothing fit for a prince. Come along, we haven't got all night. Honestly, do I have to do *everything* for you?"

With Dirit's assistance, Tristin selected a pair of dark blue breeches and a grey linen shirt. When he was dressed, at Dirit's suggestion, he brushed his hair and tied it back with a little strip of black leather.

"Yes..." Dirit circled him, hopping up on the furniture to observe him from all angles. "Of course, a proper *bath* would have been better, but if I'm to get any sleep at all, we simply haven't time. I don't expect you'll progress to the point where that's really necessary, not tonight. His Royal Virtuousness is *far* too much of a gentleman to be invading your dignity with his most impressive royal masculinity on the first encounter."

"Invading my dignity?" Tristin sputtered. "With his—"

"You'll do *quite* nicely. That really is a charming shade of pink. Lovely contrast with the shirt. Come along, then."

Tristin could only stare at the dragon, speechless. It wasn't until they'd crossed the Grand Hall and were entering the guest wing that he found his voice. "What if... what if he's gone to sleep? It must be well after midnight by now."

"A bit past two, actually," Dirit informed him. "But he's awake."

"How do you know?"

Dirit's ears flattened. "I can *feel* him. I'm *attached* to him, remember? *Bonded*. Cursed with constant awareness."

Unable to think of anything else to do, Tristin followed the little dragon through the castle's dimly lit hallways. The guardsmen posted at regular intervals said nothing, but Tristin hunched his shoulders, certain they were watching and judging. They probably thought he was off to some clandestine meeting of the most sordid kind, and he couldn't help feeling conspicuous and rather overdressed. Face flaming, he trudged miserably down the hall after Dirit.

When they reached the door of the Rhiva party's suite, Tristin stopped. "Surely the door will be locked," he said in a low voice. "And I wouldn't want to wake anyone. Perhaps it would be better to come back tomorrow." He started to turn away, but Dirit took wing and flapped in his face.

"*I* will let you in. You have only to be patient for a moment and I shall unlock the door for you." The dragon narrowed its gleaming black eyes. "If you run off, I shall make a *terrible* scene, and everyone will come running."

"Y-you wouldn't," Tristin stammered, glancing up and down the hall to see if any of the guardsmen had noticed him talking to himself outside the door.

"Try and see," Dirit invited.

"Oh, very well. But no good will come of it, I'm sure."

Dirit disappeared through the door, and a moment later, it swung open. "You must come! We must get help!" The little dragon was twitching in agitation as he darted across the room to a dark shape on the floor.

Tristin's heart stuttered as he stepped into the room and realized he was looking at a man. He lay face down on the floor, long black hair in disarray, the handle of a small throwing knife protruding from his back. "Mikhyal?" he whispered.

Tristin was in the room, kneeling at the man's side before Dirit could say another word. He reached for the knife, intending to pull it free, but the moment his fingers closed on the handle, he was engulfed in a maelstrom of despair, hatred, and anger so hot and so strong it blotted out his awareness of everything else.

Dirit was right, damn him.

And if the little pest decided to stir things up, it was up to Mikhyal to make sure it didn't cause some sort of diplomatic incident. Tristin might not call himself a prince, but it was quite clear that Wytch King Garrik thought highly of his cousin. Drannik wouldn't thank him for upsetting his host or alienating his ally.

With a heavy sigh, Mikhyal rolled out of bed and hunted down his clothing. He'd just finished dressing when Dirit appeared, hovering in the air in front of him. "You must come! Your father! Tristin!"

"What? Where?"

Dirit flitted to the door. "Just outside your door! Did you not hear—"

Mikhyal grabbed the Wytch Sword and was out the door before Dirit could finish. The main room of the suite was only dimly lit, the lamps having been turned down low for the night. On the floor, Drannik lay face down, and next to him lay Tristin, a knife in his hand.

Both men lay very still.

Mikhyal checked his father first, while Dirit hopped up on Tristin's chest. Drannik was unconscious, and from the tear in his clothing, the blade had penetrated a muscle high on his back. Mikhyal tore his father's shirt open and examined the wound. It didn't appear very deep, and there was very little blood. Such a wound wasn't nearly enough to lay low a warrior as strong and fit as Wytch King Drannik.

Mikhyal couldn't understand why his father wasn't responding until he turned him over. Drannik's face was pale, and his breathing far too shallow.

"Poison?" Mikhyal wondered, and turned his head to frown at Tristin and the knife lying next to his limp hand.

"It's not what it looks like," Dirit said quickly. "Tristin was coming to see you. I was accompanying him for moral support. When we arrived, the door was locked. I came in to open it and found your father lying here on the floor. Tristin rushed to his side and pulled the knife out before I could stop him, and... well... I suppose he fainted. He does seem to have a rather delicate constitution."

"Go and fetch Master Ilya and Wytch King Garrik," Mikhyal said. "Quickly!"

"What if someone's lurking about waiting to catch you alone? What if—"

"I'm perfectly capable of defending myself," Mikhyal said grimly.

"I'm sure that's what your father thought, too," Dirit pointed out.

Mikhyal shot him a scowl. "Go! And be quick about it!"

With a low hiss, Dirit winked out of sight.

By the time Wytch Master Ilya arrived, Mikhyal had turned up the lamps and covered both his father and Tristin with blankets from his own bed. He wasn't sure if it would help or not, but Tristin, at least, was shivering as if he were freezing.

The knife lay on the table. A faint green residue going halfway up the blade had confirmed Mikhyal's suspicions. Whoever had attacked Drannik hadn't been concerned with striking a killing blow, for the knife had been poisoned.

Master Ilya arrived more quickly than Mikhyal expected. He knelt between Tristin and Drannik, examining each in turn with his healer's sight. When he'd finished, his expression was grave. "Tristin can be put to bed. He is suffering from simple mythe-shock. Your father, however, has been poisoned. Is the weapon still here?"

"Ai, it's on the table." Mikhyal fetched it and handed it to the Wytch Master.

Ilya examined it, eyes going distant as he studied the blade. "Poison. I thought as much. A foul concoction that damages the mythe-shadow as well as the body. We can help him, but we must hurry. Ambris is particularly skilled at dealing with poisons and the healing of damage to the mythe-shadow."

"What do you require, Ilya?" The Wytch King's low growl came from the doorway, and Mikhyal turned to see Garrik stride in, a heavy black cloak draped over his nightshirt. He was followed by his guard captain, Jorin, who pushed past him, eyes scanning the room for danger.

Ilya got to his feet. "I need someone to fly up to Dragonwatch to fetch Ambris and Kian."

"I shall go immediately," Garrik said. "What of Tristin?"

"Jorin, I want guards on this suite, inside and out." Ilya's voice was cool and calm as he issued orders. "Send for someone to move Tristin back to his rooms. I'll see to him while Ambris and Kian work on Drannik."

Garrik and Jorin left, leaving Mikhyal alone with Ilya and the two stricken men. "Your Highness, have you any idea who might have done this?"

"Someone who doesn't appreciate the idea of a Northern Alliance," Mikhyal said grimly. "Tristin may be able to tell us more. According to Dirit, he is the one who pulled the blade from my father. Is it possible there was some sort of emotional resonance associated with the blade? Something strong enough to send Tristin into mythe-shock?"

Ilya glanced at Tristin. "I suspect so, Your Highness, since he shows no sign of having been poisoned. If that is the case, he may be able to help us identify the culprit."

"We must make certain he is well protected, then. My father will be quite safe, with Altan's guardsmen and several dragon shifters watching over him, and there is little enough I can do to aid in his healing. I will watch over Tristin, and Dirit can relay messages between us as necessary... assuming Dirit is in agreement?" He glanced at Dirit, who had draped himself over the chandelier, from which he had a clear view of the entire room.

"Most decidedly *not*." The little dragon laid his ears back. "Dirit's sacred duty is to protect Your Most Royal Foolhardiness. He is not a messenger bird, and he will *not* be leaving your side. Not for a moment. Messages, indeed."

Tristin had never been so cold in his life, not even at Shadowspire. He curled on his side and pulled the blankets tighter about himself, but he couldn't stop shivering. Was he ill? His head was pounding mercilessly, and he couldn't quite recall whether or not he'd been feeling feverish when he'd gone to bed.

"Are you awake?" a male voice asked.

Mikhyal.

But how could that be?

Mikhyal had been lying on the floor with a knife in his back. Tristin had tried to pull it free, only to be engulfed by a hatred so deep and hot, he still felt the blazing echo of it throbbing through his veins.

His eyes flew open, and there was Mikhyal sitting beside him, looking quite uninjured.

"You *are* awake, then. Good. Master Ilya left some medicine for you to drink."

"M-Mikhyal? But I thought... I found you on the floor... and the knife... how long...?"

"Only a few hours ago," Mikhyal said, helping him sit up. "That was my father you found, though I can understand the confusion. We're often mistaken for brothers, and in the dim light..." He trailed off and handed Tristin a cup. "It's water, but Master Ilya's put something in it. He said it would help with your headache, and he apologized for not being able to give you anzaria."

Tristin shuddered at the thought. He accepted the cup and drank the contents down quickly. "Your father... is he... is he all right?"

"I'm not certain," Mikhyal said softly. "The knife was poisoned. The healers are with him now. Master Ilya called Ambris and Kian down from Dragonwatch to see to him."

Hot shards of panic lanced through Tristin's belly. "You don't think *I*—"

"No, of course not," Mikhyal soothed. "Dirit was right there. He told me what happened."

"Where is Dirit now?" Tristin asked, glancing about.

"I managed to convince him to keep watch over my father, though he wasn't happy about it. He insists it's his duty to guard the royal bloodline. I reminded him that if this alliance doesn't get signed, it's my brother, not me, who will rule after my father, and that we'd all be better off if Shaine's rule was a long time coming." He snapped his mouth shut then, as if he'd said something he shouldn't, but quickly recovered and changed the subject. "So what happened last night? *Did* you see anything?"

"No, I'm afraid not. I was..." Tristin's face heated, but he forced himself to continue. "I was coming to see you. To... to apologize for running off. I was... ashamed, I suppose. You're so very strong and... and handsome, and I'm so scrawny and weak. And I was afraid you'd seen—" He gulped and glanced down at himself. He'd been dressed in a long-sleeved nightshirt. Barely aware that he was doing so, he tugged the sleeves down to make sure they covered his scars.

Had Mikhyal seen them anyway?

Someone had undressed him. Seen him in all his naked ugliness, including the sorry tale of desperation carved in his very flesh.

Tristin cringed and looked away.

A warm hand closed firmly around his own. "And then what?" Mikhyal asked gently.

He blinked, trying to think what Mikhyal was talking about. It took him a few moments to recall what he'd been saying. "I... and then Dirit came and told me you were upset. And... and said I should come and see you, that you were still awake. So I g-got dressed and... and when we got to your suite, he opened the door, and I f-found you... well, I mean, I *thought* it was you. I reached for the knife, but the moment I touched it..." He trailed off, sickened at the memory. "It was so very strong," he whispered. "Strong enough that I felt it even through my shielding pattern. Fear. A desperate struggle to escape. And a deep anger, like fire in my veins, burning everything it touches. I couldn't break free of it."

"I don't suppose you managed to get any sense of who the knife might belong to?" Mikhyal asked.

"Ah. No, though I *can* tell you it's no one I've ever encountered before. And that whoever it is, they are full of fear and fury."

There was a long silence before Mikhyal said, "Tristin, about last night—"

A quiet knock sounded on the door. "Come in," Tristin called. *Quickly, please...*

The door opened and Ilya entered, followed by Garrik and Jaire. "Excellent," Ilya said. "I guessed you'd be awake by now."

"I've given him his medicine, Master Ilya," Mikhyal said, holding out the empty cup.

Ilya's smile was tired. "We shall make a healer of you yet, Your Highness."

"Is there any word on my father?" Mikhyal asked, and now Tristin noticed the dark circles under Mikhyal's eyes. Had he slept? Had any of them?

"He will recover," Ilya said. "Ambris and Kian are still with him. I have come to relieve you so can go to him. If you'd like to go back to the suite and wait, you can speak with Ambris as soon as he's finished."

Mikhyal turned to Tristin. "Would you mind terribly, Tristin? I know you've only just woken up, but…"

"He's your father. Of course I don't mind. Go on." Tristin practically sagged with relief when Mikhyal, with only a single, doubtful look, allowed himself to be cajoled into going to see his father.

When the prince had gone, Ilya took the seat Mikhyal had vacated and studied Tristin with that vague, unfocused look that meant he was using his healer's sight.

"You look much better than you did last night," Ilya said. "Whatever resonances you picked up from that knife were strong enough to throw you into mythe-shock."

"Are you certain he didn't pick up any of the poison from the blade?" Garrik asked, his voice a low rumble.

"I am. Tristin is suffering from simple mythe-shock. There is nothing to indicate even the briefest contact with the poison."

"You… h-have you c-come to question me?" Tristin stammered, nervous despite Mikhyal's reassurances. "About… about the attack on Mikhyal's father?"

"Of course not," Jaire said. "You had nothing to do with it."

"Dirit was quite insistent about that," Garrik said. "When I returned with Kian and Ambris, he took physical form, introduced himself to me, and then proceeded to assure me you were not involved in the attack. Not that I thought for a moment that you were. You do seem to have made quite an impression on him, Cousin."

"Anyway, if you had done it, I'd know," Jaire said. "I'm very good at telling when someone's lying."

"And," Ilya added, arching one thin, coppery eyebrow, "if barely touching the knife was enough to throw you into mythe-shock, I doubt you could have held onto it long enough to do any damage to anyone, let alone a man as fit as Drannik. No, I believe the knife was thrown from the shadows by someone who hoped to prevent the king from signing the treaty."

A chill crept up Tristin's spine. Was Mikhyal in danger, too?

Jaire took a blanket from the chest at the foot of the bed and came to his side to drape it over his shoulders. "We only came because we wanted to make certain you were all right, and to reassure you," he explained. "I know how your mind works — it's a bit like mine, always going to the worst possible case."

"Thank you," Tristin murmured, nearly overcome at the idea that his cousins had given even a moment's thought to his comfort. "Both of you. Have… have you any idea who might have done it?"

"None at the moment," Garrick said, "but we have already begun an investigation."

"And now that you've satisfied yourselves that your cousin is resting comfortably," Ilya said sternly, "you can leave him in peace."

"Yes, Master Ilya." Jaire nodded to Tristin and followed his brother out the door.

When they were alone, Ilya said, "Now then, Tristin, tell me how you came to be in the suite in the first place, and what you sensed when you touched the knife. Anything you can remember could be helpful."

Tristin took a deep breath and began the sorry tale.

When he'd finally finished, Ilya said only, "And you have no idea who you were sensing?"

"Mikhyal asked me the same thing," Tristin said slowly. "I don't think it's that simple, Ilya. I've been… experimenting since you taught me the shielding patterns, and one thing I've noticed is that the strongest empathic resonances absorbed by objects aren't necessarily the most recent. If the knife is very old, and hadn't been in the attacker's possession for very long, the things I sensed might not have anything to do with the last person to touch it. I might only be sensing the person who owned it the longest, or perhaps the strongest personality to own it."

"I see." Ilya looked thoughtful. "So your Wytch power will not be as helpful in identifying the attacker as I'd hoped."

"I... I don't think so, no."

"Well, if nothing else, this incident has shown me that while the shielding patterns you're using are sufficient for most things you'll encounter, you're sensitive enough that you clearly need something stronger. When you're feeling better, I shall endeavor to teach you a much more complex shielding pattern. It will block out everything, but you will be able to adjust it, so that if you should choose to sense the empathic resonances in an object, you can let them in slowly, a bit at a time, before they overwhelm you."

"Yes, of course, you're right, Ilya." Tristin tried to sound enthusiastic, but the thought of more lessons did not excite him. "I suppose it's best if I don't have to worry about the possibility of collapsing just from touching something that's absorbed a particularly strong impression."

When Mikhyal returned to the suite, Kian was slumped in an armchair, half asleep, but Ambris was nowhere to be seen. Mikhyal tried to be quiet, but Kian stirred the moment he eased the door shut, blinking at him with bloodshot eyes.

"Good morning, Your Highness." Kian started to get up, but Mikhyal waved him back down.

"Don't stand on ceremony, Kian. I'm sorry to have woken you. I suppose it's too early to see my father?"

"Ambris is just hunting down any last remnants of the poison staining your father's mythe-shadow." Kian yawned and stretched. "I expect he'll be finished soon. I don't suppose you could stay for a bit? I need to talk to Mistress Polina about preparing some medicine for your father, but I'm loathe to leave Ambris alone. He's at the end of his strength, and he might well fall on his nose the moment he's finished."

"Of course I'll stay. Don't worry, I'll keep an eye on him until you get back. Is there anything I ought to do for him?"

"Just make sure he waits for me before he tries to stagger back to our suite," Kian replied, getting slowly to his feet. "I'll try to be back before he's finished." He nodded good morning to the guardsmen stationed just inside the door as he left.

Mikhyal settled himself in one of the armchairs to wait. There was no sound from his father's room, and he could only hope that might be a good sign.

Not long after Kian left, a knock sounded on the door of the suite. Mikhyal went to open it and was surprised to find Wytch King Edrun and Prince Bradin standing out in the hall. They didn't look nearly as alike as Mikhyal and Drannik did; while Edrun had the black hair and eyes so common to the royal bloodlines, Prince Bradin was a blue-eyed blond.

"Good morning, Mikhyal," Edrun said gravely. "We heard what happened. Frightful business, truly frightful. How fares your father? And is there anything we can do?"

"One of the healers is still with him at the moment," Mikhyal said, "though I believe we should have word soon. Won't you come in? I'd be glad of the company. I can ring for breakfast, if you've not yet eaten."

"That's very gracious of you," Edrun said. He and Bradin settled themselves in the sitting room while Mikhyal pulled on the red cord by the door.

A servant was there before Mikhyal had a chance to sit down. Mikhyal asked for breakfast to be brought for himself and his guests, and once the servant had gone, took a seat opposite the Wytch King of Miraen.

"Has the culprit been caught?" Bradin asked.

"Alas, no." Mikhyal didn't elaborate; Tristin wouldn't want the attention, he was certain.

"Do you think the intent was to actually kill your father, or only frighten him?" Edrun asked.

"The blade was poisoned," Mikhyal said, "so I imagine whoever was behind it intended to prevent him from signing the treaty."

Edrun and Bradin exchanged a nervous look.

"Have you any idea who could have done it?" Bradin asked.

Mikhyal shrugged. "I suppose anyone who is sympathetic to the Wytch Council's goals could be suspect. If our own Wytch Master Anxin has somehow learned of what we do here, he could very well be responsible, though I've yet to see any evidence to suggest that."

"Ai, Miraen's Wytch Master Rotham would not be beyond suspicion, either," Edrun said. "He was hand-picked by my sister, Taretha, as her replacement when she became Council Speaker. Now that Cenyth leads the Council, how soon do you suppose she will replace Altan's Master Ilya and Irilan's Master Ythlin?"

"Garrik says he's been told to expect the announcement this fall, when the Wytch Kings are called to Askarra for the Fall Council," Mikhyal said with a thin smile. "Imagine their dismay when the northern kingdoms decline the invitation and announce their independence."

"There will be war," Edrun said. "The Council will not let the kingdoms of the north go free without a fight."

"No, it will not. Access to the mines alone is—" Mikhyal stopped at the sound of the door to his father's bed chamber opening. He turned in time to see Ambris slip out and close it quietly behind him.

"Prince Mikhyal, I'm glad you're here," Ambris said. "Your father is responding well to—" He stopped dead, all color draining from his face, golden eyes going wide as they fixed on Edrun.

"Ambris?" Edrun slowly rose.

Bradin stood and reached out to steady his father, who swayed on his feet. "Is it truly you, Ambris?" Bradin didn't look at all sure.

Mikhyal frowned. Ambris was *that* Ambris? He'd thought the young prince of Miraen had died tragically a few years ago, and so, apparently, did Ambris's family. He glanced toward the guardsmen, but they wore the same blank expressions Rhiva's King's Guard did when they guarded the family closely. Taking in everything, but sworn never to breathe a word of what they saw and heard.

Ambris swallowed, eyes darting from Edrun to Bradin and back.

"They... they told me you were dead." Edrun took a step forward. "Blackfrost burned..."

"It did," Ambris murmured, pressing himself against the door. "I burned it." Mikhyal couldn't tell if he was using the door for support or trying to merge with it. A bit of both, if the stricken expression on his face was anything to go by.

"But... but... why did no one tell me?"

"Because I asked them not to." Ambris's voice was barely a whisper.

"But..." Edrun brought a shaking hand to his brow and sank down slowly in his chair.

Still on his feet, Bradin demanded, "Why would you do that? Father was beside himself with grief!"

"Beside himself?" Ambris recovered enough to give his brother an incredulous look. "Really? When he couldn't even be bothered to answer my letters?"

"What letters?" Edrun whispered, dark eyes shimmering in the morning sunlight streaming through the windows.

"The letters I gave Taretha to carry back to you every time she came to give me lessons. The letters in which I begged you to come and see me so I could tell you how sorry I was about... about Mama. The letters in which I begged for some sign that you might one day find it in your heart to forgive me. But there was nothing. Never a word from you."

Edrun shook his head. "Ambris... I never received any letters. I asked Taretha to let me come and see you. She told me... she said the mere mention of me visiting sent you into fits. She told us your guilt had driven you mad."

Ambris closed his eyes, swaying against the door. Mikhyal rose and went to him, putting an arm around him. The healer was trembling. How much of it was shock, and how much exhaustion from the complex healing he'd just performed?

"What do you want to do?" Mikhyal said in a voice pitched for Ambris's ears alone. "I can ask them to leave, or I can ask one of the guardsmen to escort you to your own suite, but either way, I think you had better sit down before you fall down."

"I... yes. I had better sit." Ambris clung to Mikhyal's arm, leaning heavily against him.

Edrun shot a worried look at Mikhyal. "Is he all right?"

Mikhyal bit back a sharp retort, and said only, "He's been with my father all night, and I gather it was a rather difficult healing. He's exhausted himself, and seeing you has clearly been a shock." He helped Ambris into an armchair. When he started to pull away, Ambris held his arm even more tightly, so Mikhyal remained, standing by the healer's side.

Tears slipped down Ambris's face. "She lied to us both."

"I don't understand," Edrun said. "She was teaching you. What could she possibly have to gain by keeping us apart?"

"My power," Ambris said, a bitter edge to his voice. "She stole my power under the guise of teaching me. She had her guard captain beat me until I was injured enough to force the shift. Then she would hold me there in agony, half-shifted and unhealed, so she could siphon off the power I should have used to finish the shift. She told you I was incapable of learning, but truly, the only thing stopping me was her wish to use me as a power source. Master Ilya taught me in a single afternoon the patterns she withheld from me for five long years. Five *years*, Father. And I'd be there still, if it wasn't for Kian."

A choking sound escaped from the Wytch King's throat, and a moment later, Edrun was on his feet. Bradin offered his arm, but Edrun pushed it away. "Ambris, I had no idea." Edrun closed the gap between them and dropped to his knees in front of his son. "If I'd known... I never would have... I'm so sorry." The king's voice broke on the words.

Ambris stared at his father, disbelief written all over his delicate features. "I thought... I thought you hated me. The fire... Mama... my fault."

"*Not* your fault," Edrun whispered. "It was an accident. A terrible, horrible accident. I never blamed you, Ambris. But in my grief, I never made that clear to you." He lifted his eyes to meet his son's. "Can you ever forgive me?"

Ambris's shoulders shook. He let out a broken sob before sliding out of the chair to join his father on the floor. Edrun wrapped his arms around his son, and Ambris melted into his father's embrace, his arms creeping around the Wytch King and holding on tightly.

A gasp came from the door, and Mikhyal looked up to see Kian standing there, staring at the two of them, dark eyes wide and scared. Ambris and Edrun broke apart, and Kian took a few hesitant steps forward, stopping as Edrun helped Ambris back to his chair.

Bradin approached Ambris and embraced him briefly. "I can't believe it's really you."

"It is a good thing for Taretha that she's already dead," Edrun said in a hard voice. "Had I known what foul things she was doing to you, I'd have put a stop to it and avenged you immediately."

"She... she died by my hand, Father," Ambris said in a low, trembling voice. "I took back what she stole from me."

"And for that, I am proud of you. And I will be proud to welcome you back home to Miraen, as well. Ferrin will be thrilled to see you alive."

Ambris's eyes darted across the room to Kian. "I... I'm afraid I won't be going back to Miraen. My home — and my husband — are here in Altan."

"Your husband?" Edrun's eyes followed Ambris's gaze, then snapped back to his son. "And you have been here all this time?"

"Ever since Blackfrost burned, yes," Ambris said. "Garrik gave us sanctuary. And before you go breaking off your alliance and making declarations of war, I would have you know that he has been trying to convince me to come and see you ever since he arranged this meeting. It was *my* choice to stay away."

"But... why?" The pain in the Wytch King's eyes went straight to Mikhyal's heart.

"I feared you had given Taretha permission to use me the way she did. I... thought you were complicit in the abuse I suffered at her hands."

"Never." Edrun looked shocked. "I swear it, Ambris. Had I but known…"

"And here I thought *your* family was dysfunctional." Dirit's voice drifted down from somewhere above him. Mikhyal glanced up to see the little dragon perched on a high shelf, watching the Wytch King and his son with rapt attention. Mikhyal shook his head slightly, but dared not speak.

"Surely you must realize," Edrun said, "that if I had been complicit in Taretha's plans, I would not be here to commit Miraen to the Northern Alliance."

"So Garrik advised me when he came to see me the other day," Ambris said. "He argued quite convincingly on your behalf. It was my choice to remain hidden. He did not agree, though he assured me that he would respect my wishes."

"And he has," Edrun said. "He's not said a word." He sighed heavily, then said, "But you have a husband. You must introduce us."

A flash of panic crossed Ambris's face, but he quickly controlled it. He got to his feet and crossed the room to stand beside Kian. "Father, this is Kian. He is the healer Taretha brought to Blackfrost after Cyrith's death. He's the only reason I'm alive."

Kian dropped to one knee and bowed his head. "Your Majesty," he whispered.

"Rise, Kian, you must not kneel to me, regardless of your station. You saved my son and have kept him safe and happy these past few years. For that, I am in your debt."

Kian rose and gave Ambris a worried look. "Ambris, you need to rest. Shall I escort you to our suite, or will your father do it?"

"I shall see to it," Edrun said. "Come, Ambris, you can lean on me and tell me the way."

Ambris shot a pleading glance at Kian, who said, "I'll stay here and watch over Wytch King Drannik until Ilya returns. I'll be along shortly."

"Have no fear, Kian," Edrun said. "I'll see that he rests. It's the least I can do. I have… much to make up to him."

Prince Bradin followed them, a bemused look on his face. After the door had closed behind them, Kian cleared his throat and said,

"You can go and see your father now, Your Highness. If you don't mind, I'd like to stay here until he wakes up. I believe we have dealt with the poison, but there are some things we cannot know for certain until he regains consciousness."

"Of course," Mikhyal said. "You are his healer. You must do as you think best." He rose and crossed the room, but paused at his father's door. "Are you all right, Kian? That meeting seemed to be a bit of a shock for all of you."

"I... I'm sorry you had to witness it, Your Highness. It was not planned."

"No, I rather gathered that. Will Ambris be all right, do you think?"

"Revealing his whereabouts to his father was not what Ambris desired, but... I think it is for the best." Kian hesitated, then added, "Though he will not admit it, he has missed his father terribly."

"As I would miss mine, were anything to happen to him," Mikhyal said gravely. "Thank you, Kian, for saving his life. You and Ambris have the gratitude of myself and all of Rhiva."

Chapter Seven

Tristin closed his book at the sound of a knock on his bed chamber door. "Come in!" A visitor might be a pleasant diversion, especially if it was someone he enjoyed talking to.

One day in bed was quite enough, and the prospect of another had left Tristin bored and irritable. He'd much rather be in the gardens with Master Ludin, but Ilya was concerned about the strain of mythe-shock on his still-weakened constitution. He'd ordered Tristin to bed for another day, much to Tristin's consternation.

The door opened to reveal a serving girl with fiery red hair carrying a tray. She was followed by Prince Mikhyal.

"Thank you, Leyka. Just set it down on the table, there," Mikhyal directed the girl.

"Will there be anything else, Your Highness?"

"No, I'll see to Tristin, thank you."

The girl bobbed in a low curtsy and left the two of them alone. Tristin peered about. "Where's your little entourage? Still guarding your father, is he?"

"Ai, and you should have heard the grumbling when I asked. Of course, Garrik's assigned guards to the suite, but since we have no idea who was behind the attack or how they got in, I thought it a sensible precaution." Mikhyal brought the tray to Tristin and set it on his lap. "And speaking of precautions, Master Ilya said you must eat all of this."

Tristin glared at the steaming soup. "Of course he did." The scowl only lasted until his first taste of the savory mixture of leeks, potatoes, and sharp, tangy cheese. Along with a chunk of fresh bread, it made the perfect lunch. Garrik had certainly been right about his kitchen staff. Tristin couldn't remember ever eating so well, not even when he'd lived with his mother at Falkrag.

Mikhyal settled himself in the armchair at Tristin's bedside. "How are you feeling today?"

"Better," Tristin said between mouthfuls. "What about your father? Is he recovering?"

"Ai, well enough to be giving the healers a hard time of it."

"Oh, good. I feared he might have taken a turn for the worse. Kian was here earlier to check on me, but he only stayed a few minutes, and he seemed very distracted."

"That's nothing to do with my father." Mikhyal paused for a moment as if debating with himself. "I suppose it's no secret. Ambris met his father yesterday morning. I… got the impression he would have preferred not to."

"Oh." Tristin lowered his spoon. "Oh, dear. How did that happen?"

"Bad timing. Edrun and Bradin came to our suite to inquire after my father just as Ambris was leaving. It was quite a shock to all three of them."

"I can imagine," Tristin said. "Ambris was adamant about not letting his father know he was alive."

"You knew?"

"He spoke of it while I was at Dragonwatch. Kian was trying to convince him to come down to the castle and meet with his father, and Ambris wasn't having any of it. How… how did it go?"

"It was rather moving, actually," Mikhyal said. "I was nearly in tears, myself. It turns out the Wytch Master who was supposed to be teaching Ambris lied to both Ambris and Edrun to keep them apart."

"Oh…" Tristin let out his breath on a long sigh. "That's a relief." He flushed and brought a hand to his mouth as he realized how that sounded. "Oh! No, I don't mean… *not* a relief that they were lied to and manipulated, but that Ambris's father didn't know what was going on. Ambris feared Edrun might have been complicit in his abuse." Tristin stared down at his lunch, wishing he had better control over his mouth.

Mikhyal didn't seem at all bothered, though. "Edrun seemed genuinely shocked to learn that not only was Ambris alive, but Edrun's own sister had been using him for her own gain. To be honest, I thought Edrun a bit naive. Rhiva's Court is a nest of snakes, and I can't imagine Miraen's being any better."

"No, I don't suppose it is," Tristin murmured. He knew nothing of either kingdom's politics, but Garrik's scathing comments about Altan's Court suggested that *nest of snakes* might actually be a compliment. "What of the treaty? Ambris feared if Edrun learned that Garrik had been sheltering him, it would put the alliance at risk."

"No danger of that," Mikhyal said. "The Northern Alliance was signed into existence this morning, over breakfast served in my father's bed chamber. He insisted they do it as soon as possible. I think the attack shook him. He hasn't said much about it, but I know he's been brooding about what will happen to Rhiva if my brother takes the throne. With the alliance in place, he can name the heir he chooses without Council interference."

"Ah. Your brother is not his first choice, then." Tristin realized then just how limited his knowledge of the royal families was. He wasn't even certain how many brothers Mikhyal had. He would need to remedy that, he supposed, if he was to live here at the castle.

"No, he is not," Mikhyal said grimly. "Shaine will not honor the treaty. Once, there would have been no question, but… ever since the accident, he's changed, and not for the better."

Tristin opened his mouth to ask a question, but snapped it shut again before anything could escape. *Should* he ask? Or would it be more polite not to? He nibbled at his lower lip, excruciatingly aware of the seconds passing while he dithered. Mikhyal must think him a perfect fool. His face burned at the thought.

"A year ago, Midsummer, it was," Mikhyal said, saving him from having to make a decision. "Shaine had a riding accident. He was thrown from his horse and knocked unconscious. We feared he might never wake, but after nearly a week, he did. He was different, though. Before the accident, he and I were close. I'd been raised to take the throne, and when he was confirmed the heir eight years ago, he was terrified. He needed guidance, and my father was too angry and disappointed to provide it. I took it upon myself to mentor him, to prepare him to be the best king he could be."

"You sound like a very good brother."

"Ai, well, Shaine had no one else. Father had always been a bit cool to him. Up until the accident, Shaine was one of my closest friends. Afterward, he wanted nothing to do with me. Instead of being reluctant to take the throne, he became almost eager, as if he could hardly wait for Father's death. And instead of turning to me for support and instruction as he used to, he turned to Wytch Master Anxin."

"Was there nothing the healers could do?" Tristin asked.

"Nothing more than to explain that this sort of thing can happen after a severe head injury, and that there was nothing to be done. My father had other healers brought in, but they all said the same thing." Mikhyal stared down at his hands.

"That must have been very difficult for you," Tristin said softly.

"Quite. And I fear once we return home and my father makes his intentions clear, Shaine will not take the loss of his position well. A year ago, it would have been a relief to him, but now? He will be beside himself. I shudder to think what he might do."

Tristin's breath caught in his throat as the pieces came together, and he grasped the situation. "Your father means to name you his heir." The words came out in a choked whisper, but Mikhyal didn't seem to notice his growing discomfort.

"Ai, and I fear he also means to protect me to the point where he fears any risk to me at all. Which doesn't bode well, if I am to be his military commander. I told you Vayne had said he could perform his transformation on me. I would gladly move forward with it, but my father is opposed. He means to declare me his heir tomorrow, at the betrothal ceremony, and once that's done, I suspect he will not allow me out of his sight for fear of losing the only heir he trusts."

Tristin dropped his gaze to his bowl, suddenly feeling very self-conscious. Mikhyal might not have realized it yet, but alliance or no, once he was the heir, friendship with someone like Tristin would reflect badly on him.

The heir of Rhiva could hardly be consorting with the half-mad, bastard son of a traitor. Even if Mikhyal didn't see him that way, the rest of the nobility would, and that was what mattered. Tristin might have grown up far from the intrigues of Ysdrach's Court, but he'd heard enough whispered gossip in his early years to have grasped how important one's breeding was to the nobility of Skanda. That attitude wasn't about to change because of a few signatures on a treaty.

"That's enough talk for now," Mikhyal's voice cut into his thoughts. "You need to finish your lunch, or Master Ilya will be after both of us.

"You s-sound like one of the h-healers." Tristin kept his eyes on his bowl. "Perhaps you've missed your calling."

Mikhyal laughed. "No, I don't think so. Although I must admit my motives are not entirely altruistic."

Tristin froze, spoon halfway to his mouth. "Oh?"

"I was promised a dance after the betrothal ceremony tomorrow. It's in my best interests to make sure my dance partner is well enough to attend."

"Ah." Tristin's face grew hot, and he kept his eyes fixed on his bowl and applied himself to his soup, which had suddenly lost all flavor.

An awkward silence followed. Tristin ate as quickly as he could, painfully aware of the heir's scrutiny. When he'd finished his last bite, Mikhyal rose.

"I'm sorry to have to leave you so soon, but my father is expecting me. We have much to discuss, and I think he wants to take advantage of the fact that here, we can speak freely without fear of being overheard."

"Of course," Tristin mumbled. "You mustn't neglect your duties on my account."

"I'll see you at the ceremony tomorrow afternoon, then."

Tristin swallowed, not sure what to think of the fact that the prince still wanted to see him. "I... I... um..."

Mikhyal's pale eyes widened a fraction, as if he'd only just realized something. "I'm sorry, Tristin, I didn't mean to push. If you're not comfortable going to the ceremony, I understand. It must be frightful, having to go among a crowd of people when you've been used to only your own company for so long."

"Ah. Yes. I… that's very true." Tristin kept his eyes down, unable to look at the prince.

"Well, I did offer to come to you at Dragonwatch to claim my dance. I could come to you here just as easily."

"No… it's all right. I… I'll be there. I… I've promised Jaire. He'll be dreadfully disappointed if I don't go."

Mikhyal frowned, but said only, "If I can get away from my father, I'll come by and see you later on. We can discuss it then."

Tristin gave him a wordless nod, but he still couldn't bring himself to meet Mikhyal's eyes. Surely the prince was only being kind. He'd offered the dance, and he'd stick to his word, but it couldn't possibly mean anything.

Since Mikhyal seemed unwilling to protect his own reputation, Tristin would have to do it for him. He would attend the ceremony as planned, but only long enough to watch Prince Jaire and Prince Vayne say their vows, and to swear his allegiance to his cousin. The moment the official business had been concluded, he'd take his leave. A celebratory feast would be held before the dancing, so there would be plenty of time to slip away.

Yes. That would be best. It might not be exactly what Tristin wanted, but he liked and respected Mikhyal far too much to want to cause the prince any difficulties. And that was all Tristin was ever likely to be to Mikhyal: a difficulty. As a traitor's bastard, no matter what he did, he would always be viewed with suspicion. He'd never be anything more than Wytch King Garrik's rather awkward relation.

All the way back to the guest wing, Mikhyal mulled over that conversation with Tristin, and wondered where he'd gone wrong. They'd been talking quite happily, but all of a sudden, Tristin had gone quiet, and when he did speak, it was in whispers, or short, stammered sentences. Mikhyal must have said something to make him uncomfortable.

He reviewed the conversation as he crossed the Grand Hall, barely noticing the bustle of the preparations for tomorrow's ceremony and the dance that would follow.

Dance.

Everything had been fine until he'd mentioned the dance.

Mikhyal stopped dead in the hall. He'd thought Tristin was interested, but... could he be mistaken? Perhaps he'd read too much into Tristin's shy, sweet smile. The uncertainty... the nervousness...

The more he thought about it, the more sense it made. Tristin had, after all, spent the last fifteen years in almost complete isolation. If he'd been locked away at seventeen, he'd never had a chance to interact with people as an adult before.

He'd thought he'd been flirting with Tristin, but perhaps he'd only been making the poor man uncomfortable. Perhaps Tristin wasn't being coy at all. Perhaps he was bewildered and embarrassed, and had no idea how to tell Mikhyal to get lost.

Oh, Mik, you blithering idiot...

A glance at the clock in the Grand Hall told him he didn't have time to go back and apologize before he was due to meet his father for lunch. He'd just have to make time later.

He arrived in the guest suite to find Dirit lounging on the chandelier. "All is well, Your Royal Diligentness." The little dragon leapt down from his high perch to land upon Mikhyal's shoulder. Though Dirit rarely manifested physically, Mikhyal couldn't help but flinch away to avoid being hit.

"I shall never tire of that game," Dirit said, settling himself.

"How's my father?" Mikhyal asked.

"He is quite safe, thanks to me." Dirit puffed his little chest out. "Although I do think he might have stayed in bed a bit longer. He's looking rather wilted, and he's only been up for an hour or so."

Mikhyal was about to knock on the door of his father's bed chamber when it opened to reveal Wytch King Drannik. The king looked very pale.

"Should you be up?" Mikhyal asked. "The healers said—"

"To the Dragon Mother's coldest hell with the healers," Drannik growled. "Garrik is joining us for lunch in an hour, and I'll not have him seeing me still abed like an invalid. Bad enough they all had to see it this morning."

"But the treaty is signed," Mikhyal reminded him.

"Ai, it is, and it will be made public tomorrow. Garrik plans to make the announcement before the betrothal. I will certainly sleep easier tonight knowing that my allies know who is to rule Rhiva after me. They will fight for your right to the throne, should the need arise, Mikhyal. They have all sworn it."

"Ai, and now your work here is done and you can rest." Mikhyal eyed his father critically. "Will you at least allow me to help you to a chair?"

"Looking particularly haggard, am I?" Drannik laughed, but it was a very tired sound. He didn't protest when Mikhyal helped him back into his bed chamber and settled him in the armchair next to the bed.

"If you overdo it now, you could set yourself back. Ambris did warn you about that. Several times." Mikhyal pulled a blanket off the bed and was about to drape it over his father's legs, but Drannik pushed it away.

"Stop your fussing, Mikhyal. I may still be a bit tired, but I'm not nearly as infirm as everyone seems to think. And I *will* be attending the betrothal ceremony tomorrow."

Mikhyal knew better than to argue, so, using his most diplomatic tone, he said, "That's two attempts on your life."

"Are we certain they were attempts on *my* life and not yours?" Drannik countered. "If the bandit attack was arranged — and the presence of the Wytch Sword suggests it was — then either one of us could have been the target. As for the other night, the room was dim, and the two of us look so much alike… it could well have been you they were after."

"I think we should operate under the assumption that they sought to eliminate *you*, Father. The Council has far more to gain from your death than mine."

"Yesterday, you might have been correct," Drannik conceded. "But as of this morning, you are my heir, and once word of that gets out, you and I will both be targets."

Mikhyal hesitated for just a moment. He hated to use the situation to press his case, but then again… "Which is why I think we should go ahead with the transformation Vayne offered to perform."

"An excellent idea!" Dirit chirped in his ear. "Think what *fun* we could have frolicking in the sky with Prince Tristin of the New Flower Bed!"

Oblivious to Dirit, Drannik gave him a long, appraising look. Mikhyal held his breath. Had this second attack been enough to change his father's mind? "The gift of the Dragon Mother would certainly give you a way to defend yourself from attack," the Wytch King said thoughtfully.

"And a weapon the Council will be ignorant of until I use it," Mikhyal said. "The element of surprise may work in our favor."

"Ai. I've been speaking with Prince Vayne. He's assured me several times that the transformation is completely safe, though I still have some misgivings about that. Given the circumstances, however, I think the benefits outweigh the risks. You have my permission to proceed."

"Excellent," Mikhyal said with a nod. He'd intended to proceed with or without his father's approval, but moving forward with Drannik's blessing would certainly be less trouble. "I'll make arrangements with Prince Vayne immediately."

"Oh, how very exciting!" Dirit leapt from his shoulder and skipped across the Wytch King's bed.

Drannik waved his hand dismissively. "There is no urgency. We still have battle plans to discuss, and even if we did not, Ilya won't allow me to leave until he's satisfied that I'm fully recovered."

"He would be remiss in his duties to let you go before you're ready, Father. As far as your health goes, I trust Ilya and his healers to know what's best."

"Ai, but Ilya doesn't have to contend with the thought of Shaine and Anxin running roughshod over the people of Rhiva in our absence, does he?"

Mikhyal started to respond, but was interrupted by a commotion in the suite's main room.

"The changing of the guard?" Drannik asked, raising an eyebrow. "They're usually so quiet, I don't hear them."

"No," Mikhyal said, heart sinking as he recognized his brother's voice barking orders. "It sounds as if Shaine has arrived. What in Aio's name is he doing here?"

Drannik's mouth tightened in disapproval. "That boy had orders to remain at the summer palace." He started to get to his feet, but Mikhyal set a firm hand on his father's shoulder.

"No, you rest. You're looking a bit pale. I'll deal with him." Mikhyal turned and left before his father could protest, closing the door quietly behind him.

Shaine was standing in the middle of the suite giving orders to the servants. Garrik's guardsmen were nowhere to be seen. The suite was now guarded by men wearing Rhiva's colors.

"Shaine," Mikhyal said smoothly. "How good to see you."

Shaine turned to give his brother a cold smile. "I'm surprised to see you on your feet, Mikhyal. Last I heard, you were gravely ill. Father said something about awakening Wytch power?"

Mikhyal hesitated. Should he tell Shaine the truth? No... Drannik would want nothing revealed to the Wytch Council, and if Shaine knew about the Wytch Sword, he would certainly tell Anxin. "Father was mistaken," Mikhyal said. "I have exactly as much Wytch power as I did when you saw me last. None."

A fleeting expression of disappointment crossed his brother's face. "Well," Shaine said, pulling off his riding gloves and tossing them carelessly on the table, "as soon as I'm settled, you can tell me what's been happening."

"What are you doing here? Father left you in charge of things at the summer palace."

"Ai, but with both of you having arrived here on dragonback, you've no safe way of returning home. I put together an escort, and here we are. I'm sure you and Father will be much more comfortable knowing you're guarded by men loyal to Rhiva."

Mikhyal glanced at the guardsmen. Two were positioned at the main door of the suite, and two had taken up posts near the bed chambers. He didn't recognize any of them, which was odd, as

Mikhyal made it a point to personally interview every single guardsman who was stationed at the palace.

"Who are these men?" Mikhyal demanded. "These are not the men I assigned to the King's Guard. And where is Captain Rhu? I must speak with her immediately."

"I had your captain arrested on charges of negligence and suspicion of treason," Shaine said flatly. "She and the rest of the King's Guard are being held in the dungeon pending further investigation into the attack on the royal caravan."

"On whose authority?" Mikhyal asked in a low voice. "Rhu and the King's Guard saved us. We were ambushed and outnumbered."

"You were saved by someone weaving the mythe," Shaine corrected him. "If it wasn't your Wytch power, as Father thought, then I've no idea what it was, but mysterious use of a power that dangerous needs to be reported to the Wytch Council and investigated immediately. Have no fear. Anxin will inform the Council as soon as I've spoken to him, and they will deal with it. Really, Mikhyal, I'm surprised Father trusts your judgment on military matters, when you've obviously no idea. Now, where is Father? I must speak with him."

Mikhyal clenched his jaw, struggling to hide his dismay and his anger. "He's in his room, resting."

"Resting?"

"He was attacked two nights ago."

"Attacked?" Shaine's hard, green eyes narrowed. "By whom? Why was I not told? I am his heir — I should have been informed the moment I arrived!"

Mikhyal considered his response carefully; the last thing he wanted was Shaine interrogating poor Tristin. "We haven't managed to determine that just yet, but Garrik's Captain Jorin is conducting an investigation."

"I shall need to speak with him immediately."

"Everything is under control, Shaine. I trust Garrik's captain to do his job."

"You don't think Garrik was behind it, do you?" Shaine asked.

"Aio's teeth, no!" Mikhyal exclaimed.

Shaine's eyes narrowed again as he studied his brother. "You seem very certain of that."

"I am as certain as I can be," Mikhyal temporized, realizing that even though it wouldn't matter after tomorrow, he still couldn't breathe a word of the Northern Alliance or his own change in fortune to his brother. Not in front of guardsmen he neither knew nor trusted. "Father was very good friends with Wytch King Dane when he was alive, and—"

"Oh, do calm down, Mikhyal. I only ask because Wytch Master Anxin has spoken of rumors of a rebellion brewing in the north, and Altan has always been notoriously... *independent.*"

"I've seen no evidence to suggest a rebellion," Mikhyal lied, hating the circumstances that made it necessary. "But if you have doubts, you should speak them to Father. It isn't as if *I* have any power here." The bitterness in his own voice didn't surprise him, but the way Shaine flinched as he turned away did.

The Wytch King of Rhiva and his soon-to-be-deposed heir were arguing, and Mikhyal, standing at his father's side, was having a difficult time keeping his own expression neutral. At least Dirit, listening avidly from his perch atop the dressing table mirror, was keeping his mouth shut for the time being.

"I never said I did not appreciate the gesture, Shaine," Drannik said, for perhaps the third time. Though he didn't raise his voice, his tone made it clear that his patience was wearing thin. "What I object to is your decision to leave the affairs of the kingdom in the hands of Wytch Master Anxin. I left *you* in charge. Not Anxin."

Shaine pressed his lips tightly together. His light green eyes darted to Mikhyal and then back to their father. Mikhyal couldn't decide if his brother was furious or struggling to come up with an explanation.

When Shaine remained silent, Drannik continued, "You will gather your men immediately, and you will make your way back to the summer palace with as much speed as you can muster."

Shaine struggled in silence for a few more moments before saying in a strangled voice, "Father, even if you think it best that *I* return to the palace, surely you can see the sense in my leaving some men behind to serve as an escort. How are you to get home safely if you have no one to protect you?"

Drannik sighed and leaned back in the heavy armchair next to his bed. "Wytch King Garrik has kindly offered me an escort. Now, go, Shaine. That is a direct order from your king. I am still recovering, and I am tired of arguing with you. If you cannot obey me, I shall send your brother in your place. He, at least, will not argue with me."

Shaine's face paled, and it was with obvious reluctance that he turned on his heel and left the room. He shut the door firmly behind him, not quite slamming it, and a few moments later, he was barking orders at the guardsmen he'd posted about the suite.

As soon as the door was shut, Drannik wilted a bit.

"Oh, dear," Dirit commented from his perch. "This sounds positively *dire*. Your royal brother is in *quite* a temper."

Mikhyal shot Dirit a warning look before saying quietly, "Was that wise, Father? Shaine could have already been here for days, skulking about, listening in, with no one the wiser. If he has overheard anything, he will take it straight back to Anxin, and Anxin will take it to the Council."

"The thought did cross my mind," Drannik said. "But it hardly matters now. The Council will know soon enough. If there are spies or sympathizers in Altan's Court, the secret will be out tomorrow, when we announce the alliance. I am content that we are as prepared as we can be."

"Ai, but are you prepared to face a coup when we return home? Shaine's imprisoned the King's Guard and Captain Rhu. With Anxin in charge, I fear what we may find upon our return."

"There are enough men loyal to Rhiva within the palace guard and among my staff that I don't think we have cause to worry," Drannik said. "And after witnessing what the Wytch Sword is capable of, I have no concerns regarding our personal safety."

"Very intelligent man, your father," Dirit commented. "Clearly he appreciates my unique abilities. I don't imagine *he* would insult me by asking me to carry messages."

Mikhyal rolled his eyes and managed to refrain from comment.

Drannik started to get up, but fell back in his chair with a groan. "Help me up, Mikhyal. Garrik will be here for lunch shortly, and I will greet him on my feet."

"Father, don't you think—" Mikhyal broke off at Drannik's scowl, but made a mental note to have a word with the healers later on. Ambris would make certain Drannik rested, even if he had to slip something into his tea.

When Garrik arrived, Drannik went to greet him, clasping his forearm and drawing him into the suite. "Come in, come in, Garrik. Mikhyal will be joining us."

Garrik frowned slightly, and glanced at Mikhyal, indicating Drannik with the slightest motion of his head. Mikhyal read the question immediately, and it was the same as his own: *Should he be up?*

Mikhyal could only lift his shoulders in reply.

"It's good to see you on your feet, Drannik," Garrik said. "You're looking... not exactly *well*, but better than you did this morning, at least."

"The credit goes to your healers," Drannik said. "They are very thorough and very skilled. Especially that young fellow, Prince Ambris."

"I shall pass the word along. I am sure he will be gratified to know that you appreciate his services."

Drannik studied the Wytch King for a few moments. "Quite a surprise that was, him running into his father like that."

"I can imagine," Garrik said mildly.

Drannik laughed. "That took stones of iron, Garrik, hiding a prince of Miraen from the Council. Whatever did Edrun think?"

Amusement flickered in Garrik's dark eyes. "Once the situation had been explained to him, Edrun was grateful. I merely offered his son my protection when he asked for it."

Noting his father's unsteadiness, Mikhyal moved surreptitiously to his side to offer him his elbow. Drannik batted his arm away and moved to the table. "Shall we sit down?"

"Ai, we shall," Garrik said. "Lunch will be along shortly. Will Prince Shaine be joining us? I was informed of his arrival an hour ago." He glanced about the suite as if he expected to see Shaine.

"He will not," Drannik said flatly. "He is on his way home to Rhiva. Or at least, he had better be." Drannik went on to explain the nature of Shaine's Wytch power and the very real possibility that Shaine already knew of the Northern Alliance.

"What of the attack on you, Drannik?" Garrik asked. "The timing leads me to believe that whoever was responsible intended for you to die before you could sign the treaty. Could Shaine have had a hand in that?"

"I don't like to think it," Drannik said slowly, "but it is a possibility we must consider." He glanced at Mikhyal. "What do you think?"

"Before the accident, I would have told you exactly what you could do with those suspicions, Father. Since then?" Mikhyal shook his head. "I fear he sees me as a threat, and I don't know how far he would go to secure his position."

Garrik shifted uncomfortably in his seat. "In light of the suspicious timing of Prince Shaine's arrival and the attack on Your Majesty within the very walls of my stronghold, I fear the escort I initially offered may not provide adequate protection. I think, perhaps, it would be better if Kian and I were to fly you both home so you don't have to risk a lengthy overland journey."

Mikhyal shot him a grateful look, which Garrik acknowledged with the subtlest of nods.

"That is a handsome offer," Drannik said, apparently oblivious to the younger men's exchange. "One I will gladly accept. I cannot imagine anyone daring to attack a man guarded by two dragons." He glanced meaningfully at Mikhyal. "Or three. Mikhyal and I have spoken at length, and I believe we are ready to take Prince Vayne up on his offer to perform his transformation procedure on Mikhyal."

Garrik regarded Mikhyal with a raised eyebrow. "Excellent. I shall inform Vayne as soon as our meal is over. He will come and explain the procedure to you so you will both know what to expect."

Mikhyal had to bite back a groan. Between the meetings scheduled with the other Wytch Kings and his responsibilities to his father, it didn't look like he was going to get a chance to speak to Tristin before tomorrow's ceremony.

Tristin stood on the dais before the throne and tried not to faint. Although, now that he thought about it, fainting might actually be better for all concerned. He'd never had to speak in front of so many people before, and he dreaded to think what might emerge from his mouth if he wasn't vigilant.

"His Royal Fractiousness says to remind you to breathe." Dirit's voice was right next to his ear. "That shade of blue isn't at all becoming. And don't lock your knees. It wouldn't do to have you fall in a heap at the king's feet, now, would it?"

Tristin glanced to the side to see Dirit perched on his shoulder, but he dared not answer. If even one word slipped out, the dam would break, unleashing a torrent of nonsense. Rumors of his madness must surely have followed him. The last thing he wanted was to prove them true. That wouldn't do Garrik's reputation any good at all.

For the first time since his rescue, he found himself longing for the relative safety of his prison at Shadowspire. At least there, it had been just him and his hallucinations, and *they* certainly weren't going to spread gossip.

Garrik rose from the throne and gave Tristin an encouraging smile before he began speaking. It sounded as if he might be welcoming his long-lost cousin, but Tristin was far too anxious to focus on the words, and barely heard them. His knees were trembling, and beads of nervous sweat were forming on his brow and on the back of his neck. The finely tailored formal clothing felt tight and uncomfortable, and he was finding it difficult to breathe. Worse, he couldn't remember what he was supposed to do.

He'd practiced before breakfast. Garrik had been there, and he'd told Tristin exactly what would happen, and even had him repeat the words of the oath of fealty back to him. Now, Tristin's mind was blank, and his eyes darted from side to side as he considered which direction would be best for his flight. The exit to the left was closer. If he dove off the dais—

A slender hand slipping into his own arrested his thoughts of escape, and Tristin turned his head to see Prince Jaire smiling up at him. The prince wasn't dressed for the betrothal ceremony yet, but his white-blond hair was done up in an intricate style involving dozens of narrow braids, all gathered at the nape of his neck.

"It's all right," Jaire murmured, giving his hand a reassuring squeeze. Tristin squeezed back, and the tightness in his chest eased enough that he could breathe again. "That's it. Slow, deep breaths. You can do this. Time to kneel now."

Tristin did as he was told, thankful that Jaire had stepped in before he'd had a chance to put his flight plan into action.

"Good. Now look up at Garrik and repeat the words of the oath."

His ears burned as he stumbled over the ritual phrases he'd thought he'd committed to memory, and then Jaire's hand was squeezing his shoulder.

"Now kiss the ring on Garrik's hand," Jaire murmured in that same soothing tone, "and then stand up and turn around."

When he bent his head to kiss the ring, Garrik's other hand rested on his head for the briefest moment, and then Jaire was pulling him to his feet and surreptitiously guiding him in his turn, making sure he was facing the right way. Tristin stared out into a sea of unfamiliar faces as the gathered nobility and royalty all bowed in acknowledgment. Jaire squeezed his hand again and whispered, "Look at Dirit. He's on the chandelier."

Tristin glanced up and saw the little dragon, hanging upside down by his tail over the gathering, waving at Tristin and waggling his tufted eyebrows.

It took everything he had not to burst out laughing, but it was enough of a distraction to get him through the rest of the ceremony. Thank the Dragon Mother he didn't have to do anything else but stand there and do his best to keep himself on his feet with his mouth firmly shut.

Then Jaire was pulling him off the dais and behind the throne. "I have to go and get dressed for the betrothal ceremony now," he whispered. "Garrik and the rest of the kings are going to announce the treaty, and they'll be yammering on about that for ages. You can either go and sit in the family section over there" —Jaire pointed to a small grouping of chairs along one side of the Grand Hall— "or you can follow me through the back hall, and escape to your suite. It's all right. I understand how hard that was for you, and I won't mind if you're not here for the betrothal."

"I'll be here," Tristin said firmly. "I said I would, and I will."

Jaire's face lit up, and he squeezed Tristin's hand again before slipping through the door at the back.

Tristin took advantage of the lull to make his way to the group of chairs Jaire had pointed out. To his relief, the section reserved for the royal family was nearly empty. The only occupant was an older lady dressed in a revealing gown more suited to a young maid in search of a husband. Tristin sat as far from her as he could, which didn't turn out to be far enough, for the moment he was seated, she leaned over and said in a low voice, "So you are Garrik's long-lost cousin, are you?"

"Ah. Well. Yes. I'm—" He gulped and just managed to stop himself from introducing himself as Prince Tristin of the New Flower Bed. "Tristin, my lady."

Cold black eyes raked over him, and the corners of her mouth turned down. Her hair, done up in an elaborate creation of braids and fine gold chains, was jet black, without even a single thread of silver. "Vakha's bastard, or so I hear."

Tristin's face warmed as he tried to think who this woman might be. He'd not attended any formal dinners, and so had yet to make her acquaintance. "Y-yes, I'm told my f-father was Prince Vakha, my lady. I never met the man, though." He remembered his manners then, and added, "I... I'm afraid I haven't had the pleasure of m-making your acquaintance."

She raised a little jeweled fan and waved it about in front of her. "I am Lady Saphron. Vakha's widow."

"Ah. Yes. Well." Tristin wished now that he'd escaped to his suite as Jaire had suggested. If this was his father's wife, he doubted she'd want to be anywhere near him. "I'm sure we'll get along famously, then." The words fell out of his mouth with reckless abandon, and Tristin was helpless to stop the flow. "You can tell me all about my father, since I never met him, and I don't even know if he was told about me, and then I can regale you with tales of my hallucinations, which were my only companions for years upon years, and then, if it pleases you, you can make sympathetic noises and order tea and cakes for us, and perhaps I shall escort you on walks around the gardens and call you *Auntie*. I can hardly wait to begin!" He stopped to draw breath and stretched his mouth wide in what he hoped was a brilliant smile.

Lady Saphron's eyes narrowed. "If you think I would have anything to do with my husband's tragic mistake, you can think again. You will never be anything to me but a bitter reminder of the follies of my husband's youth. That little chit from Ysdrach certainly had ambitions, to snare Vakha in her web of deceit. Garrik may accept you into the family with open arms, but you will not find me nearly so welcoming."

Tristin swallowed, face flaming as he looked helplessly about to see if anyone else had heard. Before he could come up with a thing to say, a voice said, "Tristin! There you are! Come on, you're supposed to be sitting with us, or had you forgotten?" And there was Mikhyal, helping him up and tugging him away from Lady Saphron.

Tristin pulled free just long enough to give Lady Saphron a stiff, formal bow. Mikhyal led him through the crowd to where Drannik was sitting. The Wytch King of Rhiva still looked pale, but his black eyes were bright and alert, and fixed upon the two of them, gaze resting for a few moments on their joined hands.

To Tristin's consternation, Mikhyal kept hold of his hand even after they were seated. "Th-thank you for that," Tristin murmured.

"Prince Jaire was mortified when he remembered that Lady Saphron would be sitting there." Mikhyal gave his hand a reassuring squeeze. "He would have come himself, but he didn't have time. He sent Dirit to tell me you might be in need of a rescue."

"I was, rather. She doesn't seem to like me at all."

"Prince Jaire told me she was always bitter about never having any children of her own, so I suppose a certain amount of resentment is to be expected. I'm sure it's nothing personal."

"I... I suppose." Tristin had doubts about that, but there was no time to continue the conversation, for at that moment, Garrik rose and called the other three Wytch Kings of the north forward to announce their alliance.

Drannik nodded to his son and rose, making his way steadily toward the dais. Tristin glanced about, heart sinking as he realized he'd lost his chance to leave unnoticed. So much for slipping off quietly before the dancing started. Mikhyal would, no doubt, insist he sit with him at dinner. With a sigh, Tristin turned his attention to the dais, where Master Ristan, surrounded by the four Wytch Kings, was reading the treaty out for the assembled Court.

When the reading was complete, Garrik announced that the first official act of the Northern Alliance was to recognize Prince Mikhyal of Rhiva as Drannik's heir. Mikhyal was called forward to kneel before his father as the ritual words declaring him the heir of Rhiva were spoken.

"He does look most regal, doesn't he?"

Tristin turned his head to see Dirit perched on the back of the chair Mikhyal had vacated, tail lashing with excitement. "He does indeed," he murmured under his breath.

After swearing his allegiance to both his father and the alliance, Mikhyal got to his feet and embraced his father, then clasped arms with Ord, Edrun, and Garrik, in turn.

That was it then. Mikhyal was officially the heir, and so far above Tristin that it certainly wouldn't do for them to be seen together in public. He glanced about, seeking any possible way out, but given the number of people present, leaving without being noticed looked to be an impossible feat. He settled himself in a miserable huddle, determined to wait it out until he could make his escape.

❖   ❖   ❖

Mikhyal started to offer his father his arm as they stepped down from the dais, but withdrew it at Drannik's fierce glare. The Wytch King of Rhiva was adamant that no further sign of weakness be shown before his peers.

Tristin was right where Mikhyal had left him, hunched over in his chair, looking as if he was trying to make himself as small and unnoticeable as possible. It must have taken a considerable amount of courage for him to attend such a large gathering when he'd only recently left the isolation of his prison tower. Mikhyal's respect for him went up a few notches, and he gave Tristin a fond smile as he took his seat.

Dark eyes met his briefly before shifting downward. Mikhyal didn't get a chance to ask him what was wrong, for at that moment, the music began, and the princes made their entrance at the far end of the hall. They were dressed in clothing Mikhyal had only seen before in history books, from the time Prince Vayne had been born into: tight-fitting breeches, high boots, and shirts with elaborate lace ruffles. Jaire was dressed entirely in white, and Vayne in black.

"Look at all that lace," Dirit said with a sniff. The little dragon was perched on Mikhyal's shoulder between himself and Tristin. "And those cuffs! Ridiculous! Imagine trying to keep them out of your soup!"

Tristin's mouth curved in a small smile, and he murmured to Dirit, "No wonder Jaire called it *frippery*."

Mikhyal had to smother a bark of laughter with a cough.

The princes had adopted an older hairstyle consisting of long, narrow braids were gathered at the napes of their necks to cascade down their backs. Vayne's jet-black hair was a stark contrast to Jaire's white-blond, and the two made a striking couple as they faced one another to speak their promises to wed.

Mikhyal leaned toward Tristin. "It must have taken ages to do all those braids," he whispered.

"Oh, it did, indeed," Dirit said. "I stopped by to watch some of the preparations this morning. You should have heard all the moaning and whining."

The ceremony was conducted by Altan's Wytch Master Ilya, with Wytch King Ord standing as Vayne's witness, and Garrik standing as Jaire's. It sounded as if they'd borrowed some of the wording from the betrothal ceremonies of Vayne's time. It was a far more romantic ceremony than Mikhyal was used to hearing. Modern betrothal ceremonies, at least among the nobility of Skanda, tended to be conducted like the business arrangements they were rather than the joining of hearts and minds that Ilya now spoke of.

When the ceremony was over and Jaire and Vayne had sealed their promises with a chaste kiss, Garrik announced the wedding would take place in the fall, during the same week the Wytch Council normally summoned the Wytch Kings to Askarra to hear the Council's bidding. None of the kingdoms of the north would be attending the Fall Council this year, and Mikhyal imagined there would be much consternation in Askarra when the Northern Alliance made its formal declaration of independence.

Consternation, and likely, plans of military action.

The guests were ushered into the formal dining room for the celebratory feast, and Mikhyal and Tristin found themselves seated at the head table, side by side, along with the rest of the royal families. From the grin Prince Jaire shot his way, Mikhyal guessed the prince had been responsible for that, and he nodded his thanks. Jaire's grin widened, and he turned to whisper something to his promised husband, who also gave Mikhyal and Tristin a nod and a smile.

A bit farther down, next to Wytch King Edrun and Prince Bradin, sat Ambris and Kian, both of them looking a bit nervous. Edrun seemed to be in very good spirits, and kept leaning over to speak to his son, or brush his arm, as if he still couldn't quite believe Ambris was alive.

When everyone was seated, Garrik rose to address the gathering. "It's no secret that I have never supported the idea of arranged marriages," he started. "And those of you who know me well are aware that since the day I took the throne of Altan, one of the greatest points of contention between myself and the Wytch Council has been my brother's marriage. Today's events bring me great pleasure. Not only am I no longer bound to obey the dictates of the Council, but my brother has managed to find himself a husband of his own choosing, marriage with whom can only strengthen

Altan's already-strong ties with the kingdom of Irilan, thus adding strength and substance to the foundations of the Northern Alliance."

Garrik raised his glass in a toast, after which he continued, "In the spirit of forming a firmer foundation for our alliance, Wytch King Edrun has a few words to say."

Wytch King Edrun nodded at Garrik and rose from his seat. "I did not wish to take the focus away from Prince Jaire and Prince Vayne's betrothal, but since their promised union helps to strengthen the Northern Alliance, it seems appropriate for me to officially welcome my youngest son, Prince Ambris, back into the loving arms of his family. I cannot tell you how pleased I was to learn that the son I believed to have perished in the flames at Blackfrost, does, in fact, live. Unbeknownst to me, Ambris was granted sanctuary by Wytch King Garrik five years ago, after Council Speaker Taretha, whom I entrusted with his care, instead sought to use and abuse him."

A low murmur rippled through the dining hall. Ambris turned bright red and stared down at his plate. Kian rubbed his back encouragingly.

"I had thought it would be most convenient if Ambris was free for an alliance marriage," Edrun continued, "perhaps with a noble lady of Altan. But I have been informed that is not the case."

Now it was Kian's turn to squirm. He gave Ambris a panicked look and practically shrank into his chair, no mean feat for a man of Kian's stature.

"While in hiding from the Wytch Council, Ambris has married the man who saved him from suffering further abuse at Taretha's hands. Kian of Aeyr's Grove, I would like to publicly acknowledge my debt to you. You have my heartfelt thanks, and you will always have a place in my family."

"I... I... thank you, Your Majesty," Kian mumbled, and ducked his head.

Garrik chuckled. "As to your wishes for an alliance marriage, Edrun, I fear I can do nothing to change the fact that Kian is not a lady, but I can do something about his status. Kian, how do you feel about lands and a title? Lord Kian has rather a nice ring to it, don't you think?"

Kian lifted his head to stare at Garrik, eyes wide.

"If you and Ambris are so inclined," Garrik continued, "you can reaffirm your handfasting with a royal wedding the same week Jaire and Vayne marry. Ilya and I shall also be speaking our marriage vows that week, so it will be quite the celebration." Garrik gave his Wytch Master an affectionate look, and Ilya smiled up at him and took hold of the king's hand.

Ambris stared at Garrik, open-mouthed, as if this was the last thing he was expecting.

Jaire got to his feet and raised his glass. "Our own harvest festival certainly promises to be much more exciting than the Wytch Council's stuffy Fall Council. To Garrik and Ilya, and to Kian and Ambris. May all these unions forged in love bind the Northern Alliance and help us hold true when the Council tests our resolve, as they surely will."

Mikhyal raised his glass, and so did Tristin.

"Royal weddings seem to be all the rage this season," Dirit said, appearing on top of Mikhyal's plate. "How very tiresome. I suppose you two will be next."

Mikhyal choked on his wine, and Tristin turned bright red. He barely looked at Mikhyal for the rest of the meal.

When the guests had eaten, they were invited into the Grand Hall, where the orchestra was already playing soft music, and an array of desserts and pastries waited on long buffet tables.

Dirit flitted off to inspect the pastries, and Mikhyal grabbed hold of Tristin's hand and followed the rest of the guests to watch Jaire and Vayne's first dance. The two princes proceeded directly to the center of the dance floor, and the music began. The dance was an old, intricately choreographed mirror dance, which had been popular in Vayne's time, but was rarely performed anymore. It was very romantic, and Mikhyal found himself wondering what it might take to get Tristin to perform such a dance with him.

Jaire and Vayne executed the complex steps flawlessly, their contrasting black and white finery only adding to the drama of the dance. When the music stopped, they bowed to each other, turned and bowed to their guests, then moved into the crowd to claim new dance partners.

"Would you do me the honor of dancing with me?" Mikhyal asked Tristin.

Tristin's eyes went wide, and he pulled his hand away. "I'm not sure that's... ah... well, I mean... not like that!"

Mikhyal laughed. "No, I don't imagine any of us will be dancing like that. Not without a lot of practice, anyway." He looked directly into Tristin's eyes. "Tristin, I've been looking forward to this ever since you promised me a dance in the garden at Dragonwatch, but if you'd rather not—"

"It's not that," Tristin said quickly, eyes darting away and then lifting cautiously to meet Mikhyal's once more. "It's just... well. I'm the bastard son of a traitor, and you're the heir to the throne of Rhiva. I'm sure you can find someone more suitable to dance with. They'll gossip, you know, if they see us together, and if your father has any hopes of making any sort of alliance marriage for you, they'll be—"

Mikhyal shut him up with a kiss.

Tristin stiffened for a moment, and then his arms slowly crept around Mikhyal. He was clearly inexperienced, but just as clearly interested, and eagerly followed Mikhyal's lead when Mikhyal deepened the kiss.

When Mikhyal finally pulled away, Tristin's eyes were wide and stunned. "Ah. Yes. Well," he said softly. "About that dance..."

Mikhyal smiled and led him out onto the dance floor.

It was just as well the first dance was a slow, romantic one. The complex steps of the mirror dance Jaire and Vayne had performed would have been completely beyond Tristin. He'd never attended a formal dance before, nor had he been given any lessons in his youth. Hidden away from Ysdrach's Court at Falkrag and later exiled to Shadowspire, he'd never attended any of the formal events that honed the social skills of Skanda's young nobles.

Mikhyal led, and Tristin did his best to follow. One of his arms was around Mikhyal's waist, which was nice in some ways, but quite distracting in others. His hand, now damp and warm with nervous sweat, was firmly clasped in Mikhyal's.

If he'd only had to worry about his hands, he might have managed. But dancing also required the moving of one's feet, and Tristin couldn't quite decide what to do with his. As he shuffled about, trying his best not to step on Mikhyal's boots or tangle their legs, Mikhyal smiled at him.

That bright, happy smile was his undoing. Tristin put his foot down wrong and trod on Mikhyal's foot. Mikhyal's arm tightened around him, supporting him as Tristin struggled to regain his balance. Once Tristin had his feet under him, Mikhyal guided him into the next sequence of steps, barely missing a beat. Tristin's face flamed. He was certain he could hear snickers as they continued their awkward lurch around the dance floor.

By the time the music stopped, he was sweaty, out of breath, and completely flustered. Mikhyal led him off the dance floor to one of the little alcoves around the edge of the Grand Hall. "I'm sorry, Tristin," he said, before Tristin could apologize for being such a dreadful dance partner. "I never thought. You've probably never danced before in your life, have you?"

"Um. Not... well. No. There's, um, not much call for dancing when you're locked in a tower like some damsel in a fairy story." At Mikhyal's contrite expression, he added quickly, "I'm quite good at languishing in my bed chamber, though. And sighing wistfully as I gaze out the window toward the distant horizon, dreaming of handsome princes." Aware that he probably sounded ridiculous, Tristin clamped his lips together and vowed to keep a tighter leash on his mouth.

But Mikhyal just gave him a sad smile. "I might have found that amusing if I didn't know it was the truth. You don't appear at all comfortable. Why don't we go back to my suite? My father's busy holding court from an armchair in the corner over there. He's not going to need me. I can fetch us a bit of dessert from the buffet table and we can go and enjoy it away from all these prying eyes, ai?"

Tristin could hardly believe Mikhyal still wanted to spend time with him after he'd so spectacularly failed to deliver the promised dance. "I... um... yes," he said shyly, ducking his head. "I... I'd like that."

"Right," Mikhyal said in a conspiratorial tone, "you wait here, and I'll go and steal us something to sustain us. What do you like best?"

"Cream puffs," Tristin said promptly. "Oh... and blackberry tarts, if there are any."

"Excellent choices." Mikhyal grinned. "I'll return shortly. If I'm captured, I shall endeavor to stuff all the evidence in my mouth and swallow it before they can wrest it from me."

Tristin returned the grin as his mind conjured an image to go with Mikhyal's stated intention. "If you are captured, my prince, they'll not get a word out of me."

"Good man. Wish me luck." Mikhyal turned to scan the crowd. "It appears I shall have to cross this rather perilous ballroom filled with enemy agents disguised as revelers." He stepped out of the alcove, looked both ways, and made his way with exaggerated caution to the dessert table. Tristin stifled a giggle as Mikhyal stopped halfway to the table and looked about furtively. He turned back to Tristin, gave him a broad wink, and continued on his way.

Still fearing himself to be a source of speculation that Mikhyal really couldn't afford, Tristin stepped back into the shadows to wait.

"He seems quite taken with you."

Tristin looked around to see Dirit clinging to the curtain at the side of the alcove. "Good evening, Dirit. I wondered where you'd gotten to."

"Oh, well, His Royal Bossiness has set me to watching over his father, who is currently being guarded by four large, well-armed men who hardly need my help. This dance is turning out to be far more tiresome than I'd anticipated." The little dragon's lip curled. "I shall never understand the fascination you humans have with your social conventions. Rules for everything. What you must wear, how you must walk, how you must drink your tea. It's all quite—"

"Frivolous?" Tristin guessed.

"Pointless." Dirit flattened his ears. "Where I come from, if something doesn't like the way you're doing something, you either get mythe-whacked or set on fire. Or, if you're really unlucky, eaten.

Usually before you can apologize." A delicate shudder rippled over the little dragon's body, beginning with an eyebrow twitch and working its way down to the tuft at the end of his tail.

"That sounds rather unpleasant," Tristin ventured.

"It is, but it does guarantee that the truly hopeless don't survive long enough to be a bother to the rest of us. That was a very interesting dance you were doing. Does it have a name?"

Tristin's face had only just cooled down, but now his cheeks burned again. "Ah. No. Not... not really. I've... not had very much practice, you see."

"Well, His Royal Gallantness doesn't seem too bothered. He's all ready to take you back to his lair and have his evil way with you."

Now Tristin's ears were on fire, too. "Oh," he said faintly. "Is he? I hadn't really... I've tried to explain to him why that would be a terrible idea. I mean, it isn't proper for him to let himself be seen in public with me. I'm not at all respectable. Not with my family history. He doesn't listen, though."

"No, he doesn't," said Dirit. "As I said, he's quite taken with you. I must admit, I'm rather intrigued to see what happens next."

A feeling of dread crept over Tristin. "You're not going to, um... *watch*, are you?"

"Why?" Dirit blinked at him, one furry eyebrow twitching. "Will there be something to see?"

"I don't... ah, that is—"

"My curiosity is now most assuredly piqued, Prince Tristin of the New Flower Bed. Perhaps morning shall find you prince of another sort of bed entirely."

"Mission accomplished!" Mikhyal sounded triumphant as he entered the alcove holding a large plate loaded with cream puffs, blackberry tarts, and crispy little sugar-biscuits. "Is Dirit here? I thought I caught a glimpse of him as I was returning."

Tristin glanced about, but there was no sign of the little dragon. "He *was*. He's gone now. He was harassing me, as usual."

"Well, I've asked the little monster to keep an eye on my father. We'll have the suite to ourselves."

"W-we will?" Tristin stammered, becoming flustered all over again at the thought of the rumors that would spread if anyone should catch sight of them leaving the dance together. He ought to plead a headache and retire to his own suite, but… he liked Mikhyal, and he'd had so few friends in his life. So instead of offering up an excuse, he returned Mikhyal's smile with a tentative one of his own. "I… I think I'd like that."

Since Drannik was at the celebration, most of the guardsmen Garrik had provided were busy watching over him, leaving only two on duty outside the suite. Mikhyal invited Tristin in and set the plate of pastries on a low table in the sitting room.

"Would you like some dessert?" Mikhyal asked. "Or can I get you a glass of spirits?"

"D-dessert would be n-nice." A glass of spirits was the last thing he needed. His tongue was already problematic enough; the Dragon Mother only knew what sort of nonsense would come flying out of his mouth if he dared have a drink of anything stronger than watered wine.

While Mikhyal went to the sideboard for dessert plates, Tristin took a moment to loosen the laces of his shirt. It was a warm evening, and the Grand Hall had been hot and stuffy with all those people packed elbow to elbow for the dancing. He squirmed, trying to get comfortable on the narrow couch, acutely aware of every sensation: the slight tightness of the new boots he wore, the stiff, starched linen of his shirt, the prickle of unease rippling through his middle.

Mikhyal handed Tristin a plate holding a huge cream puff.

"Thank you," Tristin whispered, staring down at it. Was he expected to eat it? And talk at the same time? Or should he leave it until he was finished talking? What did one talk about with a royal heir when one had been invited to said heir's suite while everyone else was still at the dance?

Had anyone seen them leave together?

Aio's teeth, what would it do to Mikhyal's reputation if they *had* been seen? Word would spread through the Court like wildfire.

"I shouldn't be here," Tristin blurted out.

"Why ever not?" Mikhyal asked.

Tristin risked a glance up. A frown marred Mikhyal's handsome features, and he was immediately sorry for having put it there. "I don't mean I don't *want* to be here, just that it might not be a good idea, I mean people will talk, and I'm quite sure they all saw us leaving the ballroom, they might have even seen me talking to Dirit, I forget sometimes that not everyone can see him, and there I was happily chatting away to him, and you wouldn't want people thinking you were doing anything untoward with—"

Mikhyal took the plate from Tristin and set it on the table, then leaned in and pressed his lips to Tristin's in a soft, chaste kiss.

"Oh." Tristin said when Mikhyal finally pulled back to stare into his eyes. "That was nice."

"I don't care what anyone else thinks," Mikhyal whispered. "I'm only interested in what *you* think."

Tristin swallowed. "I think... I think I might like another of those."

"The cream puff or the kiss?" Mikhyal teased.

"Can I have both?"

Mikhyal grinned. "Your wish is my command, my prince."

"I'm not really a—" Tristin never finished his sentence, for Mikhyal leaned over toward the table, dipped a finger into the creamy filling of the pastry, and lifted it to Tristin's mouth. Tristin froze, mesmerized, as Mikhyal spread the cream over his lips, then leaned closer to lick it off with delicate swipes of his tongue.

The air in the room became close and warm, and Tristin's clothing felt tight, especially his breeches. He closed his eyes, and when the tip of Mikhyal's tongue pushed gently at the seam of his lips, he parted them and let out a little whimper.

He'd never done much in the way of kissing, and Tristin had no idea what he was supposed to do. Should he kiss Mikhyal back? Or should he simply sit there and let Mikhyal keep doing all those intriguing things with his tongue? Was he supposed to tilt his head? What if he did and their noses bumped?

Frozen with indecision, Tristin did nothing. Mikhyal didn't seem to mind. He continued exploring Tristin's mouth with his tongue. Heat pooled low in Tristin's belly as he hesitantly poked his own tongue out. It stroked Mikhyal's, and Mikhyal let out a little moaning sound as he finished licking the cream from Tristin's lips.

When Mikhyal had thoroughly explored Tristin's mouth, he drew back, pale eyes burning. "You were saying?" he whispered.

Had he been saying something? Tristin's thoughts were so scattered, he couldn't recall. In fact, he wasn't entirely sure he'd be able to repeat his own name, if asked. "Yes?"

A smile played about the corners of Mikhyal's mouth. "Yes, what?"

"Yes, I liked that, and yes, I'd like some more, please," he said without thinking.

"Good." Mikhyal pulled him into his arms and kissed him again.

Tristin lost himself in that kiss. It was everything he'd ever dreamed a kiss could be. Sweet and gentle, but it set off a yearning heat deep inside him. Tristin might be inexperienced, but he was a quick study, and it wasn't long before he was making hesitant overtures of his own. His hands wandered across Mikhyal's broad back. It was difficult to feel the contours of his body beneath the layers of formal clothing. What would it feel like to touch Mikhyal's bare skin?

As his hand traveled lower, he wondered if he dared try to loosen the prince's shirt. He'd just about worked up the courage to start tugging it free from the waist of Mikhyal's breeches when Dirit's voice hissed in his ear, "The Wytch King is heading this way!"

Mikhyal cursed as they pulled apart. "How far away is he?"

"He just left the ballroom," Dirit said, flitting up to perch on top of the tall bookshelf from which he commanded a view of the entire main room of the suite.

"I... I sh-should really b-be going," Tristin stammered.

"You don't need to leave," Mikhyal said. "Whom I entertain is my own business."

"Yes, well... it's also the business of the entire C-Court."

Mikhyal sighed and straightened his clothing, and Tristin did the same. He'd only just finished when the door of the suite opened and Wytch King Drannik entered, looking pale and tired.

"You may have been right, Mikhyal," the Wytch King said sourly. "Perhaps attending the ceremony *and* the dance was a bit much."

Mikhyal moved to his father's side. "Do you need any help, Father?"

Drannik tried to shrug Mikhyal off, but Mikhyal insisted on seeing the king to his bed chamber. He shot Tristin an apologetic look, and mouthed, *Tomorrow.*

Tristin nodded and took the opportunity to slip away, hoping his presence in the suite wasn't going to cause problems for Mikhyal. He returned to his own rooms by way of the Grand Hall, and hung about on the fringes of the gathering, just in case anyone who had seen them leave together was watching to see if either of them returned.

By the time he arrived in his bed chamber, he was too tired to do much more than fall into bed.

Chapter Eight

Much to his consternation, Mikhyal didn't see Tristin the day after the betrothal, nor the day after that. The Wytch Kings of the Northern Alliance wasted no time after the announcement of their treaty. The very next morning, Mikhyal was summoned to the first of a series of strategy sessions that took up most of the next week. The time was spent discussing military assets, vulnerabilities, and defensive plans.

In their first act of open defiance of the Wytch Council, Altan's Wytch Master Ilya and Irilan's Wytch Master Ythlin joined them in plotting their rebellion.

Drannik recovered his strength quickly, and indeed, by the end of the week, it was Mikhyal, rather than his father, who was falling asleep at the strategy table.

When the last session finally ended, late in the evening, the Wytch Kings had planned for every contingency they could think of, and each would return to his kingdom with a list of tasks to complete.

The first order of business was to increase the forces on their borders and send the Wytch Council their declaration of independence. The plan was to deliver the document along with a prison carriage containing three Wytch Masters, each with a blood-chain locked around his neck to prevent him from using his power. Edrun would take Wytch Master Rotham into custody the moment he returned to his palace at Mir. Drannik was to do the same with

Wytch Master Anxin, who would be escorted to Mir, as would Wytch Master Faah, who was still being held beneath Castle Altan.

Ord and Edrun planned to leave the following morning, but Drannik would wait until Mikhyal's transformation was complete before taking Garrik up on his offer to fly him home. If Mikhyal was fit enough to accompany him, he would do so. Otherwise, Drannik would go on ahead to get things moving in Rhiva. With the attacker still loose, Mikhyal was not thrilled at the prospect of Drannik returning to the palace alone, but his father would not be dissuaded. Shaine and Anxin, he said, had already arrested the King's Guard, and he was loathe to give them more time in which to damage the kingdom.

As the meeting broke up, Vayne pulled Mikhyal aside and said, "Ambris and I can perform the transformation whenever you are ready, though from the sound of things, your father is eager to return to Rhiva, so perhaps the sooner the better, ai?"

Mikhyal's pulse jumped. "Ai," he said, swallowing. "At your convenience."

"Tomorrow, then?" Vayne said cheerfully. "I'll speak with Kian and have him bring you up to Dragonwatch first thing. We've been performing the transformations there. Less chance of being disturbed. Or seen by prying eyes spying for the Council."

"Tomorrow," Mikhyal agreed, gut twisting in apprehension as he started to turn away.

Vayne's expression softened, and he reached out to touch Mikhyal's arm. "Don't worry, Mikhyal. You are well-suited for this. Most of the patterns are already there in your mythe-shadow. Your transformation will be easy and painless, and you will sleep through it, I promise."

The reassurances were not enough to assuage Mikhyal's fears, and he wished it wasn't so late. Tristin had been through this, and even if he couldn't set Mikhyal's mind at ease, his company would be a pleasant distraction.

He saw Drannik off to bed and was about to seek his own bed chamber when there was a knock at the door of the suite. Mikhyal nodded to the guardsman standing beside it, and the door was opened to reveal Tristin standing in the hallway, shuffling his feet.

"Ah…" Tristin flushed and glanced at the guardsman before addressing Mikhyal. "G-good evening, Your Highness. I-I heard you might… I mean, someone suggested to me that you might be in need of a bit of… um… reassurance. About tomorrow."

"I was just thinking that some reassurance would be most welcome," Mikhyal said, smiling broadly. "I considered seeking you out, but it's late enough that I didn't want to disturb you if you'd already gone to your bed."

Tristin came in, and Mikhyal sent the guardsman outside to stand watch in the hall so they could have a bit of privacy.

"I'm sorry I haven't had a chance to talk to you all week," Mikhyal said. "These bloody strategy meetings have been interminable. There's so much to consider, and as you can imagine, everyone is eager to return home to prepare for the Council's reaction. We've been starting early, finishing late, and working through mealtimes."

"It's all right," Tristin said, ducking his head. "Jaire's been keeping me apprised, and I've plenty to do. Master Ludin's been showing me around the royal gardens and the greenhouses, and we've been planning a new garden for Dragonwatch. Dirit's been giving me regular reports, too. He popped in a little while ago and said you looked rather sweet, half asleep over the maps."

"Well, we'd all but finished, but Ord *would* keep droning on and on. I swear, the man has to repeat everything at least three times, just to be sure everyone understands."

"Jaire said the same. But he also said he thought it was a very productive series of meetings."

"It was, indeed. We've plans for the defense of the Northern Alliance, and we've all got our marching orders. We've discussed as many contingencies as we've been able to imagine, and I think we are as prepared as we can be. Garrik's first priority is to establish a communications network of dragon shifters across the northern kingdoms. We'll be able to send messages and adjust our plans much more quickly than we could if we were sending messages by courier on horseback."

Tristin's eyes went wide. "That's brilliant!" He gave Mikhyal a rueful smile. "That's why it's a good thing Garrik's on the throne. I'd never have thought of anything that clever."

"Don't put yourself down, Tristin," Mikhyal said gravely. "You're clever, too. Your strengths just lie in different areas than Garrik's."

Tristin flushed and stared down at his feet. "Oh, but you want to hear about the transformation, don't you? It was a long time ago for Vayne, and I don't think his experience was very pleasant. He has a much better idea of what to do than the Wytch Master who transformed him all those years ago. I didn't feel a thing when he did me. In fact, Ambris put me to sleep for it. He'll probably do the same for you. It's that easy. You fall asleep, and when you wake up, you're a dragon shifter."

Mikhyal found it hard to believe it would be so simple. "There's a tattoo involved, isn't there?"

"Ai, there is. The patterns are inked into your flesh and your mythe-shadow at the same time. But you'll be asleep, so you won't feel it."

"Might I... might I see yours? I didn't... the night you shifted for me, it was... it was too dark." The moment the words fell from his lips, Mikhyal regretted them. Tristin had been quite upset that night, and had fled, and with the attack on his father and all that had followed, Mikhyal had never really had a chance to find out what, exactly, had distressed him so.

Was he just painfully shy? Or was there more to it than that?

He'd certainly responded eagerly enough when they'd kissed the night of the dance.

"Oh. Um." Tristin licked his lips and his eyes darted to the door of the Wytch King's bed chamber.

"I don't think he'll be getting up," Mikhyal said. "He was very tired. But if you'd feel more comfortable, we could go into my bed chamber."

Tristin hesitated.

"It's all right if you'd rather not. I'm sure Vayne would show me his. Or—"

"No, it's all right," Tristin said quickly. "Just... yes, I would feel more comfortable if there was no chance of anyone walking in and seeing..." he trailed off and stared back down at the floor.

When they were safely inside Mikhyal's bed chamber, Mikhyal closed and locked the door. "There. Now no one will bother us."

"Thank you. I... I'm sorry I'm so... it's just... I don't normally... and you're so... and then there's the... oh, dear, I'm doing it again."

"Tristin... it's quite all right. I understand. I can turn my back, if that makes it easier."

Tristin blinked at him in the dim lamplight. "I... no, I need to... I mean, eventually, you'll... and I'll just have to... Oh, bother. Look, it's just that there are some rather ugly... *marks*... on my arms. It's... it's nothing, really, just that when I was kept captive in Shadowspire, I grew desperate. I was so weak and... and afraid... I... I might have broken the, um, window and tried to use the glass to... well, I mean..." He swallowed hard. A moment later, he shoved his sleeve up, baring his arm to the elbow, and held it out for Mikhyal to see. "There, you see? That's how weak I am. I'm sorry I'm not..."

The scars told the story more succinctly than Tristin had, and Mikhyal instantly grasped what had happened. A wave of fierce tenderness washed over him, and he took hold of Tristin's arm by the wrist and very gently drew it to his lips, turning it so he could kiss the scars.

Tristin's eyes went huge.

"You are not weak, Tristin. These marks don't make me think anything of the sort. On the contrary, they tell me how truly desperate your situation was, and how strong you are to have survived it." Mikhyal bent his head to kiss another of the silvery-pink lines. "Don't hide yourself from me, for you are strong, and so very beautiful."

To his surprise, Tristin didn't pull away. He remained still, but for his trembling. When Mikhyal lifted his head to look at him, tears glinted in Tristin's eyes. "I do believe that's the nicest thing anyone has ever said to me," Tristin whispered.

Mikhyal pulled him into his arms and held him tight. "You have not been properly cared for. Or loved. I would see that change."

Tristin's arms crept around him, and he hung on to Mikhyal. "I... I think I might like that."

When they parted, Tristin took a step back and began unlacing his shirt.

"Tristin, you don't have to—"

Tristin reached out and pressed a finger to Mikhyal's lips. "I want to," he said softly. "I believe I can trust you."

I believe I can trust you.

Knowing some of what Tristin had been through made those words all the more precious. "I swear to you, I'll do my best to be worthy of your trust."

Tristin gave him a hesitant smile and slipped off his shirt, then took a deep breath and turned around. The tattoo on his back was stunning. It depicted a brilliant, ruby-red dragon with its wings spread wide. The ink was like nothing Mikhyal had ever seen before, almost glowing in the lamplight.

"Beautiful," Mikhyal breathed. His fingers itched to touch, and he started to reach out, but stopped just before he brushed Tristin's skin. "May I... may I touch?"

"Yes," Tristin whispered. "I'd like that."

Mikhyal traced the lines of the image inked into Tristin's back, noting the way Tristin shivered at his touch. When he bent to press a kiss to the top of the dragon's head, Tristin let out a little whimper. Mikhyal moved up to his shoulder and kissed and nibbled his way to Tristin's neck. Tristin moaned and practically melted against him.

Holding him close, Mikhyal let his hand wander around Tristin's trim waist to brush over his flat stomach and nearly hairless chest. Tristin let out a little sigh and let his head fall back against Mikhyal's shoulder.

"I would like to touch you everywhere," Mikhyal whispered, "but I don't want to frighten you away. Tell me what you want, Tristin."

Without hesitating, Tristin whispered back, "I think... I think I'd like you to touch me everywhere. Please. Only... could we... can it be dark?"

"Of course it can." Mikhyal reached out to douse the lamp, leaving the room in darkness but for the faint shimmer of moonlight coming in the window.

He began by running his hands over the smooth skin of Tristin's chest and his belly. Years of addiction and inactivity had left his ribs prominent and his muscles weak and underdeveloped. Mikhyal looked forward to seeing what a few months of activity and good food would do for him.

"Can you..." Tristin sounded breathless, his voice husky and trembling. "Can you take off your shirt, too? I've never... I want... I'd like to feel your skin against mine..." He pulled away, and Mikhyal quickly fumbled with the laces of his shirt and drew it off. He tossed it to the side and pulled Tristin back against his chest.

"So warm..." Tristin murmured.

Mikhyal resumed his exploration of Tristin's body. Tristin moaned as Mikhyal's hands stroked his belly and meandered slowly down toward his hips. When he brushed his fingertips lightly over Tristin's groin, he was pleased to note the shape of a hot, rigid cock pressing tightly against Tristin's breeches. Tristin let out a little gasp, and Mikhyal let his fingertips linger, stroking him softly through the fabric.

"Oh... oh, yes..." Tristin whispered.

When Mikhyal cupped Tristin's cock in his palm, Tristin began rutting against it. His body trembled, his skin was scorching against Mikhyal's chest, and the little whimpers falling from his lips were all it took to send a storm of heat crashing through Mikhyal. The motion of Tristin's backside against his erection was enough to have him flexing his hips, seeking the sweet friction that would eventually lead to his own release.

Tristin turned his head, mouth seeking Mikhyal's. It was an awkward angle, to be sure, but it didn't matter. All that mattered was Tristin pressed against him, writhing in his arms.

Mouths met, tongues clashed, and husky moans filled the air until Tristin suddenly stilled and let out a choked cry. Moments later, Mikhyal pulled Tristin hard against him, his own release a blinding flash of pleasure that left him panting and struggling to support Tristin's weight as well as his own. With a groan, he hauled Tristin to the bed and collapsed, pulling Tristin down with him.

They settled in a tangle of limbs, Mikhyal's arms loosely around Tristin, so as not to make him feel trapped.

"That was... that was lovely," Tristin murmured. "No one's ever done that for me before. I... might have done it myself a few times, but then the drugs made it impossible to feel anything... and I couldn't... and of course, locked up in Shadowspire, there was never anyone..."

The mixture of wonder and regret in his voice made something in Mikhyal's chest tighten. How lonely Tristin's life must have been. He lifted Tristin's hand to his lips and pressed a kiss to his palm. "Then I am honored to have been the first."

"Will you be the second, as well?" Tristin whispered. "And the third? And—"

Mikhyal silenced him with a kiss.

A fat raindrop spattered on one of the flat grey stones surrounding the herb garden, and Tristin paused in his weeding to squint up at the overcast sky. It was bright enough to the west that the afternoon might be sunny, but the dark clouds directly overhead meant he'd have to take cover for now if he wanted to stay dry.

He brushed his hands off and went inside. At the kitchen door, he stopped and poked his head in. "Is there any word on Prince Mikhyal, yet, Alys?"

Alys turned from the tray of pastries she was preparing. "Not yet, Tristin. I checked with Wytch King Drannik a few minutes ago to see if he'd like some tea. Ambris and Prince Vayne were still in with the prince. I don't suppose you'd be willing to carry the pastries for me?"

"Of course, Mistress Alys, I'd be happy to help." Tristin came all the way into the kitchen in time to see Dirit creeping across the work table toward the pastry tray. "Dirit, don't you dare."

Dirit flattened his ears and turned his head to look at Tristin, gleaming black eyes full of reproach. "I was only *watching*," he said, sitting on his haunches near the tray. "You always think the worst of me, but I've done nothing wrong. Nothing at all."

"*Yet*," Tristin corrected.

"Is that little rat about again?" Alys eyed the work table suspiciously. Though Tristin noted no difference in his appearance, Dirit must have chosen that moment to materialize, for Alys gasped and jumped back. "Out of my kitchen with your dirty little feet, you!" she said sternly. "Or you'll find yourself with a broom up your backside."

Dirit drew back. "You wound me, Madam. I only wished to compliment you on your most impressive pastry-making skills."

"Trying to sweet-talk me, more like," she muttered. "Tristin, get that tray before he has his grubby paws all over it."

"*Grubby paws?*" Dirit's whiskers drooped. "I'll have you know I am far cleaner than any *human* I've ever met."

Alys ignored him and picked up the tea tray. "I shall be having another word with His Highness about his pet rat as soon as Prince Vayne has finished with him."

Tristin lifted the pastry tray. "Have you been in to check on Mikhyal lately?" he asked Dirit.

"First you accuse me of stealing pastries, and now you want information," Dirit complained.

"Oh... oh, I *am* sorry, Dirit. I didn't mean to accuse you, but you *were* slinking across the table, and you did have a rather furtive look in your eye."

"*Slinking? Furtive?* Well, I *never*," the little dragon huffed. "You're very lucky I happen to like you, Prince Tristin of the New Flower Bed, or I should decline to say a word. As it happens, I was in to see His Royal Transformedness only a few moments ago. They're almost finished, and he slept like a baby through the entire procedure."

Tristin let out a tiny sigh of relief. He'd been worried in spite of Vayne's reassurances. He remembered all too well what Jaire had told him about Kian's transformation. Kian had very nearly died, and Jaire had spent the entire time listening to his screams, unable to help him.

"Tristin! Are you coming?" Alys called from the hall.

"Yes, Mistress Alys, sorry!" Tristin hurried after her, nearly dropping the tray in his haste.

"As long as you're coming with me," Alys said over her shoulder, "do you think you could keep His Majesty company? He's looking a bit on edge. I'd try to reassure him myself, but I'm not sure how he'd take it, coming from the help, and all. And since you've already been through the transformation, you can probably set his mind at ease better than I can."

"Ah... well... I..." Tristin tried to swallow past the knot of panic rising in his chest. He'd been out in the garden for a reason: avoiding having to talk to Mikhyal's father.

Tristin had no idea what the oath he'd sworn to Garrik meant to his own status. Did it mean he could initiate conversation with the Wytch King of Rhiva without giving offense? Or must he wait for the king to address him? All he knew about the nobility of Skanda was that their interactions were governed by a tangled web of complex rules he'd never had the occasion — or the need — to learn. Jaire had tried to explain some of it to him in the days leading up to the betrothal ceremony, but Tristin hadn't managed to make sense of any of it yet. He'd already decided the best course of action was to simply keep his mouth shut around anyone who looked to be of the noble class, but if Alys wanted him to entertain Drannik, that strategy wasn't going to work very well.

Life had been a lot less complicated when the only people he'd had to talk to came from his own imagination.

"I'll try, Mistress Alys, but I'm not sure I'll be very good company."

Alys stopped when they reached the suite and patted his arm. "Just keep His Highness's rat out of sight, and I'm sure all will be well." She pushed open the door of the suite before Tristin could respond.

He waited, awkwardly holding the pastry tray while Alys arranged the tea things and poured a cup for Wytch King Drannik.

Alys handed the Wytch King his tea and took the pastry tray from Tristin. "There you are, Your Majesty." She set it down on the low table and set out two plates and two napkins. "If you need anything else, just send Tristin to the kitchen. He's going to keep you company while you wait."

And with that all too brief and surely inadequate introduction, she left him alone with the Wytch King of Rhiva.

"Have a seat, then," Drannik said. "Tristin, is it? Vakha's boy, Garrik says. You certainly have the look of him."

"I... I w-wouldn't know, Your Majesty," Tristin stammered. "I n-never met him. Alys said you were worried. About Mikhyal." Tristin froze, aware that he may have just committed an error. Was he supposed to use Mikhyal's name? Or his title? "Er... I mean, His Royal Highness, Prince Mikhyal."

Drannik's lips twitched. "No need to stand on ceremony, Tristin. You're Garrik's cousin, and he seems to think a lot of you. As does my son."

Tristin's face burned. What did the Wytch King mean by that? Had he heard them last night? He wanted to sink into the floor at the thought. Had he been noisy? He couldn't remember anything but the feel of Mikhyal's hands on his body and the scorching heat burning through him. *Had* he cried out in his ecstasy? "Ah. I... I see. Um."

He stared down at the table in time to see Dirit reaching for a pastry. The little dragon hooked a blackberry tart with one long claw and began dragging it toward him. Tristin glared at him and shook his head ever so slightly.

Not slightly enough, for the motion caught Drannik's attention. The Wytch King followed Tristin's gaze, eyes widening as he leaned forward to peer at the little dragon. Dirit froze, then turned his head, looking first at Tristin and then at Drannik. Very slowly, he unhooked his claw and drew his arm back.

"I was rather hoping you'd be too busy with introductions and awkward conversation to notice my nearly inconsequential transgression." Dirit's eyebrow tufts drew together, and his little pink tongue darted out.

"Amazing," Drannik murmured. "Is this the little creature that lives in the Wytch Sword? The same creature that saved us on the road to Altan?"

"Ai, Your Majesty," Tristin said, relieved to have the king's attention on something besides himself for the moment. "This is

Dirit. Dirit, may I present Wytch King Drannik of Rhiva, Mikhyal's father."

"Yes, I *am* aware," Dirit said, still staring longingly at the pastry. "I've been watching over him, at his Royal Stubbornness's insistence."

"Have you, now? Well, for that and your other services to the royal line of Rhiva, you have my most heartfelt gratitude." Drannik chuckled, a low, rich sound. "Help yourself, Master Dirit. You saved us all when those bandits attacked us on the road. I believe you are owed far more than a bit of pastry."

"Why, *thank* you, Your Most Gracious Majesty." Dirit rose up on his haunches and executed a neat little bow. Formalities completed, he dropped to all fours and minced back to the tray, snagged the tart, and devoured it in three bites. "Mmm, that Alys does have a way with pastry. We shall have to see about hiring her for ourselves, don't you think?"

"I imagine Garrik would have something to say about that," Drannik said with a smile. "I had better taste one and see for myself. Tristin, please sit down. I'm not about to bite you. Though I cannot say the same for Master Dirit, here. Look at those teeth! Quite marvelous."

"The better to defend your line with, Your Majesty," Dirit said. He lifted a claw to his mouth and began licking. "Sticky again. I cannot abide *sticky*." And with that, he faded from sight.

Drannik leaned back in his armchair, still gazing at the spot Dirit had occupied. "Fascinating," he murmured.

He might have said more, but at that moment, the door to the bedroom opened and Ambris slipped out and closed it quietly behind him.

"Prince Ambris." Drannik got to his feet. "How fares Mikhyal?"

"He is very well," Ambris said with a reassuring smile. "He slept through the procedure, and he should wake soon. You may go in and sit with him, if you like. Vayne is just tidying up his inks."

Drannik nodded to Tristin and went off to the bedroom.

"You're looking much brighter than the last time we talked," Tristin said.

Ambris's smile widened. "I'm feeling much brighter, too. Things went better with my father than I expected them to. I was horrified to run into him down at the castle. It was as much of a shock to him as it was to me, but it's turned out to be for the best. He had no idea what was happening at Blackfrost, and not only is he overjoyed to have me back, but he's welcomed Kian into the family, as well. If there wasn't all this alliance business going on, I think he would have liked to stay longer. He's invited us to come and visit the palace at Mir as soon as we can be spared, and of course, he'll be here at harvest, when we reaffirm our vows. Oh, but you already know all that — you were there at dinner."

"I was," Tristin said, "and I was pleased to see him officially welcome you both. I know how wonderful it feels to find a family after believing you have none."

"Garrik and Jaire both seem very fond of you already," Ambris said. "And I couldn't help but notice how much attention Prince Mikhyal was paying you at the betrothal ceremony. I saw you dancing. You make a very handsome couple, if I might say so."

Couple? Tristin's ears went hot. Was that what people thought? "Ah. Well. I think... well. I'm not sure it's... I mean, well. People *will* talk, won't they?"

The knowing look Ambris gave him said he was well aware it was more than talk.

Unable to think of a thing to say, Tristin settled for, "He... he *has* been very kind to me."

Ambris burst out laughing. "Tristin, you are a master of understatement. I'm sorry if I've made you uncomfortable. We can talk about something else, if you'd prefer. Tell me about your plans for the garden. Garrik said Master Ludin has put you in charge of designing a proper garden for Dragonwatch."

Pleased to have something else to talk about, Tristin began detailing his plans, sketching the shapes of the proposed flower beds in the air as he spoke.

I'm going to throw myself off the top of the tower and fly.

It didn't seem real, even though Mikhyal had seen the reflection of the magnificent sapphire-blue dragon tattoo adorning his back. A shiver that was equal parts excitement and dread rippled through him as he followed Tristin and Master Ilya up the smooth-worn stone steps of the watchtower. All three men wore nothing but cloaks.

The clouds parted, and the sun came out just as they emerged on the roof. Mikhyal chose to see that as a good omen as his bare feet slapped on the still-damp stones. He followed Ilya to the edge of the rooftop and stared down at Dragonwatch's courtyard, where Kian waited, already in dragon form. Mikhyal watched in wonder as the muscular black dragon took to the air. Strong enough and large enough to support a foundering dragon, Kian was there in case something went wrong.

Mikhyal tried not to think about that, but as he let his gaze travel down the mountain to the castle so far below, his stomach began to knot in dread. He was truly expected to step off the edge and… and *fly?*

"You'll be fine," Tristin said, reaching for his hand and giving it a gentle squeeze. "Vayne has etched the patterns into your mythe-shadow. Even though your human mind can barely imagine it, your dragon body will know exactly what to do. It feels a bit odd the first time, but all you have to do is let go and let it happen. Ilya and I will be right here with you."

"And Kian is down below," Ilya added. "A precaution we've not needed thus far. Everyone Vayne has transformed has come through the process with the instinctive abilities to shift and fly. Would you like to try shifting now?" Ilya stepped back to give him room, and after giving his hand a final squeeze, Tristin, too, stepped back.

"I cannot wait to see your dragon form," Tristin murmured, meeting Mikhyal's eyes. "You will be *magnificent.*"

"As magnificent as you?" Mikhyal whispered, and Tristin flushed and smiled as Mikhyal undid the ties of the cloak he wore and cast it aside.

"Think about taking dragon form," Ilya said. "You should sense a glowing core of light. Vayne will have given you the patterns and the ability to use them."

Sure enough, a glowing ball of light hung in the back of his mind. Patterns danced around it like golden snowflakes. The one to shift was there, and he instinctively *knew* that in order to shift, he had to take hold of it and mentally *push* it into the light.

The shift was smooth and didn't feel at all strange. Jaire had described it to him as just another way of being, and indeed, that was exactly how it felt. His new form felt familiar in a way Mikhyal couldn't explain, like drawing on a comfortable pair of gloves he'd worn many times before. He knew exactly what to do with it, and though he'd wondered how he would ever manage to walk on four legs instead of two, that, too, felt completely natural.

As natural as gliding through the sky on a river of air.

His fears, it seemed, had been shed along with his human skin. When Mikhyal turned to look out over the mountain slope with his dragon eyes, instead of seeing a suicidal drop, he saw freedom only a leap away.

Tristin came up beside him, already shifted. His iridescent ruby hide gleamed in the sunlight. Mikhyal looked down at himself to see his own sapphire-blue scales shimmering and glinting.

<I knew you would be beautiful.> It was Tristin's voice, but in his head.

Mikhyal didn't even have to think about how to respond; he *knew*, the same way he knew how to launch himself from the top of the tower and let the wind flow beneath his wings to buoy him up. *<I could say the same for you.>*

In dragon form, Tristin couldn't blush, but Mikhyal guessed if he were in his human form, his cheeks would be glowing, and he'd be shuffling his feet and looking everywhere but at Mikhyal. Tristin launched himself into the air. Fear forgotten, Mikhyal followed him with his gaze, hungry to experience flight for himself.

A hard blink brought down the inner eyelids that filtered the light, allowing him to see the air currents as flowing rivers of color. Fascinated, he watched Tristin climb higher and higher, following a lazy spiral of orange, then gliding gracefully down on a river of indigo.

With a trumpeting cry of triumph, Mikhyal leapt off the edge of the tower and spread his wings.

Tristin could barely watch Mikhyal's first attempt at flight. Despite his reassurances to Mikhyal and his own firsthand knowledge of how deeply ingrained his own dragon instincts were, his heart was still hammering in his chest when the sapphire-blue dragon dove off the top of the watchtower.

Mikhyal, however, didn't even hesitate. He spread his wings to catch a rising air current, looking every bit as sleek and graceful as Master Ilya.

<*Look at me, Tristin! Look! I'm flying! Oh, this is wonderful!*>

<*Oh, look at His Royal Dragonness!*> Tristin glanced up to see Dirit flitting alongside him. <*He does make a handsome dragon, doesn't he? Only don't tell him I said so. I'd never hear the end of it.*>

<*You look magnificent,*> Tristin told Mikhyal. He cast a sly, sideways look at Dirit before adding, <*Dirit thinks so, too.*>

Mikhyal's laughter bubbled in his mind. <*Does he, indeed? I believe that's the first compliment the little monster has paid me.*>

Dirit's ears flattened. <*Now you've done it, Prince Tristin of the New Flower Bed. There'll be no living with him after this.*>

While Ilya tested Mikhyal on the basic maneuvers and taught him how to breathe fire, Tristin circled and watched, with Dirit flying alongside him, offering a detailed critique of Mikhyal's performance. It wasn't long before Ilya was satisfied, and Tristin and Mikhyal spent the rest of the afternoon chasing one another through the air and gliding over the mountains. The clouds had moved on, and the sun was warm on his back, a delightful contrast to the cool mountain air. Tristin had never felt quite so alive.

When they finally returned to the watchtower, it was late in the afternoon. Tristin landed lightly on the roof, and Mikhyal touched down beside him only a few moments later. Mikhyal shifted back almost immediately. Mindful of the bright sunlight that would hide nothing, Tristin hesitated. Mikhyal might not have minded his scars in dim lamplight, but now, in the clear light of day, he wasn't so certain.

Mikhyal bent to retrieve their cloaks. His grin was huge, and with his sparkling eyes and tousled hair, he looked like a boy who'd just been given everything he'd ever dreamed of. "That was exhilarating! I can see why you all enjoy it so much." He shot Tristin a questioning look, perhaps wondering why he hadn't shifted back to human form yet.

Before Tristin could decide what to do, Mikhyal's eyes widened. He took a few steps closer to lay Tristin's cloak at his feet, then swung his own cloak over his shoulders and moved aside, turning his back to Tristin to look down over the mountain.

Tristin shifted and snatched up the cloak, which he wrapped quickly around his gaunt frame. "I... you can turn around now. Th-thank you." Face burning, he stared down at his big, bony feet and wished his blushes didn't always give him away.

Mikhyal turned to face him, a gentle smile curving his lips. "The last thing I want to do is make you feel uncomfortable. When can we do this again? My father's expecting me at the castle for dinner tonight, but we should be finished with all the meetings now."

"Tomorrow?" Tristin said hesitantly. "I could... I could ask Alys to make a picnic lunch for us? If... if that would be all right?"

"That sounds wonderful." Mikhyal leaned in to kiss him, but drew back at the sound of a draconic cry in the air above them. He looked up to see the shimmering, opalescent dragon form of Prince Jaire circling the tower.

A few moments later, the prince landed gracefully on the roof. He shifted immediately and went to fetch a cloak from the chest by the stairs. "I saw you two playing in the sky!" Jaire's eyes were bright and his grin was huge as he flung the cloak over his pale, slender shoulders. "You looked magnificent! Mikhyal, you're *beautiful* in the sunlight. Like a glowing sapphire. I thought you'd be green, like Vayne."

"Vayne said some of the patterns already existed within my mythe-shadow," Mikhyal said. "He just reinforced them, rather than having to burn new ones in. He said I might well have been a dragon shifter, had they only been a little stronger."

"Like me and Tristin." Jaire nodded enthusiastically. "I wonder how many members of the other royal families might have the same patterns... and how many dragon shifters were erased from history by the Wytch Council. It might be interesting to ask the kings of the Northern Alliance if they have any old books squirreled away. From before the Council seized power."

"I can certainly open Rhiva's vaults to you, if you're interested," Mikhyal said. "I've only been down there once or twice, myself, so I've no idea what you might find. My father might have a better idea."

"That would be wonderful!" Jaire's eyes sparkled. "I shall have to arrange a visit as soon as I can be spared. Oh... yes, and speaking of your father, he's sent a message for you. That's why I'm here, actually. Vayne's reassured him that you're fit to travel, and His Majesty asked me to let you know he'd like to leave in the morning. He wants you to come down to the castle and speak to him when you've finished practicing."

"Thank you, Jaire," Mikhyal said gravely. "Will I see you at dinner tonight?"

"Ai, I'll be there," Jaire said. "And I can't stay long here if I'm to be ready, but since I'm here, I'm going to the kitchen to see Alys. I do love her blackberry tarts."

"She served a great plate of them to me and Drannik this morning, so there should be some left," Tristin said, smiling. "Assuming, of course, that Dirit hasn't eaten them all."

An offended sniff came from nearby. "I heard that!" Dirit appeared, perched on Jaire's shoulder. "Honestly. I only ate *one*. And only at His Majesty's invitation. Tristin was there. He'll tell you."

"Ah, yes, well, I only actually witnessed the going of one," Tristin said.

Jaire laughed and headed for the stairs. "Come on then, Dirit. We'll see if we can talk Alys into parting with a few more, shall we?"

Mikhyal turned back to Tristin, pulling him into his arms for a kiss. When they broke apart, he pressed his forehead against Tristin's. "I'm sorry, but it sounds like our picnic will have to wait. If things weren't so tense and busy at the moment, I'd stay on for a few more days and follow my father home at my leisure, but I fear what we might be facing once we arrive home. The Dragon Mother only knows what Shaine has been up to in our absence, and we still don't know who was responsible for the attacks."

"Or who the target really was," Tristin reminded him. "You be careful."

"I will. Look, Tristin... I'm the commander of Rhiva's army, so I doubt I'm going to get the chance to get away again, not now that the treaty has been signed and we're putting our defense plans in motion. I fear I'm going to be terribly busy for the foreseeable future. Once things have settled down a bit, and it's safe to travel, I'd love for you to come to the palace for a visit."

Tristin's heart leapt. "I'd like that," he said shyly. "Very much."

"Consider it a promise, then. I'll send word as soon as I can." He lifted Tristin's hand to his lips and kissed his palm.

"The sooner, the better, my prince," Tristin whispered.

Chapter Nine

"Absolutely not." Garrik's black eyes narrowed as he stared down Wytch King Drannik across the breakfast table.

They'd finished eating, and Mikhyal was itching to leave, but his father was not happy with the travel arrangements.

"There have been two attacks and no culprit yet found." Garrik's tone was perfectly reasonable, but his expression was implacable. "My soldiers will escort you all the way to the palace. This is not negotiable, Drannik. I would be remiss in my duty as your host and your ally if I were to allow you to return to your home unprotected."

"If your dragon warriors escort us home," Drannik explained patiently, "then you tip our hand to Wytch Master Anxin, and through him, the Council."

"Assuming it hasn't already been tipped," Garrik said drily.

"They may soon know of the Northern Alliance, but we can hope they do not yet know of our plans for a dragon army." Drannik looked to Mikhyal for support, but Mikhyal was torn. He wanted his father protected on the journey home, but giving away their advantage to the Council before they were ready would be a terrible mistake.

Drannik rolled his eyes at his son, and continued, "If we are to have any chance of taking them by surprise, we must act under the assumption that the Council still knows nothing of the dragon army, which means Wytch Master Anxin cannot be alerted."

Garrik regarded him with a faint frown. "You will be arresting Anxin upon your return. Ilya gave you the blood-chain that will prevent him from using his power, did he not?"

"He did, and given the opportunity, I will use it," Drannik said. "But there is no guarantee I will have the opportunity."

"And that is precisely why I will not loan you horses to make an overland journey. It is not safe. Whoever is behind these attacks waited until you were on the road, and then tried again here. My mind is made up. You will return home on dragonback *with* an escort, or not at all. What if you return to find your palace overrun with Council troops?"

"There hasn't been time," Drannik said. "Shaine is not a skilled enough rider to make the journey in less than ten days. We may even arrive before he does."

"Regardless, I will see you safely home," Garrik said.

Before Drannik could open his mouth to argue, Mikhyal said, "What about a compromise? We travel on dragonback until we reach the estate at Brightwood. That will take, what, about eight hours? And then it's only a two-hour ride from there to the summer palace. At the estate, we can switch to horses, and you and your dragon warriors can head home, or spend the night and head out in the morning. There are guardsmen stationed at the estate, and they can escort us the rest of the way home in safety." He looked from Drannik to Garrik. "Would that suit you both?"

"I would remind you that the first attack occurred within the borders of Rhiva," Garrik said.

Dirit hopped down from his perch on Mikhyal's shoulder and minced across the table toward the pastry tray, where he materialized and addressed Garrik. "I would remind Your Most Gracious Majesty that *I* will see to it that the Wytch King of Rhiva and his heir come to no harm. It is my sacred task to protect them, after all. The presence of you and your dragon warriors, while a most appreciated gesture, is entirely superfluous."

"Thank you, Dirit," Mikhyal murmured.

With a sharp nod, the little dragon settled himself on his belly, head between his outstretched front legs, and gazed longingly at the blackberry tarts.

Garrik burst out laughing. "Well said, Master Dirit. I suppose I cannot argue with a creature who leaves naught but a pile of clean-picked bones behind when those he watches over are in danger. Go on, help yourself to a tart. I know you're quite partial to them."

Dirit sat up very prettily and bobbed his head respectfully. "Why, thank you, Your Most Gracious Majesty. I don't mind if I do."

And with that, the little dragon proceeded to devour three blackberry tarts in very short order. When he'd finished his meal, he carefully groomed his claws and whiskers, much to the amusement of everyone around the table.

"Very well," Garrik said finally. "A compromise, and only because you have such a fierce and valiant little defender. We will escort you as far as Brightwood, and leave you in Dirit's very capable claws for the remainder of the journey."

Dirit made a very proper bow and faded from sight.

Garrik turned to Mikhyal. "I've taken the liberty of having a harness made for you for times when you might wish to travel in dragon form. I believe it is waiting for you in your suite."

"Thank you, Garrik. That's very kind of you," Mikhyal said. "I'd never have thought of that myself."

Back in their suite, Mikhyal and Drannik packed their things in the saddlebags Kian and Garrik would carry. Eager for any excuse to use his new abilities, Mikhyal would have preferred to make the flight in shifted form. Drannik, however, was adamant about keeping Mikhyal's transformation a secret until after Anxin had been dealt with.

When he'd finished packing, Mikhyal examined the harness Garrik had sent up for him. It was identical to those used by Garrik's dragon warriors, with places to attach saddlebags and a cleverly designed holder that would accommodate a sheathed sword and sword belt.

"A handsome gift for a dragon commander," Drannik said, fingering the neatly stitched leather.

"As was the transformation," Mikhyal murmured. "What will they be saying at home, do you suppose? Surely there will be rumors about Dirit's performance during the bandit attack. Shaine knew all about it, although he seemed to be under the impression that my

Wytch power had awakened. When I told him it hadn't, he said Anxin would want to investigate."

"Anxin will have difficulty investigating anything with a blood-chain locked around his scrawny neck." Drannik's smile was grim. "And as for rumors, the only witnesses were the King's Guard, and I forbade them to speak of what they saw."

A knock sounded at the suite door. Mikhyal opened it to find Tristin standing in the hallway. "I'll just be a minute, Father," he called, and didn't wait for an answer before slipping out to join Tristin. The two of them walked a little way down the hall, out of earshot of the guards.

"I, ah, just wanted to see you once more before you leave," Tristin said quietly, cheeks going pink. "I imagine it will be some time before we can see one another again. If there's a war—"

Mikhyal stopped and pressed a finger gently to Tristin's lips. "There *will* be a war," he said quietly. "I fear we cannot avoid it at this point. But our hope is that we can win it quickly and decisively."

"And if you cannot?"

"I will find a way to come and see you. I'll be commanding my troops in the field, but that does not mean I cannot slip away now and then. I am not waiting until the end of the conflict to see you again."

Tristin managed a tremulous smile.

Mikhyal leaned in and pressed a kiss to the corner of his mouth. "We will be together again before you know it," he whispered.

"I hope so," Tristin whispered back, and flung his arms around Mikhyal before tearing himself away and hurrying off down the hall.

Mikhyal stared after him, fingers pressed to his lips, and wished with all his heart that the conflict was over and those he cared for were all safe.

The afternoon sun was warm as Mikhyal, Drannik, and their escort made their way toward the summer palace from Drannik's Brightwood estate later that day. Garrik had clearly been torn about leaving them, and once they'd arrived at Brightwood, he'd renewed his arguments of the morning. In the end, Dirit had materialized and convinced him that he could remove any threat much faster than the Wytch King could, and without the risk of accidentally roasting those he was trying to protect.

The journey had been uneventful thus far, but they were nearing the palace, and despite his assurances to Mikhyal, Drannik was clearly becoming nervous.

When the narrow track through the forest widened enough, he brought his horse up alongside Mikhyal's and said in a low voice, "I don't suppose you can send Dirit ahead to check the palace?"

"Alas, no. He doesn't have that kind of range. When the sword was in our suite at Castle Altan, he could only roam as far as the edge of the castle grounds."

"Unfortunate. They'll have seen us by the time we get that close."

"Dirit will serve us better if he stays nearby," Mikhyal said. "He's been patrolling our immediate surroundings ever since we left Brightwood, you know."

"Has he?"

"Every so often, he comes to perch on my shoulder to assure me that all is well."

Drannik nodded and lapsed into thoughtful silence.

Mikhyal dared not bring up the possibility of facing an armed force at the palace. He was certain his father was already brooding upon the possibility. Personally, Mikhyal would welcome an open challenge. It would be far less nerve-wracking than having to constantly watch his own back and his father's.

Did the fact that both of the attacks had occurred far from the palace mean their enemies hadn't been able to penetrate the palace security? Or was that only what they were meant to think?

Perhaps it would have been better to follow the queen to Castle Rhivana in the mountains. Though Mikhyal loved the summer palace, it wasn't nearly as secure as the castle. A sprawling, mostly single-level construction of light stone and pale, polished wood, the palace boasted open breezeways and large windows to let in the cool summer breezes of the northern forest. Many of the rooms opened out into courtyards and walled gardens. The entire compound was surrounded by a high, heavily guarded wall, but Rhu had confided in Mikhyal many times that the place was a security nightmare. She hated it, and would much rather have the royal family safe at the castle year round.

Mikhyal was in complete agreement, but he'd given up suggesting it to Drannik, who wouldn't dream of giving his enemies the pleasure of seeing him run for the safety of his castle like a whipped dog.

As they came in sight of the palace wall, a group of guardsmen rode out to meet them, joining the Brightwood escort. They rode through the main gates and into the courtyard with a clatter of hooves. Shaine awaited them in front of the main doors, Wytch Master Anxin at his side.

A vague feeling of disquiet stirred in Mikhyal's belly as he swung down from his horse and two men in the uniform of the King's Guard — men he didn't recognize — moved closer, as if to assist him.

"Put your weapons down, Mikhyal. And you, Father." Shaine's voice was loud and steady, and Mikhyal turned his head to see his brother approaching. Behind him, Anxin stood watching, a small, satisfied smile on his face.

Mikhyal's hand dropped to the hilt of the Wytch Sword, but Shaine said, "I wouldn't do that if I were you. There are crossbowmen on the roof."

With a sinking heart, Mikhyal looked up to the roof overlooking three sides of the courtyard. At least a dozen men were arrayed around the perimeter, their weapons trained on the king and his son.

"Cooperate, and no one will be hurt," Shaine said.

"Oh, I think not," Dirit whispered in Mikhyal's ear.

"What is the meaning of—" Drannik's words cut off abruptly as a fog descended over the courtyard.

Screams filled the air, echoing off the stone walls of the palace. Mikhyal could see nothing through the fog. He squeezed his eyes shut and loosened the reins of his borrowed horse, afraid the animal might try to bolt, but the mare didn't seem at all bothered.

The screaming ceased abruptly. Mikhyal's breath hitched as he opened his eyes. The men on the roof were gone, and the courtyard was filled with neat little piles of polished bone, gleaming in the sunlight. His father stood not ten paces away, face pale, eyes wide. The guardsmen they'd brought from Brightwood shifted position until they were surrounding Mikhyal and his father, all of them scanning the courtyard for further threats.

In front of the main doors, Wytch Master Anxin sat slumped, the blood-chain Master Ilya had given Drannik locked around his neck. Beside him, on his knees, with his hands bound behind him, was Shaine, eyes wide with shock.

Drannik recovered first. "Go and see what the situation inside is," he ordered their escort. "Carefully — they may have set up another ambush within."

"There is no ambush inside, Your Majesty," Dirit said, materializing on the back of Drannik's horse. Dangling from one claw was a ring of keys, which he offered to the king. "Not anymore."

"Thank you, Master Dirit," Drannik said, taking the keys.

"I have removed the traitors from the palace," Dirit said. "You'll want to check the dungeons at your earliest convenience. You've quite a few loyal men locked in the cells."

"You," Drannik said, pointing to four of the Brightwood guards. "Take the Wytch Master and Prince Shaine to the dungeon, and release the King's Guard." He offered the most senior of them the ring of keys.

Both Shaine and Wytch Master Anxin appeared to be in shock. They had to be pulled to their feet and guided into the palace.

Mikhyal choked down bile as he regarded the courtyard. Piles of bone lay everywhere, but there was nothing to distinguish one from another. No clothing, no weapons, in fact, the only thing that seemed to have survived Dirit's swift, uncompromising defense of the men he was bound to protect was the ring of keys he'd given to the king. How many men loyal to Rhiva had Dirit destroyed in his defense of the royal bloodline?

He glanced over at Dirit and found the little dragon watching him. "Don't mourn them, Your Highness. They were all Drachan. Council troops, dressed in the uniforms of the King's Guard."

"How can you be sure?"

One eyebrow tuft twitched. "They have a certain… *flavor.*"

Mikhyal's stomach churned as he moved slowly through the courtyard. "Does Shaine have the same flavor?"

Dirit's snout wrinkled. "I would have to eat him to find out. Would you like me to?"

"No, Dirit, that won't be necessary. He'll be quite safe in the dungeon."

A few moments later, Rhu arrived, followed by the rest of the King's Guard. They were all dressed in rumpled, ill-fitting clothing, and Rhu looked furious.

"Your Highness, Your Majesty," she said, executing a bow. "Thank the Dragon Mother you're safe. I feared Prince Shaine meant to be rid of you both."

"We were drugged," Rhu said as she stood before the king. She and the rest of the King's Guard had been given time to tidy themselves and don their uniforms, and now she and her lieutenant, Takla, were reporting to Drannik and Mikhyal in the king's study. "My best guess is they drugged either the food or the ale we were given for dinner. We woke to find ourselves in the dungeon. That was two nights ago."

"Two nights?" Mikhyal frowned at Drannik, then at Rhu. "When he arrived in Altan, Shaine told me he'd arrested you before he left the palace."

"He lied, Your Highness. He made no move here until he returned from Altan, two days ago. Everyone I was able to talk to reported the same experience: a wave of sleepiness, and then nothing until we all woke up in the cells yesterday morning. Anxin's doing, I'd imagine."

"I wonder how much Shaine overheard when he was in Altan," Mikhyal said grimly. "And whether or not he's sent word of it to the Council yet."

"If Anxin is involved — and I have no doubts about that — he will not have sent word yet," Drannik said. "Anxin never notifies the

Council of anything he attempts until he is certain of a favorable outcome. And he will not have expected us to arrive this quickly."

"He may not have expected us to arrive at all," Mikhyal said. "Why else would Shaine have brought an escort of men I never approved, rather than the King's Guard? Drachan, I imagine, if the men awaiting us here were any indication. With orders to see us dead. Possibly within the borders of Altan, so Garrik would be blamed."

"A foul plot, indeed," Drannik growled.

"Your Majesty, may I speak freely?" Rhu asked, and at Drannik's nod, continued, "I've considered Prince Shaine to be a possible risk to your security ever since the accident last summer. The men of the King's Guard have observed enough inconsistencies in his behavior to put us on edge. It would not surprise me in the least to learn he was involved in the ambush of the royal caravan."

"Thank you for your honesty, Rhu." The king let out a heavy sigh and turned to his son. "Mikhyal, arrange for Anxin and Shaine to be transported to Mir as soon as possible."

"Very well, Father." Much as it grieved him, Mikhyal could see no other option; Shaine's treachery could have undone the Northern Alliance before it had even begun. "Since we have no idea how much Shaine overheard in Altan, and no knowledge of Anxin's resources here in Rhiva, I will accompany the prison caravan. I can scout ahead in dragon form and protect our men in the event of an attack."

Rhu turned a speculative eye on him. "Dragon form, Your Highness?"

"Ai. We'd rather not have it leaked to the Wytch Council, but I suppose word of it will get out soon enough." Mikhyal gave Rhu and Takla a brief overview of the events of the past few weeks: his bond with the Wytch Sword and Dirit, the forging of the Northern Alliance, the attempt on Drannik's life, and his own transformation.

Rhu's eyes got wider and wider as the story unfolded.

"It is Garrik's aim to build an army of dragon shifters," Mikhyal finished. "We will be accepting volunteers from across the Northern Alliance. I'll be giving the men a demonstration and asking them to consider volunteering as soon as we've delivered Shaine and the Wytch Master to Mir."

"You've had an eventful few weeks, Your Highness," she said when he'd finished. "I'm pleased to see you've managed to survive the experience." She cast a dubious look at the sword belted to his hip. "I don't suppose I'll have to worry about you losing your edge anymore, will I?"

Mikhyal laughed. "No, you won't. I have quite a fierce little protector right here." He gave the Wytch Sword an almost affectionate pat. "Now, Father, if you don't mind, I'd like to change and unpack my things. After that, Captain Rhu, Lieutenant Takla, and I have a prison caravan to organize, so I'll see you at dinner."

Drannik's dark brows drew together. "When do you intend to leave?"

"The sooner the better. By now, Faah will be on his way to Mir. I would not delay the delivery of the Northern Alliance's first official message to the Council. We'll let the men have a good night's sleep to recover from their time in the cells, and leave first thing in the morning."

"Having only just gained the heir of my choice, I find myself loathe to allow you to put yourself at risk," Drannik said slowly. "But as your little defender has proved himself so capable, I will not quarrel with you."

"Thank you, Father."

Mikhyal made his way back to his apartment with Dirit perched on his shoulder. In the bedroom, the little dragon curled up on the bed, watching Mikhyal pack the things he'd need into a small, leather backpack which would be loaded on the supply wagon. As he'd be spending most of his waking hours in dragon form, a few changes of clothing and his weapons should be sufficient.

"Well, at least there's no argument about whether or not I should accompany the prison carriage to Mir," Mikhyal said to Dirit.

"Did you expect there to be?" Dirit asked. "As your father said: I've proved myself *extremely* capable. You have nothing to worry about as long as *I* am protecting you, Your Royal Adventurousness."

❖ ❖ ❖

Mikhyal could hardly bear to watch his brother being led into the courtyard from the dungeons, but as the commander of Rhiva's army, he didn't have the luxury of hiding away. He stood stiffly next to his father, whose face was impassive as he watched the prisoners being escorted to the waiting prison carriage.

Shaine shuffled past, blinking in the bright sunlight. His head was bowed, and the guards on either side of him were helping support him. Heavy chains bound his wrists and ankles, and the anzaria he'd been given to prevent him from touching the mythe had clearly left him dazed and dizzy.

When he reached Mikhyal, Shaine lifted his head briefly. His pale green eyes were dull, his shoulders slumped in defeat. Not even a trace of the brother Mikhyal had once loved so fiercely remained in those eyes.

Shaine didn't speak, which was just as well; Mikhyal had no words to express either his disappointment or his grief. There would be no coming back for Shaine, and the loss of that last tiny flicker of hope was a cruel blow. Shaine's actions yesterday had crushed any remaining hope Mikhyal might have harbored, leaving him with nothing but the bitter knowledge that the brother he loved was truly lost to him.

Anxin came next, still wearing the blood-chain Ilya had supplied. He, too, appeared defeated and subdued.

Dirit must have sensed Mikhyal's mood, for the little dragon was nowhere to be seen. The Wytch Sword was nearby, already secured in its place on the harness Rhu had brought out in preparation for Mikhyal's departure.

Once the prisoners were secured inside the carriage, the guardsmen assigned to escort them mounted up, and the carriage rolled out of the courtyard and onto the road.

"Well, that's done," Drannik said as the last of the escort passed through the gates. "You had better have Rhu see to your harness if you still intend to accompany them."

"I do, but only as far as Mir," Mikhyal assured his father. "Garrik's sending a contingent of dragon warriors to take over from there. I should be back within ten days or so."

"Good." Drannik embraced him briefly. "Give my regards to Edrun, and then hurry home. There is much work to do. May Aio protect you."

"And you, Father."

Drannik left the courtyard, and Mikhyal nodded to Rhu and quickly stripped out of his clothing and shifted. Rhu politely averted her eyes until he snorted at her to let her know he was ready.

She strapped the harness on and checked that the Wytch Sword was properly secured. "You'll do, Your Highness. Be careful out there. We're going to need you."

Mikhyal dipped his head and waited until Rhu had stepped back before launching himself into the air.

Mikhyal didn't sleep well that night. He couldn't stop staring at the prison carriage. Was Shaine also lying awake in the darkness, perhaps regretting the choices he'd made over the past year? Or wasn't there enough left of the brother he'd loved to feel regret?

Dawn finally arrived, and the men rose from their bedrolls to break camp. Mikhyal dressed quickly and approached Lieutenant Takla.

"Before we get underway again, I'd like to take to the air and scout ahead to check the surrounding forest and make sure nothing's crept up on us in the night."

Takla pursed his lips. "Is there any point, Commander? Yesterday you complained of not being able to see anything through the forest canopy."

"Yes, *do* listen to the lieutenant," Dirit counseled from his perch on Mikhyal's shoulder. "There is no reason to scout. I will be flying ahead of the procession, and I promise you, if anything is hiding in the forest, I will find it and deal with it long before it can threaten you."

Mikhyal ignored him and focused on Takla. "Ai, but the Wytch Sword can help me with that. I'm afraid you'll have to indulge me, Lieutenant. I'd never forgive myself if we were caught in an ambush I could have seen if I'd only taken a few minutes to look for it. That's how they got the drop on us on the way to Altan, you know. They were hidden in the forest, not far from the place we'd stopped for the night."

The lieutenant looked doubtful, but once Mikhyal had shifted, he helped him into the harness and fastened the straps. Mikhyal stood still and tried to be patient while the complicated leather contraption was draped over him and the straps adjusted so they were comfortable. Finally, Takla was satisfied. He checked the Wytch Sword was secure one last time, then patted Mikhyal on the flank and said, "Good enough."

Mikhyal swung his head around to glare at Takla, who gave him a sheepish look and a slight shrug.

"Sorry, Commander. When I see you like this, I can't help but think of you as a rather magnificent steed."

Uncertain as to whether he should take offense, Mikhyal snorted and took to the air.

Scouting from the air was a grand idea in theory, but the reality had proved to be problematic. For one thing, much of their route toward Mir took them through dense forest. While Mikhyal could keep track of the prison carriage winding its way along the road, he couldn't see through the dense canopy to either side. Dirit, however, could go wherever he wished, and Mikhyal was relying on the little dragon to tell him if anything lurked beneath the trees.

While Dirit explored the forest below, Mikhyal scanned the treetops for any sign of smoke, or for a clearing where a group of armed men might make camp.

<I'm not seeing anything suspicious from up here,> he reported. <What about you, Dirit?>

<Nothing so far, Your Royal Recklessness.> Dirit's mind-voice dripped with disapproval. <But I shall be sure to — oh, do watch out!>

The bolt came out of the dense canopy of green, tearing through the delicate membrane of his right wing. A second bolt quickly followed, this one lodging in his chest. The tough hide and the thick layer of muscle underneath it prevented the bolt from piercing his heart, but the pain was enough to cause every muscle in his body to seize up.

Dirit was beside him in an instant, flitting about and chittering away about a crossbowman hidden in the trees. Mikhyal was too busy struggling to slow his descent to wonder why Dirit hadn't simply eaten the man. He crashed through the canopy, his thick dragon hide protecting him from being impaled by twigs and branches.

The impact with the ground was hard enough to stun him. Worse, the burning cold spreading slowly through his body from the wound suggested he'd been poisoned.

No choice but to shift. If he shifted, he'd heal, though he'd be naked and helpless in his human skin for as long as that took. He dithered for only a few moments before instinct overruled intellect. The shift wasn't nearly as smooth as usual, and it took longer than it should for him to feel the sharp twigs on the forest floor poking his human skin.

He lay amid a tangle of leather straps, the Wytch Sword underneath him. His wounds had healed in the shift, but the poison was still burning through his veins, and his vision was beginning to blur. Mikhyal vaguely remembered Vayne warning him that while the shift could heal even the most grievous physical injuries, it could neutralize only the simplest poisons.

He started to roll over in an attempt to free the Wytch Sword.

"Don't move," said an unfamiliar voice.

Mikhyal looked up to find himself staring at the business end of a crossbow. The man holding it was dressed like a common bandit, though the way he held himself suggested he might be something more. Why in the Dragon Mother's name hadn't Dirit dealt with him?

He reached for his center, intending to shift and roast the man, but it was gone. The glowing ball of power burning within him was nowhere to be found.

"Do as he says," Dirit hissed in his ear. "I cannot help you. I have never encountered a human like this before... *all* living things have a mythe-shadow... he *must* have a mythe-shadow, and yet he does not. I cannot eat him for you."

"Shift again and you're dead," the soldier told him.

A heavy paralysis crept through Mikhyal's limbs and his mind, making everything feel heavy and slow. "What do you want?" he demanded, words slurring as his tongue began to go numb. His attacker said nothing, merely stood there waiting, crossbow pointed at Mikhyal's chest.

Mikhyal's mind screamed for action, but his body refused to obey. Soon, a warm lassitude spread over him, dulling his senses and sapping his strength. His mind ceased to protest as the darkness slowly engulfed him.

"What do you make of this?" Master Ludin held out a limp, torn leaf.

Tristin took it and examined it carefully. "It looks almost as if something's eaten it. Except..." he peered at it more closely, noting the red, powdery substance at the very edges of the tears. "I don't think bite marks would have left that red powder along the edges, would they?"

"Very good, m'lord."

In the two days since Mikhyal and his father had departed, Tristin had spent almost every waking hour in the gardens. When Garrik had first introduced him to Master Ludin, the old man had been quite distressed at the notion that the Wytch King's cousin meant to get dirt on his royal hands. It had taken the Wytch King himself to reassure Master Ludin that working in the garden was what Tristin wanted, and that the healers were of the opinion that it would help complete his recovery. Once that was understood, Tristin and Master Ludin had become fast friends. But the old man still refused to call Tristin by his name.

"It's a fungus," Master Ludin said. "I've seen no sign of it on the other plants, so we may have caught it before it can spread. We'll treat it and keep a careful watch on the rest. I thought this morning I'd show you how to mix a paste we can smear on the leaves to kill the fungus."

Tristin hesitated for a few moments before asking tentatively, "Would...would smearing it on the leaves of the uninfected plants prevent them from succumbing?"

"It would indeed, and that will be our job this afternoon."

"Tristin!"

Tristin turned to see Prince Jaire standing at the greenhouse door, his face pale and strained. "What's wrong, Jaire?"

"We need to talk." The prince's gaze flicked to Master Ludin. "Quietly, if you please."

Tristin excused himself and followed Jaire outside. Jaire shut the greenhouse door, and they'd only gone a few steps before he said, "Dirit's in trouble."

Tristin went cold. "What kind of trouble?"

"I don't know." Jaire's voice was high and tense. "He's frightened and frustrated, but that's all I can tell."

"Can you talk to him? When you're shifted, I mean?"

"No, I tried already. He's in Rhiva... it's much too far away. I... I felt something odd yesterday afternoon, but it was there and gone so quick, I wasn't sure if I'd imagined it. But this is different. It's been going on since breakfast, and it's only getting worse. What if something's happened to Mikhyal? We have to go to him."

"*Now?*" Tristin stared at Jaire. "It will take us all day to get to Rhiva."

"Yes. If we leave now, we'll arrive just after dark."

"Shouldn't we check with Garrik first? I don't think—"

"Garrik will have to have a meeting and a committee, and he'll want discussions and maps and... and I don't think we can wait." Jaire bit his lip. "If you won't come with me, I'll go alone."

"You really think it's that serious?"

"I don't *know*," Jaire said, shaking his head again. "But Dirit's really frightened, and knowing what he can do, I can't think of anything much that would frighten him. We *must* go and help."

Tristin dithered for only a few moments. If Dirit was in trouble, then it stood to reason that Mikhyal was also in trouble. "Very well. Should we pack anything?"

"What would we bring?" Jaire asked. "Neither of us is any good with weapons. We're only dangerous in dragon form."

"Fair point. What about a change of clothes?"

"Mikhyal's in trouble, and you're worried about your clothes?"

"No, but think for a moment," Tristin said. "We can't land too close to the palace. They won't be expecting us, and if there's been a coup of some sort, do we really want to show ourselves to the Council? Better if we land a short distance from the castle, get dressed, and walk the rest of the way. It'll only take a few minutes for us to fetch some clothing."

"I'm not going back inside," Jaire said. "If Ilya sees me, he'll know something's wrong. You can fetch clothing for both of us. Pack it in my saddlebags and bring my harness. It's a long flight, and I'd rather not have to hold a bag in my claws all the way there. I'll wait for you at Riverwatch."

Tristin frowned. "Where's that?"

"The watchtower just across the river from Dragonwatch. It's all falling apart, so don't try to land on the roof. I'll wait for you at the bottom of the tower." Jaire began unlacing the ties at the neck of his shirt.

Tristin waited for him to undress and shift, then gathered up the prince's clothing and boots to pack up and bring with him. Jaire launched himself into the air. The trees prevented Tristin from following his progress, but he imagined the prince would be flying as close to the treetops as possible to avoid being spotted.

With a heavy sigh, Tristin started back toward the castle.

Mikhyal jolted awake. His mind was fuzzy, his mouth was parched, and he was freezing cold. He stared into the dimness and dredged his memory for some hint of where he might be.

He was lying naked in a heap of straw in a stuffy, dark room — no, that lurching motion that kept pushing him against the wall suggested he was in a wagon of some sort...

It all came back to him in a slow cascade of memories: Dirit's hissed warning, the bolt piercing his chest, his fall through the canopy, the crossbowman standing over him...

He was inside the prison carriage.

And it was moving.

Every rut in the road made the vehicle lurch, sending shards of pain lancing through Mikhyal's head. His whole body ached, and he rolled over, struggling to find a comfortable position. Straw and dirt stuck to his sweat-slick skin, and something tugged at his neck. It was a slim metal collar, and he shuddered as his fingers slid over smooth, ice-cold stones. This was a blood-chain, probably the very same one they'd locked around Anxin's neck. It would prevent him from touching the fiery core inside himself and shifting.

Shifting...

His heart stuttered. He'd shifted back to human form on the forest floor after he'd been shot...

Where was the Wytch Sword?

Mikhyal felt about himself, but there was nothing in the carriage but the pile of straw he lay on. Was the deep cold gripping him an effect of the blood-chain? Or was it coming from the increasing distance between himself and Dirit?

Dirit's absence suggested the latter.

Panicked, Mikhyal scrambled to his knees, groaning as his stiff muscles protested the sudden movement. Where were they taking him? A heavy iron cuff was locked around his ankle and bolted to the carriage floor by a length of chain just long enough to let him crawl to the door. The tiny barred window was too small to allow for much air flow, and he could see nothing but thick forest moving by. Nausea and dizziness forced him back down to the floor.

The light coming in the window was beginning to dim before the bone-jarring motion of the carriage finally changed. Mikhyal was thrown to one side, hitting the wall as the vehicle lurched off the road. Pain shot through his skull, and stars exploded in his head.

By the time the pain receded, the sickening motion had stopped. Someone barked orders to open the carriage, and a key rattled in the lock. Moments later, the door opened, letting in cool, fresh air and dim, evening light.

"Looks all right to me," an unfamiliar male voice called.

"See that he gets some water. And something to eat, I suppose. He'll need his strength to answer the Council's questions." That voice he knew: Wytch Master Anxin.

"Let me see him." And that was Shaine. His brother pushed the Wytch Master aside and peered into the carriage, holding up a lantern. Mikhyal blinked at the light, but the fog dragging at his mind made both thought and speech impossible.

"He looks sick." Shaine frowned. "Are you sure he's all right?"

"It's the blood-chain," Anxin said. "And we dare not remove that."

Shaine stared down at him, his features softening. He started to reach out. "Mik, I—"

"Shaine." Anxin's voice was soft, but Shaine jerked his hand back as if he'd been burned. "Go and wait inside the shelter. I need to speak with your brother alone."

Shaine handed Anxin the lantern and retreated.

"Get him out," Anxin ordered.

Still naked, Mikhyal was dragged from the carriage and forced to stand before the Wytch Master, half supported by the men who flanked him.

Anxin's face betrayed no emotion as he studied Mikhyal with sharp, dark eyes. "What foul weapon did you use to kill my men at the palace? And who gave it to you? Garrik of Altan, was it?"

Mikhyal shook his head and pressed his lips together.

Anxin nodded, and the man his right drove a fist into Mikhyal's gut. The pain was enough to steal his breath away and bring tears to his eyes. Only the men gripping his arms stopped him from collapsing to his knees.

"You will answer," Anxin said softly. "If not me, then a Council Inquisitor. And you will tell them everything you know. It will go easier on you if you speak willingly."

"I would rather die," Mikhyal ground out.

Anxin laughed. "Oh, no, Mikhyal of Rhiva. Dying is not an option. Not for you."

If they took him too far from the Wytch Sword, it might be. Should he point that out?

No. He knew too much about the Northern Alliance's plans. Better to die of mythe-shock on the journey than betray the Northern Alliance in the Council's dungeons. If Anxin thought it was the effect of the blood-chain, then so much the better.

At another nod from Anxin, Mikhyal was thrown back into the carriage. The door slammed shut, leaving him in near-darkness once more. He curled up in the straw and closed his eyes, shivering with cold. His duty was clear, his only regret that there would be no more dances with Tristin.

Chapter Ten

Tristin and Jaire had been airborne for less than an hour when Jaire faltered in the air. For one heart-stopping moment, Tristin thought he was going to plummet to the ground, but with a great flap of his opalescent wings, Jaire righted himself and recovered his rhythm.

<*Are you all right?*> Tristin slowed until he was flying level with Jaire and eyed him with concern. <*Do we need to stop?*>

<*I'm not sure. Dirit feels... he's not just afraid now. He's in pain.*>

<*Why?*> Tristin's heart stuttered. <*What's happened? What about Mikhyal?*>

<*I can't tell which of them is hurting, but I don't think it matters. They're bonded. Vayne told me about it. If one of them is injured or... or worse, the other would feel it, maybe be thrown into shock. Maybe even...*> Jaire didn't finish the thought, but with two mighty beats of his wings, he pulled ahead of Tristin. <*We have to hurry! We might not have much time!*>

Tristin needed no more urging than that. He blinked hard, bringing his inner eyelids down, and studied the colors of the air currents to determine which would assist him the most. Jaire must have had the same thought, for they both turned toward a ribbon of yellow-green streaming east, toward Rhiva.

They flew in silence, communicating only when they needed to adjust speed or direction, or when Jaire had something to report. Dirit's condition seemed to be deteriorating as the day wore on. The lack of information was maddening, and Tristin's dragon belly was a burning, writhing knot of anxiety, which only grew hotter and tighter with every report from Jaire.

In the early afternoon, as they crossed into Rhiva, heavy clouds began to build. Tristin eyed the darkening sky. A storm would ground them, and he couldn't bear the thought of anything preventing him from reaching Mikhyal.

Jaire, too, eyed the sky. <We have to beat the storm, Tristin. We don't have time to wait it out.>

<What are you getting from Dirit?>

<My sense of him is flickering in and out. It ought to be getting stronger as we get closer, not weaker. If I lose him entirely...>

<Then we'll have to start at the palace and go from there.> The thought made Tristin's belly churn. What if the Council had already moved against Rhiva? What if they approached only to be seized and imprisoned? Worse, what if they were shot down? How would Garrik ever know what had happened to them?

He wished now that he'd thought things through before leaving, and perhaps told someone.

It was well into the evening when Jaire said, <We're close... come on!> He veered south and circled a small clearing. <Down here! Dirit! Dirit, it's Jaire, I'm here!>

Tristin followed Jaire down into the clearing where they found Mikhyal's empty harness and the Wytch Sword lying atop a broken tree limb. Of the prince of Rhiva, there was no sign.

Jaire didn't shift, but moved toward the harness and nudged it. Something pale and nearly transparent flickered on the ground next to the Wytch Sword.

<Is... that you... Prince Jaire?> It was a very sorry-looking Dirit that appeared in the middle of the tangle of straps and buckles, flickering in and out of sight. The little dragon's once-bright silver scales had dulled to grey, and he was almost transparent. His ghostly appearance reminded Tristin of the way Prince Vayne had appeared when he'd been trapped in the mythe.

<Dirit, what's happened?> Jaire exclaimed.

<His Royal Highness... escorting Wytch Master's prison carriage... trouble most dire...> Dirit's voice was heavy and slow, as if every word was an effort almost beyond his energy.

<What kind of trouble?> Tristin asked, stomach clenching as his worst fears were confirmed.

<Ambushed.> Dirit groaned. *<Shot down. Poisoned... invisible soldier... casts no shadow in the mythe... never encountered... one like that before... could not sense him... could not fight him. Could only... watch him carry His Royal Highness away. Too far... bond is fraying... will break soon... he will die.>*

Jaire shot Tristin an anguished look, then turned back to Dirit. *<Can you lead us to him? Can you point the way?>*

Dirit looked down at the Wytch Sword. *<You must... bring this. Fly... that way.>* The little dragon pointed with one extended claw toward the southwest. *<I will... get stronger as you get closer... come to you... when I can.>*

<I'll get the sword,> Tristin said, and shifted back to human form before Jaire could. "You're the one with the harness, and if time is against us, we don't want to have to worry about getting you strapped up again."

Jaire nodded in understanding and waited while Tristin bent to retrieve the Wytch Sword. The moment Tristin's fingers closed on the grip, a flash of desperate fury followed by the sense of a fierce, ongoing struggle nearly overwhelmed him. It was a horribly familiar sensation. Tristin squeezed his eyes shut and pushed the most complex shielding pattern he knew into place the way Ilya had taught him.

When he opened his eyes again, he was on his knees, and Jaire was nudging him gently with his snout.

"I'm all right," Tristin managed to gasp out. "Thanks to Ilya's lessons. But someone besides Mikhyal has touched this blade." He raised his eyes to look at Jaire. "The same person who threw that knife at Wytch King Drannik in Altan."

Jaire cocked his head, but Tristin didn't expect to hear a response. None of the shifters he'd met could hear dragon mind-voices when they were in their human forms.

Dirit flared brightly, and for just a moment, he looked almost solid. "Prince Jaire wants to know... if you can tell... who it was."

"I'm afraid not," Tristin said apologetically. "Not any more than I could the first time I sensed it. But the anger, the sense of futile struggle... it's the same feeling. The same... *flavor*, if you will. But that must wait. We have more important concerns at the moment."

With his mind properly protected, Tristin picked up the sword once more and secured it to Jaire's harness. Mikhyal's harness went into one of Jaire's saddlebags. He checked Jaire's straps once more before shifting back into dragon form so that he and Jaire could confer without making Dirit translate.

<We can't go on to the palace for help,> Jaire said. <That will only strain the bond even more, and if we tell Drannik what's happening, he'll be as bad as Garrik with meetings and plans. You go on to the palace and let them know what's happened, and I'll follow Dirit to Mikhyal.>

<That's a dreadful idea, Cousin,> Tristin said flatly. <Garrik would never forgive me if I let you go alone.> In fact, Garrik would probably never forgive either of them for going this far without telling him, though Tristin didn't bother to give voice to that thought; Jaire knew as well as he did what Garrik's reaction to their adventure would be. <We have no idea who has taken Mikhyal, though I can guess Rhiva's Wytch Master might have had something to do with it. If we're going up against a Wytch Master, two dragons are more likely to succeed than one.> Especially one as gentle as Jaire, who was untried in battle, and might not be able to bring himself to kill, even to save his own life.

<Three...> said a weak little voice. Tristin glanced about and saw Dirit perched on Jaire's head, still flickering in and out of sight. <Three dragons... once we get... closer to His Royal Highness... my strength will return... I shall turn his captors... into pretty little piles... of bones.>

<Three,> Jaire said, dipping his head in acknowledgment. <Let us be off, then.>

Tristin glided low over the trees. Just off his right wingtip, Jaire kept pace with him, Dirit perched on his head. The little dragon was no longer flickering, and the closer they drew to Mikhyal, the more he perked up.

<Veer left a bit,> Dirit said, his mind-voice sounding much stronger than it had when they'd first found him. *<Toward that tree sticking up above the rest. See it?>*

He did see it, and thought for perhaps the dozenth time since they'd taken to the air with Dirit that it was a very good thing dragons could see in the dark. Lightning-laced storm clouds hung low in the sky, and the air felt thick and heavy.

Tristin banked left, aiming for the tree, and a moment later, Jaire followed suit. Dirit's directions had nothing to do with roads; he was going by the only guide he had: the tug of the bond he shared with Mikhyal.

It wasn't long before Jaire said, *<I sense someone up ahead.>*

<Mikhyal?> Tristin asked quickly.

<No… it feels like a Wytch Master.>

<That will be Anxin,> Dirit hissed. *<They will have set him free. How many do you sense with him, Prince Jaire?>*

<Anxin is strong enough to overwhelm everything else. I can't pick out any individuals.>

<What of Mikhyal?> Tristin's heart hammered in his chest. *<Can you sense him?>*

<No, sorry.> Jaire sounded apologetic. *<I can't.>*

<He is there,> Dirit said. *<My sense of him is muffled and faint, but I feel him.>*

<Is he conscious?> Tristin asked.

<I can't tell,> Dirit said. *<They may have drugged him. Or perhaps used that horrible blood-chain. If they've any sense at all, they will have made certain he can't shift.>*

<If he's wearing a blood-chain, I'm surprised you can sense him at all,> Jaire said.

<The bond runs far deeper in the mythe than any human-made device can reach,> Dirit said. *<Only death can cut him off from me entirely.>*

Only death… Tristin shivered. It wouldn't come to that. It couldn't. There were too many things he still needed to say to Mikhyal, too many hours they hadn't spent together, too many dances left to dance.

<There!> Dirit launched himself from Jaire's head to fly out in front of them, pointing to a clearing just ahead. *<See the shelter? Circle*

*it. Keep low, and don't get too close. You don't want the Wytch Master
sensing you. I'll go down and have a look.>*

The little dragon disappeared before either of them could protest.

With a silent curse, Tristin followed Jaire in and circled the clearing, gliding just above the trees. The shelter was close to the road, with a fenced pasture behind it for the horses. The carriage sat maybe thirty paces away from the shelter, and the guardsmen had arranged their bedrolls around it. Ten paces beyond the carriage was a campfire.

<I suppose there will be sentries,> Tristin said, studying the heavy canopy. Not even the excellent night vision of his dragon form could pierce through the dense treetops.

<Probably,> Jaire replied. *<We should wait for Dirit. He'll tell us how many we're dealing with.>*

Dirit appeared just after the first low growl of thunder rolled across the sky. He perched on the end of Tristin's snout and said, *<We are badly outnumbered, so we shall have to be sneaky and underhanded.>*

<If it saves Mikhyal's life, I'm quite willing to be sneaky and underhanded,> Tristin said.

<So am I,> Jaire agreed, though his mind-voice wavered, as if he wasn't quite certain of that.

<Anxin and Shaine are asleep inside the shelter,> Dirit reported. *<There are six sentries hidden in the trees around the clearing, about twenty paces out, and six more sleeping beside the carriage. Not that His Royal Highness is going anywhere. I couldn't rouse him.>* Dirit sounded worried. *<He's wearing that horrible collar, and they've chained his ankle to a heavy ring fixed inside the carriage.>*

<Can you get rid of the sentries?> Jaire asked. *<The same way you got rid of the bandits?>*

The little dragon nodded. *<I can, but they are too far apart for me to take them all together. I shall have to deal with them one at a time, very quietly. The man who shot down His Royal Highness is with the group by the campfire. One of you will have to deal with him, for I cannot. He is completely cut off from the mythe.>*

<I can take the ones by the campfire,> Tristin said.

<You must wait until I've finished,> Dirit cautioned. *<If the Wytch Master wakes up, he will sense the disturbance I make in the mythe. He will not be able to stop me, but he will come and have a look. You may have to fight him.>*

<What about going after the Wytch Master first?> Tristin suggested.

<Bad idea,> was Dirit's response. *<He's warded and shielded. A direct attack will wake him, and he'll warn the sentries. And I may not be able to get through his shields.>*

<What if I land and spray fire all over the shelter?> Tristin asked.

Dirit laid his ears back. *<Can you guarantee you won't roast His Royal Highness in a moment of mindless battle lust? Or start a forest fire, trapping him inside the carriage? In case you weren't paying attention, he's unconscious and he's chained. He won't be able to escape the carriage on his own.>*

Tristin shuddered as he thought back to the last time his dragon instincts had swept him away. During the tense confrontation on top of Dragonwatch, Prince Jaire had put himself between Tristin and Wytch Master Faah, intent on keeping Faah alive for questioning. In his mindless fury, Tristin had very nearly flamed them both.

As if following his thoughts, Dirit said sternly, *<You must keep your head this time, Prince Tristin of the New Flower Bed. The moment you hear screams, you must land and do your best to defend the carriage without turning the forest into a fire trap. Use your claws and teeth.>* Dirit snapped his little jaws for effect. *<And be careful. These men are all Drachan soldiers. They are the best the Council has, and they will fight like it. Don't worry about me — your dragon fire cannot touch me.>*

<This is a terrible plan,> Tristin said.

<Well, at least it's a plan,> Dirit retorted, and promptly vanished.

<What if we—> Jaire started.

<Too late,> Tristin told him. *<He's gone. Let's tighten our circle. If you see movement below, you can be sure it's an enemy. The only man we care about saving is chained inside that carriage.>*

Thunder rumbled overhead as they closed in on the shelter. If Dirit had begun killing the sentries, there was no indication of it. Tristin scanned the treetops, thankful for the cloud cover and the heavy canopy, even if it did make it more difficult to see what was going on below.

A cry came from inside the shelter, a scream of rage and desperation.

<That was Shaine,> Jaire said. <He's terrified... and the Wytch Master is furious... Tristin, I think Anxin has some kind of hold over him.>

Shaine's cry had alerted the guardsmen bedded down around the carriage. They erupted out of their bedrolls and had weapons ready in the blink of an eye.

Before Tristin could protest, Jaire swooped down to land on the roof of the shelter. At the sight of the dragon, the men guarding the carriage reached for their crossbows. A barrage of lightning from Jaire forced them back behind the carriage.

While they were occupied with Jaire, Tristin circled the clearing once more and landed on the other side of the carriage from the guards, his only thought to protect Mikhyal.

The moment he'd landed, Jaire took to the air, raining lightning down around the guardsmen who were using the carriage for cover. Two crossbow bolts flew past Jaire, narrowly missing him. Another round of lightning sent the men shouting and scurrying into the forest.

Mindful of Dirit's warning about setting the forest alight, Tristin held his fire, trusting Jaire to keep the guardsmen occupied while he freed Mikhyal. He was still determining the best way to extract the prince from the carriage when another scream came from the shelter. The door flew open, and a half-dressed figure tore out, sword gripped tightly in his hand.

"Mik! Mikhyal!" The man sounded desperate.

Shaine.

Jaire spit lightning again, hitting the ground behind Shaine, just missing him, then spit another barrage into the forest. Tristin spun around and planted himself between the carriage and Shaine, all the while growling low in his throat. Shaine skidded to a stop, eyes wide with horror. "Please..." he started, holding out a hand toward Tristin. "Don't hurt him!"

A moment later, a man dressed in the black robes of a Wytch Master strode from the shelter. "Shaine!" he barked.

Shaine reacted as if he'd been slapped. He jerked to attention and made a choking sound in his throat. His eyes remained fixed on Tristin, desperate and imploring, but he didn't move forward.

Anxin's eyes narrowed as they fixed on the dragon guarding the carriage. The Wytch Master barely hesitated before a glowing green ball appeared in his hand. He raised his arm and hurled it directly at Tristin.

Tristin flinched and tried to dodge out of the way, but he wasn't fast enough. The ball exploded against his side, sending thousands of tiny shocks radiating through him. Roaring in pain, Tristin reared up on his hind legs, only to see the Wytch Master readying another ball of light. He drew in a breath to blast Anxin with his flames, but there in front of the Wytch Master, still rooted to the spot, was Mikhyal's brother, eyes still fixed on Tristin.

Please... Shaine's desperate plea echoed through Tristin's mind.

With a shout of triumph, Anxin released the ball of light. The moment it left the Wytch Master's hand, one of Jaire's lightning bolts intercepted it, and it exploded in a shower of green and yellow sparks.

Anxin scowled and readied another attack, this time turning toward Jaire. Tristin had only a moment to make the decision. The primal sense of struggle he'd sensed when he'd touched both the throwing knife and the Wytch Sword flashed through his mind.

Shaine?

Praying to the Dragon Mother that he was right, he charged forward and launched himself over Shaine to land in front of Anxin. His claws gouged deep furrows in the dirt as he skidded to a stop and let loose a great gout of fire.

Anxin's robes caught fire immediately. The Wytch Master screamed and began beating at the flames. A moment later, lightning rained down from above, wreathing his body in mythe-light. He twisted and writhed, fighting to escape, as Jaire continued to bathe him in lightning.

All at once, Anxin's scream cut off, the lightning stopped, and the Wytch Master crumpled to the ground in a heap of smoking fabric. At the same moment, Shaine dropped to his knees and let out a cry that sounded like equal parts anguish and triumph.

Dirit appeared, hovering in the air in front of Tristin. *<Oh, excellent job on the Wytch Master! That's it, then. His men have all been neutralized. They were all Drachan, you know. They're not anymore. Now they are nine tidy little piles of bone, all polished and arranged very nicely, and three lightning-blasted corpses, compliments of Prince Jaire.>*

Tristin glanced at Jaire, who had returned to the roof of the shelter, and was scanning the forest for any sign of threat. *<Perhaps keep that last bit to yourself, hmm, Dirit?>* Tristin suggested.

<Of course. Our tender-hearted prince might not appreciate the knowledge that he's made his first kill.> Dirit cocked his head. *<He'll have to get over that in a hurry. There's a war coming, you know.>*

<Ai, I know,> Tristin said sadly. *<It'll happen soon enough... but let's give him a little time, shall we?>*

<Very well, Prince Tristin, Guardian of Tender Hearts. I shall take full credit. What shall we do with Prince Shaine? Shall I make another pretty pile of bones?> Dirit's ears flattened to his head. *<Or... seeing as you've managed to roast the Wytch Master, perhaps you'd rather hang onto him for information?>*

Tristin stared at Shaine, who was still on his knees, tears streaming down his face, great sobs shaking his slender body. Swirling air currents had him looking up to see Jaire gliding down to land lightly between himself and Shaine.

<Don't hurt him, Tristin. I don't think any of this was his fault.> Jaire turned to Dirit. *<Is it safe to shift back, Dirit? Or are there more Drachan in the forest? I don't sense any, but you said one of them was invisible to the mythe.>*

<They have all been dealt with, Your Highness,> Dirit said. *<I counted them myself.>*

<Thank you, Dirit. I don't like to think how that would have gone if you hadn't been here.> Jaire shifted back to human form just as the first raindrops began to fall. "I felt something break when Anxin died. There was a connection of some sort running deep in the mythe between him and Shaine, but it's gone now." Jaire quickly untangled himself from his harness and dug into his saddlebags for his

clothing. "Are you all right?" he asked Tristin as he pulled on his shirt and breeches. "Anxin hit you with something."

<Tell him I'm fine, Dirit,> Tristin said. <It still stings a bit, but I don't think it's done any permanent damage. And if it has, it will heal when I shift. If you're certain Shaine is no danger to you, I'm going to see to Mikhyal.>

Dirit repeated his words to Jaire, who patted Tristin's flank and gave him a sad smile. "Shaine is no danger to us. You can't feel him the way I can. He's devastated. Go and see to Mikhyal. I'll see what I can do here." Jaire knelt on the ground beside Shaine and began speaking to him in soothing tones.

Tristin turned his attention to the carriage. The door was locked, but its hinges didn't look strong enough to impede a determined dragon. Tristin wrapped his claws around the bars of the window and pulled. With a loud squeal of straining metal, the door came free. He tossed it aside and turned his attention to the interior of the carriage. His dragon body was far too big to fit inside the opening, but he could see Mikhyal, sprawled in the corner, naked and vulnerable. He shifted back to human form, entered the carriage, and crawled to Mikhyal's side. "Mikhyal, wake up," he whispered, pulling Mikhyal into his arms. "It's Tristin. It's all right, I've come for you."

While he was cradling Mikhyal and wondering how he was going to remove the chain from his ankle, Dirit flitted in, two keys clenched tightly in his little jaws. Tristin held out a hand and Dirit dropped them in his palm.

The moment the metal touched his flesh, Tristin flinched and adjusted his shielding pattern. The keys carried the same traces of empathic resonance he'd felt on the Wytch Sword and the knife that had struck Drannik. He frowned at Dirit. "Shaine gave these to you?"

"He gave them to Prince Jaire. One is for the carriage door, which it doesn't look as if you'll need, and the other is for the chain."

"But they feel like… oh, dear… that means Shaine was the one who threw that knife at Wytch King Drannik. You didn't leave him alone with Jaire, did you?"

Dirit didn't seem the least bit concerned. "You needn't worry. Prince Jaire is convinced that Shaine is entirely free of the Wytch Master's influence."

A small, glowing ball of mythe-light appeared above Tristin's head, and he quickly located the lock and used the key to free the prince. To his disappointment, Tristin wasn't strong enough to carry Mikhyal himself. Dirit had to fetch Jaire to help. Between the two of them, they dragged Mikhyal's limp body from the carriage. They were only halfway to the shelter when a brilliant flash of lightning split the sky. Rain pelted down, drenching them.

They hurried into the shelter, where Shaine waited. He watched with wide, haunted eyes as they dried Mikhyal off and settled him on one of the bedrolls. Mikhyal moaned as they gently arranged his limbs and covered him with blankets. The blood-chain was still locked around his neck, ruby-red stones glowing dimly, tiny flecks of gold swirling deep within them.

Dirit perched on Mikhyal's chest, twitching his whiskers and looking quite agitated. "We *must* get that abomination off of him. Quickly!"

"Do you know how to remove it?" Tristin asked Jaire.

"No. Ilya does, though. I can fly back to Altan and fetch him. We could be back here tomorrow afternoon."

Tristin hated to think of Mikhyal suffering for that long. "We can't do anything until the storm passes. Then you'll need to let Wytch King Drannik know where we are and what's happened. And you should really sleep before you fly all the way back to Altan." That would take even more time. Tristin lifted a hand to Mikhyal's forehead to brush dirty, sweat-soaked hair away from his brow.

"I don't want him to wear that thing for one minute longer than he has to," Jaire said vehemently. "I wore one once, and it was *horrible*."

"I... I can free him." The soft, trembling voice came from behind them.

Tristin turned to see Prince Shaine take a hesitant step forward. "I can take the blood-chain off of him. I-I know the p-pattern to do it. Anxin showed me. I-I'm the one who put it on him in the first place. I d-didn't want to, but... I didn't... I couldn't..." His voice dropped to a whisper. "Anxin forced me. He wanted to make Mikhyal hate me so he wouldn't try to help me break free." A fat tear slid down his cheek.

Jaire beckoned Shaine forward. The young man knelt at his brother's side and reached out with shaking hands to gently rotate the collar a quarter turn. He closed his eyes, brow wrinkling, and a moment later, Mikhyal heard a faint click. The swirling golden flecks within the stones faded and winked out, and Shaine withdrew the collar and offered it to Jaire, who drew back, shaking his head.

"I can't touch it," Jaire whispered. "It hurts."

"Hand it to me, Shaine," Tristin said quietly.

Shaine gave it to him, and Tristin crossed the room and threw the thing into the fire, vowing to destroy it before they left the shelter.

"Tristin?" The hoarse voice coming from the bedroll had Tristin turning to see Mikhyal's eyes fluttering open.

"Mik?"

Mikhyal knew that voice. It was Shaine's, but he hadn't heard his brother sound so young and uncertain since the accident that had stolen him away and left a cold stranger in his place. He groaned and forced his eyes open to find himself in a room lit by flickering firelight. Blankets had been piled on top of him, and the terrible, icy weight that had dragged so painfully at his mind was gone.

"Mik... oh, Mik, I'm so sorry." Shaine knelt at his side, holding his hand tightly, tears streaming down his face. "Please be all right, you have to be all right, you can't die thinking I hate you! All those horrible things I said and did... Anxin did something to me when I was recovering from the accident. I've been fighting to escape him ever since. Sweet Dragon Mother, please, don't take him before I can tell him the truth!"

"I'm not dead, Shaine," Mikhyal whispered.

"Mik!" Shaine bent forward, pressed his face to Mikhyal's chest, and wept as if his heart would break.

Mikhyal struggled to free his arms so he could get them around his brother. "It's all right," he murmured. "I've got you." While Shaine sobbed against him, Mikhyal glanced about the room, relief surging through him as his eyes came to rest on Tristin, who was kneeling on the floor next to Shaine.

Tristin smiled sadly. "He speaks the truth. It was his struggle I felt when I touched the Wytch Sword and when I pulled the knife from your father's back. That's why there was so much fury and despair in what I felt... Anxin was controlling him, and he was struggling to break free with all his strength."

"I didn't want to hurt anyone," Shaine whimpered. "I'd never have hurt Father if I'd had any choice. Anxin made me take the sword to use as payment to the bandits he hired to attack you on your way to Altan. He said... he said only the line of Rhiva could use it properly, and he wanted it out of the way."

"It's all right, Shaine. I believe you," Mikhyal said, heart breaking a little as his brother trembled in his arms.

Tristin's eyes were dark with pain as he rested a gentle hand on Shaine's trembling shoulder. "Another victim of the Wytch Council."

"One of the last, at least in the north," said another voice, and Mikhyal's gaze moved past Tristin to settle upon Prince Jaire. "The Northern Alliance will no longer tolerate such atrocities."

"Prince Jaire," Mikhyal said.

"Prince Mikhyal," Jaire said, giving him a nod. "Tristin, since Shaine is free of Anxin's influence, I'm going to the palace to speak with Drannik."

"I'm not sure that's a good idea," Tristin said. "We have no way of knowing if it's safe. What if Anxin's men have taken the palace?"

"They tried," Mikhyal said, "but Dirit stopped them. He killed all the men Anxin had waiting for us at the palace. Whether there were more stationed outside of Dirit's range, I don't know."

"If you killed the twelve he had here, then that's all of them," Shaine said quietly. "Anxin was furious that you managed to get rid of the entire force he had at the palace. He thought it would be so easy."

"It might have been if you hadn't taken the Wytch Sword from the vaults," Mikhyal said, smiling at the little dragon sitting beside him.

"Yes, poor Wytch Master," Dirit said, settling himself on the bedding next to Mikhyal's head. "Engineered his own downfall, he did. I find it rather ironic that if he'd just left the sword in the vaults, his plan might well have succeeded."

"The Northern Alliance owes you a debt we can never repay, Dirit," Mikhyal said.

"All part of my sacred duty," Dirit said, preening. "Now that you are revived to my satisfaction, I shall be outside, patrolling the grounds and protecting my bond-mate." The little dragon vanished with a snap of his jaws.

"You see, Tristin?" Jaire said. "The palace is safe. There's no reason why I shouldn't—"

"You're about to have company!" Dirit chirped as he reappeared, this time perched on Jaire's shoulder.

A moment later, there was a loud knock on the door. Jaire flung it open. "Ilya!"

Altan's Wytch Master stood in the doorway, stark naked and dripping wet. "I've found him!" Ilya called to someone outside. "Found them both. Or perhaps I should say, found them all." A loud draconic snort came from outside, and then a large, orange-gold dragon appeared behind Ilya, nudging the Wytch Master into the shelter with its snout so it could get its head through the door to have a look at the shelter's inhabitants.

"I'm *fine*, Garrik," Jaire said, stroking the big dragon's snout. "You don't have to always come looking for me, you know."

"We were worried," Ilya said. "I was able to track you through the mythe. I would have come alone, but of course, Garrik wouldn't allow it. What happened?" His gaze settled on Mikhyal and Shaine. "No, that can wait. You have wounded men here. Let me see to them first." He leaned out the door and called, "You might as well shift, Kian. You, too, Garrik. It looks as if we'll be spending the night here, at least. Kian, bring the saddlebags in with you, if you would. I'll want some dry clothing."

Jaire found Ilya a cloak, and the Wytch Master settled beside Mikhyal and Shaine.

"Check Shaine first, if you wouldn't mind," Mikhyal murmured to the Wytch Master.

While Ilya examined Shaine with his healer's sight, Jaire and Tristin told their tale. Dirit took up his spot next to Mikhyal so he could listen and make comments and corrections. When Jaire and Tristin had finished, Mikhyal filled in his own account of what had occurred when he and Drannik arrived at the palace, and how he had been captured.

Shaine squirmed when Mikhyal told them how he'd been shot down and collared. "Anxin knew about your alliance because of me," Shaine whispered. "He made me spy on your meetings in Altan, before I attacked Father. I didn't want to, Mik, you must believe me! I tried to stop, but he was too strong. And when I arrived back here, I tried not to tell him anything, but he just... he pulled it all out of my head."

"It wasn't your fault, Shaine," Mikhyal said quietly.

"He sent that Drachan soldier out to shoot you down. Said you wouldn't be expecting a man you couldn't sense. He was to take you alive for the Council Inquisitors. Anxin knew you'd been made an offer to be transformed, and he guessed you'd do it. I'm so sorry. I've betrayed you and Father. And Rhiva." Shaine ducked his head, silent sobs shaking his body.

Mikhyal shot a helpless look at Ilya. "What can we do?"

"I can dose him with anzaria and send him to sleep," Ilya said quietly. "He is both traumatized and suffering from mythe-shock."

"Do it," Mikhyal said with a nod.

"I shall be dosing you, too, Your Highness. You are suffering from the after-effects of both the collar and the poison they used to bring you down."

Ilya gave each of the brothers a dose of anzaria, and once Shaine was curled comfortably at his brother's side, the Wytch Master touched his brow and sent him into a deep, healing sleep.

"Will he be all right?" Mikhyal asked, stroking Shaine's flame-bright hair.

"It will be a few days before he recovers from the mythe-shock," Ilya said gravely.

"Ai, I know that, but... I mean afterward. Will I ever have my brother back the way he was before the accident?"

"That, I cannot say for certain."

"But Anxin is gone," Mikhyal protested. "He no longer controls Shaine... is that not right?"

"Anxin wasn't controlling him in the sense you mean," Ilya said quietly. "If that was the case, Shaine would have broken free of him the moment the blood-chain cut off Anxin's access to the mythe. No, what Anxin did to your brother was far more cruel and insidious. He imposed a pattern on him, burning it into his very mythe-shadow, and then tying it to his own so it was continuously reinforced. The pattern set the bounds of Shaine's behavior, and it sounds like your brother was fighting all along to break free. Unfortunately, as long as Anxin lived, that was not possible."

Mikhyal's chest tightened painfully as understanding began to dawn. "That's why I saw glimpses, every now and then. It was as if he was trying to speak to me, only something always stopped him."

"The pattern," Ilya said. "He could only break free of it for the briefest moments, and even that would have taken a tremendous effort on his part."

"But... why wouldn't the blood-chain break the connection?"

"For the same reason Dirit was able to lead Jaire and Tristin to you even though you wore the blood-chain — because the connection between them went far deeper than the blood-chain could reach. Deep enough that only Anxin's death could break it."

Mikhyal shuddered and blinked back tears, furious at the way Shaine had been violated. How horrible it must have been for him, to be forced to make his own brother hate him, and to be powerless to stop it. "How do I help him?"

"You must be patient with him." Ilya's voice was gentle and reassuring. "He will need time to come to terms not only with what has been done to him, but what he was forced to do under Anxin's influence. He will likely blame himself for not being strong enough. The burden of guilt he carries is already crippling. I will do what I can to reassure him that it was not his fault, but he will need to hear it more than once. And from more than just me."

"He will hear it from me every hour of every day, if that is what it takes," Mikhyal vowed. "I will do everything I can to help him."

"That is as much as anyone can ask, Mikhyal." Ilya gave his shoulder a squeeze and said, "Sleep now. Shaine won't wake until you are both safely home at the palace."

The anzaria was beginning to make him drowsy. Mikhyal listened to the rain on the roof and the murmur of voices as the other dragon shifters determined what must be done next. After very little discussion, it was decided that once the storm passed, they would depart for the palace, with Garrik and Kian transporting Mikhyal and Shaine on dragonback.

"Do you hear that, Shaine?" Mikhyal murmured. "You'll be riding on a dragon."

But Shaine was deeply asleep, and didn't stir.

Mikhyal tightened his arms around his brother. "It'll be all right," he whispered. "Now that I've got you back, I will make it all right. I swear it."

Chapter Eleven

Mikhyal listened in silence to Tristin and Jaire's account of the events at the shelter. The anzaria Ilya had given him had sent him into a deep sleep, and he'd only woken when Ilya had roused him for the flight back to the palace that morning. Upon their arrival, they'd been given breakfast and then ushered into Drannik's study.

Despite the thick cloak he wore over his clothing, Mikhyal was still shivering with cold. Mythe-shock, Ilya had said, and gave Mikhyal permission to attend the meeting only after receiving his assurance that he would rest for the remainder of the day.

Learning that Lieutenant Takla and his men were all dead had been a blow. While Mikhyal and the others were eating breakfast, Kian had taken Rhu out on dragonback to search for them. They'd returned shortly after to report that they'd found the remains of the camp and the men.

Guilt gnawed at him. If he hadn't insisted on scouting ahead, might he have saved them? No. He'd done what he thought best at the time, and he must make an effort to remember that. If he allowed himself to fall into the trap of questioning every decision, he'd lose his edge, and Rhiva needed him sharp and decisive. Shoving away the guilt, he brought his focus back to Jaire's account of the previous day's events.

"… and after Tristin set him on fire, I… I finished him off," Jaire said quietly from his spot across the table. "He might have hurt Mikhyal and Shaine, but… I couldn't bear to watch him burn." He sounded very young and uncertain, and when he'd finished, he bit his lip and stared up at his brother. "You're right, Garrik. I don't think I'd make much of a soldier. I haven't the stomach for killing."

Garrik's arm went around Jaire, and Mikhyal's heart stuttered painfully in his chest as the brothers' display of affection reminded him of how he and Shaine used to be.

"You did well," Garrik said. "Compassion is not a weakness. It's one of the things that sets us apart from the Wytch Council."

Jaire swallowed hard. "Then... then when Anxin was... was dead..." he trailed off, eyes filling with tears.

Tristin said softly, "If... if I might continue, the tale, Your Majesty?" At Drannik's nod, he said, "Once Anxin was dead, Dirit reported that he had dealt with the rest of the Drachan."

"You're certain they were Drachan?" Drannik asked.

"Dirit said they were," Tristin said. "He said they, um, had a... a *flavor*."

"Ai, he said the same to me after he dealt with the troops Anxin had brought into the palace," Mikhyal said, reaching for Tristin's hand under the table and giving it a squeeze.

"And so they do," Dirit said, appearing on the table in front of Mikhyal. "A nasty, musty, *oily* flavor. I shall have to eat blackberry tarts until the aftertaste has gone. It still lingers, and I fear I shall have dreams most frightful until it abates." The little dragon gave Mikhyal a meaningful look, and Jaire's lips twitched into a small, watery smile.

"Is that creature speaking to you again?" Drannik asked.

"Ai, he's just putting in his breakfast order," Mikhyal said drily.

"Indeed." Drannik's eyebrows lifted slightly. "And what would he like?"

"Blackberry tarts," Tristin, Mikhyal, and Jaire said almost at the same time.

"Well, then. We shall have to see that the kitchen staff are notified," Drannik said gravely. "Master Dirit shall have his pastries."

Dirit materialized long enough to perform an elaborate, sweeping bow to the Wytch King, and then vanished.

Garrik, who had been mostly silent up until now stirred and said, "Since it appears that Anxin knew of the Northern Alliance and of our ability to create dragon shifters, it might be best to operate under the assumption that the Wytch Council also knows."

"Ai," Drannik said with a sharp nod. "Our advantage lies chiefly in meeting their superior numbers with our dragon army. If Anxin did have the opportunity to pass along what he learned, we might expect them to strike soon, before we have had a chance to transform more men."

"I will stop at the palace in Mir and at Castle Irila on my way home and inform Edrun and Ord that they must be vigilant. We may need to meet again, sooner rather than later."

Drannik inclined his head. "I will be available at your convenience."

"I'll also have a word with Vayne," Garrik said. "If we could find him an apprentice or two, we might be able to build our army more quickly."

A sharp rap on the door was followed by Ilya's entrance. "I'm sorry to interrupt, Your Majesty, but Prince Shaine is beginning to stir. He's been calling for his brother."

Mikhyal got to his feet. "I'll go and see to him. Finish your meeting, Father. I've already told you all I can recall. Ilya wishes for me to rest for the remainder of the day, but if we need to discuss strategy, there is no reason I cannot do that from my bed."

Ilya shot him a disapproving look, but Drannik said, "I'll stop by when we've finished here."

Mikhyal gave Tristin's hand another squeeze under the table and whispered, "Come to me in Shaine's apartment when you've finished here. There are things we need to talk about before you return to Altan."

Tristin nodded mutely, ears going pink.

The moment he and Ilya were alone in the hall together, Mikhyal asked, "How is Shaine?"

"He has yet to awaken fully, Your Highness," Ilya said. "I see nothing in his mythe-shadow to concern me, but I would like to have Prince Vayne come to Rhiva to examine him, just to be sure all of Anxin's hooks died with him."

"If you can spare him, we would appreciate that," Mikhyal said.

Shaine looked very small in the big bed in his apartment. His flame-bright hair was unbound and scattered across his pillow, framing his pale face in a fiery halo. He was murmuring in his sleep, eyes fluttering half open now and again.

"He'll be awake before long," Ilya said. "It might reassure him if yours is the first face he sees."

Mikhyal settled himself on the big bed next to his brother, and took hold of his hand, stroking it gently. "Come on, Shaine. Time to wake up."

Shaine's eyes fluttered and opened. He blinked up at Mikhyal, frowning. "Mik?"

"Who else? Welcome back. I've been worried about you." Tears filled Shaine's eyes and spilled down onto the pillow. Mikhyal pulled his handkerchief from his pocket and gently wiped Shaine's face. "I used to wipe your tears away when you were small. Do you remember?"

"I... I remember." Shaine's voice was a hoarse whisper.

"You used to run after me, always trying to keep up with me, and never quite managing it. I thought you were a bit of a nuisance at the time, but I'd give anything to have my little brother back. He was so quick to smile, and he had the most infectious laugh."

Shaine turned his head away. "You don't want him back," he whispered. "Haven't you heard? He's a traitor and a coward of the worst sort. He tried to murder his king. He ordered his own brother shot down, and he locked a blood-chain around his brother's neck with his own hands. If he'd been more of a man, he'd have found a way to break free of Anxin instead of allowing him to hurt those he loved."

"Do you really believe that?" Mikhyal asked softly. "Shaine, look at me." He waited patiently for Shaine to turn his head and open his eyes. When he did, Mikhyal locked gazes with him and said, "Anxin used the power of the mythe to bind you to his will. He manipulated you in ways you had no hope of fighting."

"Your brother speaks the truth," Ilya said from the foot of the bed. "You had no chance against the full might of Anxin's power. What happened was not your fault. Your brother knows that."

Shaine closed his eyes and curled up on his side, back to Mikhyal. Ilya managed to convince him to drink some medicine, and Mikhyal stayed close until Shaine's deep, even breathing told him his brother was asleep.

Ilya withdrew slowly, beckoning to Mikhyal, who gave his brother one last, lingering look, heart breaking a little. He'd only just gotten him back. Was he to lose him to despair now, when there was so much to hope for?

Dirit appeared on the bed and settled himself beside Shaine, curling up on the pillow next to his head. "Go and talk to Ilya," he said. "I shall watch over Prince Shaine, and I will fetch you if he needs you."

"Thank you, Dirit," Mikhyal murmured, and followed Ilya into the main room of Shaine's suite. When he'd closed the door quietly behind him, he said softly, "I suppose it was too much to hope that he would be... unchanged. Unaffected."

"He's been through things you cannot even imagine, Your Highness," Ilya said. "As I told you last night, it will take time and patience."

"I wish..." Mikhyal stared down at the floor, guilt at his own ignorance nearly overwhelming him. "I should have known. He was so different after the accident. But the healer said a blow to the head like that... and I asked one of the healers down in the village, and she said the same. I had no idea. All that time, he was trapped in his own body. Watching me, all the while silently begging me to see... and I *didn't*. How could I have been so blind?"

"You had no way of knowing," Ilya said gently. "Do not blame yourself, Mikhyal. Shaine needs you to be the strong, confident brother he remembers, now more than ever. He needs you to believe in yourself so that he can feel the truth of it when you tell him you believe in him."

Mikhyal barked out a laugh that turned into a sob. "You make it sound so easy."

"Do I? I do not mean to mislead you. It will not be easy. Recovery from something like this is a long, difficult journey."

"But it can be done?"

"It can, but he cannot do it alone. He will need your strength. He will need you to convince him that the journey is worth taking. That the darkness he must stumble through will eventually end, and he *will* emerge into the light."

"Do you really believe I can be that for him?" Mikhyal whispered.

"I do." Ilya's voice was firm and full of conviction. "You have one weapon Anxin did not have."

"And what would that be?"

"You love him. And deep inside, Shaine knows that. In the end, it may be the only thing that matters."

"Might I stay with him, then, Master Ilya?" Mikhyal asked. "I know I promised you I'd rest today, but I think I could do that just as well watching over my brother as I could worrying in my own apartment."

Ilya gave him a long, appraising look, perhaps studying him with his healer's sight. "I think," he said finally, "that is an excellent idea. It would be good for Shaine to have someone who cares for him nearby."

Mikhyal turned to go back into Shaine's bedroom, but before he could take a single step, the apartment door opened and Drannik strode in.

"How is Shaine, Ilya?" Drannik asked.

Ilya pulled no punches in his description of what Anxin had done. He told Drannik exactly what he'd told Mikhyal, finishing with his recommendation to have Vayne come out and examine the prince.

"Anxin," Drannik growled when he was finished. "Damn him to the Dragon Mother's coldest hell. Is there no end to the Council's treachery? I knew he was influencing Shaine, but to burrow into the boy's mythe-shadow like a parasite? And right under my nose?" The Wytch King shook his head. "I should have seen it."

"With respect, Father," Mikhyal said in a low voice, "You never wanted to look at Shaine closely enough to notice. I tried to tell you he'd changed after the accident, and you said he'd finally grown up and decided to take his responsibilities seriously."

"Ai, that I did. I'd long suspected the boy wasn't mine, and when the Council decided Shaine would be my heir rather than Mikhyal, I resented him even more."

"Nevertheless, you did acknowledge him," Mikhyal said. "He is yours by right, if not by blood, and you are the only father he's ever known."

Drannik stared at his son, dark eyes wide and stunned. "Ai," he said finally, in a very small voice. "That I am. And I've not been a good one, I fear."

"There is still time," Ilya said quietly.

"Perhaps," Drannik said, looking thoughtful. "Perhaps there is, at that."

Tristin emerged from his bedroom in the guest suite of Rhiva's summer palace to find Garrik, Jaire, Kian, and Ilya busy devouring breakfast.

"You should have woken me," he said reproachfully as he took a place at the table.

"Ilya said we should let you sleep as long as you could," Jaire said.

"You were so tired, you were falling asleep in your dinner last night," Garrik added.

"But-but we're leaving right after breakfast, aren't we?" Tristin almost wailed. He'd wanted to say goodbye to Mikhyal properly, but it didn't look as if there was going to be time.

"Well... *we're* leaving," Garrik said, indicating himself, Jaire, and Kian. "Ilya's staying on for a few days to keep an eye on Prince Shaine. And Wytch King Drannik stopped by last night, after you'd gone to bed. He and Ilya and I had a long talk about Shaine's recovery. He's going to need much in the way of support, and he may find it helpful to have someone to talk to. Someone who isn't family, and has also been used and abused by the Wytch Council." Garrik gave Tristin a meaningful look. "Drannik wanted me to ask you if you'd have any objection to spending some time here at the palace."

"Ah... well." Tristin swallowed, hardly able to believe the Wytch King would want *him* to stay on to help his son. "I think... um..."

"Mikhyal will be here," Jaire pointed out with an innocent smile.

Tristin's face felt like it was on fire, and he slouched a bit in his chair. "I... yes?"

"Is that an answer?" Garrik inquired. "Or a question?"

"I would... I mean, I think... I'd be very happy to help. And of course, Mikhyal being here would be... well, that is... Oh, but can Master Ludin spare me from the greenhouse?"

"I will speak to him," Garrik said gravely. "I'm certain something can be arranged. Your only obligation to me is to put in an appearance at the harvest festival for Jaire's wedding."

Jaire turned big grey eyes on Tristin. "You'll be there, won't you, Tristin? I want all my family there when I marry Vayne."

All my family. Tristin's eyes filled, and he smiled at Jaire. "I'll be there, Cousin. I wouldn't miss it for anything."

"Plan to stay for the entire week, then," Garrik said. "There will be much to celebrate, including a special ceremony to recognize you as Vakha's legitimate son and heir."

"Whatever for?" Tristin frowned at his cousin. "My father never wanted anything to do with me, and I want nothing to do with his name or his titles. Why should I care about any of that?"

"*You* may not care, but the nobility of the Northern Alliance undoubtedly will," Garrik said. "How am I to ensnare you in an alliance marriage if I haven't legitimized you?"

Tristin's heart stuttered, and a shiver of dread rippled through him. Was he to be married off and sent away like some unwanted piece of furniture? Of course, it made sense for Garrik to make such use of him; Tristin was more of an embarrassment than anything. "Alliance marriage?"

Garrik leaned forward, eyes glittering with mischief. "I hear Rhiva has a prince of marriageable age. Recently declared heir to the throne, if I'm not mistaken." He winked. "Of course, if you object, we can certainly drop the matter."

"*Rhiva?*" Tristin's voice was almost a squeak. "Y-you mean Mikhyal?"

"Indeed," Garrik said with a grin. "If you and Mikhyal are in agreement, of course. There's no need to rush into anything. Unless, of course, you *want* to rush into it."

Tristin's tongue knotted up and his face burned so hot he had to loosen his shirt. Jaire patted his arm comfortingly and shot his brother a glare. "Leave him alone, Garrik. He's not used to being teased."

"Sorry, Tristin." Garrik didn't look at all sorry. "You feel like one of the family already. I forget you're still new to all this."

Family.

There was that word again, this time coming from Garrik. Tristin gave his cousin a shy smile and said, "It's all right, Garrik. I don't mind your teasing. I... I don't know about the other, though. I think... I think it's a bit early to be making plans. I hardly know the man. Although... I'd, um, I'd like to see a lot more of him." He flushed again, realizing that what he'd said would probably be misinterpreted. "Um. I mean, I'd like to get to know him better."

Garrik's lips twitched, but he managed to keep a straight face. "See as much of him as you like, Cousin."

An hour later, Tristin said goodbye to his family in the courtyard of Rhiva's summer palace. Kian had already shifted, and Jaire was busy settling the saddle on the big, black dragon's back.

Garrik hugged Tristin hard. "Take care of yourself, Tristin. You can expect Vayne in the next day or so. We'll send along some of your clothes and things for you. And I imagine you'll be seeing Jaire, as he'll probably talk Vayne into bringing him along."

"I'll have the staff prepare a suite for them," Mikhyal said, coming up beside Tristin.

Garrik nodded to Mikhyal, then stepped back, threw off his cloak, and shifted. Heavily muscled, with orange-gold scales glinting in the sunlight, Garrik's dragon form was just as impressive as his human one.

Tristin lifted the saddle, settled it on his back, and secured the straps. Mikhyal helped him heft the saddlebags and get them attached. When he'd checked all the straps to make sure they weren't digging into Garrik or rubbing anywhere, Tristin gave his cousin a playful slap on the flank. Garrik whipped his head around with an indignant snort.

Jaire laughed. "That's the way to deal with Garrik," he said happily. "Goodbye, Tristin. I shall probably be back with Vayne in a day or so, but if not, I'll look forward to you coming home for the wedding."

"Coming home," Tristin murmured. "I like the sound of that."

"You'll bring Mikhyal with you, won't you? And... and Shaine, if he'd like to come. If he's well enough."

"I will be sure to let him know he's welcome," Tristin said.

Jaire hugged him, then stepped back next to his brother and shifted. Jaire's dragon form wasn't nearly as big as Garrik's, but his coloring was breathtaking. Shimmering opalescent scales caught the light, reflecting all the colors of the rainbow, and brilliant violet markings shaded from light to dark across his body.

Mikhyal watched the three dragons launch themselves into the sky. "They are beautiful, aren't they?" he murmured.

"Ai, they are," Tristin agreed.

"I'm still not used to the idea that *I* can take dragon form."

"We shall have to practice, then," Tristin said shyly. "I wouldn't mind helping you get used to the idea."

Garrik and Jaire circled the palace once, and Tristin waved. As they turned west toward Altan, Mikhyal's arm slipped around Tristin's waist. "Will you miss them?"

"Ai, but Altan isn't far for a dragon. I can be back with them in a day if I wish. If... if it's all right for me to visit them." Having never lived anywhere he loved enough to miss, homesickness wasn't something Tristin had ever experienced before. He might miss his suite at Castle Altan, though, and he would definitely miss his cousins.

"Of course you can visit them," Mikhyal said. "Whenever you like. Shall I give you a tour? I thought you'd enjoy seeing the palace grounds. We have some lovely gardens."

Tristin couldn't help the smile that spread across his face. "I'd love to see the gardens. But... are you up to it?"

Mikhyal scowled. "Not if you listen to Ilya, I'm not, but a slow stroll shouldn't hurt."

"Then I'd be delighted." Tristin adjusted himself so that his arm was around Mikhyal. "There you are. You can lean on me if you get tired. Only, do let me know if you feel faint, as you're quite a bit heavier than I, and I'm not sure I could sweep you up into my arms. We might end up in a rather ungainly heap on the floor."

Mikhyal laughed, a full, hearty laugh. "That would make quite the picture."

The palace gardens were quite different than those surrounding Castle Altan, making more use of colorful leaves than flowers, which, with the short growing season in the north, made perfect sense. Tristin found himself studying them carefully and making mental notes. Master Ludin would be fascinated, and Tristin wondered how the old man would feel about riding a dragon to Rhiva to meet with Drannik's royal gardener.

In the sunny rose garden, they found Shaine and Drannik, sitting on a stone bench talking quietly. Shaine appeared tense and pale, but broke into a tentative smile at something his father said, and Drannik reached out hesitantly to put a hand on Shaine's shoulder.

"I hope Shaine is able to find himself again," Mikhyal murmured as they hurried past so as not to disturb them.

"He's surrounded by people who love him and want to help him," Tristin said.

"Do you really think that will make a difference?"

"Garrik and Jaire's kindness certainly made a difference to me. Without knowing I had their support, I'm not sure I'd have had the strength to get through those first few weeks at Dragonwatch."

"I'm glad you did," Mikhyal said. As they passed into the palace, he leaned closer to Tristin. "What shall I tell the staff to do about your accommodations? You can have your own suite, if you'd like. Or... or a room in mine. I've a spare. I, ah, went to the trouble of having it prepared as soon as I returned from Altan. In case you decided to pay me a visit. We never did get to have that picnic. I was hoping we might rectify that in the very near future."

"I... I'd like that." Tristin's face heated. "The picnic, I mean. And... I... could I? Stay with you? If... I mean, if you would be... Oh, but I don't have to, of course, and I would never want to impose. I can't imagine how anyone could—"

Mikhyal pulled Tristin into his arms and silenced him with a kiss. When he drew back, intense blue eyes fixed on Tristin's, holding him immobile. "I want you, Prince Tristin of Altan," Mikhyal said, his voice a low, husky growl. "In my suite and in my life. Is that clear enough for you?"

"Ah, um, ai, Your Highness, it is indeed."

"Then would you like to see your room?"

"Oh, a tour! How very exciting!" Dirit appeared hovering in the air in front of them. "*Do* lead on, Your Royal Predatoriness. I'm sure Prince Tristin of the New Flower Bed is quite eager to be lured into your lair." The little dragon's eyebrow tufts waggled suggestively as he eyed Tristin.

"Your timing is impeccable, you little monster," Mikhyal muttered.

Dirit's gleaming black eyes went wide. "*Monster?* Me? Well, I never! Monster indeed. I'll have you know your royal father calls me *Master Dirit.*"

"You have far too many teeth to look properly innocent, Dirit," Mikhyal told him.

"Well, *really.*" The little dragon's whiskers twitched. "I'm quite insulted. In fact, I'm not sure if I shall ever deign to speak to you again."

"If you don't speak to me again, how am I to thank you for leading Tristin and Jaire to me?"

One eyebrow tuft lifted. "I *could* make an exception, I suppose... Especially if there will be groveling. And blackberry tarts."

"No groveling," Mikhyal said firmly. "But you do have my heartfelt gratitude, Dirit. You saved my life."

"Well, that *is* my sacred duty, after all." Dirit looked very pleased. "Then, if you're planning to have your way with Prince Tristin of the New Flower Bed—"

"Prince Tristin of Altan," Tristin cut in. "Garrik's promised. He'll be making it official at Prince Jaire's wedding."

"Oh, so we're going to be true royalty now, are we?" Hovering in midair, Dirit made a very formal bow toward Tristin. "Legitimized and everything. Lands and titles. Nobility. Well. *That* changes everything. If His Royal Manliness is planning to have his evil way with the soon-to-be Prince Tristin of Altan, then I shall be off to entertain myself for a bit."

"Dirit, would you... would you mind keeping an eye on Shaine?" Mikhyal asked. "Let me know if he's alone or sad, or if he might need someone to talk to. After all he's been through, I fear for him."

"I will, Mikhyal." Dirit nodded solemnly, and pressed one of his front claws against his chest. "I will watch over him for you."

Mikhyal's eyebrows flew up. "I think that's the first time you've addressed me by name. What's the occasion?"

Dirit sniffed. "Against all expectations, I do believe I've become rather fond of you." And with that, the little dragon disappeared.

Mikhyal took Tristin's hand, and they continued on their way. By the time they reached the royal apartments, Mikhyal was leaning heavily on Tristin. "I fear I'm more tired than I thought," he said ruefully as he handed Tristin the key.

Tristin opened the door and helped him in. "Ilya did tell you to rest. And now I'm telling you, as well. Any more tours and such can wait. I'm not going anywhere."

Mikhyal went straight to his bedroom, where he sank down on his bed with a sigh of relief.

"See if you can have a bit of a sleep," Tristin suggested. He expected an argument, and when he got none, realized he'd been correct in his assessment. Tristin was just as glad. He, too, was still feeling tired. Once Mikhyal was settled, he'd go and curl up on one of the sofas in the sitting room and see if he could have a nap.

He covered Mikhyal with a light blanket, leaned down to press a kiss to his cheek, and turned to leave.

"You said you weren't going anywhere," Mikhyal said. "Won't you stay? You look as if you could do with a rest, as well."

"Ah. Well. I... yes, I am a bit tired," Tristin said, flushing. "I was going to curl up in the sitting room."

"Whatever for? There's room here." Mikhyal patted the empty space beside him. "Come on, then."

Tristin hesitated only a moment before pulling his boots off and joining Mikhyal on the bed. He lay down on the very edge, but Mikhyal reached out and dragged him closer, then snuggled up to him, pressing the full length of his body against Tristin's.

Tristin relaxed against him, and was soon fast asleep.

Tristin woke with a start, and for a moment, he couldn't think where he was. Once he felt the warm body pressed against him, he remembered, and relaxed. Outside, it was nearly dark. He'd slept most of the day away, and so had Mikhyal.

"Did you sleep?" Mikhyal murmured, pulling him closer.

"Ai, and better than I thought I would."

"As did I. I could get used to falling asleep next to you, Tristin." Mikhyal rolled off the bed and stretched. "Let me go and see if the staff has left us anything." He padded over to the door and opened it. Warm lamplight poured in, and Mikhyal turned to give him a grin. "Ah, yes. A cold supper packed in a picnic basket, just as I requested."

"A picnic basket?"

"I promised you a picnic, did I not? A picnic you shall have, my prince." Mikhyal stepped out to retrieve the basket, and when he returned, he shut the door firmly behind him and brought the basket to the table beside the bed, then turned up the lamp.

Tristin sat up, blinking in the bright light. "In here? You mean to have a picnic on your bed?"

"Well, it's a bit dark to be off into the forest," Mikhyal said, "and I don't suppose Rhu would allow it anyway. Now that I'm the heir, I'm sure I won't be allowed nearly as much freedom as I've been used to." The expression on Mikhyal's face was almost wistful. "I suppose we could go and sit in the gardens and pretend we're in the forest, but it won't be nearly as private as staying here would be."

"Private?" Tristin flushed and looked around. "Oh, dear. Dirit *did* try to warn me about you luring me into your lair."

"He did, indeed," Mikhyal said gravely. "And here you are. But you're free to go whenever you wish. Regardless of what Dirit says, I hope you know I would never try to take advantage of you, Tristin."

"I, um, I might not... um, actually *mind* that," Tristin whispered. The moment the words were out of his mouth, he cringed, certain he'd been much too forward.

"Mind what?" Mikhyal's voice was gentle.

"Ah. Having you, um, take advantage."

"Oh?"

"There was... um. That night. When you... when we... and then you took your shirt off, but... and it all felt very nice, but... but I never got to see the, um." He ducked his head, and the last bit came out in a jumbled rush: "I would have liked to have seen a bit more of you."

A long silence followed, and when Tristin dared to look up at Mikhyal, the heat in the prince's blue eyes was scorching. "Your wish is my command," Mikhyal breathed, and began shedding his clothing.

Tristin's cheeks flamed, but he kept his eyes fixed on Mikhyal, warmth already beginning to pool low in his belly at the thought of the kisses and touches that might follow.

Mikhyal removed his shirt and tossed it aside, and Tristin drew in a sharp breath as his gaze roamed over the prince's chest and shoulders.

"Could you..." Tristin trailed off, not sure how to ask. Was there some sort of protocol for these things? "I-I mean... might I... might I see your dragon?"

"My *dragon*?" Mikhyal's lips twitched. "I've never heard it called... *Oh*... Oh, you mean... sorry, of course." He turned around and sat on the edge of the bed, his back to Tristin.

The tattoo was every bit as lovely close up as Tristin had thought it would be. "Beautiful," Tristin murmured, reaching out to trace the lines with his hands.

"No more beautiful than yours." Mikhyal rose and turned to face Tristin, hands moving slowly to the laces of his breeches. "Can I show you my dragon now?" he whispered, eyes locking onto Tristin's.

"Please..." Tristin whispered back. He stared, transfixed, as Mikhyal undid the laces and eased the breeches down over his hips. Mikhyal was as aroused as he was, which both pleased and relieved Tristin.

"Do you think I might see yours?" Mikhyal asked.

Tristin swallowed hard, suddenly feeling painfully shy and self-conscious, which was ridiculous, considering Mikhyal was the one with no clothing on. Without a word, Mikhyal turned down the lamp beside the bed. The room filled with shadows, the only light now a dim, golden glow.

"Is that better?" Mikhyal murmured.

"Y-yes, th-thank you."

"If you're uncomfortable, I can get dressed."

"N-no, I think I'd like... I'd like to... show you..." Tristin's heart was pounding so hard he feared he might faint. "I'm just not sure... I mean, I've never done anything like this before and I'm not sure what the rules are, and I'm terribly afraid I'll do something wrong, and I can't help worrying—"

Mikhyal leaned forward and kissed him. "May I begin by undressing you?"

Tristin gulped. "Um. Yes?"

Mikhyal climbed onto the bed and pushed Tristin down. He began undressing him slowly, starting with his shirt, and covering each revealed bit of skin with tender, reverent kisses. When his shirt was off, Mikhyal straddled his hips and leaned down to press a kiss to his lips. "Is this all right?"

"Yes," Tristin breathed.

"Might I explore a bit farther?"

"Please..."

Mikhyal slowly worked his way down Tristin's body. Tristin's entire skin came alive at his touch. The contrast of warm, soft lips with the rough scrape of stubble was almost enough to undo him.

His hips began to flex slowly, pushing his throbbing cock against Mikhyal as he sought the friction that would lead to release.

Mikhyal placed a line of kisses across Tristin's chest, stopping only to tease a nipple or nip at his belly. He moved slowly down to the laces of Tristin's breeches, then stared up at him. "Might I see what's under here?"

"Oh, yes…" Tristin moaned softly, then gasped as Mikhyal began undoing the laces with his teeth, pausing every so often to press his mouth against Tristin's cock.

Tristin squirmed and moaned, gasping at the pleasure shivering through him.

With agonizing slowness, Mikhyal eased his breeches down over his hips, exposing his hot, rigid cock. "Oh, Tristin." Mikhyal's voice was a husky growl that sent a searing heat straight to Tristin's groin. "I want to touch you. May I?"

"Please…" he whispered.

Mikhyal pulled Tristin's breeches the rest of the way off and tossed them aside, then leaned forward and pressed a single kiss to his cock.

Tristin could barely stand it. A hot, gritty tension was growing inside him, as if something was stretched so tightly it must surely break. "Mikhyal," he whimpered, arms creeping around Mikhyal, "I want…"

Before he could even begin to articulate what he wanted, he was in Mikhyal's arms, the prince's bare skin scorching him. In the heat of his desire, Tristin's fears were reduced to ash.

"I want you, Mikhyal," he said, his voice sounding strong and certain. "Please."

"Yes…" Mikhyal whispered. His mouth found Tristin's, and then those big, strong hands were everywhere, pressing, stroking, squeezing…

Mikhyal pushed a thigh between his legs, and Tristin thrust hard against his hip, desperate now for release. Mikhyal's hands skimmed over his hips before he leaned forward, teeth closing lightly on the meat of Tristin's shoulder.

Heat surged through Tristin, and he thrust harder. Mikhyal moaned against his shoulder and shifted him to his side, pulling him close with a leg hooked over his hips. Mikhyal's cock pressed against his own, and then Mikhyal took them both in one big hand and Tristin could no longer think.

It was sweat and power and animal lust, and Tristin wanted it to go on forever. They came together in a blinding flash, and Mikhyal swallowed the hoarse cry that tore from Tristin's throat in a deep, possessive kiss.

After, they drifted on the edge of sleep, limbs tangled, sweat drying, until finally, Mikhyal kissed him and gave him a sleepy smile.

"Much as I'd love to fall asleep again, we should probably eat something before we do."

Tristin's stomach growled at the thought of food, and Mikhyal laughed as he got to his feet. He didn't bother to dress, moving about the room in a completely unselfconscious manner, turning up the lamp and closing the curtains on the evening.

The picnic basket was still sitting on the little table near the bed, and Mikhyal gave it a rueful grin. "I'd still like a picnic in the gardens. I suppose there's always tomorrow."

"Or the next day," Tristin said with a lazy smile. "Or the day after that."

"Mmm. I think I shall have to have a long recovery from my ordeal." Mikhyal's blue eyes twinkled with mischief. "I wonder if Ilya can be bribed to order me to my bed for a few days." He set the basket on the bed and began unpacking the food.

Tristin's stomach growled again at the sight of fresh bread, thick slices of meat and cheese, and blackberry tarts. "Good thing you sent Dirit off on a mission. He'd devour those blackberry tarts in a few seconds, and not leave a crumb for us."

"He is a funny little thing, isn't he?" Mikhyal said, settling himself next to Tristin. "I quite resented him at first, but I find I've grown surprisingly fond of him."

"Which is a good thing, as it sounds as if he'll be with you for the rest of your life."

"He's certainly proved his worth. I... I suppose I should ask you before things go much further... how do you feel about... about sharing me with him?"

Tristin flushed, but he kept his eyes fixed on Mikhyal's. "Considering he's already saved your life twice, you won't hear me complaining. And anyway, I will have to learn to share you, regardless. You will be the Wytch King of Rhiva one day, and then I'll have to share you with the entire kingdom."

"Can you?" Mikhyal asked, a worried frown wrinkling his brow. "You're not very comfortable at Court, I know."

Tristin took hold of Mikhyal's hand and drew it to his lips, kissing it gently before saying, "If the Dragon Mother wills it, I shall have plenty of time to learn. Believe me, Mikhyal, when I think back to what I thought my future would be just a few short months ago, being here like this with you is... it's like a dream. I still have to pinch myself to make certain it's real, and that you're not one of my hallucinations."

"It's real," Mikhyal whispered, leaning over to kiss him. "And so am I."

Tristin kissed him back, and for the first time since he'd left Shadowspire, he didn't feel the need to pinch himself.

~ The End ~

Acknowledgments

Thanks to my awesome beta team: Tully, K, Eric, Jill, and my (still) favorite minion, Michael. You guys rock! Thanks to Jill McCarl for general nit-picking, encouragement, and proofreading.

And huge thanks to Chinchbug for bringing Dirit to life on the cover.

Author Bio

Jaye McKenna was born a Brit and was dragged, kicking and screaming, across the Pond at an age when such vehement protest was doomed to be misinterpreted as a paddy. She grew up near a sumac forest in Minnesota and spent most of her teen years torturing her parents with her electric guitar and her dark poetry. She was punk before it was cool and a grown-up long before she was ready. Jaye writes fantasy and science fiction stories about hot guys who have the hots for each other. She enjoys making them work darn hard for their happy endings, which might explain why she never gets invited to their parties.

CPSIA information can be obtained
at www.ICGtesting.com
Printed in the USA
FSHW010644060520
69871FS